Outrageous Fortune

LULU TAYLOR

arrow books

Published by Arrow Books 2012

4 6 8 10 9 7 5

First published in Great Britain in 2012 by
Arrow Books
Random House, 20 Vauxhall Bridge Road,
London SW1V 2SA

www.randomhouse.co.uk

Addresses for companies within The Random House Group Limited
can be found at:
www.randomhouse.co.uk/offices.htm

The Random House Group Limited Reg. No. 954009

A CIP catalogue record for this book
is available from the British Library

ISBN 9780099550464

Penguin Random House is committed to a sustainable future for
our business, our readers and our planet. This book is made from
Forest Stewardship Council® certified paper.

Printed and bound in Great Britain by Clays Ltd, St Ives plc

To Lizzy Kremer

Part One

Part One

1

1985

In London's exclusive Portland Hospital, Lady Julia Dangerfield lay propped up on the Siberian goose-down pillows covered in white silk cases she had brought with her, along with all other manner of home comforts. She wasn't about to feel any more uncomfortable than she had to. She wore a gauzy white wrap trimmed with white marabou and was perfectly made up; her short blonde hair, frosted with highlights, had been blow-dried into place by her personal hairdresser that morning. She did not look like a woman who had given birth only sixteen hours previously.

From her well-padded position, she gazed at the television set that was mounted on the wall and angled so it could easily be seen from the high hospital bed, but she was not really taking anything in. A tumbler full of clear liquid over a stack of ice cubes sat by her bedside and every now and then she lifted it to take a sip. There was a knock at the door of the private room. Julia clicked off the television with the remote control and said, 'Come in!'

The door opened and a nurse entered, smiling broadly, holding a large bouquet of pink roses and ranunculus in her arms.

'Not another one!' exclaimed Julia, rolling her eyes. She gestured around at the dozens of other bouquets all over the room. 'And they're all in bloody pink! Why can't someone send me a bunch of bluebells, for God's sake! Everything is pink – pink cashmere blankets, pink teddies, pink clothes, pink booties . . . Everything except pink bloody gin, more's the pity.'

'Oh, they're beautiful, Lady Julia,' cooed the nurse, ignoring the gin comment, 'and everyone knows it's pink for a girl!'

'Yes, I am aware of that, thank you,' she snapped. 'But all this pink is making me ill. People are so unimaginative.' She sighed. 'Put them over there. Wherever you want. We'll be taking them away soon anyway.' She gestured at the pile of Gucci luggage waiting in the corner. 'My maid came in earlier and packed. I'm leaving when my husband gets here.'

'Yes, ma'am. With your precious little bundle.' The nurse went over to the cot next to Lady Julia's bed and gazed down with melting eyes at the sleeping baby inside. 'Ooh, isn't she beautiful?'

Julia watched her, shaking her head. 'I can't think how you manage it. You must see hundreds of babies all the time, but you really sound as though you think she's beautiful! Don't they all look the same?'

'Oh, no, ma'am, each one is unique! And this one's a jewel. Look at that little mouth!'

Julia looked over at her daughter. The baby,

dressed in a beautiful white lawn nightdress and covered with a pale pink cashmere blanket, lay on her back, tiny fists to either side of a downy fair head, eyes closed and little rosebud mouth half open. 'Well . . . she *is* sweet, I do agree. Her mouth is rather adorable. But still – she's just a tiny baby. We don't really know what she's going to look like or who she is. She'll probably be rather boring until she starts to talk.' Julia lifted the glass to her lips, ice cubes clinking, and took a long sip. She shrugged. 'I suppose that's what nannies are for, and thank God I've got three.'

The nurse gaped at her, obviously astonished by the new mother's attitude to her little miracle.

Just then a man walked through the open doorway and at once the room seemed to be filled with his presence. He was of medium height and full-figured, his perfectly tailored suit not quite able to hide the rounded stomach and chunky back, and striking to look at: although in late middle age, he still appeared youthful and vibrant. His skin was tanned and scarcely lined and his black hair was luxuriant, receding only slightly at the hairline and tinged with grey at the temples. It was not simply his appearance, though, that drew all attention to him. He radiated a magnetic quality, a force of personality, that was intensely powerful. The nurse seemed to feel it as she almost shrank away from him, obviously hoping she would go unnoticed.

Julia had sensed him there almost before he had walked in. Now she turned to him with a bright but slightly brittle smile. 'Darling!'

He stood still and opened his arms in an expansive

gesture, a broad smile crossing his face. 'My dear!' he declared. 'Where is our little angel?'

Julia nodded towards the cot. 'Asleep.'

'Ah!' The man quickly skirted the bed. He bent over the cot, his expression softening as he gazed at the baby. 'She's gorgeous. You've excelled yourself, my love. This is the best birthday present you could have given me.'

'It was rather lucky, wasn't it? I didn't plan to have her on the same day as your birthday, but it's worked out rather well.'

'Perfectly,' he said with satisfaction. He put one of his great brown hands on a tiny curled fist. 'She and I will always have a special bond. People who are born on the same day do.' He smiled tenderly.

Julia studied her husband's expression with interest. She had been fleetingly worried that the baby was not a boy. She'd feared he might share the same attitude as her father – boys good, girls a tiresome drain on resources. But as soon as the baby had been pronounced healthy, her husband had been elated. One of his greatest ambitions had been realised: this little child connected him by blood to some of the great society families, even to a King of England although it was centuries ago and very much on the wrong side of the blanket. To him it didn't matter what sex the child was; this baby symbolised the fact that the Dangerfield family now officially belonged.

He looked up. His dark brown eyes, so often hard and determined, were now soft and moist with emotion. 'My darling,' he said in a low voice. 'What a precious gift you've given me. I cannot hope to match it, but perhaps this will go a little way towards expressing my feelings.' He slipped a hand into his pocket and brought out a long slender jewellery box of dark red leather edged with gold, stamped with the unmistakable livery of Garrard and Co., the Crown Jewellers.

'Oh, a present, how lovely!' cried Julia, clapping her hands. 'Thank you, darling.' She took it from him, opened it and gazed at the jewels inside. 'How beautiful. Diamonds . . . and they're pink.' Her gaze slid swiftly over to meet the nurse's, watching quietly from her corner of the room, and then back to the bracelet and earrings that lay sparkling on the ivory silk lining.

'Do you like them?' asked her husband, smiling proudly.

'Of course I do, Daddy.' Julia turned one soft peach cheek up towards her husband so that he could kiss it. 'They're simply stunning.'

'Do you want to put them on?'

'Oh . . . yes . . . but not now. I want to go home first.' She gazed up at her husband plaintively. 'Is the maternity nurse here?'

'Waiting outside.'

'Then call her in so that she can be told about the baby and what she needs, and we can leave.' Julia pouted and gave her husband the beseeching look she knew he could never resist. 'Then we can start being a family.'

'Very well. Whatever you want.' Daddy Dangerfield was evidently in the best of moods and his wife's appeal to his new status as head of the family was just the ticket to get her what she wanted. 'I shall order the arrangements to be made at once.'

7

2

Across town, the maternity ward of the Royal London Hospital was full. Each bed had a curtain around it to separate it from the one next to it, but the thin material did little to shut out the mewling cries of newborns, the chatter of family groups come to admire the baby or the other noises that came from behind it: sobbing, anguished demands or loud complaints.

Elaine Drovey found this part of her job one of the hardest. She hated coming to the maternity ward. While most families were celebrating and enjoying the special moment that a new arrival marked, the people she was visiting were usually either terrified or furious at the sight of her. Social Services appearing in the maternity ward was never good news.

She walked down the aisle between the dull grey baggy curtains, trying to count beds as she listened to the babble of voices coming from behind them. The East End had large Asian communities and the languages spoken here were many and various. She stopped beside one particularly limp curtain. No sound came from behind it. There was no visiting family here, she noted grimly. No anxious husband hovering about, worried about his wife and new son or daughter. Well, that was hardly surprising.

She pulled back the curtain and stepped forward. 'Miss Hughes?'

Lying on the bed under the meagre hospital blanket, her face buried in the thin pillow, was a young woman. She was completely still and all that could be seen of her were two scrawny arms marked by multiple wounds and scratches, and a nest of bleached-blonde hair streaked through with strawberry red.

'Miss Hughes?' said Elaine again, a little more loudly. She stepped into the little cubicle, pulling the curtain to behind her, and sat down on a black plastic chair by the bed.

The figure on the bed moaned, then the head was lifted and turned to face Elaine so that she could see two bleary eyes and an exhausted face. 'Whad the fuck do ya want?' said the woman from between dry lips. 'I've just had a fuckin' *baby*.'

'I know that, Miss Hughes. That's why I'm here.' Elaine reached for the capacious bag that was always stuffed with case files, folders and the piles of paperwork that blighted her life. She tried not to appear shocked by Michelle Hughes's appearance. The girl couldn't be older than twenty-two but she looked at least forty, her face lined and thin, great dark circles under her puffy eyes and her mouth set in a line of exhaustion. Of course, she had just given birth and Elaine had seen enough new mothers to know that they rarely looked like the mums in glamorous soap operas, who seemed to have done nothing more strenuous than walk up a flight of stairs. But it wasn't the ordeal of birth that had aged and ruined this poor young thing.

'Where the *fuck* is my baby?' demanded Michelle Hughes, pushing herself up on her thin, track-marked arms. 'Where've you taken her?'

Elaine's sympathy began to melt away. 'Your daughter is at present in the emergency neo-natal unit,' she said briskly. 'She's been born addicted to heroin, Miss Hughes, and that's something we take quite seriously.' She had just been to see the poor little mite herself: the baby girl, born late the previous night, lay in her high-tech incubator, connected by lines to drips and monitors. A hospital bracelet hung loosely around one miniature wrist and she was dressed only in what looked like an absurdly large nappy, her spindly legs emerging from it like two matchsticks. As she slept, her little chest rose and shuddered before falling again, and she made small shivery mewing noises. It had been quite heart-rending to watch.

Elaine pulled a typed form out of her bag and scrutinised it. 'The doctors say that your daughter has an unusually low birth weight and shows the signs of opiate withdrawal. So far there are no signs of Foetal Alcohol Syndrome.' She smiled tightly. 'So that's one good thing.'

'What ya talking about?'

'Did you drink much in pregnancy, Miss Hughes? Alcohol, I mean. Not orange juice. Sadly.'

'Alcohol?' Michelle Hughes laughed in a hollow tone, and fell back on her pillows. 'Couldn't afford booze if that's what you're saying. No one can, on the fucking pittance this government gives us to live on!'

'Yet you found money for heroin,' sniffed Elaine. 'Some people might consider that rather expensive.'

'No, I fuckin' didn't!' snarled Michelle, her eyes blazing as she turned to glare at the social worker. 'I haven't touched it for months! Not since I found out I was knocked up. I *haven't*,' she insisted, seeing the look on Elaine's face. She assumed a hurt expression. 'I haven't used since the fucking test came out positive.'

Elaine just stared at her, and at the fresh track marks on her arms. She said more gently, 'Then it's a mystery how your little girl came to be addicted to it.'

'Is she all right?' There was a flicker of anxiety in the girl's eyes.

'They don't know yet,' Elaine replied, glancing back at her notes. 'The first forty-eight hours are the most critical. They'll give her intravenous fluids, a high-calorie formula milk to make up for her low birth weight, and keep her very calm in a low-stimulation environment. She'll be prone to fits, seizures, breathing problems, muscle pain and distress. We'll have to see how she progresses. She'll be in hospital for a week at least.' Elaine fixed Michelle with a look over the top of her glasses, interested to see how the mother responded to news of her baby's condition, but Michelle seemed unmoved. She simply sighed heavily and closed her eyes.

'When can I get out of here?' she murmured. 'I'm in fucking agony and I'm bleeding like a pig as well. How long does that go on for?'

Elaine remembered the aftermath of her own first delivery. No one could be prepared for the physical consequences of giving birth, the great trauma it caused to both mind and body. Michelle groaned and rolled over, obviously in pain.

'Is there anyone to come in and see you?' asked Elaine, more sympathetically.

'Nah.'

'The baby's father?'

The girl made a snorting sound that Elaine took to be a derisory laugh.

The social worker sighed. It was a sad story. What kind of life did the fatherless baby face with this sad, lonely creature for a mother? What sort of future awaited her? The child would be safe enough here in hospital, and checks would be carried out before she could be allowed to go home with Michelle. If there was inadequate housing and the mother still showed signs of addiction, the child would be put immediately into foster care. Elaine would be happy to bet a size-able sum on that outcome. 'So,' she said a little more brightly, 'have you thought of a name for her?'

'Yeah.' Michelle looked round, a spark of interest in her eyes. 'I'm gonna give her a really nice, glamorous name. Something that don't sound like she comes from round here. I'm gonna call her Chanelle.'

'Chanelle. Very pretty.' Elaine picked up her pen and snapped the nib out. 'Now we've got a name, we'd better get on with filling out some of these forms then, hadn't we?'

3

Daisy Dangerfield liked this game very much. She called it 'Being Like Daddy', and it was a game she and her father both enjoyed. They always played it when Daisy came to stay in London. It would start the same way: Nanny would dress her up in her best pink coat with the velvet collar, pale pink leather shoes and a big pink bow in her fair hair. Then she would be summoned downstairs where Daddy was waiting in the hall in his huge grey overcoat and black hat, a cigar clenched between his teeth.

'Here's my princess!' he'd yell as she came skipping down the stairs, giggling. Then she'd put her tiny hand in his huge one and they'd go down the front steps of the house to where the Rolls-Royce was waiting for them. The driver, Ted, opened the door for her and she'd climb into the vast interior and on to one of the slippery pale leather seats. Once Daddy was beside her, he would open the silver drinks cabinet that was recessed in the panelling in front of him, and pour himself a grown-up drink from a crystal decanter, one of those liquids that looked as pretty as honey but smelled bitter and nasty.

While he sipped it and shouted through the dividing window at Ted about the traffic and the state of the markets, Daisy would press her face up against the cool glass window and watch the reactions of the people on the pavement as the car glided past them. In Belgravia, where they lived, there were plenty of cars like this and no one took much notice, but as soon as they were passing along busy shopping streets and through crowded squares, she would see people stare, their mouths dropping open and their eyes widening at the sight of the magnificent golden car with its unmistakable Spirit of Ecstasy mascot on the bonnet. Ted would drive them to a smart, modern building in the City of London, the place where Daddy's company, Dangerfield Property Investments, had its headquarters, and a doorman would come and open the door of the Rolls and hand Daisy down exactly as if she were a real, grown-up lady.

Inside, she held Daddy's hand all the time, and, when he sat behind his huge mahogany desk, she would perch on his knee, pretending to help him run the enormous empire of Dangerfield holdings even though she was only four years old. All the grey-haired businessmen in their dark striped suits and silk ties would smile at her fondly and burst into roars of laughter whenever she spoke.

Today was a special day for Daisy. Daddy had promised her a surprise and she was eager to find out what it was. When the Rolls stopped at the entrance to the Dangerfield headquarters, she was ready to jump out as soon as the car door was opened.

'Hey now, don't be in such a hurry,' laughed Daddy in his deep, booming voice. 'It'll keep, Princess. Another five minutes won't make any difference.'

But Daisy couldn't wait. She hurried in, her little leather shoes tapping on the marble floor of the entrance hall, and went straight to the special lift that only Daddy used, pushing the button for the top floor. The security guards and receptionist smiled fondly at her as Daddy followed behind, his laugh echoing in the vast atrium.

'I wish all my employees were as eager to get to work!' he declared, coming up to Daisy and taking her hand in his.

By the time the lift doors opened on the top floor, people had gathered to meet them: executives, assistants and the secretaries who followed Daddy around whenever he was at work. And they always beamed at little Daisy, their affection for her blazing out of their eyes. Each one of them took every opportunity to tell Daddy how much they adored his little girl.

'Here we are,' he announced, smiling at his staff. 'Is my surprise ready?'

They were led along the carpeted corridor to Daddy's vast office, with its three glass walls and panoramic view over the city: St Paul's Cathedral lying almost immediately below in its splendour, with the river stretching away beyond, spanned by bridges; skyscrapers to the east and the less dominant skyline of Westminster to the west. But they didn't go into Daddy's office this time. They stopped instead at a door next to his, and Daddy pointed at an engraved nameplate.

'Can you read that, sweetheart?' he asked.

Daisy recognised her own first name written out in capital letters, although she could not yet read her surname. Nanny had taught her the alphabet and how to scrawl out her name, but she wouldn't learn to read properly until September when she started at her exclusive girls' prep school.

'Daisy! Me!' she announced proudly, and everyone laughed.

'Clever girl,' said her father fondly. 'Let's go in.'

They stepped into a perfect miniature office. There was a small but beautifully made dark wooden desk inlaid with scarlet leather, and tucked under it was a child-size replica of Daddy's own carved mahogany chair but this one had a little scarlet cushion. On the desk was an ivory pen pot with a miniature Mont Blanc pen in it, a Smythson scarlet leather writing pad stamped with 'Daisy Dangerfield' in gold letters, and a shiny black modern telephone. On the wall hung a pretty painting of a pot of daisies.

'Oh!' exclaimed Daisy, clapping her hands with joy. The watching executives murmured their admiration of the adorable little set up. She ran to the desk, pulled out the chair and sat down. She swung on it happily and it turned smoothly, without a squeak. Laughing, she beamed up at her father.

'Do you like it, darling?' he said, his expression soft.

'Yes, Daddy, yes!'

'Look, I'll show you how it works.' Daddy came forward and picked up the telephone receiver. He showed her how one of the buttons would connect her to Lorraine, her personal assistant, who would

16

fetch whatever she wanted. Lorraine stepped out from the crowd of onlookers and smiled.

'Can I have betsy cola?' asked Daisy quickly.

Her father laughed heartily. 'Well, if you are a very good girl and make lots of lovely profits for Daddy, then you'll be allowed a Pepsi-Cola. And this button is for when you want to speak to me. Your telephone is directly connected to mine and we shall be able to speak whenever we want to. Now, what do you think?'

Daisy gave herself an extra strong swing and put out her legs as she revolved in her little chair. 'I think . . . I like it here!'

Everyone laughed again, then Daddy picked her up and carried her along the corridor to his own office. The others left them, to go to the boardroom in readiness for a meeting. Daddy and Daisy were left alone, the little girl in her father's arms as they stared solemnly at the portrait over the fireplace. It showed a man who looked like Daddy: dark hair, strong features and a determined look in his black eyes below the thick dark brows. But this man had a neat black moustache, small gold-rimmed glasses and wore old-fashioned clothes.

'My father,' said Daddy softly as they looked together. 'The man who passed on his gifts to me and made me what I am today. He was a brave man, Daisy. A man who struggled every day of his life, and who gave us all the blessings we enjoy. He gave me so much, and what he gave me, I pass on to you – my daughter. There are some Dangerfields who aren't true members of the family and we must beware of them. But you are, and one day, my dear, all of this – the Dangerfield inheritance – will be yours.'

Daisy thought for a moment, trying to understand what had just been said. Then something occurred to her. 'And Sarah's?' she said brightly. 'And Will's?'

There was a pause. She felt her father's shoulders stiffen under the soft wool of his business suit. She wondered if she'd said something wrong. Surely Daddy meant for her brother and sister to have something too – that was always how it was at home. If one of them got a biscuit, they all got a biscuit.

'Yes, of course,' he said gruffly. 'Will's and Sarah's too. But you, Daisy . . .' His hand tightened around her small one. 'You are the special one. Try to understand that, my dear – *you* are the special one.'

4

Little Nelly Hughes was playing in the sandpit in the garden. Her father had built it for her 'specially, and she loved it when he pulled off the wooden cover and let her climb in with her feet bare, the cold dampish sand squelching up between her toes. Inside was a collection of toys: buckets, little pots, plastic spades and some toy cars and tractors. A naked Sindy doll kept smiling despite the fact that her nylon hair was matted and dull with sand. Nelly liked to make the dolly have adventures in the sandpit, muttering to herself in a long, ceaseless stream of chatter as she played.

She was lost in her own world when her mother came to the sliding patio doors and called for her.

'Nelly! Nelly! Come inside, please!'

Nelly heard a note of anxiety in her voice and looked up. Her mother stood just inside the house, wiping her hands on the apron she always wore during the day, unless there were visitors. As Nelly watched, her mother carefully untied the strings and took the apron off, folding it up neatly as she did so. The little girl got up obediently and climbed out of the sandpit. Her feet were scratchy with sand, so she wiped them quickly on the grass, picked up her sandals and came skipping back over the lawn.

'What is it, Ma-ma?' she asked chirpily. If visitors were here, a plate of the best biscuits appeared on the glass coffee-table in the lounge, and that meant one for Nelly. She hoped there were the round short-bread ones, with the window of sticky jam in the middle like a little red cushion or a shining jewel. She liked those best of all.

'The lady's here, darling,' said her mother, her expression worried. 'She says she phoned to tell us that she was coming this morning but we thought it was tomorrow. Oh dear, oh dear . . .' Her mother's eyes filled with tears.

Nelly didn't say anything but gazed up, hoping and trusting that whatever was wrong, her mother would make it all right.

'Come along.' She bustled Nelly through the dining room, smoothing down the child's hair as they went. Outside the lounge, her mother kneeled down and helped Nelly put on her sandals as she muttered that it couldn't be helped. Then she stood up, took a deep breath, smiled and ushered the child into the sitting room.

It's always cold in here, Nelly thought. It was only used for best, and there was a chill in the air that never went away. The family lived mostly in the kitchen or else in the room her mother called the snug – a small cosy room with a squashy sofa and a television.

In the lounge sat a plump lady in a flowery dress

and glasses, a big bag by her side. She stood up with a smile as Nelly and her mother came in.

'Hello, dear,' she said cheerfully. 'How nice to see you again. Do you remember me?'

Nelly nodded silently. She did remember her. The lady had come here before and asked to see her. There had been questions, dull ones, and she'd been made to sit still and answer them with the promise of a jam biscuit as a reward if she answered nicely. It was never the way it was when one of her mother's friends came round and the adults ignored her as they chattered away, pouring endless cups of tea and not noticing when she slipped another pink wafer off the plate.

This lady had also been there when Nelly had been taken to a place like a doctor's waiting room: a bright room, with toys and tables and chairs in it. Another lady had been there, asking to play with Nelly and telling the little girl to call her 'Mum', but Nelly hadn't wanted to. The skinny, shabby woman, smelling of cigarettes and with her nose pierced, was nothing like Nelly's own clean and comforting mother. Instead, the little girl had played with the dolls and ignored her.

Nelly expected a question from the visitor, but the lady turned instead to her mother.

'Is she ready?'

'No, not really . . . we thought . . . tomorrow . . .' Her mother sounded helpless.

'You should have warned her in advance,' reproved the lady. 'That's the policy we advise.' She shook her head. 'It's going to be worse for the poor little thing now.' She turned her attention to Nelly again, the big smile spreading over her face. Nelly didn't trust it.

Did the lady think she couldn't hear anything? What was going to be worse? She felt a flicker of apprehension.

'Have you had a lovely time here?' the lady said in a stickily sweet voice. 'Have you enjoyed it?'

What does she mean? Playing in the sandpit? Nelly just stared back and said nothing.

The lady turned to her mother again. 'She has lovely eyes, hasn't she? Very striking, that greeny-blue colour. You've done an excellent job, Mrs Thornton, you really have. You'd hardly know it was the same child. Remember how she was as a baby!'

Her mother looked down and Nelly saw pain deep within her eyes and felt cold clammy fear crawl over her. 'Yes,' said her mother in a strange, tight voice. 'I thought she'd never stop crying. It took four months before she stopped suffering. Now you'd never know what she'd been through. It's taken a lot of love and care.'

The lady looked sympathetic. When she spoke it was in a low, soft voice. 'I know how difficult this is. I'm very sorry.'

'We . . . we had hoped . . . to adopt.' Nelly's mother's voice sounded choked.

'That's what we all thought would happen,' the lady said, shaking her head. 'But the mother really has turned her life around, quite unexpectedly. And her petition to have the child back to live with her was granted.' The lady shrugged. 'You know and I know that the best thing for the poor mite is to stay here with you. But what the judge says . . . well, that's what happens, I'm afraid.'

Nelly reached out for her mother's hand. She had

grasped that they meant her when they said 'poor mite'. 'I want to stay with you!' she said quickly, clasping Ma-ma's fingers.

'When does she go?' asked Nelly's mother in a shaking voice, putting her own hand over Nelly's.

'This afternoon, I'm afraid. We can wait until your husband gets back so he can say goodbye.'

'So soon?'

The lady nodded, and Nelly saw to her horror that her mother was crying.

'I don't want to go!' she cried, nestling into the warmth of her mother's body. 'Where am I going? I won't go! I won't.'

Her mother suddenly pushed her away, stood up and ran out of the room, sobbing. Nelly watched her go, staring after her with wide eyes, confused and frightened. The lady in the armchair opposite leaned towards her, her eyes grave and sad.

'Now, Chanelle,' she said softly. 'You must be very brave. Do you understand? You must be a very brave girl indeed.'

5

The parties held in honour of Daisy's birthdays were legendary: in the grounds of Thornside Manor, a modern William-and-Mary-style palatial mansion in the greenest, plushest part of Surrey, whole fair-grounds and circus tops appeared. One year, a fairy-land was built in the grounds, with tiny houses where real little people lived, along with a miniature castle with a moat for Daisy and her friends to play in. Another year, a dozen over-excited eight-year-old girls were dressed and made up as miniature Disney Cinderellas, before being driven around the grounds in a glass coach pulled by white ponies, and then enjoying a party in the ballroom of the house. And the celebrations weren't confined to birthdays. People still talked of the Christmas extravaganza that Daddy organised one year: fake snow, husky dogs, sleigh rides and a skating rink were all conjured into existence, along with stalls handing out hot chocolate or hot blackcurrant and endless ice cream. Father Christmas himself came from Lapland to sit in a beautiful, twink-ling, snow-covered chalet and hand out splendid presents to everyone. Daisy had a sense that anything was possible – Daddy could always make her dreams come true.

For her twelfth birthday, she asked for something a little more grown-up. Her entire class was invited to a smart hotel in London where Daisy's favourite pop group, a chirpy quartet, performed on the stage and then mingled with the party goers. Familiar faces were everywhere, tucking into canapés and seeing if they could get anything harder to drink than lemonade: they were the stars of Daisy's favourite television soap opera, flown over from Australia to be guests at her party.

'Thank you, Daddy!' she'd said, squeezing him tight in a gigantic hug.

'You're welcome, my princess. Anything for you,' he'd replied, kissing her cheek and beaming with pleasure.

Everybody thought how wonderful it was to be a Dangerfield and have such a loving, indulgent father. But they didn't see what it was like at home, when Daddy wasn't the expansive, generous giver of gifts and thrower of parties. They didn't see his rages.

Daisy was thankful that these were never directed at her. When Daddy wanted to let rip with his lacerating tongue, he directed it at Julia, criticising her looks, her clothes, and almost every choice she made. Or he took out his bad temper on Will and Sarah, his children by his first marriage. Daisy's half-brother Will was five years older than she was and seemed very grown-up. Sarah came next, with three years between her and Daisy, although her shyness and reserve made her seem a little younger. Daisy loved being with her big brother and sister, but some of the time they lived with their mother, Elizabeth, who had been divorced from Daddy before Daisy was born. Will and Sarah were both at boarding school and divided exeats and holidays between their parents.

When they arrived at Thornside or London or wherever, Daddy would be happy to see them at first but soon he would start becoming irritated, and before long his temper would ignite because once again they'd fallen short of his expectations, and then the raging would start. It made poor Sarah clumsy and frightened and prone to bursting into tears, provoking her father even more. His remarks to her could be cruel and cutting, but he seemed to take a particular pleasure in putting Will down, questioning his choices, dismissing his achievements and demanding ever higher standards.

Daisy saw the way her half-brother handed over a good report with a glow of pride, hoping for praise from his father, and the hurt and sadness that filled his eyes when Daddy ignored the good and focused on one low mark, working himself into a rage and tearing the report to pieces. It was worse when Will brought friends to the house. As everyone sat down to lunch, Daddy would set about criticising Will in front of the visitor, mocking him and making the poor guest join in the laughter directed at his son.

He would declare that Will was useless, that he hardly knew the boy was his son sometimes. Then he'd list Will's failings and flatter the unfortunate friend: 'I expect your parents are very proud of you, you seem a very well-rounded, diligent boy. You should teach Will not to be so lazy. He needs to push himself! I'd be proud if *you* were my son.'

Daisy wondered why Daddy couldn't see that this had the opposite effect on Will to what was intended. The boy wasn't motivated to try harder. He simply hardened his heart against his impossible-to-please father, and decided it wasn't worth the effort trying to win his praise. And the pain of being found wanting, no matter how hard he tried, was obvious in his eyes.

Julia remained remote from her stepchildren, watching the way they were bullied with a distant look of sympathy in her eyes, though she never intervened. More and more these days, she looked beaten and broken, and no one blamed her for not wanting to draw Daddy's fire.

Only Daisy escaped the rages. Only she rushed into his arms, beaming with delight. Only she said, 'I love you, Daddy!' with sincerity in her eyes.

As she grew older and her position as Daddy's favourite more entrenched, Will and Sarah began to avoid her. Even her mother seemed to find it difficult to be with her sometimes, and certainly when Daisy and Daddy were together. It seemed that his love for her only increased the others' hurt at his indifference to them.

Daisy didn't know why it should be this way and there was nothing she could do anyway, so with childish logic she simply accepted it. Daddy wasn't nice to the others. Perhaps they should try a little harder to please him, and then he might love them as much as he loved her.

Daisy was lounging around in her sitting room in the Belgravia house, watching afternoon telly before she had her supper. She thought that at thirteen she was too old to have a nanny, but Daddy wouldn't hear of getting rid of Nanny Johnson, who was humming away in the next-door kitchen as she cooked for Daisy. When the house telephone rang, the light that denoted her father's study flashing on the base, Daisy leaped over the sofa and whisked it up at once.

'Yes, Daddy?'

'Come down here, darling, right away.'

She hurried downstairs, skipping down them three at a time, lithe and energetic in her cropped jeans and ballet pumps, and burst into the study to find Daddy, standing before the fireplace, puffing away on his usual big cigar.

'Princess!' he said, beaming, as she came in and rushed over to kiss him. 'How would you like a little treat tonight?'

'Ooh, what?'

'A trip to the opera.' Her father's face darkened. 'Your mother was supposed to come. But she's . . . unwell.'

Daisy knew what that meant. Her mother was frequently unwell these days, staggering and unfocused not long after lunchtime, her breath bitter and her eyes bloodshot. She wasn't often seen in the evenings and, if she was, would always say that she felt ill and that her sleeping pills were making her drowsy. The pills were supposed to explain the way her mother's head tilted and swung slowly, and the slurs and drawls in her speech, but Daisy wasn't fooled. She knew that the drinks tray in the drawing room held an irresistible allure for her mother. There was one in each of the family homes: the Belgravia house, Thornside Manor, the villa in Tuscany, the estate in

Thailand, the chalet in Gstaad – a little folding table tucked discreetly behind a sofa or beside a cabinet, laden down with bottles of spirits, little cans of mixers, a soda siphon, an ice bucket, a supply of crystal glasses and saucers of lemon slices put out freshly each day. Three or four visits to the tray would turn Julia from an articulate, sharp-witted woman into something else altogether.

Daisy hated her mother's inability to resist the lure of those bottles – not just because of the drawling, drowsy creature who then took her place but because she knew her father despised it too. Sometimes her mother didn't become slow and slurry but hysterical, full of laughter and jokes, although the laughter and gaiety always turned eventually to screaming rows. Daisy knew them well, even though they usually took place when she was supposed to be asleep in bed. In London, the voices would bounce off the marble floors and soar up the main staircase, reverberating off the white-painted walls. The thick carpets of the corridors and their sturdy doors absorbed some of the noise, but Daisy would still know that three floors below her parents were screaming and yelling at each other. Sometimes she heard them clearly.

'I don't know why I ever let you take me away from him!' her mother shouted once. 'You only did it to satisfy your own fucking pride, not for me!'

Her father's booming tones were harder to distinguish but she heard him say some dreadful words: 'You crazy bitch!. . . Disgusting tramp . . . Why don't you go and live on the Embankment with all the other winos? You're mad, you should be locked away!'

In Surrey, her bedroom was far away in the east

wing, but she still seemed to be particularly attuned to the frequencies that carried her parents' voices. She always knew when another humdinger was underway, and would bury her head under her pillow, muttering 'stop, stop, stop, stop . . .' through gritted teeth, until she could at last shut it out and go to sleep.

They won't be rowing tonight anyway, Daisy thought with a stab of relief. *Not if Mummy has already gone to bed and Daddy's going out.*

'Well, what do you say?' asked her father, smiling. 'Do you want to come?'

'Yes, please!' she said, excited. The opera! Staying up late! How exciting. 'What should I wear?'

'Tell Nanny you need a long dress,' Daddy said, putting his cigar between his lips. 'We'll be leaving in half an hour, so you'd better hurry.'

Upstairs, Nanny tutted because the supper she'd cooked for Daisy was now not needed. 'You'd better have a mouthful or two, though! Goodness knows if Mr Dangerfield will remember to feed you.' But she said it without rancour as she liked life with the Dangerfields. Apart from looking after Daisy's things, there wasn't much for Nanny to do; she whiled away hours in front of the nursery television, enjoying the daytime game shows, ordering food from the kitchen and growing ever more plump.

Nanny went to the large walk-in wardrobe to find something suitable. Daisy was measured every six months and the measurements sent to a Parisian boutique; a few weeks later, a huge powder blue box would arrive, its insides thick with tissue paper that concealed beautifully made dresses, skirts, blouses, cashmere cardigans and pairs of soft kid shoes in white and pale pink. Daisy was beginning to scorn such babyish things, and had persuaded Daddy to let her go shopping with her friends instead once or twice. Nanny flicked through the rail of clothes. 'You should wear your black velvet, I think. It's not long, but long's no good for a girl your age anyway. It's below the knee and will look very nice.'

'Can I wear my hair up?' Daisy asked excitedly, pushing her fair hair on top of her head, blonde tendrils escaping through her fingers.

'No,' said Nanny firmly. 'A nice brushing out and hairclips will be best.'

Daisy descended the stairs twenty minutes later feeling tremendously dressed up. Her black velvet dress felt very sophisticated, and Nanny had been persuaded to let her wear the tiniest smear of cherry lip gloss on her lips, so she felt like a proper lady. She wished she was wearing something with a heel like Mummy's spindly party shoes, but her ballet slippers had bows on them and looked a little like the shoes the older girls at school wore, so she was happy.

Daddy was downstairs waiting for her. He'd changed into his dinner jacket and black silk bow tie, a white silk scarf draped round his shoulders. Daisy always thought Daddy looked terribly impressive and handsome in his evening clothes – and tonight she was going out with him! She wanted to dance down the stairs, but walked as elegantly and carefully as she could instead.

'You look beautiful, my darling,' he said, smiling as she came towards him. 'Now come here.'

When she reached him, he leaned forward and

pinned something to the front of her dress. When she looked down, a diamond brooch sparkled on her chest.

'Oh!' she gasped, hardly able to speak.

'I was going to give that to your mother,' Daddy said. 'A little piece I picked up in Paris – it's vintage Van Cleef and Arpels. Art Deco. Do you like it?'

'Yes,' Daisy breathed, hardly able to take her eyes off the delicate setting that curled around the glittering diamonds.

'I think it suits you best,' he said with a smile. 'Now, come along. The traffic can be terrible at this time of night.'

She couldn't stop looking at the sparkle of her diamond brooch all the way to the Royal Opera House.

6

The girl ran nimbly through the Peckham estate, racing along the well-known paths, her brown hair streaming out behind her as she went. She knew where to skip the broken paving stones, or when to leap over a flowerbed, and where she could cross the road most quickly, ignoring the lights as she dashed to the central island, then over the far lane between slow-moving cars. She wove in and out of the people in her way: mothers pushing buggies, small children dawdling in their wake, the strolling elderly.

She knew which places to avoid – the ones where kids hung out when they ought to be in school. Everyone knew. Whenever she reached the children's playground – painted in bright brave yellow and red against the grey concrete and grime of the estate – she always speeded up. Today it was difficult to imagine how she could go any faster, but when she saw the boys there, she pushed herself as hard as she could, despite her thumping heart and the pain burning in her chest.

'Hey, girly! We can see you!' shouted the tallest. He

must be sixteen at least – almost a man – a gangly black boy in a leather jacket and pristine white trainers, his trousers slung so low they were round his thighs. He laughed.

She felt her blood chill at the sound of his voice.

'You can't run fast enough,' yelled his friend, a white boy with a close-shaven head and a skin dotted with red spots. 'We're gonna catch you one of these days, you better believe it.' Then he laughed loudly. 'Gonna do what you know you want.'

'Your pussy ever been fucked?' demanded another. 'You wanna taste of my dick, huh?'

She tried not to shiver, but pulled in another burning breath and ran even faster. When she reached home, a small shabby terrace house, she pushed her key into the lock, rushed in and slammed the door behind her, shutting out the chill winter weather. It was almost Christmas and a string of limp fairy lights flashed around the hall mirror.

'Chanelle! Chan-*elle*! You back from school?'

It was the usual shriek, coming from upstairs. Still catching her breath, Chanelle cast her eyes in the direction of the noise.

'Come up here, girl, I heard you come in!'

Chanelle sighed and climbed the stairs to her mother's fusty, filthy bedroom. Opening the door, she saw Michelle sitting up in bed in a bedraggled nightie, her hair all over the place and her eyes bleary.

'What is it?' the girl asked, lolling against the doorframe, one skinny leg tucked behind the other.

'Bring us a cuppa tea, will you? I'm bloody parched up here, and so's Bill.' Her mother gestured to a musky snoring lump next to her under the duvet.

Chanelle sighed. 'All right.'

She pulled the door shut and went back downstairs, feeling angry. She was always angry these days, from the moment she woke up till she flung herself down on her thin mattress to go to sleep. It was hard to remember a time when she hadn't been full of rage and spitting with fury at the horribleness of everything. Sometimes she was sure that life had once been different for her: she recalled warmth, sunlit days, and a comfortable feeling of love and security that had felt like being hugged. In her nightmares, she was being ripped away from a soothing presence. She would wake sobbing and more lonely than ever.

In the kitchen she turned on the radio. Music flooded out. It was one of her favourite pop songs and she started to relax as she put the kettle on and washed up a couple of mugs, pouring away the dregs with their sour flotilla of cigarette butts. Her mum and Bill had been up till the early hours, drinking and smoking, which explained why they were still in bed at close on four o'clock. They'd kept her awake until after midnight and then she'd overslept and almost been late for school. She couldn't afford to get another late card. Her teacher had said that the council officers had reviewed the register and noted her punctuality problems. Then there were all the unauthorised absences. They didn't understand that Michelle could decide on a whim that her daughter wasn't going to school that day – that she wanted to take her shopping, or else had errands to be done. And Michelle didn't care if the truancy officers came calling or not. Nothing seemed to bother her – she didn't take them seriously when they said that they could take her to court if Chanelle's attendance didn't improve. They said she could be fined or even put in prison if she didn't make sure her daughter got to school on time every day.

A small part of Chanelle hoped her mother would be put in prison, and then she herself would be taken back to that lovely sunny place she recalled from her earliest memories, but she knew that would never happen. Michelle was very good at playing the game. She sensed just when things were getting dicey, and then she would work hard at making a good impression. When the social workers came to visit, Michelle knew exactly how to play the flawed but loving mother who was only trying to do her best for her little girl and striving to manage her life as well as she could. Once the social workers were satisfied and out the door, then it was business as usual.

Chanelle moved in time to the music and sang along as she made the tea: one bag dunked into two stained mugs until the water turned dark, some milk sloshed in and a spoonful of sugar. She carried the mugs upstairs to her mother's darkened bedroom, where the only light came from the gaps where the curtains were hanging off the rail. Her mother's boyfriend was still asleep. Michelle, sitting up, took the mug Chanelle held out to her.

'Thanks, love. What's that bloody racket down there? You're always listening to that stuff too loud.'

Chanelle shrugged, thinking it was kind of rich when her mum had music blaring into the early hours with no thought for her daughter trying to get to sleep upstairs, let alone the neighbours.

Michelle took a sip and put the mug down. 'That's

the business. Just what I needed.' She reached over to her cigarette packet, took one out and lit it. As she blew out her first lungful of smoke, she said, 'Nice day at school?'

'Mum . . .' Chanelle began tentatively, sitting down on the bed and plucking nervously at the duvet cover.

'Yeah?'

'I was wondering about . . . about the dancing class.'

Michelle frowned. 'Not this again, Chanelle.'

'Please, Mum,' she begged. 'I really want to do it, and Mrs Ford says it's only twenty-five pounds for the half-term—'

'Twenty-five pounds!' Michelle took an indignant drag of her cigarette, looking scandalised. 'Fucking cheek, that's a fortune! I've told you, I can't afford it. It's not just the classes . . . you'll need dancing shoes and Christ only knows what else. I'm sorry, Chanelle. No.'

There was a silence as Chanelle contemplated the dark disappointment that was settling on her. Then she said in a small voice, 'But Mrs Ford says I should do the classes . . . She says I'm talented. She says I have a natural gift for it.'

'Mrs Ford can shove it up her fucking arse!' snapped Michelle. 'How can you be so selfish, Chanelle, when you know what I'm going through?' Her eyes filled with tears and the corners of her mouth turned down.

Chanelle stared back guiltily. Her mum had been worse than ever lately, drinking and taking drugs and generally losing it. It was because they'd come and taken another baby away – the third that had been born and taken away before it had even come home. This latest was Zara, a little red, scrunch-faced thing that Chanelle had glimpsed only for a moment in the hospital, just after she'd been born. Social Services said that Michelle couldn't provide a proper environment for a baby, that her lifestyle was too chaotic, and they'd taken little Zara off to be fostered, just like they'd taken Sonny and Jacob, the boys who'd arrived last year and the year before that.

Each disappearance had led to weeks of tears and depression for Michelle and endless drinking, when everything at home would have broken down altogether if it had not been for Chanelle. And there was no talk of taking her away any more. People seemed to have forgotten she was only thirteen. They treated her more like the mother than the child these days, and that was what it felt like sometimes, as she cleaned up the house and tried her best to cook meals and keep her mother functioning.

'Sorry, Mum,' she muttered. 'It's just . . . it's just something I really want. That's all.'

Michelle sniffed. 'I know, love. I'm sorry too. Maybe . . . well, let's see come Christmas, shall we? Maybe things will be better then.'

7

Christmas at Thornside Manor was always a lavish affair, and this one promised to be no different.

Even though she was getting too old to bounce around, Daisy came down the stairs feeling excited. There were going to be some gorgeous new treasures for her to take possession of, and it was also a proper family day here at Thornside. Although she liked it when they spent Christmas skiing at the Gstaad chalet, it was best when everyone was here, where it felt most like home with all the proper Christmassy things.

'Happy Christmas!' Daisy chirped as she came into the drawing room, where Sarah was already sitting on a sofa reading one of her pony books.

Sarah looked up, smiled shyly and returned a 'Happy Christmas' in her quiet voice, then went back to her book. She was quieter than ever, and seemed to want to shrink into herself and disappear behind her glasses and the thick fringe that fell over her brow. She had always been kind enough to Daisy, but seemed happiest when alone with her horses. Daddy had bought her two – a grey mare called Mindy and a white pony called Bobo – and they were kept at the stables of an adjoining farm. Most days in the holidays, Sarah was to be seen pulling on jodhpurs, riding boots and a thick jumper, grabbing her riding hat and heading off to be with her beloved horses. She would spend all day at the stables: cleaning, mucking out, grooming the horses, caring for the tack and exercising Mindy and Bobo. She had taken Daisy out on Mindy once, but Daisy had been frightened to find herself so high up with only the reins to hold on to, and Mindy hadn't helped by galloping off with her when an irresistible open field had presented itself. When Daisy had finally been able to pull the mare up, she had slid to the ground, trembling, promising herself she would never get on a horse again.

Without a love of horses to bond them, Daisy and her half-sister had always remained a little distant from one another, and that had only increased as they grew older. Perhaps, Daisy thought, it was because it was so obvious that she was Daddy's favourite. Nevertheless, she was sure Sarah felt some affection for her.

She wondered if her sister had noticed her new outfit. Daisy and her best friends had been allowed to go shopping in Harvey Nichols, flitting around the upstairs floors where the cool stuff for teenagers was on display, and she'd bought an amazing Moschino tunic dress which she wore with a loose chain belt slung round her hips, and some Lanvin flats. Last year she'd been done up like a kid in a smocked floral number, but now she felt grown-up and trendy – a lot more so than Sarah, who despite being nearly sixteen was in a plain skirt, high-necked blouse and a red jumper, like some kind of old biddy.

Daisy looked over at the fireplace where five fat Christmas stockings were propped up. Here at Thornside, stockings appeared at the ends of beds but were kept like vast overstuffed sausages to be opened when the family were together. Big presents would be given later after lunch, when they all gathered in the great hallway where the twenty-foot Norwegian spruce reached up almost to the second floor.

'Where's Will?' she asked, looking about for her half-brother.

'Upstairs of course,' replied Sarah. Will was seventeen now and in the sixth form at Winchester. He had become even more silent and intense, interested only in the computer he had in his room, and his music, to which he was almost obsessively devoted. He had lately moved to a big space in the attics which had been soundproofed and laid out with state-of-the-art electronics, where he could play his music and hunch over his computer for hours on end without bothering anyone. Even though Daddy had arranged the new rooms for Will, he seemed to resent the hours his son spent there, and was always ordering him downstairs to spend time with the family. Will just sat there in furious silence, clearly longing to be back upstairs again.

When he was around, Daisy found herself in awe of him. He had always been a mysterious character, five years older and hardly caring about her existence. Her first memories of him were of a freckly, messy-haired boy, who was always off on private adventures in which she could have no part. Some strange physical transformation had overtaken her half-brother since she had last seen him. He was much taller than before, having shot up over a foot to a towering six foot three inches, and skinnier, as though he had depleted his fat stores with the rapid growth. He was strong, though; she could see well-formed muscles on his arms and across his chest and shoulders as a result of the rowing he did. His hair had darkened from bright ginger to a chestnut auburn, and in certain lights Daisy could see golden glints on his chin and cheeks where red-gold stubble was breaking through the skin with its light dusting of freckles. Sarah had the same hair colour, though hers was long, pulled back into a thick chestnut ponytail that curled down her back like a river.

Daisy was never quite certain that Will even liked her. He sometimes shot her looks of such coldness and near resentment that she felt he must hate her – but then, a few minutes later, he would speak to her in a perfectly friendly way and she would wonder if she had imagined those other feelings of his.

The room filled with an unmistakable presence as Daddy came in, imposing in his navy blue velvet jacket and red silk bow tie, a pair of monogrammed slippers from Church's peeping out at the bottom of his dark trousers. 'Happy Christmas!' he boomed, and opened his arms. The girls ran to him, covering his smooth face with kisses. He laughed and then frowned. 'Where's Julia?' he asked gruffly. 'And that rascal Will?'

'Here's Mummy!' said Daisy, seeing her mother coming down the stairs. She noted with relief that Julia looked composed and elegant in a red Dior shift dress. Her fair hair was shiny, brushed into the usual sharp bob framing her delicate, heart-shaped face. She was thin to the point of bony but Daddy was proud of his wife's aristocratic elegance and slender proportions. 'I can't stand women who turn into plump milch cows!' he would sometimes bellow. 'Now, *your* mother, Sarah . . . that's a woman who didn't care and who turned to fat as a result.' Sarah would blush scarlet and seem to sink back into herself, as though painfully aware of her own puppy fat.

Julia Dangerfield moved delicately on her kitten heels across the flagstoned hall, her blue eyes unsmiling despite the curve to her scarlet lips. 'Merry Christmas, everyone,' she said lightly as she offered her cheek to Daddy for a kiss.

'Where's that boy?' he growled. 'He's driving me to the limits of my patience.'

'He's just a teenager,' Julia said in a reasonable tone. 'You must give him a little leeway.'

'I've never given anyone leeway in my life!' declared Daddy loudly, puffing out his huge chest. 'And I'm not about to start with some angst-ridden adolescent!'

Julia's jaw seemed to set and there was the faintest lift of her eyebrows and a small sigh. She looked over at the girls. 'Happy Christmas, Daisy . . . Sarah.' They went obediently to kiss her, Daisy breathing in the familiar and rather intoxicating scent of Fracas, which her mother always wore.

'Sarah,' commanded Daddy, 'go upstairs and get your brother. Tell him he'd better come here now or there's going to be merry hell to pay.'

Sarah went at once, running up the stairs.

'I won't have that boy spoil Christmas,' growled Daddy. 'Where's the bloody champagne?' He frowned. 'Drake knows we're here, doesn't he? Julia, ring the bell.'

Things had to go exactly as Daddy wanted them or he would be swift to show his anger. Already Daisy began to feel nervous at the way his face was darkening. Once the storm started, it could quickly worsen and then anything might happen.

Julia pressed the button by the fireplace and an instant later the butler was there, outwardly calm but, Daisy could tell, a little flustered. He was carrying a tray of crystal flutes and an ice bucket containing a bottle of vintage Dom Perignon, its neck wrapped in a pure white linen napkin.

'Sir,' Drake murmured as he came in, placed the tray on a small table and prepared to open the bottle. 'Merry Christmas, sir.'

'Sod your Merry Christmas!' snapped Daddy. 'Having a lie-in, were you? Come on, man, get on with it.'

Drake nodded politely and untwisted the wire around the neck of the bottle. A second later, he had removed the cork with the faintest popping sound and was topping up the glasses with the fizzing liquid. The girls were given a drink as well – half a glass for Sarah and Daisy, while a full flute waited for Will.

'M'lady,' Drake murmured, placing a glass by Julia's side. She had sat down on one of the gilded Louis XVI chairs by the fireplace and was staring into the flames that flickered in the grate.

There was the sound of footsteps and then Will and Sarah came into the room.

'About bloody time!' said Daddy. 'Come on, boy, get your glass . . . everyone, get your champagne.' When they were all ready, Daddy made the traditional Christmas toast – 'To the ongoing, eternal success of the Dangerfields, and to my father who gave us all the blessings we enjoy!' – and they all drank.

The cold bubbles prickled Daisy's tongue. She was sure she'd learn to enjoy champagne eventually – after all, everyone else seemed to love it – and she liked the slightly fuzzy feeling it gave her.

'And now,' Daddy said, happier once the day was back on track and all were present and correct, 'stockings.'

The bulging stockings were handed out and they each took a turn to extract a present and open it. As usual, Daddy had spoiled them all. Julia unwrapped her diamond-encrusted Cartier watch with raised eyebrows and a smile. Among many other trinkets, Sarah received a Gucci purse and a pair of diamond earrings, Will a Dunhill wallet and an Armani belt, and Daisy a necklace of pure pink pearls and a beautiful antique Fabergé egg to add to the collection that her father had been building for her since she was little. This one was set in turquoise enamel and gold, and opened to reveal a golden couple, the woman in a ballgown, the man in tails, dancing on a miniature turntable while a Viennese waltz chimed away from somewhere inside.

'It's beautiful, Daddy!' she said with a beaming smile, breathless with excitement. 'Thank you.' She rushed over and kissed him. 'I love it *so* much.'

He smiled, gratified. 'These are just little things. Your big presents are waiting for later.'

'Drake!' said Julia, holding out her glass. The butler came over obediently and poured in more champagne. She had put the watch on and it glittered around her wrist.

Daddy watched, then said sharply, 'That will be all, Drake.'

The butler bowed. 'Very good, sir. Lunch will be served at one o'clock precisely.'

'See to it that it is.' Once Drake had gone, Daddy turned to his wife and said, 'Don't start, Julia.'

'What do you mean?' She smiled sweetly. 'It's tradition to have champagne on Christmas Day, isn't it? And I know how you like things done properly.'

He stared at her, his dark eyes glittering with anger, but made an effort to control himself. 'Let's just try to be a happy family today, shall we? For one day in the year.'

Daisy heard a snort and turned to look at her half-brother. Will was sitting hunched on the sofa, his expensive presents lying discarded on the floor next to him, as though the costly designer leather meant nothing at all.

'What is it?' Daddy said sharply.

Will shrugged. 'Nothing.' But the expression in his eyes and the petulant thrust of his lower lip said everything.

Why is he so angry? Daisy wondered. *When Daddy's so good to us?* She knew that it must be horrible to have your parents not live together, to have your father marry again to someone who was not your mother, but surely Will couldn't remember a time when things had been any different? And, after all, he spent just as much time with his mother as with his father, when he wasn't at school . . .

'Be careful, boy,' Daddy said in a menacing voice. 'I've had just about as much of you as I can take. Any more attitude from you, and the Ferrari that's waiting outside is going straight back.'

A scowl creased Will's face and his green eyes sparked, but he said nothing.

'Mustn't make Daddy cross!' Julia said gaily. 'We all know what happens when Daddy gets cross!' She tipped back her head and emptied the contents of her champagne glass.

'I warned you, Julia,' Daddy said, his voice low. Daisy shivered. Julia got up and walked to the drinks tray. She picked up a bottle of vodka and poured herself a large tumblerful. Then she turned and smiled at her husband.

'I know, darling,' she said, her eyes icy. 'I know it *very* well.'

Daisy stared at them both, frightened. Surely they weren't going to start one of their rows today, were they? She felt torn between her parents. She loved her mother but had never felt from her the warmth and adoration she received from her father, and as a result was far more likely to run to her daddy for hugs and kisses. It was as though there was an invisible force field around Julia that kept everyone, even her daughter, away from her.

Daddy seemed to be working hard to control himself. He said through gritted teeth, 'Please, let's try and get through today without any tantrums or bad behaviour.'

Will got up from the sofa. 'Come on, Sarah,' he said, his voice startling Daisy with its deep masculine timbre.

'Where are you going?' demanded his father, frowning.

'To call Mum. She's on her own today, remember? We're going to wish her a Happy Christmas.' He

47

stalked out of the room, Sarah following timidly behind.

Daddy watched them go, then beckoned Daisy over. 'Come on, Princess. Bring that egg of yours, I want to see it up close.'

By the time Will and Sarah had returned from their long phone call with their mother, Julia had made several more trips to the drinks table and it was getting harder to ignore the evidence of her condition. She'd begun to slur her words and her usual elegant walk was marred by swaying and stumbling.

Daisy knew that Daddy was trying to ignore it, but she could also tell by the stiffness of his shoulders and the set line of his mouth that he was growing more and more furious.

Drake appeared and announced that lunch was served, and they went through to the dining room which was laid out in the Christmas best: gleaming silver, fine linen, heavy crystal, and long tapering candles burning in the candelabra. Crackers from Asprey, each containing a solid silver trinket, sat by every plate. A vintage Sancerre was chilling in the giant silver ice-filled cooler while a decanter containing Château Haute Brion '82 stood to breathe on the cabinet, waiting to accompany the main course. Three maids in black uniforms stood with their backs against the wall, watching the family take their places at the table and waiting for Drake to give them the nod.

Daisy settled herself into her chair, hoping she might be allowed to taste a little of the wine, although she wouldn't be too unhappy with a glass of fizzy cola.

The sight of the table in all its finery seemed to

cheer up her father, and when the staff began to bring in the food – plates of Scottish smoked salmon with a prawn and salmon mousse, and tiny poached quails' eggs on miniature circles of rye bread, dripping in hollandaise – he seemed happier.

'Happy Christmas, everyone!' he said, when they had been served. 'You may begin.' He piled up a forkful of salmon as Drake moved discreetly about, filling up glasses. 'How was your mother?' he asked, looking at Will as he shovelled food into his mouth.

Daisy sliced through the soft pink flesh of the salmon and put it in her mouth, savouring the sweet, smoky flavour.

'She was fine,' Sarah said quickly.

'I asked your brother. Can't he speak for himself? He's said precious little today.' Daddy smiled coldly.

'Mum is all right, considering she's spending Christmas on her own without us,' retorted Will, flushing.

Daddy chewed slowly. When he'd finished, he said, 'Your place is here with me. You spend plenty of time with your mother. Today, she is at liberty to make her own arrangements.'

Will glowered at his father but said nothing.

'I've had enough of this ridiculous side-taking,' Daddy announced, his eyes hardening. 'You are my son and daughter – you are both Dangerfields.' He put down his cutlery. 'I've decided. From now on, you will spend the majority of your time here at Thornside. Your mother is exerting too much influence on you, that's clear. You're both becoming spoiled, bolshie little monsters.'

Sarah's face went bright red and her eyes filled with

tears. She bit her lip and stared hard at her plate, letting her chestnut hair fall in front of her face to hide it from her father.

'You can't do that,' burst out Will, furious. 'We're not babies! It's up to us how we spend our time and where we live!'

'I don't think so,' said his father in a voice of steel. 'You will do as you're told or regret it.'

Daisy felt a nasty shiver run down her spine. Daddy had never spoken to her like this. She didn't know what she would do if he did.

'Leave the poor little fuckers alone,' said Julia suddenly from her end of the table. She lifted her glass to her mouth and took a great gulp of the white wine Drake had just poured her.

Daddy looked at his wife. 'What did you say?'

'You heard me! Why don't you take a break from ruining everyone's lives today? It's fucking Christmas after all!'

'Julia, control yourself,' hissed Daddy, his eyes fierce.

She threw back her head and laughed. 'Sorry, am I being naughty? Everyone must behave, mustn't they? We all know what the punishment is for being bad.'

Daddy rose to his feet. Daisy cowered in her chair, fearful at the sight of the rage on his face. She wished with all her heart that Mummy would stop talking when it was making Daddy so cross.

Julia smiled at her husband and gave a careless shrug. 'It's about time someone told you how it really is. Haven't these children of yours been through enough? You divorce their poor, long-suffering mother because you fancy a change. A bit of posh, to buff up the Dangerfield bloodline. Well, it was looking a bit ropey, wasn't it, what with your brother being born on the wrong side of the blanket? So you chose me.' She thumped herself in the chest with her hand. 'And I fell for it, like the idiot I am. What was wrong with your last wife, huh? I'll tell you. She was from hearty peasant stock, just like you, and you couldn't bear that. But your father chose her for you, and as long as he was alive – making everyone's life a misery, just like you – you did what he said.'

Daddy's fists clenched and he stared at his wife from under beetling brows. 'You'd better shut up . . .' he growled.

'What are you going to do about it?' cried Julia, a strange merriment dancing in her eyes. 'Huh? Well? Will I be wearing long sleeves and high necks and make-up . . . to hide the bruises?'

'You're drunk. Get out of here. Now!'

She put her head on one side in a coquettish way and blinked at him. 'And miss this delightful Christmas meal? How could I?'

He flung his napkin on to the table and roared, 'Get out, NOW!'

Drake appeared as if by magic at Julia's side and gently took her arm, lifting her up.

'Get your hands off me, you shit!' she screamed, trying to shake him off, but the butler was too strong for her. She glared at Daddy. 'Always get your bloody heavies to do your dirty work for you, don't you?'

'Take her upstairs, Drake,' commanded Daddy. 'Lock her in the bedroom with a bottle of vodka. That's obviously what she wants, the disgusting drunkard.'

Julia went pale with rage, unable to speak. As Drake

pulled her to her feet, she managed to free her arm enough to rip the diamond-encrusted watch from her wrist and fling it across the table towards her husband. It hit one of the solid silver candelabra with a clink and bounced off to land with a plop in Daddy's glass of Sancerre, where it sank to the bottom, like a strange glittering fish. 'That's what I think of your bloody present!' she spat, as Drake hustled her out of the room. A moment later they were both gone.

They all stared at the magnificent piece of jewellery as it bobbed gently beneath the surface of the wine.

Daisy realised her hands were trembling. She was scared. Then she caught sight of Sarah who was weeping, her shoulders shaking and tears running down her scarlet cheeks. Will was stony-faced but his eyes betrayed that he too was shaken by what they had seen. He and Sarah had never shown any affection for their stepmother; they were polite to her, but the most that could be said was that they tolerated her. For her part, Julia had pretty much ignored them in return. Arrangements were made that included them when necessary, but otherwise life continued in much the same way whether Will and Sarah were there or not. Now Julia had just defended them in a way that had never been seen before, and it looked as though she was going to pay a nasty price for it. Will's mouth tightened.

As Daisy watched her half-sister crying on to the plate of salmon before her, she felt her spine stiffen.

Daddy isn't going to see me like that, she told herself fiercely. She knew her father well enough to be sure that Sarah's display of weakness was only going to infuriate him further. He hated it when his children quailed before him, and always had – he was far easier to placate if he felt that they had showed spirit, even if it meant he had to punish them. *But not me. He doesn't punish me.* It was true. Daisy had never done anything to warrant it – or not that he had seen anyway.

Daddy pulled the Cartier watch from the wine glass and tossed it on the table, wiping his wet fingers on the tablecloth. Then he sat down, his face like granite, put his napkin back on his lap, picked up his cutlery and took a mouthful of salmon. There was silence apart from the sound of silver rattling on china and some mournful whimpering from Sarah. After a few moments, Daddy could stand it no longer.

'Stop that blasted blubbering!' he yelled, throwing his cutlery back down. 'Do you hear me? Shut up immediately!'

Sarah jumped in fear and knocked over the crystal wine glass that Drake had filled with elderflower cordial. It toppled over slowly, hitting the silver cooler and smashing. The tablecloth was immediately soaked and shards of crystal glittered everywhere like scattered ice.

Daisy gasped. Sarah stared at the mess, horrified by what she'd done. Daddy jumped up again, now properly irate. He strode over to Sarah and grabbed her by the shoulders.

'How can you be so clumsy?' he cried. It was obvious that she was going to become the target of the rage that had been building within him all morning. 'You stupid, clumsy oaf! This is all because of your bloody mother . . . Julia's right, she's just a peasant – and so are you! Look at you. You don't even look like a Dangerfield with that damn' hair of yours!'

Sarah seemed frozen with fear, her eyes wide and her mouth open.

'Go on!' he screamed. 'Go upstairs and get out of my sight!'

'Don't you bloody well touch her!' Daisy looked over to see Will getting to his feet. 'Get your hands off her.'

He had gone white, his freckles showing up as pale blotches. He had pulled himself up to his full height, and had set his broad shoulders. The muscles that he had worked into iron strength with his rowing bulged beneath his suit jacket. He looked suddenly more like a man than a boy.

'Keep out of this,' shot back Daddy, but he let go of his daughter's shoulders. 'Sarah – upstairs. Now.'

Will put up a hand. 'You stay right here, sis.' He stared defiantly at his father. 'She's not going anywhere.'

'How dare you?' snarled Daddy. 'You're just a boy. You and your sister will do as you are told, do you understand?'

'No,' Will said stubbornly. 'You can't control us. You're our father, not a dictator.'

Daddy went scarlet in the face and seemed to be struggling for breath. He slammed his fist down on the table so that the crystal tinkled. 'You . . . you . . . *will* do as I say! I *will* be obeyed. Don't you understand that without me you've got nothing?' He waved towards the ceiling. 'That fancy equipment upstairs, the thousands of pounds worth of computer nonsense – I *paid* for all that. Everything you have, everything you own, every bloody thought that school of yours put in your head – I paid for all of it!'

'No, you didn't,' Will said calmly. The more his father raged, the more in control of himself Will seemed, as though he was drawing his own power from Daddy's fury. 'Grandpa did.'

Daisy turned her eyes automatically to the portrait of Joseph Dangerfield that hung in pride of place against the far wall, a life-sized oil painting of the old man sitting in his favourite armchair in the drawing room of this very house. He was wearing a perfectly cut Savile Row suit, his leather shoes shining and glossy, his grey hair cut short and neat, his expression serious. Josef Mzareč, who had left Czechoslovakia in the twenties and come to seek his fortune in England, had become an English gentleman – or tried to. He had changed his name to Dangerfield, bought expensive houses, thrown lavish parties and sent his only son to public schools and Cambridge, but he had never belonged. His accent, still apparent despite his attempts to lose it, and his unpolished ways had shut him out of high society as effectively as an iron door.

Grandpa had died before she was born, but Will and Sarah had known him when they were very little.

'What did you say?' said Daddy to his eldest child in a choked voice.

'You heard me. Grandpa made our money. You've just lived off it. And he put money in trust for me and Sarah too – and when it's time for us to have it, we'll be rid of you forever.' Will suddenly smiled, and his face was transformed. 'In fact, I don't know if I can wait that long. You know what? I've had just about enough of all this. You've treated me and Sarah like shit for years while you spoil that little brat out of her senses.'

He means me! Daisy thought, shocked. *Am I spoiled?*

Daddy gaped at him while Sarah stared, her eyes frightened.

'Do you think we haven't noticed?' Will's smile vanished and his face hardened again. 'You act as though we're nothing . . . people you can cast aside when someone else takes your fancy, just like you did with Mum. Well, I've got news for you. We're *not* nothing. We're part of this family and we matter. Grandpa knew it – which is why he put the family fortune in trust for all of us. Maybe he knew you too well. No one cares what the fuck you do, Dad. There's nothing you can do about the fact that we're Dangerfields just as much as your little princess, and we're entitled to everything Grandpa wanted for us.'

Daddy's mouth had dropped open as though he was unable to believe what he was hearing.

Will stepped out from behind the table and walked around it towards his sister. 'Come on, Sarah. I've had enough of this. Let's go.'

She looked at him and then at her father, obviously scared to move. Will came up to her and took her hand. 'Come on.'

The two of them headed for the door. Daddy watched them go and then hurried after them into the hall. Daisy leaped out of her own chair and ran after everyone. She was in time to see Will scoop up a set of keys from the vast china bowl on the hall console table.

'What the hell do you think you're doing?' shouted Daddy. 'Those are the keys to my Aston Martin!'

When Daddy wasn't being driven by Ted in the

Rolls, he used his British Racing Green Aston, speeding along the roads as though he owned them.

'I know,' Will said pleasantly. 'I've always wanted to drive it, and now I'm damn well going to.'

'You've only just passed your test!' cried Daddy. 'You can't . . . you can't . . .'

'You're so keen on telling me what I can't do,' Will said, grabbing his coat from the stand. 'But you know what? I don't give a damn. Tell you what – why don't you just keep that Ferrari you got me for Christmas? We'll do a swap.'

He opened the front door as Sarah slipped on her coat. The next moment, they were both skipping down the stone steps to the driveway. Daddy's Aston Martin had been brought to the front by Ted earlier and Will pointed the fob at it so the doors clicked obediently to unlocked.

'If you climb into that car, that's it!' screamed Daddy, his face puce. Daisy hid herself behind him, watching all that was happening, shivering a little in the cold December air. 'Do you hear me? *That's it*! You can consider yourselves no longer part of this family!'

Will climbed into the low-slung driver's seat as Sarah slipped in beside him and pulled the passenger door shut. She looked much happier than she had five minutes before.

Will looked up at his father and grinned. 'I don't think that's your decision to make actually, Dad. Sorry!'

He put the key in the ignition and fired up the engine. A moment later, the car roared over the gravelled drive, spun a little on the stony surface and then leaped forward as Will powered her round the turning circle. The Aston Martin headed out on to the asphalted drive that led between an avenue of limes, out to the great gates and the open road.

Daisy stood beside her father and watched the little car zoom away, still hardly able to believe what had just happened. Had they really gone? And from what Will had said, he meant for ever.

Her father seemed equally disbelieving and stood for a long minute staring after his car as it disappeared into the distance. When it was certain that his two eldest children were gone and not coming back, he seemed transported by fury, his hands with their little tufts of black hair on each finger shaking uncontrollably. Then, without a word, he went back into the house and climbed the stairs. Daisy followed him at a distance, not sure what she was meant to do now. Daddy climbed all the way up to the attic space that had so lately been converted for Will, went inside and shut the door. Then, from inside, came the sounds of wanton destruction, as he carefully and painstakingly destroyed every last piece of Will's treasured equipment and ripped the room to shreds.

8

Chanelle knew that her mum had made an effort for Christmas. She'd gone to the supermarket on Christmas Eve and bought the last turkey joint on the shelves. It came in a ready-to-roast tray with a packet of stuffing and some grey-looking chipolatas wrapped in pallid bacon, and she'd also bought some frozen vegetables and a Christmas pudding. There was even a tin of cheap chocolates.

And at least I don't have to cook them too, Chanelle thought.

One thing her mother didn't have any trouble remembering was the booze. That appeared every year without fail, even when the food didn't. This year there were big litre bottles of whisky and vodka, cans and cans of beer, and great plastic barrels of cider. Because it was Christmas, there was also a bottle of wine.

She tries, Chanelle thought, but knew nevertheless that elsewhere people were having better Christmases than this. Her mother was still in bed although it was nearly noon, because she and Bill had not been able to resist all the alcohol in the house and had started as soon as Michelle had returned from the supermarket with it. Friends had dropped by later and they'd caroused into the early hours, singing and shouting, the air thick with cigarette smoke and toxic with the fumes of alcohol and skunk. The house was grey, cold and acrid-smelling when Chanelle had awoken, still drowsy from her interrupted sleep, and gone downstairs.

On the kitchen table was a present, shambolically wrapped but obviously intended for Chanelle. She pulled off the flimsy paper and saw that underneath was a pink teddy bear with a big heart appliqué-ed on its chest. She stared at it for a while. It was a rare present from her mother and she liked it for that reason, but it wasn't what she'd asked for. She'd wanted a Discman so she could listen to her CDs but her mum had said it would just be nicked, so there was no point. Or else she'd wanted a pair of new pink Nike trainers, or some jeans with sparkles on the pocket and embroidery tattooed over the legs. Or the dancing slippers she stood and stared at in the cellophane-covered window of the dusty little shop on the high road that sold tutus, leotards and sparkly silver tap shoes.

Not a teddy.

She put the bear back down on the table and sighed, then opened the fridge and took out the cold, clammy tray of turkey, turned it over and read the instructions. It seemed easy enough. The only problem was guessing when her mother would be conscious enough to eat their Christmas meal. She cocked an ear and listened. There was no sound from upstairs.

No point just sitting around here waiting, she thought. She put the turkey on the side and turned the oven on to heat up. Then she picked up her coat and headed outside, pulling the door of the tiny terrace house shut behind her.

Her hands dug deep into her pockets against the wind that always blew bitterly around the sharp concrete angles of the Blacksmith Estate. It flicked her mousy brown hair into her eyes and she tried to shake it away without using her hands. For once she didn't feel the usual nervousness when she was outside. The estate seemed deserted today: everyone was inside, eating their Christmas dinner, or glued to the television. All around houses were glinting with coloured lights, or had their windows sprayed with snowflakes and Santa stencils. Christmas trees were silhouetted against net curtains, and the silvery flickering rectangles of television screens glowed through from the rooms beyond.

The loops of flashing stars that hung from door jambs or were entwined in scrawny bushes by front doors lent the bare, harsh-looking estate a touch of sparkle and joyfulness that was usually lacking. Chanelle stuck her chin down into the collar of her coat and looked stubbornly at the ground. She didn't want to think about families where children were looked after, where mums cooked meals every day, did laundry and made sure that all was well, or where there were dads . . . Chanelle tried not to think about that ever. The knot that twisted in her belly was too painful.

She rounded the corner of a row of terrace houses into the square where the playground was. Above the front door of each house was a long blue plastic case with a light inside. The lights were all off but it was still possible to read the white lettering on the cases that would be illuminated when the lights were switched on: 'Help needed – call the police.' Panic alarms. Every now and then, late at night, one would flash and after a while, if anyone could be bothered to call, a police car would draw up, blue lights twirling on its roof, and the officers would get out in a leisurely fashion, ready to deal with the latest domestic drama. There was always something going on around here. Last year, a woman had been knifed by her ex-partner in front of their kids, even though she had a court order against him to stay away from her.

Chanelle wandered over to the deserted playground and sat down on one of the swings, moving it idly as she wondered when she should start to head for home. She was about to get up and retrace her steps to the house when she heard a voice.

'Hey, you! Girly.'

She turned and saw the tall black boy who often hung out here with his gang. A tremor of fear ran through her as she saw him strolling towards her, though he was on his own. She would have to be brave. She put her chin up and said, 'Yeah? Whatchu want?'

He came closer to her. He had fine clear skin and bright brown eyes, his black hair shaved close to his skull with the back patterned in wavy lines like the contours of hills on a map. There was a blunt cut through one of his eyebrows. As he approached, he grinned. 'What you doin' here? It's Christmas Day, innit?'

62

'Yeah, well, what are *you* doin' here?' shot back Chanelle.

The boy sat down on the swing next to hers. He shrugged and reached into the pocket of his leather jacket for a packet of cigarettes. 'It's a bit crowded at mine. I came out for some air, laike. All my aunties and uncles and cousins and, laike, whatever. It was doin' me head in.' He offered the packet to Chanelle. 'Want one?'

'Nah.' She shook her head, her fear of the older boy subsiding as she realised he wasn't interested in being aggressive to her.

'Hey, I'm sorry about what that boy of mine said to you the other day, you know? 'Bout your pussy. He shouldn'ta said nuffink like that to you, I told him. Some of the kids round here, don't matter if their balls have dropped or not, they still want to pretend they can fuck someone.' He lit his cigarette slowly, observing her for a while before he said, 'You're at St Stephen's, innit? I seen you in the playground. Them girls were giving you trouble.'

Chanelle shrugged and looked away. School was no picnic, it was true. She was picked on, perhaps because she was small and pale and scrawny, or because the others sensed her loneliness and the anger that ran through her like molten lava in the core of a volcano, waiting to be spewed forth when the eruption came. The playground had become a place of torture for her as she waited for whatever new torments the gangs of girls had devised for her. More than once, she'd been hustled round the back of the toilet block and kicked, pinched and spat on while they hissed insults

63

until she couldn't help tears of pain and fury running down her face. They liked that.

'Why do you let 'em do it?' the boy asked, shaking his head. 'Them lot are bitches but they ain't tough.'

'Not tough towards you maybe,' retorted Chanelle, flushing red that he might have witnessed her ordeal. 'But most of 'em are bigger than me.'

The boy laughed. 'Yeah, maybe you's right. Listen, next time they give you grief, you come to me, ahright? I'll make sure they don't trouble you no more. Whass your name?'

'Chanelle.'

He nodded approvingly. 'Yeah. Naice. I'm Jamal. You come to me any time, and I'll help you, yeah?'

She smiled at him. He didn't frighten her any more. 'Yeah. OK. Thanks, Jamal.'

'No worries.' He ground out his cigarette and stood up. 'I better get back. You coming? I'll walk you, if you like.'

'Yeah. My mum'll probably be awake by now.' She remembered the turkey joint waiting on the side for her to put it in the oven.

She got up and the two of them walked slowly out of the playground together.

After they'd shared the Christmas dinner that Chanelle had cooked, eating it while wearing flimsy paper crowns from the cheap crackers, Michelle announced that they were going out.

'We're going to Gus's,' she said loudly while Bill sat back replete in his chair and lit a fag.

Chanelle brightened. 'Are we?' She didn't go to Gus's very often but she always liked it when she did.

Chanelle didn't know how her mother had come to have a friend like him, he wasn't like anyone else they knew, but he'd always been there, a friendly presence in the background of their lives. He had a house round the back of the estate, not a modern one but an old Victorian place, battered and ramshackle and full of unusual things: a piano, glass cases with stuffed animals and birds in them, old skulls, and strange sculptures of bone and wax. There were books and pictures everywhere, piled on tables and on the floor, along with heaps of yellowing newspapers and dusty magazines. Gus had painted all the walls with murals of country landscapes from some hot place where there were vineyards, castles and soft green hills melting into hazy blue skies. It wasn't exactly homely but it was interesting.

It was already almost dark when they walked around to Gus's, a sharp cold wind ruffling their hair and pinching their noses and ears. The house was lit up and a late-afternoon party was going on, plonky jazz playing on the ancient stereo, people all over the house, puffing on cigarettes and clutching glasses of wine or whisky.

'Ah, Michelle, come in!' Gus cried, when he saw them pushing their way through the crowd in the hall. 'Welcome, welcome! Merry Christmas!'

Chanelle was glad to be in the warmth and light. She followed her mother and Bill down the hallway into the kitchen at the back, where Gus was standing at the stove, stirring a saucepan of mulled wine, an aroma of oranges and cinnamon wafting up from the pot. He sported a gold paper crown that perfectly encircled his bald spot. He was old – Chanelle didn't know how old, but old. He had white hair and bushy white eyebrows with stray wiry black hairs sticking up from them. His dark brown eyes were almost lost in pouchy, wrinkly skin. His nose had swollen and turned red from years of drinking and he'd let the white stubble grow over his chin and cheeks so that today he looked like a tipsy Father Christmas. He was wearing an ancient yellow jumper that had clearly once been very good quality, and a pair of stained old jeans. 'And here is the lovely Chanelle.' His eyes looked almost black as he leaned over and put a hand on her shoulder, giving it a friendly pat. 'How are you, my dear?'

He didn't speak like anyone else she knew, except maybe for a couple of teachers at school, his accent all rounded and his words clear. 'All right,' she mumbled, suddenly shy.

'Have you had a splendid Christmas, dear?'

'Yeah.' She smiled. It had been rubbish really, but there was no point in telling anyone that. They weren't interested. Gus was distracted for a moment, directing Bill to the glasses and the whisky bottle, then turned back to her.

'Now,' he said in a warm tone. 'Someone told me that you wanted something very special for Christmas.'

Chanelle frowned, puzzled, and shot a glance at her mother, who was grinning as she lit up a cigarette.

Gus went on. 'Someone told me you would like some *dancing lessons*. Is that right?'

'Yeah . . . yeah,' Chanelle said, suddenly breathless. 'That's right . . .'

'Well, well. The funny thing is, I had a visit from Father Christmas last night,' Gus said, tapping his nose. *He thinks I'm a stupid kid,* Chanelle thought with a touch of scorn but she pretended to lap it up, grinning at him eagerly. 'And he asked me to give you this . . .' He picked up a brightly wrapped parcel and gave it to her.

She took it, excited, and opened it quickly. Inside lay a pair of pink satin ballet slippers, their shell-pink soft slippery ribbons tied around them. Next to them was a small card on which was written: *IOU dancing lessons for one year.*

Her eyes were suddenly wet and stinging, and her throat felt tight and painful. 'Oh, thank you. Thank you, Gus,' she said in a choked voice, clutching the slippers to her chest. She was delighted but surprised. He'd never given her anything before, so why should he start now? 'Thank you. I dunno what else to say.'

He patted her shoulder again. 'You're very welcome. A little present from your uncle Gus, that's all.'

'Happy now?' asked Michelle, puffing out smoke as Chanelle nodded, still scarcely able to believe that her dearest dream had come true. 'Hope that's the last we'll hear of you complaining for a bit now, anyhow!'

9

Daisy giggled as Lucy held up the magazine picture. They were in Lucy's study, supposedly doing revision for their exams, but actually leafing through gossip mags, looking for anything about themselves and their friends.

'"Are these Britain's craziest heiresses?"' queried Lucy in a silly booming voice, reading out the headline on one article.

'Hmm,' Daisy said, 'we *might* be, I suppose!' She balled up a piece of paper and threw it at the picture. It showed her and Lucy attending a charity ball the previous week. Daisy had worn a shimmering floor-length Rachel Gilbert gown, a scene-stealer in silver sequins, and she'd accessorised it by carrying an antique silver birdcage containing two miniature parakeets, their green and scarlet feathers providing a wonderful contrast to her metallic dress. Lucy had sported a tame white owl, which sat on her shoulder throughout the evening, blinking its amber eyes at the bemused partygoers. She'd returned it to its cage during the dancing.

Lucy continued reading. '"Fifteen-year-old beauties"—' She raised her eyebrows at Daisy. 'Ooh, beauties, get us! "Fifteen-year-old beauties Daisy Dangerfield and Lucy Critchlow-Browning had all eyes on them last night thanks to the eccentric additions to their costumes. The heiresses caused quite a stir at the charity event, which raised seventeen million pounds for needy children."'

Daisy giggled again. 'Nice that everyone noticed. Now we just have to plan what we're going to do next time!'

Lucy sighed dramatically. 'Darling – so difficult when we've set such a fantastic precedent.'

'Oh, I'm sure we'll think of something, don't you worry.'

The door to Lucy's study opened then and Keira Bond stood there, lounging in the doorway, blonde and statuesque. She was not exactly one of Daisy's favourite people, and she felt the same way about Daisy.

'What are you doing here?' she drawled, giving Daisy a lazy, up and down look. 'I thought the day girls had buggered off by now.'

'I've got permission to stay on and revise,' Daisy replied tartly, 'not that it's any of your business.'

Keira stared at her, lips tightening slightly. 'Well, I'm glad I've found you actually because I've got something I've been meaning to say.' She put a hand on one hip and fixed Daisy with a hostile look. 'Stay away from Freddie Umbers.'

Daisy raised her eyebrows. Freddie was a deliciously handsome boy she'd been spending a bit of time with lately. Their paths had crossed at various smart parties and in Les Caves du Roy in St Tropez over the summer. He'd shown a marked interest in her, full on flirting whenever he saw her, and she didn't object. In fact, she fancied him rotten and was sure that he was going to ask her out soon, as he'd asked for her mobile number and email only last week. 'What's it got to do with you?' she returned.

'Freddie's going out with me,' Keira said. 'So paws off. OK?'

Lucy murmured, 'You're only after him because his dad's got a fuck-off yacht. *So* transparent.'

Keira scowled at her and pointedly ignored the comment.

'Oh – and does Freddie know about that?' asked Daisy. ''Cos he seemed pretty keen on asking me out last week – if the fact that he kissed me has anything to do with it.'

Keira's eyes narrowed and two spots of colour appeared on her cheeks. 'You heard me,' she spat. 'Stay away from him, you *pleb*.'

'What?'

'A pleb. A noove.'

Daisy flushed in her turn, anger flaring inside her. 'What are you talking about?'

Keira snorted. 'Come on, you know what I mean! Your dad's rich, but he comes from nothing. My father said he's a common little immigrant who got lucky when his father bought a few houses. You're just a generation away from being a poor-as-muck peasant.'

Daisy felt a rush of anger. She had suspected something of the sort was being said around the common room. Keira and her little gang had taken to whispering about her and laughing cruelly whenever she came past, calling out insults that hadn't meant anything to her but which she now guessed were jokes about her background. Questions of social status were taken very seriously in this school: exactly where your money came from and how big your house was were matters of great importance – almost as important as how thin and pretty you were, and whether or not you had a boyfriend, and what school he went to, and how much money *he* had.

So that's what it's all about! Daisy thought, burning with fury. *I might have guessed . . . stupid, stuck-up bitches! How dare they talk about my father like that?* A rush of protectiveness towards him surged through her. How could anyone think him anything less than wonderful? He was charismatic, powerful . . . the greatest man in the world, probably. And as for the story of Daisy's grandfather and his extraordinary rise from buying a few dilapidated houses in the East End to owning a magnificent real-estate empire that included leisure resorts and hotels . . . well, it was an amazing achievement and nothing to be ashamed of. It had made the Dangerfield family extremely rich. But money wasn't enough according to the girls in Daisy's school. They valued blue blood and the leisure that came from being born to inherited wealth; they sneered at hard work and a family who had arrived in this country and made its mark within two generations.

Daisy leaped to her feet, her eyes flashing. 'How dare you!' She lifted her nose in the air. 'For your information, my father is the best there is, and I'm not ashamed of his background one little bit. He works amazingly hard and does loads for charity. What does your father do? Mix a mean gin and tonic while

71

he's waiting for his turn on the tennis court? Well, excuse me while I faint with admiration.'

'And anyway,' Lucy pointed out, 'Daisy's mother *is* actually a lady.'

Keira curled her lip with scorn. 'Yeah, and my mum told me that her family cut her off for marrying a ghastly peasant. But apparently she was pissed at the time.' She turned to Daisy. 'See? You're just a common little nobody with a father who's as plebby as you are.'

Daisy flew at her and grabbed the other girl's hair. Keira squealed and tried to grasp Daisy's wrists, writhing against the strong fingers tugging against her scalp.

'Let go of me, you stupid bitch!' howled Keira.

'Not until you apologise,' Daisy said through clenched teeth, and yanked again on Keira's long locks, hearing with satisfaction the squeal of pain that resulted.

Lucy rushed up, pulling Daisy off. 'Stop it, you're going to have Miss Reed up here! We'll all be in trouble.'

Daisy let go reluctantly and Keira pulled back from her, clutching at her head, her eyes full of furious tears.

'You're going to pay for this, Dangerfield, I mean it!' she hissed, before turning on her heel and stamping away.

There was a moment of silence and then Lucy said, 'Her face was a picture. That was brilliant, Daisy, it really was!'

'She deserved it, the horrid cow!' said Daisy, still panting. 'No one says that about my family and gets away with it.'

*   *   *

72

Her father thought it was the funniest thing he had ever heard. Daisy was in his study, sitting on his knee, while he made her tell the story all over again. A fat Cuban cigar burned in the ashtray on the leather-topped desk, giving off a smell that was simultaneously fragrant and fetid.

'So you couldn't contain yourself, could you, my little firework? You rushed to defend your father's honour.'

'She was being horrible about you,' Daisy said in the little-girl voice she often used with her father, though she was hardly aware of it.

'What did she say?' He looked up into her face, his dark brown eyes sparkling with amusement, thick black brows beetling above them as they always did when he found something funny.

Daisy was pierced by embarrassment. She didn't want to repeat what that awful girl had said about her beloved father. She saw him for a moment through the eyes of her schoolmates, suddenly understanding how they might laugh at his fat stomach, always encased in a florid waistcoat, the last button carefully left undone as a gentleman always does. No doubt they sniggered at his jet black hair, too intensely dark and over-shiny to be natural, and at his tanned skin, which he kept a constant walnut brown with his trips overseas and the sunbed in the house gym.

But she didn't see any of those things – or at least, not usually. She only saw warm brown eyes and welcoming arms, and heard that deep chortling laugh or the voice calling her his princess. She smelled the comforting scent of his Hermès cologne mixed with

73

the bitter undertone of old cigar smoke, and knew that she was loved.

'Well?' he pressed, taking her hand in his. 'What did that little minx have to say about me?'

'Oh . . .' Daisy squirmed. She couldn't bring herself to say it. She was afraid that her father might feel bad about himself, or, worse, think that she might share Keira's sentiments. 'You know . . . she was just nasty. That crowd always are. The whole lot of them are catty, but Keira Bond is the worst.' She tried to change the subject. 'Daddy, did you see the pictures of the shoe designs?'

'Of course I did, darling,' he said, successfully diverted. He tipped her off his knee and went over to the computer to pull up the pictures she'd sent him. 'They're wonderful.' He scanned the images proudly as Daisy went round to join him in looking at the screen.

Displayed were a series of photographs of ballet pumps in a variety of materials, colours and finishes, along with some biker-style boots and sparkly sandals. To Daisy, they looked even more gorgeous than she remembered. The factory in China had done a marvellous job and soon they would start proper production.

'These look splendid, Daisy. Really. I'm very impressed.'

She smiled up at her father, delighted by his praise. It had been her idea to start designing a line of shoes aimed at girls her age, to be sold both on the Dangerfield website and in the boutiques on-site at Dangerfield hotels and resorts. Daddy had loved the idea, and arranged for her to meet people who could help bring her

74

designs to reality. So far, Daisy's ideas had all tested very well in market research: her shoes were filling the gap very well between little-girl styles and more grown-up, sophisticated looks sold to older women. Although there was no reason why grown-ups wouldn't want them too, the shoes looked so good.

'If this does well,' Daddy said thoughtfully, 'we can look at expanding the range and perhaps exploring other lines.' He gazed down at his daughter, his eyes momentarily stern. 'This doesn't mean I want you to forget that our main business is property. You understand that, don't you? That's what you'll be doing for me when your schooling is over.'

'I know that, Daddy,' she said.

He put one big brown hand over hers. 'It's more important than ever, Daisy. You're all I have. You know that, don't you? Now that your mother is so ill.'

Daisy nodded, her eyes wide. Her mother was more absent from her life than ever, in and out of places where Daddy said they would help her with her problems. Once or twice, she'd seen Drake wrestling Julia down the stairs and out of the house, into a private ambulance waiting to take her to a rehabilitation centre. Her mother would scream and shout and Daisy would want to run to her, but Daddy would hold her tight, whispering to her that her mother was very sick and had to see special doctors to help cure her of the alcoholism that was killing her.

And Daisy would clutch on to him, blinking back her tears, praying that Mummy would be well soon, and more thankful than ever that her father was the unchanging centre of her life.

Now Mummy was in a rehabilitation facility, a very

pretty old house with crenellated battlements, set in acres of velvety green lawns. Daisy missed her but she couldn't help feeling relieved that the house was calmer now.

Daddy looked suddenly sad.

'Are you all right?' Daisy asked, putting her arms around him, hating to see him downcast. 'It's not just Mummy, is it? Are you thinking about . . . about the others? About Will and Sarah?'

'No,' he said gruffly. 'Of course not. They made their choice and that is that. I don't dwell on it, Daisy, and nor should you.'

Daisy knew he was putting on a brave face. How could he not miss his two elder children? She had not seen either of them since that Christmas Day three years ago. The Aston Martin had been returned a few days later, collected by Daddy's staff, but he hadn't had the heart to drive it again and it had been sold. Now, all that was left was the echo of her half-sister and brother. It was strange that they had simply been erased from her life, and Daisy missed them, but had no idea how she would ever tell them so. Besides, Will's outburst on that last day had stayed with her; both he and Sarah had obviously always hated and resented her, thinking that she had monopolised all their father's attention. But what could she have done to have avoided that? She hadn't asked to be born, or to be Daddy's favourite. How could it be her fault?

Now she was, to all intents and purposes, his only child, the apple of his eye. She knew he spoiled her horribly, with the vast clothes allowance he funded and the credit card with no limit to draw upon at will. She already had a pink Range Rover of her own sitting in the garage, despite the fact she couldn't drive. When she wanted to go somewhere, she only had to call on the services of Daddy's driver or his pilot; the helicopter, plane or yacht were always at her disposal.

But Daisy knew that one day she would be more than just a pampered playgirl. There was a vast family business waiting for her to take over the reins when she was old enough. She would be expected to perform then, and perform better than anyone else. That expectation meant there would always be a core of steel beneath her glossy, designer-clad exterior.

She didn't mind that her future had been planned out for her since the time she was small.

Daddy needs me, she thought. *I have to be there for him. I'm all he has.*

10

The sounds of ballet slippers sliding and slapping on the wooden floor could be heard despite the loud piano music that echoed round the studio.

Chanelle moved as if in a trance, hearing the music somewhere deep inside herself and unable to do anything other than respond. The routine was short but demanding, and she had practised her sautés and pliés endlessly so that she could incorporate them with perfect grace into the dance.

She finished bent low, one toe pointed in front of her, arms outstretched, head bowed. As the music came to an end, she felt as though she'd floated back into her body. There was silence from the observers for a moment, then the elderly white-haired woman who'd come to watch her nodded sharply and said, 'Thank you, Miss Hughes. You can go now.'

Chanelle made the dancer's curtsey as she'd been taught, and then ran lightly to the swing doors of the studio. She turned long enough to catch her teacher's eye and see her smile and wink, before she had to leave.

In the changing rooms, another girl from her class was getting ready, wrapping her veil skirt around her while she anxiously inspected her hair bun in the mirror, making sure that not a wisp had escaped.

'How was it?' she said as Chanelle came in.

Chanelle shrugged. 'OK, I think. We'll see.'

The other girl looked sick with nerves. 'Lucky you that it's over!'

Chanelle nodded as she took off her shoes, but she didn't agree. She would have loved still to be dancing if she possibly could. There was simply nothing else in her life that made her feel that way. It alone had the power to make all the sadness and anger and drabness disappear.

She was just leaving the dance school, her bag slung over one shoulder, when Mrs Ford came hurrying out after her.

'Chanelle!' she called.

She stopped and turned. 'Yes?'

'You did very well.' Mrs Ford was smiling, her eyes shining. 'Easily the best today. I think you're in with a chance.'

'Thank you, Mrs Ford.' Excitement and pleasure bubbled up inside her.

'I'll let you know as soon as I do.'

Chanelle turned away towards the bus stop. On the one hand she was elated. Could she really win a place at ballet school? How amazing would that be? But . . . on the other . . . well, there was no way she could get the fees together. Her only hope was a scholarship but the standards were incredibly high. Girls from all over the world competed for the precious free places. She had little or no chance.

She didn't know what to fear more – getting a place, or not getting one. One way or another, there didn't seem to be much hope for her.

The letter came three days later on a Saturday morning. Chanelle heard the slam of the letter box on the front door and knew that the postman had been. She dashed into the hallway and picked up the slim white envelope with the stamp of the ballet school on the front and tore it open, her hands already shaking and her fingers clumsy with nerves.

She pulled out the letter and read it, then gasped and sat down on the floor as though her legs had suddenly given way. It wasn't a scholarship, but it was a bursary. They'd offered her a place with twenty percent of the fees paid.

Overcome, Chanelle clutched the letter close to her chest, her heart pounding. She was in! She could go! Mrs Ford had warned her not to get her hopes up, and told her that at fifteen she was old to begin her training . . . perhaps too old. She should have started years ago. But it seemed the school was willing to give her a chance.

'What are you huffing and puffing about?' Michelle came through into the hall, frowning. 'What's that?'

'It's the ballet school, Mum,' Chanelle stammered, holding up the letter.

Michelle took it, read it and then handed it back to her daughter, her face blank.

'Well . . . what do you think?'

'You know what I think. I think we can't afford it.'

'But, Mum . . .'

Michelle's face suddenly changed. She scowled, fury

80

flashing in her eyes. 'I told you not to go that fucking ballet audition! I told you what would happen, but you wouldn't listen. How the hell are we gonna pay any fees? Ballet isn't for people like us, I've said it over and over.'

'But they're giving me a bursary!'

'Money off? Money off the twenty grand or whatever it is? What's left will still be too much. I can't get that kind of cash together, you know that.' She snatched back the letter and ripped it to pieces, scattering the bits over the carpet. 'Forget about it, Chanelle. I should never have let you try in the first place.'

She watched, horrified, as the pieces of her precious acceptance letter drifted down to the floor. Sobs choked her and despair overwhelmed her. She scrabbled about, picking up the pieces, and jumped to her feet. 'I hate you!' she screamed. 'I hate you.'

'I fucking hate you too,' retorted Michelle, but Chanelle was already on her way out of the door.

She ran through the estate. It was a warm day and lots of people were out. She dodged them all as she ran, intent only on reaching her destination. Her breath burned in her chest as she ran, and her thin shoes meant her feet hurt every time she took a stride, but she didn't care.

Five minutes later, she stopped at the front door of Gus's house and pounded on the front door. 'Gus!' she panted, her voice barely audible. 'Let me in!'

She banged again and the door suddenly opened under her fists. Gus stood on the hall mat, frowning.

'Well, well, it's young Chanelle! What's all this about? You'd better come in.'

When she was sitting on one of the kitchen chairs, her breath restored, and had managed to explain, he looked relieved.

'I thought it was an emergency,' he said, bustling about, making them a cup of tea. His half-eaten bowl of muesli was on the table, the milky spoon abandoned beside it.

'It *is* an emergency,' Chanelle protested. 'I got a bursary to the ballet school!'

'Congratulations, young lady. They were right then. You do have talent.' Gus turned to smile at her, his dark eyes disappearing into the fleshy wrinkles around them. She handed him the pieces of paper, wiping away the hot tears that kept flowing from her eyes, and sniffing. 'What's this?'

'The letter. Mum tore it up. She says I can't go.'

'Oh, dear.' He gave her a sympathetic look and started to piece together the shredded paper. 'Yes, I see. There's the crest of the school. What a shame. Why did she tear it up?'

'Because we can't afford it.' Despair coursed through Chanelle and she started to cry harder. 'But it's all I ever wanted! Oh, Gus, you gave me the lessons. You even gave me two more years when you said you'd only give me one. Can't you pay for me to go to the school?' It had been her secret hope all along. After all, he'd come to her rescue once before when he'd paid for her lessons and carried on paying for them. Surely that meant that he wanted her to succeed. Why would he only give her the lessons and deny her what she wanted so much? She had nurtured an inner conviction that he wanted to sponsor her dancing career, that he'd never stop making sure she was able to do the one thing she loved and was obviously good at. In her mind, he was the fairy godfather who would make everything right for her.

He was gazing at her, dark brown eyes inscrutable. He passed her a mug of steaming tea and sat down at the kitchen table opposite her. 'I'm afraid I may have given you the wrong idea,' he said softly. 'I don't know how much ballet school costs but I suspect that, even with a bursary, it's going to be several thousand pounds a year. I don't have that kind of money, Chanelle, and I'm sorry if I gave the impression that I did.'

'But you must!' she burst out, angry despite her tears. 'You're different from the rest of us! You're rich.'

Gus stared at the table for a moment, one hand stroking his white whiskers. 'It's true that I'm not like many of the people who live around here,' he said slowly, looking up at her. 'And I did once have a bit of money. But I don't now. Not any more. I'm sorry. If I had it, I'd give it to you like a shot. But I'm not rich at all.'

Chanelle cried even harder, wiping her nose on her sleeve. She pushed back her chair and got to her feet. 'I don't believe you!' she shouted, unable to bear the fact that her hopes were dashed. 'You're just like everyone else . . . you don't care about me or what I want! You all want to ruin my life. You can all just fuck off!'

She ran out of the house, weeping, hardly knowing where she was going but desperate to be alone with her broken heart and the dreams that now lay in as many pieces as her precious letter.

11

'No school today for you, miss!' Daddy had said that morning when Daisy had come down for breakfast.

She'd been pleased even though she knew she really ought to be at her lessons with her exams approaching, but one day wouldn't matter. Besides, the school let Daddy do what he liked now that he had paid for a new library, theatre and science laboratory, named the Dangerfield Wing, all freshly finished and opened by Daddy himself in a grand ceremony marked by the unveiling of a golden plaque. That had not endeared her much more to Keira Bond and her cronies, but who cared? Keira could only gnash her teeth, aware that her plans for revenge on Daisy were coming to nothing. The other girls found the fact that she was starting her own shoe line beyond cool and there was talk that Daisy's next birthday party was going to be super-amazingly grand, and everyone wanted to be invited.

'Where are we going?' Daisy had wanted to know, before she rushed upstairs to change.

'You'll see,' Daddy had said mysteriously, draining his cup of coffee. 'Be ready in ten minutes.'

Daisy had thrown on a smart fuchsia pink shift dress and given it an edge with a studded black leather jacket and some of her own snake-print ballet pumps, and raced back downstairs in time to join her father in the new black Rolls-Royce. The gold one had been retired a few years before and this sleek new one with its snub nose and long back had taken its place. The drinks cabinet had gone, to be replaced by an on-board computer that showed constant updates on news of the financial markets.

The driver took them to the heart of Mayfair, to the flagship hotel of the Dangerfield empire, the Dangerfield Florey. It had once been simply Florey's, one of London's oldest and most prestigious hotels, but had been on its last legs in the eighties when Daddy had pulled off a major coup, buying it from the original owners and turning it into the hub of the Dangerfield business. It had so much more cachet than the string of airport hotels built by Josef in the seventies that had provided the bedrock of the family fortune, and it was grander by far than the high-rise luxury flats that the Dangerfield family had built in the most expensive cities in the world. Owning the Florey had given Daddy more satisfaction than most of his other property deals put together, even if Josef, his own father, had dismissed it as a white elephant. It cost a fortune to run and its profit margins were relatively small, no matter how expensive the rooms were, or how many crowned heads and movie stars ate in the restaurant or celebrated weddings and birthdays in the famous ballroom.

'Are we going to the Florey?' Daisy said, excited to be rounding Grosvenor Square to the Mayfair street where the grand façade of the Dangerfield Florey stretched along almost an entire block. It had grown gradually from two small hotels in Victorian terrace houses that had been merged together and then come to absorb more and more of the terrace until eventually, at the end of the nineteenth century, the Florey family had realised that the ramshackle design was no longer adequate. They'd had the old hotel demolished and rebuilt along the grand lines necessary for such a prestigious place, with lifts, en suite bathrooms, and marble, gilt and glittering glass everywhere. Now there were two hundred suites, two restaurants, a brasserie, a ballroom, three bars, and a vast ground-floor atrium where afternoon tea was served to ladies weary from shopping on nearby Bond Street, and rich tourists keen to experience the opulence of the famous hotel.

Daddy smiled and said nothing as the Rolls drew to a halt in front of the entrance, where a red carpet led from the edge of the pavement to the splendid lobby with its revolving door in glistening black and gold. The doorman, resplendent in his black greatcoat with its double rows of brass buttons and red grosgrain trimmings, came striding forward to open the car door, touching his hand to his peaked cap in salute as he recognised the boss.

Daisy climbed out, happy to see the Florey, her favourite of all the Dangerfield possessions. Above the lobby, the flat roof was covered in plants and bright flowers that looked beautiful against the cheerful red brick of the building above.

'Come along, Daisy,' Daddy said, taking her hand again. 'Let's see what we will see.'

They went through the door and into the imposing foyer where the black-and-white chequered marble floor gleamed in the light cast by the enormous crystal chandelier set above it. Through two more walnut-and-brass, many-paned doors and a turn to the left, and then they were in a long corridor where discreet boutiques were open for the custom of the hotel guests and visitors: a branch of Loro Piana, selling the finest cashmere scarves, shawls, coats and jumpers; a tiny outpost of Asprey's stocked with their exquisite bags, leather goods and silver knick-knacks – just the place to come for a gift or an indulgent treat. And, of course, there were several small but glittering jewellery shops, where a forgetful husband could select a wedding anniversary trinket or birthday gift to be wrapped and presented to his wife in their suite or over dinner.

Daddy led Daisy along the corridor. They passed the little boutiques and then stopped. Daisy stood and stared, gasping. Above the neatest miniature shopfront, she saw her name in flowing golden script, and beneath that: *Fashion for Feet*. Then she realised that the windows of the small store were full of her designs: elegant pumps displayed on brass stands and pink velvet cushions, some plain and some bejewelled. Kitten heels and slingbacks were ranged opposite biker boots and a selection of colourful wedges and easy-to-slip-on canvas shoes for the beach or by the pool.

'Oh, my goodness!' Daisy cried, clapping her hands with delight. 'This is wonderful!'

'Do you like it, darling?'

'I love it!' She flung her arms around him, laughing with joy. It was perfect.

'Is it a nice surprise?'

'It's fantastic! Oh, Daddy!' She turned back to look at her little boutique, her face flushed with excitement. She could see herself reflected in the shiny glass panes, her long fair hair falling about her shoulders, a wide grin on her face. She fizzed with pleasure at seeing her shoes actually available for people to buy – she'd only ever seen samples at home, nothing like this display. The velvet slippers in slate and charcoal, trimmed with sparkling yellow and amber crystals, looked more fantastic than she could have imagined when collected together like this.

'You should be proud,' her father told her. 'Now you'll be in charge of this, Daisy, do you understand? I've hired people to work in the boutique and a manager, but she'll report to you. You'll be the boss of everything from now on. And if this works, then we'll look at opening boutiques in other hotels in the group.'

Daisy nodded. 'I understand.'

'Good. But there's something I want from you in return. Come on. We're going back to the car.'

They arrived at Dangerfield headquarters twenty minutes later.

'I've got a little job for you this morning, my dear,' Daddy said with a smile as they rode the lift up to the top floor. 'Something that needs doing. I was about to do it myself, but I thought it would be an interesting test of your character. You're beginning to understand something of the business we do here, aren't you, my love?'

'Yes, Daddy.' She smiled back at him. She couldn't help but pick up what was going on: she was privy to so many of Daddy's conversations. Recently he'd started asking her to attend meetings and talks over rich dinners in exclusive restaurants, and she had even begun to sit in on the board meetings too. The other executives didn't seem to find it odd that Daddy was accompanied by his sixteen-year-old schoolgirl daughter, although she did look older in her expensive clothes and costly jewellery. Perhaps they understood the concept of the great business dynasty, and that the best place for the heiress apparent was at her father's elbow, learning the way of his world.

'Well, it's time you realised that business is not all about pleasant encounters. There are a lot of scoundrels out there, and we must always be on our guard against them. Do you understand?'

Daisy nodded again.

'Great success brings the jackals sniffing about. Everyone is on the make, everyone wants to be the one . . . the winner. And those of us who are top of the heap must protect ourselves by staying constantly on the alert, ready to repel anyone who attacks us. The worst threat does not come from those who appear outside the fortress with siege machines and weaponry, trying to take possession of what we own. The worst threat comes from those who are *already inside*.' Daddy patted her arm, his hand huge and rather hairy, the veins on the back prominent and purplish despite the heavily tanned skin. 'You'll soon see what I mean.'

They went to his office, greeted effusively by all the staff as they went, assistants trotting after them to take Daddy's heavy camel silk-cashmere coat, answer his rapid volley of questions and remind him of his diary commitments.

Daisy followed him into his office and Daddy dismissed everyone else, even his PA.

'What would you like me to do today, Daddy? Shall I go to my office?' Daisy enquired.

Her miniature office had been upgraded to a proper grown-up one, with a Chagall painting and a Picasso print on the wall, an elegant Regency lady's desk and a full set of Smythson desk accessories in the pink that was becoming her trademark colour with gold monogrammed Ds everywhere, each topped with a tiny gold-stamped daisy. Into her pink leather in-tray went all the major paperwork of the company – the accounts, the reports, the day-to-day activities of the business. Daddy would send the chief financial officer and other heads of department to her office to talk her through these and what they meant. She could follow much of it, but it was all very complicated and she had enough to learn at school. It would be different now that she had her own business to control, of course. She was looking forward to inspecting her sales figures and overheads, and was already hungry to see a profit on that bottom line.

'No.' Daddy looked at her with an expression that was both solemn and playful. 'I have a job for you to do first.' Then he explained what it was.

Ten minutes later, the door opened and in came one of the managing directors.

'Yes, sir?' he said brightly. He was a middle-aged man with neatly cut greying hair, discreetly framed glasses and a navy pinstripe suit. He seemed upbeat but there was the faintest flicker of nervousness in his eyes.

'Ah, Chalmers,' Daddy said, his voice almost jolly. He was sitting not behind his desk but in one of the armchairs positioned to enjoy the spectacular view over the City of London. 'Thank you for coming. I know how busy you are, running this great company of ours.'

'I've as much time as you need, sir, you know that.' Chalmers cast a curious glance at Daisy, sitting in the great green leather chair behind Daddy's desk, while he waited to be invited to sit down. There was a long pause, then Daddy spoke again.

'Chalmers, you know my daughter, don't you?'

The director looked over at Daisy with a fond smile. 'Of course I do, sir. We all enjoy her visits. She brings us luck – that's my opinion anyhow.'

'She does, she does.' Daddy pressed his fingertips together and seemed to be examining the smooth pinkness of his perfectly manicured nails. 'Now – she has something to say to you, if you don't mind.'

Chalmers looked over curiously at Daisy, his expression just a touch more relaxed. He seemed to be assuming that the boss had called him in to help the girl with her homework or something.

Daisy got to her feet. Her heart was pounding and her palms felt clammy but she straightened her spine and told herself to be brave. This was a test she was determined not to fail. Daddy was testing her mettle, making sure she had his spirit, drive and courage. She tossed her head and stared straight at Chalmers.

'Mr Chalmers, how long have you been here at Dangerfield?'

'Er, let me see now . . . twenty-five years. Yes – twenty-five years! Goodness me.' He smiled cheerfully. 'It's flown by. Feels like yesterday I arrived here as a graduate trainee, all wet behind the ears.' He glanced at the chair by the desk. 'May I sit down?'

'I'd rather you didn't.' Daisy went and stood by the vast floor-to-ceiling window. Down below, she could see tiny people, streams of traffic and the office buildings stretching away in either direction, together with the sprinkling of church spires and lead roofs reminding her that London was not simply the bustling, modern temple to money-making it sometimes seemed. When she turned back a moment later, Chalmers was looking a little uncertain. Was she imagining it, or was he paler than before? *Don't feel sorry for him, for God's sake. I can't afford to mess this up.*

She walked around the desk and stood before him – the tall, middle-aged businessman confronted by the sixteen-year-old girl – a schoolgirl, even if she was dressed in Dior.

'My grandfather started this company,' she said in a crisp, clear voice. 'He built it up from nothing and with it he's given a wonderful life to many people who've worked for him. He's given them the means to house, clothe and feed their families. And for his trusted lieutenants, his directors, there have been many pleasant perks – haven't there, Mr Chalmers? Home loans. School fee grants. Company cars and drivers. Tickets to the opera, to Ascot, to Wimbledon and all the rest.' She felt a trickle of sweat roll down the back of her neck, but hoped she was hiding her nerves. *What do I say next?* A chill of panic crawled over her skin but after a second she was in control again.

Chalmers was looking puzzled. 'Yes . . . but I don't understand?'

'Don't you?'

'No. I appreciate all the management benefits, of course, but I work very hard . . .'

'Of course. We require hard work in return for the generous salaries we pay, and all that comes with them. Also . . .' Daisy picked up a sheet of paper from Daddy's desk. Her father was watching her intently, his face impassive '. . . we demand loyalty. Absolute, total loyalty.' She held out the sheet of paper to Chalmers. He took it and she watched the blood drain from his face as realisation dawned. He looked up at once, not at her but at Daddy.

'Sir . . . sir . . . I can explain . . .' he stuttered, his hands shaking. Daddy simply stared back at him, and Chalmers moved his imploring gaze to Daisy. 'Please, let me explain—'

'I don't think you need to,' she said, raising her eyebrows. 'I think it's clear that you've been very, very careless. Fancy leaving that in your fax machine for your secretary to discover! Luckily, she knows exactly where her loyalties lie. It's just a shame you don't.' She leaned over the desk and pressed a button on the telephone. 'I believe that inciting another company to join you in attempting a management buyout counts as gross misconduct. Accordingly, you'll be leaving the premises instantly – without your company car or your security pass or any other company property.

Your employment is terminated forthwith. Your salary will be paid up until today. All outstanding loans must be paid off in full within three months, and your pension contributions will be returned – minus bonuses.'

Chalmers was now looking ill, as though he might pass out. His face was a ghastly shade of grey and his eyes were full of fear and panic.

'Please,' he said hoarsely. 'This will ruin me . . . my family . . . I have three children at school, a mortgage, debts . . .'

Daisy felt suddenly overwhelmingly sorry for him. He was totally crushed. It felt wrong that a grown man should be reduced to begging for mercy from a girl like her. *Stay strong. This is what Daddy wants. Daddy is always right,* she told herself.

'You should have thought of that before,' she replied coolly. The office door opened and two burly security guards came in. 'These gentlemen are going to take you downstairs and relieve you of your pass. Your belongings will be sent on to you.'

Chalmers seemed beaten before the guards took hold of his arms. He cast one look at Daddy and muttered, 'I'm sorry, sir, really . . .' but Daddy said nothing, merely watching as the guards walked him out of the office.

When the door had closed behind them, he turned to Daisy, a smile on his mouth and his eyes blazing with pride.

'That's my girl, Daisy! That's my girl.'

She instantly forgot Chalmers and the wreckage of his life. All that mattered was the wonderful feeling of basking in her father's approval.

12

Chanelle hoisted her dancing bag on to her shoulder and let the heavy doors of the dance school shut behind her. She hunched her thin shoulders against the wind that cut across the road with icy intensity and began to walk home.

She still lived for her dancing lessons, but some of the joy had gone out of them since she had been forced to decline the place at ballet school. Mrs Ford had been almost as disappointed as she was, Chanelle could see that, but there was nothing to be done. The school would only offer the bursary, not a full scholarship, pointing out that they were taking a risk with Chanelle anyway and that many other girls would leap at the place and pay whatever it took.

'You'll have to make it another way,' Mrs Ford had said, trying to help her be brave. 'You don't have to go to ballet school. There are other ways to succeed as a dancer, you know.'

Perhaps there were, but for now Chanelle couldn't see them. The bursary had been her route out of this place. There were plenty of girls in her class at school who couldn't be bothered even to try. They were the pack of bitches who picked on her constantly and enjoyed tormenting others, always looking out for some poor girl to victimise. They obsessed over their looks and who they were going out with and couldn't be bothered with schoolwork, turning up their noses and rolling their eyes when teachers tried to get them interested, unconcerned about what was going to happen to them in the future. Their lives were going to be all about clothes and hair and going out and boys, until the end of time.

They're stupid, thought Chanelle dismissively. *'Cos they've got brains and they're not even trying to use them.*

Chanelle wasn't like that. She didn't want a life on benefits, trapped here on a South London estate, scraping together every penny and stealing minutes of happiness through booze or drugs – the kind of happiness you paid for in the end. If she could just get on as a dancer, she could move away from here and get her own flat. She saw evidence of another world wherever she looked. Where Gus lived there were streets of old Victorian terrace houses and sometimes she walked past them at dusk, just so she could look in the lighted windows and get a glimpse of the cosy, comfortable worlds inside where children played with toys while their mothers ironed or sat on the sofa with a mug of tea. She saw televisions showing bright and jolly kids' programmes and children watching intently while they ate toast and bananas. Dads came home from work and were kissed and hugged by their families. Cats lay curled up on cushions in carefree sleep. She even saw a mother playing the piano while her little girl practised the violin next to her. And the houses – they looked clean, well furnished and warm. There were pictures, books, photos and ornaments. Chanelle longed with all her heart to walk into one of those houses and live that kind of life.

Giving up her place at ballet school had been hard for her because she'd been so certain that she would have become a famous ballerina if she'd been able to take it. Now that her dreams had been abandoned, she'd hardened her heart. She couldn't depend on anyone but herself. She'd given up ballet entirely and started modern dance and tap, changing the direction of her ambitions. Now she planned to become a dancer like the ones who supported the acts on *The X Factor* on television, and get work on the stage or dancing in big pop concerts. There would be good money in that and she'd get a break eventually, she was sure of it.

I was stupid to rely on Mum or Gus, she told herself sternly.

For a while she'd nurtured a fantasy that Gus would look after her, like the father she'd never had, but his inability to step forward and provide for her when she'd needed him had made her realise that was just a stupid fantasy. He'd paid for her dancing lessons, that was true, but the end of the year was rapidly approaching and he'd said nothing about continuing to fund them. She'd have to pay for them herself somehow.

Chanelle was crossing the park, lost in thought about how she would do this, when she saw them. They were standing in the orange puddle of light cast by a street lamp, barring her way. Amy Banks was at the head of them as usual, leader of the gang of the nastiest girls in school.

'There she is,' Amy said scornfully, her head thrown back so she could stare balefully at Chanelle. 'Thinks she's better than all of us, with her precious dancing.'

Chanelle stopped, saying nothing, but she was instantly on her guard and looking for an escape route. As her eyes slid past them towards the gate at the far end of the park, the gang moved to encircle her. She was surrounded by ten or so girls, standing in attitudes of careless malevolence.

'You're disgusting, did you know that?' sneered Amy.

'Yeah,' echoed a couple of the others.

'Smelly, too,' added another.

'That's why we don't understand why you think you're so great,' said Amy in a deceptively soft voice. ''Cos you're a bit of scum really, ain't you? Everyone knows it. The dance people just feel sorry for you, Scum, 'cos you're such a piece of dirt. But you've got a bit above yourself, haven't ya? And that's why we're going to teach you a lesson of our own.'

There was a moment of absolute stillness as the girls confronted each other, standing statue-still in the semi-darkness. Then Chanelle made a bolt for it, darting towards a gap between two of her tormentors where she sensed a weakness. For a moment it seemed that she had made it, but then she felt hands grab her coat and yank her backwards. Then she was on the ground in the centre of the gang, her bag ripped from her shoulder, a flurry of punches and kicks raining down on her while her attackers hissed curses and insults.

It hurt, of course, yet she quickly became inured to the pain. Instead, she focused on protecting herself, rolling into a small ball and thinking frantically about how she could get away and how far they would go. The kicks thudding into her back and thighs, one ringing painfully against her ear, were mounting in intensity and she was afraid the girls were driving themselves into a frenzy.

But the real panic was that her bag had been taken, and in it was her dancing kit. Something might happen to it and she could not afford to replace it . . .

Another kick hit her in the kidneys, and another in the head.

This is dangerous, she realised, feeling sick with dizziness and pain. *Could they kill me?* She knew that they could if they wanted. Two girls at her school had been jailed the previous year for kicking some poor old tramp to death under the railway arches at Waterloo.

Then she heard a different noise: shouting and barked orders. The kicking stopped abruptly and she became aware that something was happening beyond the small circle of her tormentors. She took her arms away from her face, blinking. The darkness and the stars dancing in front of her eyes from the blow to her head confused her. But the girls had stopped their onslaught and there was a different argument going on, a deep voice railing against the gang.

Then an arm came down and began to help her to her feet. She looked up and found herself blinking into a pair of brown eyes that glittered in the darkness. 'Jamal,' she said wonderingly.

'What da fuck they done to you, girl?' he said brusquely, but he was gentle as he guided her to her feet. She felt woozy and strange, but relieved to see him. Ever since that Christmas Day a few years before, he had been her friend. Distant but still a friend, someone who spoke to her whenever their paths crossed, and who looked out for her. Then he had left the school. If Jamal had been around today, the girls would never have dared attack her. What was he doing here? Chanelle blinked at him in surprise. Four other black boys stood about in hooded jackets, sloppy jeans and trainers, watching as their leader helped the girl.

'Lucky for you we was passing and heard what was going on, laike.' He turned to Amy and the rest of the gang. 'You leave her alone, ya hear me? Any one of you bitches touch her again, and you'll be answering to me, y'understand?'

'My bag,' Chanelle said weakly. 'They took my bag.'

'Where's her bag?' demanded Jamal. There was a scuffle and Chanelle's bag was produced and handed to one of Jamal's boys, who brought it forward. It was empty.

'My stuff . . .' she said desperately.

'Find her stuff,' Jamal ordered, and the other boys started looking about for the scattered dance shoes and clothes. 'Now you better get the fuck out of here,' he said to the girls, 'and don't let me see your faces again, you get me? Otherwise you gonna be sorry. For real.'

The girls stared at him sulkily but didn't dare say a word. Instead, they melted away into the darkness, muttering under their breath once they were at a safe distance.

'Thanks,' Chanelle said gratefully. One of Jamal's boys passed her the bag, its contents restored. There were her dance shoes, a little muddy but all right.

'You can brush it off when it's dry,' Jamal said, seeing the worry on her face. 'You'll see.'

'Thanks for helping me,' she said, gazing up at him. He looked like some kind of guardian angel to her.

'No worries.' He shrugged and smiled at her. 'Looks like they gave you a bit of a beatin' there. We better go see if you're all right. You come with us, OK? Just in case they're waiting for you.' He reached out and touched her cheek with his thumb. 'You gonna have a black eye there.'

Chanelle smiled back at him. Her face ached and she could feel the delicate skin around her eye beginning to swell, but she didn't mind if it meant she could feel that gentle touch of his. Jamal would protect her and keep her safe. She was suddenly more sure of that than anything else in the world.

13

The Hôtel de Crillon sparkled, every window draped in waterfalls of glittering lights. Its exuberance matched that of the funfair at the far end of the Place de la Concorde where a silvery-bright Ferris wheel turned slowly.

Inside the hotel, twenty-three well-born or well-connected young ladies were being prepared for their big night – le Bal, the French equivalent of Queen Charlotte's Ball in England, where debutantes made their first official appearance in society. When Daisy had been invited to take part by the ball's organisers, she'd jumped up and down with excitement. Her only disappointment was that none of her friends had been invited to attend. Two of the other English girls were at different schools, and a third lived in South Africa. The rest of the girls were drawn from international high society – there were two princesses, a baroness, and the daughter of a huge Hollywood star among them. They were all linked by the fact of having plenty of money, which was lucky as the ball was an expensive evening – not for the girls but for their proud parents, who footed the bills and made lavish donations to the charity the ball supported.

Before the big occasion, the girls were prepared by professional make-up artists and hairdressers. Each one had already been assigned a different designer who would provide her dress; Daisy had been allocated Marchesa, and she was delighted because their romantic gowns were her absolute favourites. She was to wear a dark grey confection of sequined tulle over a long straight column of silk, the tops of her breasts rising from the low-cut swathed bodice and her arms bare except for a light wrap of almost transparent sparkling grey tulle. When the girls were made up, they were led to a table where an array of jewels was laid out, the jeweller accompanied by two heavies to guard the pieces while the girls made their choice.

'Diamonds, I think,' he said wisely as he assessed Daisy's dress and colouring. Her hair was rolled up over giant Velcro curlers but her face was finished, eyes smoky and emphasised with swoops of dark kohl, and lips pale and glistening with shell-pink gloss.

The jeweller thought for a moment and selected a simple but stunning necklace of diamonds in a filigree design along with matching earrings. 'Allow me,' he said, fastening them round her neck.

With the earrings tucked through her lobes, Daisy turned to examine the effect. Even with the rollers in she looked stunning, and the jewels glittered enticingly.

The hairdresser bustled up. 'Come on, *chérie*, you have to go in a minute!' She led Daisy away to have her rollers taken out. A moment later, nose prickling from the acrid hairspray she'd been liberally sprayed with, Daisy was ready.

'You look beautiful,' said Olympe von Grasson-Bentick, one of the other debutantes, as they picked up their long skirts and tottered on their high heels out of the make-up room. Long dark hair curled over Olympe's tanned shoulders, her eyes looking Egyptian with their heavy cobalt-painted lids, and her dress was a halter-necked teal silk creation with a stunning jewelled collar.

'Thank you,' Daisy said, 'and so do you.'

'I'll be glad when the circus part is over,' Olympe confided.

'Who's taking you in?' Daisy whispered as they approached the salon where the young escorts were waiting: handsome, well-bred young men in tailcoats, white waistcoats and bow ties.

'Ugh, an idiot!' Olympe rolled her eyes. 'It's Maximilian de Bettencourte – and he's a giant. I'm going to look like a fool standing next to him . . . and as for the dance! How about you?'

'Freddie Umbers,' Daisy said in a careless voice, trying not to sound too pleased at her own luck. 'There he is now.'

They could see the young men standing about in small groups, waiting for the girls. There would be a series of photographs first, recording the ball goers in their finery, and then a ceremonial entrance for each debutante on the arm of her escort, when she would be announced to the room full of guests, and photographed again. Daisy caught a glimpse of Freddie, instantly notable for the fact that his waistcoat was not the pristine plain white sported by the European aristocrats, but a bright Union Jack pattern instead. And he was tall and extremely good-looking, with short dark-blond hair and intense blue eyes. He was lolling insouciantly against the wall, hands in pockets, a haughty expression on his face, but when he saw Daisy approaching, he instantly stood up straight, his eyes glittering with appreciation.

'Wow! You look amazing,' he said, kissing her cheek, an expression of frank admiration on his face.

'Thank you.' She smiled, warmed by his flattery.

He bent close to her ear so that his voice buzzed deep and almost tickly inside it. 'I'm fucking bored, though. When does this whole shebang kick off? I've been waiting for ages.'

'Ten more minutes or so, I should think. They're still finishing off the last girls. Then we have to have our pictures taken.'

'Then,' Freddie's voice buzzed even closer, sending electric shivers down her spine, 'I reckon we've got time to . . . you know what . . .'

She gave a little gasp. 'We can't!'

'Yes, we can.' He grinned mischievously, took her hand and led her out of the room, moving quickly so that none of the organisers or chaperones milling about noticed what they were doing. She laughed nervously as he led her to the lift. It arrived in seconds and they ascended smoothly to the top floor. As they came out, she took her room card from the cleverly concealed pocket in her dress and went to open the door of the Leonard Bernstein Suite, the grandest in the hotel. Daddy had insisted she have it all to herself, and the plan was to take her friends back there when the ball was over and continue partying in the drawing room and on the terrace, with its stunning view over the Place de la Concorde, the Eiffel Tower, Les

105

Invalides and the Left Bank, all glittering against the night sky.

'This is so naughty,' Daisy giggled as they went into the lavish drawing room. A grand piano once played by Bernstein himself dominated one corner of the room.

'That's what makes it such fun,' breathed Freddie as he took her in his arms and began to kiss her.

'My make-up,' she gasped. 'You're going to kiss it off!'

'You can put a bit of lipstick back on, can't you?' he murmured, then kissed her properly, pushing open her lips with his tongue and taking possession of her entire mouth, while his hands roamed appreciatively over the smooth skin of her back, arms and chest. 'God, you're gorgeous.'

She couldn't help surrendering to the delicious sensation as he kissed her. She felt tremendously sexy, knowing she was dressed beautifully and perfectly made up. Freddie's hand suddenly raised the tulle skirt and he took one peachy cheek of her bottom in his hand while he kissed her even more forcefully.

'I want to have you right now,' he muttered, pressing his strong hard body against hers, and she could feel his desire for her through the scratchy wool of his dress trousers.

'We can't!' she said breathlessly, half desperate to give in to him, and half anxious about her appearance. They would be furious with her if she reappeared with all that hard work ruined. Besides, she hadn't slept with Freddie . . . not yet. They'd done everything but . . .

'Then later,' he said, pulling back and staring at her, eyes heavy-lidded with lust. 'Tonight. Right here.'

'Yes,' she whispered back, feeling shameless but excited at the same time. 'Later.'

He sank his mouth on to hers again, pulling her tightly to him, and she felt a hot, wet desire flood her.

'Oh, my goodness,' she said on a shivering sigh as their mouths parted. 'What have you done to me?'

Freddie shot her a sly smile. 'Just getting you fired up nicely, my darling. I want you to be thinking about me all night . . . and all the gorgeous things I'm going to do to you later.'

'Not exactly pure and virginal debutante behaviour,' Daisy returned. She caught a glimpse of the small gold and mother-of-pearl Cartier clock on the side. 'Oh my God! We'd better get back. It will all be starting at any moment!'

They went swiftly back to the lifts. As the doors opened on the ground floor, Daisy could hear music coming from the Grand Salon which meant the debs were about to begin their procession. They must be taking the group photograph. She really was late.

Out came a flustered-looking organiser who saw Daisy and spluttered, 'Mademoiselle, please! Come at once! We need you here.'

'Sorry!' she called, heels clicking on the marble floor as she dashed along the hall, oblivious of the bellboys and concierge admiring the beautiful blushing English girl flying past in a cloud of tulle and glitter, like Cinderella late for her ball.

14

Chanelle leaned her forehead against the cool glass of the window pane. The city lay before her, a carpet of sparkling lights. She could see the London Eye illuminated in green against the night sky, and the floodlit towers of Big Ben and the Palace of Westminster. Everything glittered with the kind of glamour that could only be seen at night. It was hard to believe that she was in a grimy council flat twenty-five floors up in a high-rise building.

I have to believe there's a better life out there for me, she thought, staring out at the flickering lights.

'This is my gran's flat,' Jamal had told her when they'd come in. 'She's in hospital so it's empty. She don't mind if I use it.'

Chanelle had looked around. It was definitely an old lady's flat, with its powdery but musty smell, the rickety furniture, and the china ornaments and lace doilies on every surface. The walls were covered in family photographs – weddings, christenings, school photos and other gatherings, the people in them ageing accordingly. 'It's nice,' Chanelle said, and meant it. It was homely, and Jamal's gran obviously loved a lot of people. She went over to one of the pictures on the wall and inspected it more closely. 'This is you.' She pointed at a seven-year-old Jamal, who was smiling broadly and showing a big gap between his front teeth.

'Yeah. My gran loves those things. I look stupid, don't I?'

'No.' Chanelle looked at it again, the picture with its white plastic frame hung with pride for everyone to see. Her mother had once stuck a school photo of Chanelle on the fridge, but it was the trial one from the photographer – small and with the company name stamped across it. 'I think you look nice.'

'Wanna cup of tea?' Jamal disappeared into a tiny kitchen and a moment later she heard a kettle heating up. She browsed around until he came out with two steaming mugs. He put them on the coffee table, and they sat down on the sofa and looked at one another a little shyly. She'd been hanging around with him and his boys since they'd rescued her from the girl gang last week, and the air had been crackling with the attraction between them. She hadn't been surprised when he'd asked her if she wanted to come up to the flat, but she had been excited.

'Do you wanna have a smoke?' he asked, pulling a tightly rolled joint out of his pocket.

'Nah.' Chanelle shook her head. She wasn't shocked. Plenty of the kids around the estate smoked grass and weed, or were out of their heads on skunk. Loads of them had their first joint of the day walking to school. 'I don't do drugs.'

Jamal laughed. 'These ain't drugs!' He pulled a

packet of white powder out of his pocket and tossed it on to the table. '*These* are drugs, man!'

Chanelle stared at it in horrified fascination. She knew that she was looking at a lot of hard stuff, worth a ton of money. She looked up at Jamal, who was grinning back at her as though he'd just showed her a bag of sweets, not a stash of Class A. 'Is this your gear?'

'Uh-uh.' He shook his head and she noticed again the swirling lines in the black fuzz of his closely cut hair. 'Well, it's mine, but I don't use it. Mug's game, this stuff.'

'I know,' Chanelle said, with feeling. She regarded the innocuous-looking white powder with suspicion and curiosity. Was it speed? Cocaine? Heroin? Whatever, it was what her mother craved. It was what would kill Michelle in the end. It had already taken her youth, her looks, her teeth . . . it would eventually take her life too, Chanelle was certain of it. *Death in a bag*, she thought as she stared at it. *Death disguised as happiness.* 'So why've you got it?'

Jamal shrugged. 'It's what I sell, innit? Got my gang, my posse. We buy this off another guy, a big important bloke over Old Kent Road way, and then we sell it on, laike.'

Chanelle nodded. She'd guessed something like that must be going on. Jamal was boss of the local gang, called the Blacksmith Boys, after the estate, and bitter rivals of the gang over the way in the next postcode, the Righteous Crew. Last month one of the young lads had been knifed but Chanelle couldn't remember which gang he was in now. There were still rotting flowers and teddies at the site where he'd died.

'What you think?' he asked softly.

Chanelle lifted her shoulders and made a face. 'Nothing. What you do is your business.' As far as she was concerned, if people wanted to take this stuff, it was up to them. 'If no one wanted it, you wouldn't be able to sell it, right?'

Jamal laughed again softly. 'Raight. And they do want it. I make good money with this.' He leaned back against the floral print of the sofa and lit his joint. Expelling a long stream of fragrant smoke, he slid his gaze over Chanelle. 'I've wanted to get you on your own for a while, you know?'

'Have you? Why's that?' Something like excitement mixed with fear turned lightly in her stomach.

''Cos you're not like the other girls. That's why they don't like you, see? But I like it.' He leaned a little closer to her. His dark brown eyes shone and she noticed the way the light cast a patch of gold on his dark cheek. 'I like it a lot. And I wondered . . . if you want to be my woman.'

Chanelle caught her breath. She'd never had a boyfriend, not a proper one. She'd gone out with boys in her class when she was younger, but that was nothing. They only held hands and it never lasted longer than a week or so. Everyone ended up going out with everyone else. Now, here was Jamal – tall, handsome, strong – asking her to be his girlfriend. She knew it must be special because the boys usually talked about girls as bitches or whores, pussy that was there for their enjoyment. But Jamal was treating her with respect, even though loads of girls must be willing to fuck him if he wanted, because he was the boss.

She realised suddenly that she wanted to be his

girlfriend more than anything. But she had no idea how to say it. After a moment, she said, 'Er . . . yeah. OK then. If you're sure.'

Jamal laughed more heartily. 'Hey, that's why I like you, man. You ain't like those others! If I'm sure . . .' He shook his head, grinning, and took another puff on his joint. 'I'm sure. How about you? You like me?'

She gazed at him: she liked everything about him, from his soft but deep voice, his height and rangy body, to his face with those meltingly brown eyes. He had high cheekbones and a wide straight nose over a mouth that all of a sudden she longed to feel on her own.

She nodded, suddenly finding she couldn't speak.

As if he was reading her mind, he leaned over and pressed his lips to hers. A second later, she felt his soft tongue probing her mouth. She hadn't been kissed before. Too proud, the cows at school said, thought she was too good for anyone, but it wasn't like that. She'd been scared about letting anyone get that close to her. It felt right with Jamal, though. His mouth was so gentle, the feeling of his lips gorgeous, and as she tentatively returned the kiss, she began to relax. It felt natural to let their tongues touch and explore each other's mouths, and he tasted of smoke and honey. What was odd was how the kiss seemed to set her insides quivering, and hot bolts of sensation firing down her belly and into her groin. She felt almost uncomfortable there, as though it was aching with a need she didn't understand.

But Chanelle knew all about sex. Boys had cocks that they wanted to shove inside you and rub until they came. The girls at school talked about it all the

112

time. Sometimes the boys made you put their cock in your mouth and suck it. It all sounded horrible. And more than one of the girls had appeared at school with a swollen belly and then left before exams.

Chanelle pulled away suddenly, panicked. 'I won't get pregnant, will I?'

Jamal laughed softly. 'Nah, I ain't ready for that and neither are you. Anyway, we're just kissin', yeah? No need to rush it.'

She felt relieved. He wasn't going to force her to do anything she didn't want. He kissed her again, gentle pecks that became deeper and deeper until they were lost in the sensation of each other's mouth.

After that, she was Jamal's girl, and any moment she wasn't at school, she spent with him and the gang. They passed long hours hanging round the playground, or at Jamal's grandmother's flat, his unofficial headquarters. It was there they drank gallons of tea, and sometimes beer, when the business of the day was completed, and smoked endless joints – even Chanelle, who had been persuaded that it was not really taking drugs, not if it wasn't sniffed, swallowed or injected. It was in that flat, on his grandmother's bed where a crucifix hung above the pillow that she and Jamal slept together for the first time. The things that had sounded so horrible to Chanelle she now surprised herself by wanting: she longed to touch his cock when it was hard with his desire for her, to kiss it and caress it. Nothing excited her as much as the groans he made when she pressed her lips to its head, ran her tongue over the smooth top and held the hot, velvety shaft in her hand. Her own reactions surprised her. The

113

first time he'd pressed inside her, she hadn't been frightened at all, just hungry for the pleasure that her body craved. It had felt entirely right to open herself to him, to pull him closer against her so that they moved together. It was so beautiful, she felt she could never ever get enough of it.

Together they discovered how to please each other: the way her nipples responded to firm sucking, stoking her internal fire and making her desperate for him to enter her, or the way he could bring her to an exquisite climax by tantalising her pussy with his tongue and then thrusting hard inside and inciting her shudder of pleasure with firm strong movements. She loved it when he reached his own peak, his face contorting with the exquisite agony, and the delicious release.

They drove each other wild, and satisfied one another's desire many times on those pink nylon sheets, and afterwards whispered that they loved each other.

Love at last. Chanelle was happy for the first time in her life. Her world was Jamal, and she was his.

When the year came to an end, Chanelle did not ask Gus for more dancing lessons. For the only time in her life, dancing was not her only passion. Now her world revolved entirely around Jamal and the activities of the Blacksmith Boys. Every minute that she wasn't at home or at school, she was with them. The other boys looked up to her because they could tell their boss liked this girl better than any other he'd had before, and treated her with a respect they didn't often show to girls. Plenty of them hung around the gang, trying to get favour with them; they were usually slept with, passed round and then cast aside. Some stayed a while, and helped the boys in their deals – girls could sometimes go places more quickly and easily than the boys, and they were less likely to be stopped by police.

Jamal never asked Chanelle to carry anything for him, even when he showed no compunction about sending younger girls off with wraps in their purses to make an exchange in a shopping centre or round the back of a supermarket.

'You know you're precious, right?' he said to her as they lay in bed together. He stroked one large hand over her head. 'You're my girl, right?'

She nodded, full of happiness. There was nowhere in the world better than right here: in bed with Jamal, his long warm body pressed against hers, his arms around her. She'd never felt loved and cared for her in her life before now, and she luxuriated in the delicious feeling, craved it more than anyone craved the narcotics that Jamal supplied. *He loves me*, she marvelled. 'I'm your girl,' she whispered, and kissed him, the sweet soft touch of his lips sending tingles of pleasure all over her. She would never be tired of that kiss, she was certain of it.

When their lips parted, he said, 'For ever?'

'For ever. You and me. For ever.'

15

Daisy stared at the figure in the bed in horror. Her mother had deteriorated so much since she had last seen her. There had been another stay in a convalescent home and then Julia had come back to Thornside for more rest and recovery. She lay now, a thin and shrunken figure, in her vast bed with its white silk counterpane and mountains of snowy pillows. Her fair hair looked thin and faded against the sheen of the silk.

'Mummy,' Daisy said in a half whisper as she approached and sat down in the pink damask-covered armchair next to the bed.

Julia opened her eyes. They were bloodshot and yellowing, and her skin had a waxy tinge. Her cheekbones were almost visible below, as though her flesh had become very thin and almost translucent. She smiled as she looked at her daughter. 'Daisy. Darling.' Her voice was reedy and weak.

'How are you, Mummy? You don't look well.' Daisy leaned forward and took her mother's hand. It felt bony under her own smooth, warm one.

Julia sighed. 'I'm feeling better despite what those bloody doctors have done to me with their foul drugs. But I've missed you, darling.' Her mother squeezed her hand. 'You're so grown-up. Almost eighteen. Tell me, what has Daddy planned for you?'

'A big party at the Florey,' Daisy replied, smiling back. 'All my schoolfriends, the girls from the Crillon Ball . . . I don't know, hundreds. Will you be there, Mummy?'

'Of course, if I possibly can. I shall look out my best dress and make sure I take a spin on the dance floor.' Julia smiled again, though it seemed to cost her an effort.

Daisy tried not to show her sadness. It was obvious her mother would be able to do little more than sit and watch, if she managed that. How had it come to this? Her beautiful vibrant mother reduced to a shadow of herself. Daisy longed with all her heart for Julia to get better – perhaps things would be different if she did, and they could be a happy family again. But slowly, inexorably, she seemed to be getting worse.

'I'm so proud of you, darling. There's so much I want to talk to you about, to discuss . . . if only I had the strength.'

'You will, Mummy, you'll get better, I know it.'

'I want to, but it's so hard.' Her mother shifted closer towards her, her expression changing. She looked apprehensive, almost fearful. 'Tell me – is your father here?'

'Yes. He brought me down in the car.'

'And . . . and is that woman with him?'

'Margaret?' Daisy nodded. 'Of course.' Margaret was Daddy's new personal assistant and had swiftly made herself indispensable to him. Now she was always with Daddy, almost every moment of the day, brisk, efficient and almost ghostly in her ability to fade into the background whenever she wanted. Daisy couldn't warm to her – despite her perfect manners and unfailing politeness, there was something chilly about the woman – but there was no questioning her ability to run Daddy's life with astonishing smoothness. Any problem could be sorted instantly by Margaret, any arrangement put in place without fuss. Daisy rarely saw her father now without Margaret present, and they spent hours shut away together in Daddy's office. Margaret had been in the car with them on the way down, in her usual businesslike costume of neat grey suit and low-heeled pumps, her dark hair with its unusual streak of white at the front pulled back into a neat bun, and gold-rimmed glasses framing her pale blue eyes.

'I don't like her, Daisy,' Julia said urgently.

Daisy shifted uncomfortably. It was true that Margaret took up a lot of Daddy's time but she had also been careful to make sure that Daisy did not feel excluded from her father's life. In recent months, he had been asking her to accompany him to many more of his business events. It was not unusual for Daisy to board the Dangerfield jet and fly to a lavish dinner in some city where she would accompany Daddy in place of her mother, dressed in designer gowns with sparkling jewels, dining on the finest food in the world and sipping the most expensive vintages, surrounded by businessmen and their glamorous well-dressed wives. They would fly back through the night – luckily the plane was equipped with two comfortable bedrooms

– and she could be back in school the next day. Margaret's arrival had not altered Daisy's special place by Daddy's side.

'Be careful of her, do you promise me?' Julia pushed herself up on one elbow with an effort and stared earnestly at her daughter. 'And of him.'

'Daddy?' Daisy frowned, puzzled.

'Yes. Him. Daisy, I—'

The door opened and a nurse came through with a tray laden with a glass of water and a selection of pills on a silver plate. Julia broke off at once.

'Hello, Lady Julia, I've brought your mid-morning medications.' The nurse smiled at Daisy. 'Good morning, miss.'

Julia stared at the nurse, her eyes resentful. 'I don't want them,' she said defiantly.

'Now, now, Lady Julia, none of that! We have this all the time. You need your medicine. It makes you better.'

'So you say,' she retorted. 'And if I disagree, you force it on me!'

The nurse laughed cheerfully. 'What a silly story! Your daughter won't know you're joking.' She shot a glance at Daisy and said quietly, 'She's often like this. It's a side-effect of the medication. You mustn't worry.'

'I heard that,' Julia snapped. Her strength seemed to leave her then and she fell back on the pillow. 'I don't care if you eavesdrop or not, or what you report back. You're not going to stop me talking.'

'Of course not,' soothed the nurse.

'What is it, Mummy?' Daisy asked, leaning forward and clasping her mother's hand a little tighter. 'What do you want to say?'

119

Julia gazed at her earnestly and whispered, 'You know how ruthless he can be, darling. You saw what happened to Will and Sarah.'

Daisy blinked at her. 'But *they* left *us* . . . Daddy was heartbroken.'

'All the same, be careful, because—'

The door swung open again at the same moment as a sharp knocking rang out. Margaret stood in the doorway. 'I do apologise for interrupting, Lady Julia, but Daisy is required downstairs. Daisy – your father wants to see you right now.'

'Yes, I'm coming.' She released her mother's hand and stood up. 'I'll be back later, Mummy.'

'Yes, sweetheart. I'll see you then.' Julia managed a forlorn smile. 'Don't be long.'

'I won't.'

But when she finally managed to get back from the long discussion about her shoe business and its expansion, the nurse was sitting outside her mother's room. There was no seeing the patient, she explained, she was sleeping. Perhaps later. Daisy did not see her mother again before it was time to return to London and school.

'Daddy!' she cried. She looked at him, laughing. He was grinning broadly, clearly delighted with her reaction.

'Do you like it, darling?'

There on the road in front of the Belgravia house was a beautiful shining BMW 3-series convertible in a shade of palest sugar pink. A giant silver bow was wrapped around it.

'It's a customised colour,' Daddy said proudly. 'That shade is now called "Daisy Dangerfield Pink".'

'It's beautiful,' she said, still laughing, 'but Daddy – I can't drive!'

'I know. Margaret's arranged some lessons. You can start learning whenever you want.'

Daisy dashed up to him and threw her arms around him, kissing him on the cheek. 'Thank you, thank you!' she said. 'It's wonderful.' They linked arms and walked back inside the house.

Back at the breakfast table, where Daisy was indulging in a birthday treat of blueberry pancakes with maple syrup, she opened her other presents: a pink Hermès Birkin handbag in softest emu leather, customised with a stamped motif of a small gold daisy; and an exquisite necklace of eighteen diamond daisies that flashed and sparkled as they slipped through her fingers.

'Oh, Daddy,' she said, flushing with pleasure, 'thank you. It's beautiful. I'll wear it at the party tonight.'

'I have something else for you – a card from your mother.' He held out the small white envelope.

Her good mood became sombre as she took it. Opening it, she read her mother's brief birthday message. It was signed: 'With much love, Mummy'. Daisy looked up at her father. 'I wish she was well enough to be with us.'

'I know, Princess, so do I. But she's being taken good care of at Thornside. We'll send her lots of pictures of the party.' He smiled at her fondly. 'Now, don't you have an appointment or two?'

Daisy glanced down at her Cartier watch. 'Oh, yes, I'll be late.' She jumped up and kissed her father's cheek. 'I'll see you later, Daddy, at the Florey.'

'The *Dangerfield* Florey, darling. Yes, I'll see you later. Have a happy day.'

As a further birthday treat, Daisy and her three closest friends had been given one of Daddy's special black credit cards and they were taken to Bond Street in the Rolls. It followed them at a discreet distance while they made their purchases and loaded up the car with the enormous bags.

They bought cocktail dresses in Chanel, Burberry, Dior and Gucci, shoes in Prada and Jimmy Choo, silk scarves in Hermès, and evening bags in Bottega Veneta and Alexander McQueen. Daisy found herself a slinky party dress in Dolce & Gabbana to go with some extraordinary yellow Versace heels that she was going to wear to the party that night.

After the exhausting spree, they went to the Dangerfield Florey for an inspection of Daisy's little shoe shop, which her friends cooed and shrieked over, and then had a light lunch in the bistro, where they chatted about their futures over poached salmon salad and a glass of champagne.

'Can you believe we're nearly out of that *dump* of a school?' demanded Lucy Critchlow-Browning. 'Five more months and it's all over! Thank Christ.'

'Yeah, but we've got A-levels first,' said Antonia Rushton gloomily. 'I just know I'm going to fail all of them.'

'What does that matter when you're not going to university anyway?' asked Lucy sweetly. 'Haven't you got a year off to go skiing?'

'I'm helping with a friend's skiing company,' Antonia said in a hurt voice. 'Not just skiing.'

'Answering phones in the morning, skiing the best runs in the afternoon, bopping away in local night-clubs with ski instructors in the evening. Yeah, like, *really hard work*!' Lucy rolled her eyes and they all laughed, even Antonia.

Daisy picked up a piece of salmon on her silver fork. 'I can't wait to get to Brown,' she said. 'It's going to be amazing.'

'You're so lucky,' Fiamma Beaumont said wistfully. 'I can't wait to go to Aberdeen, even if Daddy has halved my allowance for not getting into Cambridge, but America sounds miles more glamorous.'

Daisy smiled at her. 'I know. It's all planned. Three years at Brown, then maybe a year at Stanford Business School, depending on my grades, and then I'm joining the family firm.'

Lucy made a face. 'I bet it's not in the post room, either! That's not really your daddy's style, is it?'

'No, not really.' Daisy laughed. 'He wants me to become a trainee director with promotion to the board the moment I've proved myself.'

'What about your shoe line?' Antonia asked. 'It's so gorgeous! You must keep doing it. I *die* for the python ballet slippers!'

'Oh, I'll keep that going while I'm at university, to keep my hand in. Later I might diversify a bit – but property will always be our priority.' She looked about. 'Hotels like this, in particular.'

'Amazing to have your life sorted like that,' Fiamma said enviously. 'Especially as it's what you want to do.'

'Of course.' Daisy gave her a puzzled smile. What on earth else was there to do? This was all that she'd ever considered. She'd never even bothered thinking of anything else.

'Come on, then,' Lucy prodded her. 'We're dying to know. What did Daddy get you for your birthday?'

'Um . . .' Daisy looked a bit abashed. Even though she was used to her father's grand gestures, she was aware that they could appear over the top to others. 'Well . . . this . . .' She picked up her Hermès Birkin and displayed it for them.

'Very pretty!' said Antonia admiringly. 'I've been staring at it all morning, you lucky thing.'

'Beautiful,' sighed Fiamma, her blue eyes envious. She reached out a hand and stroked the buttery leather. 'I want one. But Mummy just laughs when I ask.'

'Come on,' teased Lucy, grinning at Daisy. 'That can't be all! There must be more.'

'Well . . .' Daisy felt her face flush a little. 'A BMW was waiting outside the house for me this morning.'

Lucy burst out laughing. 'How fantastic!' she cried. 'You can't even drive. But I bags the first ride in it when you can!'

'And there was a diamond necklace . . . But I'm just worried that's not the last little surprise.' Daisy shrugged almost ruefully. 'What can I do? He loves to spoil me.'

The hours after lunch were all about relaxation and preparation for the party. The girls descended to the hotel basement which contained the beauty treatment rooms and spa, and spent a happy afternoon being pampered and massaged before visiting the hair salon. When they were properly smoothed and glowing, their hair glossy and swinging, they went upstairs to where

Daddy had reserved one of the grand suites for them. Waiting were a manicurist, a make-up artist and yet another hairdresser, to get them looking their best for the party that evening. A bottle of champagne was opened, some music was put on, and the girls bopped and drank happily as they prepared for the main event.

By the time they were ready to go downstairs, they were all high with excitement. The party was going to be in the ballroom, with hundreds of people invited. Daisy had been allowed fifty invitations of her own – the rest had been taken by Daddy so that he could invite business associates and various important people he was keen to entertain. He had also hired a society consultant to advise him which of the younger crowd he should invite: sons and daughters of the aristocracy, oligarchy, or movers and shakers in the arts, movie, music and theatre scenes. 'I want to make sure you have the right friends, darling,' he had said to Daisy, showing her the guest list. 'It's important you are one of the gilded circle. Don't forget, you can invite anyone you like to a private holiday in Thailand this summer – you will have the entire estate at your disposal, and the jet will be available to take you all there.'

It was almost time to go downstairs. Daisy stood in front of the mirror in the Florey Suite, assessing her reflection and thinking over Daddy's expectations of her. It was usual, she realised, for everything he gave her to come with a condition: it was hers, but at a price. The birthday party was to celebrate her eighteenth, but it was also intended to give Daddy extra kudos in his own world, and Daisy was expected to make the evening work for her on a social level. That was fine. She could do that. After all, she knew plenty of the trendy young things from school and the raves and parties she went to. Daddy didn't need to worry about that.

Her strappy, short cocktail dress shimmered lavender and silver. The shoes were a bit of a risk, but somehow they worked – big, yellow snakeskin platforms that made her legs look extremely long. She could see that the make-up artist and hairdresser had done good work – she looked fresh and young but her best features were subtly highlighted: her blue-grey eyes widened and emphasised with a little kohl and silver glitter shadow and some mascara, and her lips shining a delicate rosebud pink.

Best of all, Freddie was coming tonight. Her eyes glittered back at herself from the mirror as she remembered the pleasurable things they'd done together in the Leonard Bernstein Suite at the Crillon. It had been a delightful place to sample her first taste of sex and Freddie had proved very competent indeed in that department. They'd spent most of the next day extending her education. Later, perhaps, they would be able to sneak up here to the suite and celebrate her birthday properly.

Lucy came up, beaming. She looked elegant in a black column dress. Her hair had been softened and straightened, and the make-up artist had given her smoky eyes and cherry lips. 'How are you doing?' she said. 'Ready for the party?'

'You bet.' Daisy grinned back at her. 'But I'm feeling somewhat underdressed without a parrot or two.'

'I shouldn't worry,' Lucy replied. 'Knowing your dad, he's probably got some tame unicorns downstairs for an extra birthday surprise.'

At that moment there was a knock on the suite door and a second later Daddy breezed into the room, an unmissable presence in his dinner jacket, a bright silk waistcoat stretched across his large front and a blue silk bow tie at his neck. 'Ladies, ladies!' he roared, clapping his hands. 'You all look amazing – gorgeous! Wonderful! Have you had a lovely day? I hope you've looked after my Daisy! Now, now . . .' He grabbed each girl in turn and gave her a smacking kiss on the cheek. 'Where's my girl? Ah, there she is! Daisy – you look beautiful.' Daddy gazed at her with misty eyes. 'Beautiful.' He turned to the other girls. 'Now, ladies, I need a moment's privacy with my daughter. Would you excuse us? Just a moment, that's all.'

He took Daisy's arm and led her through the connecting door to the bedroom of the suite, shutting it behind them. Immediately his expression became grave.

'What is it, Daddy?' she asked anxiously. A prickle of fear raced over her skin and she shivered.

'Some bad news, my darling. I've just heard. I'm afraid that Mummy's been very silly. She's taken an overdose of her medication and has been taken to hospital.'

Daisy felt her stomach plummet as though she'd stepped into a lift travelling downwards at super-speed. 'But . . . but . . . how is she?' she stammered. 'Is she all right now?'

Daddy fixed her with a steady gaze and shook his head sadly. His oiled hair gleamed under the lights of the suite. 'Daisy, I'm sorry. Things don't look good at all. She's extremely ill. The doctors are not sure what the outcome will be.'

Daisy felt sick. She could hardly believe her ears. A moment ago she had been carefree, laughing, sipping champagne and worrying about whether her dress was too short. Now, she was shaking, her palms clammy and her brain whirling as she tried to process what she'd been told. Mummy ill? Possibly dying? She had not been truly close to her mother for years, but suddenly found she yearned for her with all her heart. 'Mummy,' Daisy said in a broken voice. She looked wildly towards the door and began to kick off her shoes. 'We've got to leave at once. I must go to her—'

'No.' Her father's voice was firm. 'Absolutely not.'

'Wh . . . wh . . . what?' Hot tears were stinging Daisy's eyes but she blinked them back. Only one escaped to roll down her cheek. She could hardly take in what she had just heard.

'You are to do no such thing. This is a very important party. You will dry your eyes, powder your nose, put your shoes back on and walk into that ballroom downstairs with your head held high. There's nothing you can do for your mother. She's unconscious and would not be aware of your presence one way or the other. The party must go on. You must do this for me, Daisy, do you understand?'

She knew at once that her father was deadly serious. There was no way she would be seeing her mother. It was another test, she realised. He was assessing her reaction under this awful pressure, seeing whether she had the strength to act as though nothing in the world was troubling her. She realised that the pain in her hands was the feeling of her own fingernails digging deep into her palms. *I can do it,* she told herself. *I'll never fail a challenge he sets me.*

Daddy spoke quietly. 'Are you a Dangerfield – or not?'

She took a deep breath. 'All right. But afterwards I'm going straight to the hospital.'

Daddy nodded. 'Agreed. I knew you wouldn't fail me, Daisy. Now, are you ready to go down?'

She pushed away thoughts of her mother lying in bed, alone in a cold hospital miles away, perhaps even dying while they were talking. She lifted her chin, straightened her shoulders, slipped her feet back into her shoes and stood tall. 'I'm ready,' she said, in the strongest voice she could muster.

'Good.' Daddy smiled at her, evidently relieved that she was being so amenable. 'Now, remember – no one must guess a thing.'

'No one will.' From somewhere deep within herself, Daisy managed to summon a smile. 'I am a Dangerfield, after all.'

Daddy put a hand on her shoulder and stared into her eyes. 'Never forget that, Daisy.'

Then they walked together out of the bedroom to join the others who were laughing and joking in the sitting room next door.

16

''Cos it's your birthday, innit?' Jamal said as they came out of the restaurant. Chanelle had told him off for spending all this money on her.

He put his arms around her and pulled her close to him. The next moment they were kissing, not caring that they were in the street and that passersby were having to walk round them.

'No one's ever done anything like this for me,' Chanelle said, when their lips finally parted.

'Should fuckin' well hope not!' Jamal laughed.

'I don't mean candles and dinner and all that stuff . . .' She laughed as well. 'I mean, no one's ever done anything special for me – spoiled me, like you do.'

'I do it 'cos I love you, you know that.' He took her hand in his and raised it to his lips. 'And I'm gonna look after you, I promise. You need someone to spoil you, you're a beautiful girl, Chanelle.'

She snuggled into him and he put an arm about her shoulder. 'Come on, we'll go back to mine,' Jamal said. He had moved into his own place now, a rented flat in a house off the Walworth Road, and it was their private base. The happiest hours Chanelle had ever known had been spent there, most of them wrapped up with Jamal under his duvet as they experienced all the joy of each other's bodies. He'd shown her what making love with real tenderness and emotion was all about, and she adored it.

'This has been the best birthday of my life,' she said, gazing up at him. 'The best.'

Jamal had done everything he could to make it special for her. He'd turned up for their night out with a bouquet of flowers and a bottle of sparkling wine – ''Cos you're eighteen, and someone's got to make a fuss of you!' he'd said. They had opened the bottle at Chanelle's house, and Michelle had sighed over it, and shared a glass with them, telling Jamal that he was being dead posh.

She had deteriorated further over the years. There were no more pregnancies, which was a blessing, but her health was shot from the long-term abuse to which she'd subjected her body. She was on many different types of medication to control her heartbeat, her blood pressure and the early-stage diabetes that had begun to plague her. Then there were the other symptoms: her gaunt frame, her shaking hands, her blurry eyesight and failing memory. She still drank more than she was supposed to – *Well,* Chanelle thought, *she's not supposed to drink anything at all, silly cow!* – but the only pleasure left to her came from the beer and fags she loved. Now that she was getting sickness benefit, she felt she could afford a few luxuries.

Her birthday present to Chanelle was a packet of fags and a magazine, plus a card with a badly written scrawl inside: *Luve ya, babes, happy birthday.*

It was as much as Chanelle had expected and she was pleased to get it even though she didn't smoke very much. She knew her mother could not stretch to anything more. Michelle did her best under the circumstances.

Jamal's present was brilliant, though. After the fizzy wine and the flowers, he'd taken her out. He'd already told her to dress up, so she'd put on her favourite outfit – a tight black jersey sheath that clung to every curve – and a pair of knee-high black leather stiletto boots that laced up the front. A slick of bright red lipstick finished it off.

'You look gorgeous,' he had said when she'd come downstairs.

'Oh, my little girl, all grown-up!' Michelle had said in her cracked, gravelly voice. She'd beamed with pride. 'You're a proper woman now, ain't you?'

Chanelle had certainly felt like it as they'd climbed into a minicab. They'd gone up West to a posh hotel and Jamal had waited until they were in the bar with a cocktail each before announcing what his present to her was. Chanelle had been sipping her Long Island iced tea and thinking how delicious it was when he'd said casually, 'Don't you want to know what I've got you, babe?'

'It's this, innit?' she'd said, blinking at him in surprise. 'Going out.'

He'd laughed and told her that his real present was the chance to go back to the dancing school if she wanted. She'd told him how much she'd once loved to dance and that she'd stopped going to lessons. These days she got most of her dancing pleasure from going to clubs with Jamal and hitting the dance floor.

It was so sexy to dance with him, knowing that people were looking at how well they moved together and what a great couple they made.

She'd cried a little then and hugged him, and he'd laughed and said, 'You oughta get some singing lessons too, 'cos you got a naice voice as well. You could be a star one day, I'm serious. Now, finish your cocktail 'cos we've got a table booked somewhere fancy.'

'Maybe you'll make my dreams come true,' she said as they went out of the bar and headed for the exit. On their way, they passed great wooden doors standing open on to a ballroom. Inside, hundreds of people were milling about, looking rich and glamorous in their expensive party clothes as they sipped champagne.

'Look at that,' she said to Jamal, nudging him.

He followed her gaze and nodded. 'Yeah, man. Serious fucking cash to pay for something like that.'

Just then, Chanelle turned and saw two people walking down the corridor towards them: a glossy-looking girl with perfectly done hair and a shimmering cocktail dress tottering on her heels alongside a tall, tanned man with a stomach that bulged out from under a silk waistcoat. Chanelle and Jamal instinctively stood back to let them pass. As they drew level, the girl looked Chanelle right in the eyes. For a moment, they were caught in one another's gaze and Chanelle sensed the enormous gulf between them. This girl looked like she'd never been hungry, tired, or wondered where the money she needed to live on was coming from. She looked like her biggest dilemma was choosing her nail colour or running out of phone battery. And yet, as they stared at each other, Chanelle saw something else in the blue-grey depths of those eyes. Sadness? Fear? She couldn't tell. Then the instant was gone, the pair had passed them and were approaching the ballroom doors. She heard the man say, 'Are you ready, darling?' and the girl reply, 'Yes, Daddy,' then Jamal pulled Chanelle on, down the carpeted corridor.

'Rich bitch,' he said with a grin. 'C'mon, let's get out of here. This place ain't for us.'

In the restaurant they went to, the staff had given them strange looks and the waiter had been a bit sniffy when Jamal had ordered the drinks and food, but they hadn't cared. They had candles on the table, a starched white cloth, and they'd eaten pâté and toast, then steak with chips, and chocolate cake to finish, along with a bottle of expensive red wine. Chanelle had never felt so sophisticated in her life.

'Thank you, sweetie,' she'd whispered as they emerged afterwards, full and happy and a little hazy with wine.

They got on a night bus heading back south of the river and snuggled up together at the back, murmuring to one another as the bus ground its way back through the middle of the city, stopping every few minutes to take on more passengers or drop them off. They were over the river and heading east when the bus took an unexpected left turn and rumbled along a different route from usual. Jamal frowned and sat up, peering out of the windows into the darkness.

'Hey, what's goin' on?' he muttered. 'Where da fuck are we goin'?'

'Everything all right?' Chanelle asked sleepily, aware

that he was gripping her hand more tightly than before.

'Yeah. Yeah. No problem. Don't worry about it. We're on some kind of diversion, that's all.'

The bus rolled on further off its usual route and then came to yet another stop. The doors beeped, opened so that people could get off, then beeped again and began to close, but stuck before they were fully shut. The driver opened them and tried again, but the same thing happened. He tried several times with no luck.

'What's going on?' Chanelle grumbled. 'Fuckin' muppet.' She shouted towards the driver, 'Come on, mate, let's get moving!'

'I can't move the bus when the doors aren't operational!' the driver bellowed back. Next they heard him on the radio to his controller.

'Come on!' Chanelle said with a sigh. 'We don't want to sit here all night.'

'Nah.' Jamal looked out into the darkness beyond the window. His arm tightened around her.

A moment later, the driver opened the doors again. His voice came over the speaker system. 'Everyone off, please. This bus terminates here. Mechanical faults to the doors. Everyone off. All change.'

'Ah, *fuck*,' muttered Jamal. His face had hardened and Chanelle sensed the tension in him.

'What is it, babes?'

'Nothing, nothing.' He got up, raised his collar so that it was as far over his cheeks and chin as possible, then took her hand. 'Come on, let's get off.'

They shuffled off with everyone else, and the grumbling passengers milled around the bus stop, trying to work out when the next bus might come along, while their broken-down vehicle stood uselessly beside them, its hazard lights flashing.

Jamal seemed to be hunched over, keeping himself in the centre of the crowd, and darting glances about as if on a constant state of alert.

'What's the matter?' Chanelle asked, worried.

'You got any cash?' he demanded in a low, urgent tone.

'Nah. Clean out.'

'Ah, shit. Look, here comes another bus. We'll never get on . . .'

It wasn't a question of not getting on – the crowded night bus did not even stop.

'What is it?' Chanelle asked, more nervous now.

Jamal pressed his lips to her ear. 'Do you know where we are?'

She looked about. Everything seemed a bit different at night. Besides, she never usually came to this part of town because . . . because . . . She gasped, a painful shot of cold air suddenly flooding her lungs. 'Oh my God . . .'

'The fuckin' bus took us on a diversion, didn't it? Don't say nothing. We're gonna get a taxi or something and get out of here, all right? But we need some money, yeah?'

'Let's just get a taxi, we can stop at a cash point wherever!' Chanelle said, panicked.

'We gotta find one first.'

Chanelle looked up the road. The West End was flooded with taxis, all with their yellow 'For Hire' lights glowing. Here, the taxis that passed them were taken, shadowy figures sitting in the back seats, roaring past on their way to cross the river. There was nothing to hail.

'Minicab?' she suggested, trying to hide the tremor in her voice.

'Don't be stupid. No idea who the drivers are.' Jamal was looking seriously worried. He was usually calm and collected, always in control of any situation. The fact that he was afraid made her feel sick.

But then, the situation was serious, she knew that. The bus had brought them on to the Righteous Crew's turf. That was a dangerous matter for any Blacksmith Boy. For the gang leader, it was pure recklessness. Chanelle tried to steer clear of the darker side of Jamal's life but she knew something of the run-ins with the police, the ongoing gang rivalries, and drama of the drugs trade with all its illicitness, big rewards and violence. But Jamal did not get involved in any of his boys' bloody work: when a deal had been reneged on or a payment missed, he simply instructed his lieutenants to sort it out, and they did. They told stories of their exploits, sitting round the coffee table at Jamal's place while passing big joints around – some of the boys liked white pipes, cannabis laced with Mandrax to give them a proper buzz – and Chanelle tried not to listen because the stories made her shiver with horror and fear. She thought of Jamal as removed from all that when he was with her. But now, she realised, it was frighteningly close.

'There's gonna be another bus in a minute,' she said hopefully, but Jamal was getting twitchy.

'Don't know how long I can wait,' he said. 'We gotta get out of here, Chanelle, I ain't being funny.'

'Then let's go. How far till we're off the turf?'

'Boundary is Sylvester Road. I reckon it's only ten minutes away, if we hurry.'

'We're gonna run for it?'

Jamal nodded. 'They don't know we're here. Not yet, anyway.'

As soon as the decision was made, they began to move. Jamal buried his face even deeper into the turned-up collar of his jacket, put his arm around Chanelle in a pincer-tight grip, and the two of them began to move at a fast stride, away from the crowd at the bus stop and into the black-and-orange darkness of the city night. They didn't run for fear of attracting attention to themselves, but moved with obvious urgency, Chanelle's high-heeled boots tapping rapidly on the pavement as she trotted to keep up with Jamal's long strides.

Her heart pounded, her breath came fast, and her eyes flickered to left and right. Every dark corner seemed intimidating and frightening, as though someone might lurk there unseen. It seemed to take forever to reach the end of one street and gain another. She was not sure whether she felt safer in the concealing dark of alleyways or out in the glare of the streetlights where other people and traffic passed by.

'Are we nearly there?' she panted, after they had been going for what felt like hours.

Jamal had taken his arm from round her shoulders and was now holding her hand. His grip tightened. 'Nearly, babe. Just a few more streets.'

The boundaries were well known by every gang member, and crossing them on foot was close to suicide. Chanelle could hardly believe they were actually in the other gang's territory – it felt like a nightmare – and when Jamal muttered to her that Sylvester Road was just across the road, relief flooded through her. With safety so close, they couldn't stop themselves from taking to their heels and running. An oncoming car beeped its horn at them as they raced across its path and dodged a motorbike in the other lane, but moments later they were over and into Sylvester Road. They slowed down and gazed at one another, laughing, relief evident in their faces.

'That was a close one,' Jamal said.

'Never again,' Chanelle said fervently. 'Don't want to go through that again.'

She could never remember afterwards where they came from. They seemed simply to materialise in front of them – a gang of tall boys in oversized hoodies so that their faces were shadowed and hidden, like wraiths from a horror film.

The only one whose face could be seen was the leader: his hood was pushed back to reveal an Afro pulled into tight dreadlocks, a snarl on his face and hatred glittering in his eyes.

'Stop right there, man,' he hissed at Jamal. His accent was classic South London gangsta, a cockney lilt infused with Jamaican influences. 'You think we don' know wha you bin? Huh? You know da rules, blood. It's about respec', innit?'

Jamal said nothing but he tensed from head to toe, his grip around Chanelle's hand turning to iron so that she almost cried out in pain.

The leader stepped forward until his face nearly touched Jamal's. Chanelle could smell the weed and cigarettes on his breath. She was frozen with fear, unable to move and hardly able to take everything in. She never saw exactly what happened, just a swift movement from the man who had spoken, then the gang turned and ran, scattering silently into the dark on rubber soles. Beside her, Jamal had bent over. The next moment he had dropped to his knees on the pavement, his hands clutched to his belly.

'Jamal! Sweetheart!' she cried in panic.

'Get my phone. Pocket.' His voice terrified her, it was breathless and without power. She saw that his hands were covered in a dark substance that was oozing out from between his fingers. 'Quick!'

She fumbled for his pocket, her breath coming in short painful gasps. She knew they'd stabbed him. She was not surprised – it was what happened, it was the punishment for straying – but she was in cold shock, knowing only that there were a few precious minutes to get help for him. She pulled out the mobile phone as Jamal slumped over so that he was lying on his side on the ground. She blinked at the phone, not sure how to use it. Jamal always had the latest model to flash out when he did business and it was nothing like her own basic pay-as-you-go that had run out of credit the day before. Chanelle pushed some buttons randomly but nothing happened.

'How do I switch it on, babe?' she cried. Hysteria began to grip her, and she felt herself losing control. 'How do I switch it on?'

Jamal said nothing. His breathing was coming deeply now, with a curious rattle in it as though he needed to cough.

Chanelle screamed with frustration and threw the phone to the ground. 'Help!' she yelled. 'Help us!

Someone!' Tears started flooding out of her eyes, and she began to shake. 'Help!' she cried, but her voice was weak with sobs. She kneeled down next to Jamal and took his head on her lap. Stroking it, she gazed down at him. He had paled and his eyes were shut, the horrible sound of his breathing rasping out. 'Babe, babe . . . stay with me. Don't go, baby, I love you, I need you . . .' Her voice broke over the words.

'What's happened?' A man was approaching out of the darkness.

'Call an ambulance!' begged Chanelle, desperate. 'My boyfriend's been stabbed!'

'Holy fuck.' The man whipped out a phone. 'I'll call 999.'

'Please, tell them to hurry! Please.' She ran a finger over Jamal's cheek. She saw her tears fall on it and roll down as though Jamal himself was weeping. 'Baby, stay with me . . . please . . . hold on. I can't live without you. Don't leave me.'

17

There was a knock on Daisy's bedroom door.

'Yes?' she said. She was sitting at her dressing table, putting on lipstick. It was not easy. Despite the warmth of the room, her lips were cold and the red lipstick seemed to sit waxily on her mouth. *Like making up a corpse*, she thought, and then shuddered. That was not a good analogy.

The door opened and Margaret stepped into the room. She was dressed in a sombre black shapeless suit and her usual flat black pumps. There was not even a pearl necklace or a brooch to lighten the outfit, and her dark hair was pulled back into its habitual stern ponytail, the white lock standing out against the brown.

'Yes?' Daisy asked, and repressed another shiver. Margaret had brought even more of a chill into the room with her.

'The cars are ready downstairs,' she said, in her expressionless way. 'It's time to go now.'

'Thank you. I'll be right there.' Daisy turned back to her reflection as Margaret closed the door behind her. She picked up her hairbrush and pulled it through her short fair hair. She had recently told her hairdresser, Cedric, to cut off the long light waves she had had all her life. It was time to stop being a child now. She was a grown-up. She was just over eighteen and she was motherless. It was strange how everyone in her life disappeared after a while: first her brother and sister had vanished, roaring away down the drive that Christmas Day, never to be seen and rarely spoken of again. Now her mother had gone too. There were just the two of them left, her and Daddy. And Margaret, of course.

In just a few short months, Margaret had become a constant presence. There was a room for her in every Dangerfield house, although Daisy was sure she still kept a place of her own because Margaret retained the air of someone just passing through and occasionally disappeared for a few days, though she always returned. Daddy relied on her more and more; she was constantly at his side, with an answer to every question he threw at her. She kept his diary and made every travel arrangement, every meeting and every dinner engagement. She was also responsible for the upkeep of all the property Daddy owned and his personal administration, down to selecting each gift he gave. She had quickly become embedded deep into his life, and Daisy was only just beginning to realise how completely her father now depended on his assistant.

Margaret had even been in the hospital room when Daisy's mother had died. Daisy and her father stood next to the bed, Daisy holding Julia's hand as she slipped away, never waking from the coma she had been in for four months. Margaret had been a silent presence, standing just out of sight behind the monitors that displayed Julia's vital signs.

'I think she's gone,' the doctor had said quietly. 'The brain stem is non-functioning and I'm afraid that means there is no hope of any change. Do we have your permission to turn off the machine that's keeping her breathing?'

'Yes,' Daddy had snapped brusquely. 'Do it.'

Daisy had wept as her mother's chest stopped rising and falling, and the lines on the monitors became flat; tears poured down her face as Julia died without a struggle.

Why have you left me? she wanted to cry out. *Didn't you love me enough to stay?* But she couldn't bring herself to say anything in front of the other people in the room; instead she clung to her mother's hand and wept bitterly until a nurse led her gently out.

Now Daisy stood up and smoothed down the black Prada dress that she'd teamed with a white leather belt, and black-and-white heels. On her now-short fair hair she'd pinned an ornament made of a Victorian mourning brooch and dark raven feathers.

That would have pleased Mummy, she thought. Julia had always been famously elegant and well dressed. *I wish she could see this outfit, I'm sure she would have liked it.* Daisy was hit by a rush of grief as she realised that she was only going to miss her mother more as time went by, not less. There would be no chance now to get to know one another. Her mother would never be at her wedding or hold any grandchildren or share any of her adult life. The shock hit her with sudden force, and Daisy almost bent over under its strength.

No, she told herself, holding back great shuddering sobs. *I can't give in. I must get through it. I have to put on a brave face. It's what Daddy expects.*

She blinked away the tears in her eyes, biting her lip with the effort. She closed her eyes, gathered all her courage, opened them, set her shoulders and headed for the door.

The Maybach limousine waited for her on the gravel drive. Daddy was already inside, almost filling his wide black leather seat even though he had become a little slimmer lately. An exercise room had been installed in the London house and a couple of times a week he made his way down to it, emerging red-faced and sweaty an hour later. Pills and supplements were left by his place in porcelain pill boxes at breakfast. The kitchen sent up strange sludgy green or lurid orange concoctions that Daddy drained with a look of determination on his face. Whatever he was doing was obviously having an effect.

Margaret sat next to him, her seat separated from his by a wide black leather armrest, looking thin and angular next to Daddy's fleshiness. Her feet rested on the footplate below her seat.

'Come on, girl,' Daddy said roughly. 'We'll be late.'

'Yes, Daddy.' Daisy climbed in and sat down opposite him so that she had her back to the driver and the bodyguard sitting next to him. Margaret gave a subtle nod and the limousine pulled smoothly away from the house. It was a short drive to the village church where the funeral service would take place. Daisy studied her father as they went. He looked stressed and unhappy, but that was hardly surprising.

He had shown little emotion since his wife's death, but perhaps he had been hiding his grief and only today, at the funeral, would he allow it to show.

He's amazingly strong, Daisy thought. *I'll work as hard as I can until I'm as strong as he is.* It was only a few months now until she was due to start at Brown University in America and she was already regretting that she would leave her father at a time when he obviously needed her. There had been some talk a while ago of him coming to live in the States during her studies, but nothing had been said of it lately. *He's busy, I know that. I can hardly expect him to drop everything just to be with me. I've got to learn to stand on my own two feet.*

She knew that there had been a lot of paperwork to sort out since Mummy's death, legal matters had to be dealt with though no one had said exactly what. If Mummy hadn't left a will, there would no doubt be further complications to do with whatever estate she'd had.

That's probably why Daddy looks so strung out, she thought. *More worries for him. Yet more on his plate. Poor Daddy. I must look after him.*

The journey to the church was silent. When they got there other mourners were arriving, going into the church or lingering outside to smoke or talk. Daisy realised that she knew hardly anyone there and wondered who they were all were. *They must be from a part of Mummy's life I know nothing about.*

She'd known that her mother's aristocratic family had cut her off for marrying Daddy, but that Mummy hadn't minded. She'd always been a rebellious woman, running away for a life of bohemian loucheness in London when she was just a teenager, hanging out with artists, poets and musicians. She had met Daddy when she was working as a publisher's secretary, though she'd never explained exactly how. 'We had friends in common,' she'd said vaguely when Daisy asked how her parents had met and married. 'We were introduced by a connection.' Daddy had been entranced by the leggy aristocratic blonde, and had set about wooing her with iron determination.

'Darling, I didn't stand a chance,' Julia had told Daisy. 'Your father wasn't going to take no for an answer. And as soon as my father told me he'd disown me if I married that utter shit Dangerfield, I was as good as engaged. Besides, you know Daddy. He has to win.'

As a result, Daisy didn't know any relatives on her mother's side. Were any of them here today? *Do I have a family I don't even know about?* Despite her desperate sadness, she was curious. As she and Daddy made their way down the central aisle to their pew, she couldn't help scanning the congregation, trying to discern family similarities in the faces there. Was that woman with the red-rimmed eyes and the pale brown hair tucked up into a black hat related to her? What about that man with the dark moustache and the cold green eyes? Could he be an uncle or a cousin?

Then her eyes were drawn to the pine coffin, resting on its catafalque at the front of the church. *Mummy is in there,* she thought, feeling cold and almost sick. She pushed the thought away and looked instead at the flowers on top: a wreath of white roses from Daddy, and an arrangement of daisies from her. She'd written the card herself: *'Goodbye, Mummy. I love you.'*

147

They sat down. Daisy looked at her order of service. The front was embellished with a beautiful black-and-white photograph of her mother. She was standing in front of a window, one arm draped across her body as she looked away to the left. As a result she was almost in silhouette, but it was still possible to see the fine-boned features, the long straight nose, high cheekbones, and hooded eyes. Long, dark-blonde hair fell down her back. She looked impossibly young and pretty. Daisy felt that bitter stab again, and the sense of waste, along with the feeling that she was going to miss her mother more and more as time passed.

The service began. It was short but very beautiful. Daddy went up and did a reading, booming out the words of Keats's 'Ode to Nightingale'. A woman Daisy did not know read a passage from the Bible. The choir sang exquisitely, their voices soaring up towards the hammer-beamed ceiling of the old church. Daisy fought her tears but it was difficult. The sadness seemed to grow and possess her until she hardly knew how to suppress it. She was almost overcome. It was only the presence of Daddy next to her, stern and stony-faced, that stopped her from breaking down altogether.

Afterwards they trailed out behind the coffin. The cemetery was behind the little church; an open grave waited, a pile of earth to either side covered with a green grass-like cloth, wreaths and bouquets arranged around it.

Daisy quailed. She didn't think she could stand this part, where her mother was consigned to the ground. *Surely Daddy won't miss me,* she thought, but suddenly she didn't care if he did. She needed to cry. The weight of the unshed tears was making her eyes ache and her head throb. Spotting a large funeral monument, mouldering and covered in moss, she slid behind it, buried her face in her hands and began to weep.

She had been sobbing for a few moments when she felt a hand on her arm and a deep voice said, 'Hey now . . . don't cry. Come on, it's OK.'

She looked up, startled, and blinked away her tears. She was staring at someone very familiar and yet not. 'Will!' she gasped, suddenly recognising him.

He nodded. 'Hi. Listen, don't tell Dad I'm here, OK?'

'But . . . what are you doing?' She was stunned, hardly believing that she was actually looking at her half-brother again. He had changed, filling out and gaining a manly shape, so that he seemed taller and bigger than before. His once-unruly red hair had been close cut, his boyish freckles had faded. He had become handsome and striking.

'Listen, I might be lots of things, but I'm not a monster.' He smiled, and his expression softened. 'I know we didn't always get on, but I was actually pretty fond of your mum. She had a hard time from me and Sarah, but she was always good to us. And I saw the way *he* beat her down and destroyed her.'

'Is Sarah here?' Daisy felt the first ray of happiness she'd known in weeks. Here was Will, her big brother. Did this mean they were going to be a family again?

He shook his head. 'No. She's too afraid to see Dad. Listen, Daisy.' He fixed her with a solemn green-eyed gaze. 'I'm sorry that your mum's dead. I came here to pay my respects. It was important to me to do that.

But I'm afraid it doesn't change anything between us. You're with *him* and that's the way it is. OK?'

'But—'

'That's the way it is,' he repeated firmly. 'I wasn't going to say anything but when I saw you crying like this . . . well . . . I hope I don't regret it, that's all.'

'Please, Will,' she said, suddenly desperate. She couldn't let him walk out of her life again. 'Please, stay. Talk to Daddy. Can't you make it up?'

He shook his head. 'There's a lot you don't understand, Daisy. Maybe you will one day. But for now, it's impossible. So will you do me a favour and promise me that you won't tell him I was here?'

'Yes, of course. I promise. But . . .' Disappointment began to crush her. She couldn't bear it.

'Thanks.' He smiled at her again almost sympathetically. 'You're a good kid. I'm sorry it has to be this way – but you're on his side and that makes us diametrically opposed. We can't be brother and sister. We can't even be friends. Sorry, that's not going to change. Goodbye.'

Before she could say anything more, he headed quickly away to the churchyard gate and was soon lost to view.

Daisy leaned against the cool, rough stone of the monument and wondered how she was going to bear another goodbye.

From across the graveyard, she could hear the voice of the vicar intoning the last words of the funeral service. She dried her eyes, blew her nose and took a deep breath. Then she went back towards the grave to join her father.

She had almost reached him when she saw a scuffle

going on at the back of the crowd. Daddy's driver and the bodyguard were wrestling with a man in a dark suit, wrenching him forcibly out of the churchyard. Everyone was watched in stunned silence as the burly men bundled the other man away from them and out towards the lych gate.

'Get your bloody hands off me, I've every right to be here!' cried the white-haired stranger, trying to twist out of the guards' meaty fists with no success.

Astonished, Daisy looked over at her father who had gone pale and was quivering with rage. He lifted one arm and pointed at the hapless man. 'Get out!' he roared, his eyes flashing. 'You are a stranger here, do you understand? How dare you invade my family like this? Do you hear me? Get out! Never show your face round here again!'

Before the man could say another word, he was pulled from the churchyard and out of sight, his protests muffled.

Daddy closed his eyes for a moment. Then, with his composure regained, he took a deep breath and looked at the vicar. 'You may proceed. The rubbish has been disposed of.'

As the service resumed and people pretended the odd interlude had not happened, Daisy bit her lip, more thankful than ever that Daddy had remained unaware of Will's presence. If this was how he responded to someone turning up unexpectedly, his reaction to seeing Will was unimaginable.

18

In the study of Thornside Manor, Daddy Dangerfield sat hunched over his desk. He looked as though he was in great pain, and his face was a dark, congested red. When he looked up, his eyes were bloodshot and red-rimmed. On the desk in front of him lay a sheet of thick, expensive writing paper covered in neat handwriting.

'Where did you get this?' he rasped, his voice sounding choked. His hands were clutching the sides of the desk, knuckles yellowy-white under the force of his grip.

'It was addressed to Daisy,' Margaret said calmly. 'I thought it looked as though it might be important. So I took the liberty of intercepting it.'

Daddy made a strange strangled sound in his throat. 'How could she do this to me?' he managed to say at last. 'What she's suggesting is outrageous . . . terrible! And she hasn't even given a name!'

Margaret regarded him calmly, her blue eyes cool beneath their perfectly arched brows. She was not a beautiful woman but she exuded a certain stylishness that came from her immaculate grooming and subtle, tasteful wardrobe of plain but expensive clothes, along with an evidently fierce intelligence.

'We need to be sure that she's telling the truth,' Margaret said in her low, measured way.

Daddy stared up at her, a flicker of something like hope in his eyes. 'Would she lie about a thing like this?'

'Who knows?' Margaret responded crisply. 'I must say, deciphering the thoughts and motives of a half-crazed depressive alcoholic is beyond me. But that hardly matters one way or the other. There are simple things we can do to discover the truth. And if she's lying, no one but you and I need ever know about it.'

'What things?' Daddy frowned, puzzled.

'Leave it to me,' Margaret said. 'I'll do what's necessary and have the results back with you in no time at all.'

'Thank you, Margaret, thank you.' Daddy gave her a look of gratitude that was granted to very few people in his life.

'All part of my job,' she said with a small smile.

'You know I'll show my gratitude in the usual way.'

'Of course. I'll see about it immediately.'

That evening, in the privacy of her office, Margaret typed a letter to the clinic explaining what her needs were. Then she put several small clear tubes of gel with what looked like mascara wands in them – these containing the samples – into a Jiffy bag along with her letter. She sealed it carefully, addressed and prepared it to be collected by a courier the following morning.

She gazed down at it. Her employer had the right to know the truth. And she would make sure that he did.

19

'Yoh! You OK?'

Chanelle turned round. One of the boys from the gang was sloping up quietly behind her, hands in his pockets, a baseball cap pulled low over his face.

'You shouldn't be here,' she muttered. 'It's not safe.'

'Not safe for you neither.'

She turned back to look at the dying flowers tied to the traffic bollard near where Jamal had been knifed. The cellophane was limp now and the blooms inside faded to grey and brown. The scrawled messages – 'RIP bruv, u's with the angels now', 'Neva 2 B forgotten', 'Tragic loss, taken too soon, rest in peace, From all at St Stephen's' – were smeared by the rain.

'I'll be fine,' she said at last, pushing some strands of hair away from her face.

'They know you's his girl. They find you, they rape ya, man,' the boy said, twitching and bouncing on the spot, unable to stay still, whether from drugs or nerves Chanelle couldn't tell.

'They won't find me.' She continued to stare bleakly at Jamal's memorial. He'd been cremated and his ashes taken by his grieving family. They didn't even know about Chanelle, so no one had spoken to her at the funeral and she hadn't introduced herself. It was too late for all that now.

The police had interviewed her but she'd stuck to the code. She hadn't seen any faces and couldn't identify anyone. She had nothing to say beyond a basic explanation of what had happened. No one talked to the police, that was understood. Her life wouldn't be worth much if she did. Even so, she was still in danger, she knew that.

I don't even care, she thought hopelessly. *I wish they would come and get me.*

Life had lost all meaning for her since that terrible night. She'd gone in the ambulance to King's College Hospital with Jamal, watching as the paramedics did what they could in the moving vehicle, trying to keep him with them, trying to resuscitate, but Chanelle had known it was hopeless. She'd sensed him go and knew that she was terribly, unutterably alone.

So why can't I cry? she asked herself. There hadn't been any tears since it happened. Just a strange and immediate shutting down, as though her heart had been switched off, leaving her body functioning but feeling nothing. She spent hours lying in her bed, staring dry-eyed into the darkness, wondering how she was going to go on in this state, feeling like a robot.

'Who's taken Jamal's place?' she asked suddenly, turning to look at the boy. It was Jackson, she realised, one of Jamal's favourites.

'Terence, yeah?' he mumbled.

'Oh.' She turned away again. Jamal had known the other boy was a threat to his position. Terence had a violent streak more pronounced than most of the gang displayed. He didn't care who got hurt, or even if people died. He loved the thrill of it all and was turned on by motors with blacked-out windows, and guns . . . the life of the big-time dealer. Things round here wouldn't get any better with him in charge. No doubt he was planning some gruesome act of revenge for Jamal's death right now. He wouldn't care who was killed in the process.

'I gotta go,' Jackson said, cocking his head in the direction he'd be taking.

'Yeah, sure.'

Still he lingered. 'So . . . what you gonna do, Chanelle? You don't look right.'

'I'm leaving.'

'Where you goin'?'

She stuffed her hands deeper into the pockets of her jacket. 'Dunno. Away from here.'

'Leaving school?'

'Leaving everything. There's nothing for me. It's all over. I gotta get away and start again.'

Jackson nodded as though he understood this. 'You take care, yeah?'

She managed a small smile. 'Yeah. You too. Stay out of trouble, OK?'

Jackson grinned back. 'Do my best. 'Bye then.'

''Bye.' He left as quietly as he'd come while Chanelle carried on standing, staring and remembering.

20

Daisy sat in her room in London, turning over the pages of a guide to Europe and wondering if she and Lucy should factor Vienna into their travel itinerary. They had decided to go travelling for the remainder of the summer, to help Daisy take her mind off things and get in the mood for her move to America in the autumn. She would be glad to be away from the house: Daddy hadn't been the same since the funeral, which was hardly surprising, but he was more prone than ever to violent rages and spent hours locked away with Margaret, working.

The telephone on her desk rang. It was a long single buzz, so it was an internal call. Going over, Daisy saw that the call was from her father's study. She picked up the receiver.

'Hello? Daddy?'

Instead of her father's voice, she heard Margaret's cool, measured tones. 'Daisy, could you please come down?'

'Yes, of course.'

'At once.'

The phone went dead. Daisy looked at it, frowning. Margaret's loyalties lay completely with Daddy, but she had always acted respectfully towards Daisy in the past.

She put down her travel guide, checked the mirror and ran her fingers through her hair. She looked fine in a smart dark pencil skirt and a draped olive green cardigan. As she made her way downstairs, she wondered why Daddy wanted to see her. Perhaps it was something about Brown University. After all, her move to the States was imminent. Margaret was making all the arrangements – maybe they'd finalised the house Daddy was buying her in Providence, Rhode Island. Even though she'd be living on the campus, it had been decided that Daisy should have a bolthole, somewhere to retreat to if she needed privacy and where she could spend some of the vacation if she didn't want to come home. They'd found a beautiful white clapboard Colonial-style house in extensive grounds. There was even a cottage nearby for her guards to stay in: Daddy insisted on maximum security when Daisy was out of his sight.

Crossing the chequered marble floor of the hall, she felt a flicker of nervousness. Things hadn't been the same lately. Daddy had been in a dark mood, the kind she feared most because it usually heralded a massive explosion after which there were always casualties. Drake the butler had been the latest – fired by Daddy in a screaming fit when supper wasn't served at eight o'clock precisely. Margaret had made sure Drake was out that same night, and a new butler was attending to the breakfast table by morning. There was, Daisy realised, no one else left now for his anger to land upon – only herself.

But Daddy has no reason to be cross with me. I've never done anything wrong.

He was always delighted with her, particularly as the shoe line had been successful in the Florey and new boutiques had been opened in some of the other Dangerfield hotels and resorts. Daisy had been wondering about the possibility of designing a line of jewellery as well. She'd always been drawn to the glitter of fine stones and interesting designs, ever since Daddy had given her that diamond brooch years before.

Besides, he wanted to prepare her for taking on the company. Once she was properly educated, she was going to be inducted into the reality of what the family owned and where. Very few people were privileged enough to understand the full extent of the Dangerfield wealth, but she was going to be one of them.

She reached the heavy oak door to her father's study. He had a study in every one of their properties, each devoted to a different theme. His London one celebrated fox hunting, the walls covered with old hunting prints and etchings. On top of the bookshelves was a selection of antique velvet-covered riding hats, and cabinets displayed brass hunting horns, and a collection of hip flasks. On the wall was a framed display of stock pins and lapel badges, while over the fireplace three stuffed and mounted fox masks bared their sharp teeth and stared glassily out over the room.

Daisy knocked on the door, two sharp raps, and waited.

'Come in!' It was Margaret's voice, faint through the thick oak panels.

Daisy pushed open the door and went in. Daddy

was standing behind his desk with his back to her, gazing out of the window that gave over the garden below. Just outside, its branches pendulous with cushions of pink blossom, a tree swayed gently in the fresh morning breeze. Something about the way her father's hands were clasped behind his back and the rigid set of his shoulders made Daisy worry.

Margaret gave her a thin smile and ushered her towards the desk. As usual Daddy's assistant seemed almost invisible herself in a plain grey suit and without make-up.

Daisy stepped forward on to the antique Persian rug before her father's huge desk.

'Daddy?' she ventured. 'You wanted to see me?'

There was a long pause, then her father turned round. She could barely restrain a gasp of fear: the expression on his face was something she had never seen before. He looked ill, his skin yellow and waxy, his face haggard. Great dark circles bagged out under his bloodshot eyes. Within their depths was a coldness Daisy had never known to be turned on her.

He fixed her with that cold, cold stare.

Ruthless. The word slipped unprompted into her mind.

Then he spoke in a voice like ice. 'Never call me that again.'

'Wh-wh-what do you mean?' she stammered.

'You heard me. You have no right to call me that.'

She shook her head, confused. 'But Daddy—'

'Didn't you hear me?' he shrieked, and slammed his hand down on the desk with terrifying force. 'I'm not your *daddy*.' He spat out the word with terrible bitterness.

Daisy's mouth dropped open and she felt as though she had been punched in the stomach. All the breath seemed to leave her body.

'That's right,' he hissed, eyes now burning with icy fire. 'You're not my daughter. That bitch of a mother of yours was unfaithful. There's no way you're a Dangerfield. Look!' He picked up a letter and tossed it towards her. 'That's the lab report. Your sample and mine were analysed. There's no chance in hell that you are my daughter.'

Daisy fought for calm despite the panic that was building inside her. She stepped forward and picked up the paper. It was headed with the name of a laboratory and there was a line that read 'DNA testing reference' and a string of numbers. Her eyes dropped to the line at the bottom: 'Statistically impossible that Subject A is the daughter of Subject B'. She felt dazed. 'But . . . but . . .'

'She couldn't keep a secret.' Daddy's voice had dropped to a menacingly quiet tone. 'Even from beyond the grave. She punished me all those years with her drinking, and now she has to destroy the one thing she gave me as well.' He pointed at another letter lying on his desk. Daisy recognised her mother's handwriting sloping across the page, but she couldn't make out any words or see to whom it was addressed. 'The bitch had to make sure I suffered. This letter explains that you're not my child.' He looked as though he wanted to spit on the paper to show his contempt for the woman who had been his wife. 'She meant it for you, so that you could go on posing as my daughter.'

'I don't understand,' Daisy said, fighting to keep

control. *Mummy left me a letter and they took it?* She feared that tears might come and she knew how much Daddy hated them, but then, quite suddenly, she was certain that she wasn't going to cry. Survival instinct kicked in. She felt a strange serenity along with a heightened awareness: her skin seemed to prickle with a sudden alertness to everything around her. She felt as if she could see every hair on Daddy's knuckles, every pore on his great nose; she felt as if she could see Margaret quite plainly as she stared impassively at the scene before her, even though the woman was standing behind Daisy. *You must handle this very carefully,* a little voice seemed to whisper inside her head. *What happens in the next few moments will decide the future course of your life.* She wanted to ask who her father was, but something told her this was unwise. *I must act as though this changes nothing.*

She forced herself to smile at her father. 'Oh, D—' She caught herself just in time. There was no point in antagonising him. 'You poor darling, what a horrible, horrible shock. How could Mummy do that to you?'

Daddy looked faintly startled, then his eyes narrowed and hardened again. 'Yes. Yes, it *is* a terrible shock. I feel utterly betrayed.'

'But this needn't change things between us, surely,' Daisy said. Despite her desperate desire to stay calm, she could feel herself begin to tremble. Her stomach churned with horrible nausea. 'You're my father in every possible way. You've brought me up to be like you, to think like you and understand things like you. That's the important thing, isn't it? And perhaps she made a mistake. Perhaps you *are* my father.'

There was a pause while Daddy seemed to consider this. For a moment, she thought she saw a softening of his expression.

'To me, you're my father,' she said gently, with a sudden hope that everything was going to be all right. 'I love you. I'd do anything for you. Can't we go on as we are?'

His face was instantly stony. 'No!' he rapped out. 'No. I don't know who you are . . . whose spawn you are. You could be anything! I'm not passing off some other man's bastard as my own. The lab results can't be wrong!' His face began to darken as the blood rushed to his cheeks. He banged both palms on the desk and leaned towards her. 'Don't you understand what being a Dangerfield means? It means sharing blood with *him*.' He cocked his head towards the photograph of his father that was displayed in an ornate silver frame on the sideboard. 'It means belonging to our family, our tribe, our clan. You are a pretender. An imposter.' Fury seemed to grip him then and he began to snarl at her. 'You're a bastard, I tell you! The fruit of some disgusting liaison with God knows who . . . that whore of a mother of yours, opening her legs for anyone! How could she, how could she? The brazen slut! And you . . . the sight of you makes me sick.' He gathered a wad of saliva in his mouth and spat it towards her.

Daisy recoiled as it landed on the front of her cardigan and lay there, a bubbling mass, before it started to slide down in a slippery trail. She gasped and stared up at her father, unable to believe this was actually happening.

'But, Daddy!' she implored. Her control began to

crumble. Her heart pounded as her eyes burned and stung. Despite her best efforts, tears began to pour down her face. 'No! No . . .'

'Yes, yes,' he mimicked back in a high squeaky tone. Then his voice turned harsh again. 'You've lived off the fat of the land for long enough. None of this is yours. You're a parasite and nothing more. I want you out of here immediately. At *once*. And when you're gone, I never want to see you again, do you understand? I never want to see your face again!'

Daisy sobbed. He couldn't mean it. Surely this was a passing fury that would blow over and be forgotten. He adored her! She was his princess! Could he really cease loving her just like that?

'Daddy,' she whispered through her tears, 'please . . .'

He began to shake violently. 'Say that again, and God help me, I will punch you,' he thundered. His fist clenched as though in readiness to carry out his threat. 'Get out! Get out, do you hear?'

Knowing that she was on the brink of losing her self-control completely, Daisy could only obey. She turned and stumbled towards the door, her shoulders slumped, half-blinded by her tears. As she went, she saw Margaret's expression. In the other woman's eyes, there was a strange mixture of amusement and pity.

Don't pity me! Daisy felt her defiance return. Despite her weeping, she lifted her head, straightened her shoulders and stiffened her spine. *I can't show them they've won.*

As she reached the door, she realised that this might be the very last time she would ever see her father. She turned and looked at him, taking in his reddened face, dark, embittered eyes, the strong features submerged in a layer of fat. She looked at his over-dyed black hair, the meaty shoulders stuffed into his jacket, the paunch jutting out from under his burgundy waistcoat. He was a strange combination of strength and weakness, of manliness and childishness. Despite everything, she loved and felt sorry for him. He'd had only her to care for him. Now who would he have?

'Goodbye, Daddy,' she said softly. 'You'll always be my father, no matter what some test says.'

'Get out!' he roared. 'Or I'll have you thrown out!'

'I'm going, don't worry,' she said. Then she opened the study door, walked out and closed it behind her. In fifteen short minutes, her life had been utterly transformed.

Part Two

21

Two years later

Coco wrapped her leg high around the silver pole and leaned back, swaying from side to side so that her breasts swung invitingly while she snaked her arms in time to the music. She wore only a small silver thong, a scrap of fabric covering her pubic mound with the string cutting between her buttocks, and a pair of very high heels. That was not including the ton of make-up she'd plastered on. The girls had to wear heavy make-up so that it could be seen in the dim lighting of the club: thick blue glittering eye shadow, kohl pencil and false eyelashes, streaks of blusher and lots of sticky dark red gloss on their lips. It was what the punters liked: their idea of glamour. And when the lights caught the sheen on the girls' lips, it looked as though they were moist and parted in arousal.

Coco ground her hips in a rotating motion and pulled herself up the pole so that she could spin back down gracefully to the ground. It took a lot of practice and strength to do this so that it looked effortless, but

Coco had been dancing at the club for a while now and she was, so Roberto said, a natural. It helped that she had a figure that seemed made for pole dancing: long legs and a slender torso, the golden expanse of her stomach pierced at the belly button with a silver bar, and full ripe breasts and graceful arms. Her hair had been dyed peroxide white and she wore it in a shaggy, shoulder-length style that gave her a vaguely seventies, punkish air. The customers seemed to like it, anyway; she was one of the girls most called upon to give private dances in the back room.

The rule there was no touching: the man was supposed to sit watching while she gyrated only centimetres away, thrusting her pelvis at him and twisting her hips, running her hands over her breasts while she pouted, gazing at him through half-closed eyes. Sometimes, she got a strange thrill from the power she had over the male sitting there, his glassy gaze fixed upon her, first on her tits and then on her mound. He would be stock still, trying to control his breathing and unable to conceal the bulge in his pinstripe trousers – most often they were wearing suits. Usually they were City boys from along the road, slumming it in the East End for a laugh, taking in a lap-dancing club as the perfect way to finish their evening.

Sometime she tortured them a little bit further, rolling down her briefs or her thong, so that they could glimpse the prize inside, watching them as their pupils dilated and they became even more choked.

That happened rarely, though. Mostly she couldn't stand the punters. She disliked the ones who sat there as though they didn't give a toss that a beautiful near-naked girl was dancing right in their face. They looked almost bored, as though they'd perfected the art of staying unaroused, and simply stared at her with something like contempt. But weirdly, those were the guys who gave her the most money: the ones who would tuck a couple of fifties into the strap of her thong or toss a wadge of tenners on to the table afterwards.

The ones she hated most were the leery, lusty bastards who thought she was there to be touched and pawed, as though she were nothing more than a piece of meat. They thought a private dance meant they'd bought her for whatever they wanted – they reached up to tweak her nipples or tried to thrust their hot fingers inside her pants. One even reached up, grabbed her round the neck and tried to pull her face down to his crotch, where she could smell the rank mustiness of his cock and the dried piss on his underwear.

She'd call them fucking shitheads and push them away while yelling for Sam or Roberto. Roberto was not much use, to be honest, but at least his presence would stop the groping. Sam would intimidate with his size and explain very carefully the no-touching rule, but the punters were rarely thrown out. It was understood that another girl might be a bit more amenable, perhaps with another tenner or a twenty changing hands. Coco wasn't one of them. She didn't sell it. At least, not until recently.

Coco did a last spin around the pole, ending with her feet pointing up towards the ceiling and her head almost touching the floor, and then as the music faded out, her dance was over. She got down and strode off the stage, passing Kandy who was bouncing nervously in the wings as she limbered up for her turn. In the dressing room, Blanche was putting on her make-up. She was six foot tall, a statuesque black girl with skin that shimmered in the lights, especially when she rubbed baby oil into it.

'How did it go?' Blanche asked, gazing at her own reflection as she painted a thick layer of turquoise glitter on to one eyelid.

'Good.' Coco shrugged. 'Usual, I guess. It's not busy yet.'

'It'll fill up later, right?' Blanche smiled at Coco in the mirror. 'Listen, honey, I got an invitation for later. You interested?'

Coco picked up her towel and rubbed her arms with it. She had managed to work up quite a sweat. Pole dancing was a good way to keep slim. 'What's the deal?'

'Usual thing. It's our man from Spitalfields, remember a few weeks back? He liked it very much. He wants the same again.'

'Uh huh.' Coco began to rub down her legs. She owed Blanche a lot. The other girl had got her this job when she'd had nothing else and nowhere to live. It was Blanche who had told Roberto to train her and suggested their on-stage double act, which always went down fantastically well with the punters. Blanche had come up with her new name too.

'It's funny, innit?' she'd said. 'I'm black and I'm called Blanche, which means white. And you're white, and we can call you Coco, which is, like, black. Dark brown, really, but you know, it works, yeah?' Blanche had smiled with that irrepressible good humour of hers. 'And it's funny, 'cos it fits with your real name. Chanelle. Coco. Like Coco Chanel.'

Coco had liked it at once. She had wanted a new start and she was certainly getting one: she'd left South London behind and come east. She'd known that she couldn't stay in Peckham, surrounded by the memories and watching Terence, the new gang leader, taking over Jamal's position. Despite what all those notes on the flowers had said, Jamal would be forgotten soon enough, she'd realised that.

Michelle had not seemed unduly bothered by Chanelle's announcement that she was leaving, telling her to take care and not to wait too long before coming back for a visit. She hadn't asked how Chanelle intended to look after herself, perhaps she just assumed that the girl would be applying for a flat, signing on for benefits, getting pregnant, starting the kind of life she herself had led. She was living in a cloud of cheap vodka and strong lager most of the time, so perhaps she hadn't thought about it at all.

Chanelle had felt nothing as she left the tiny house with her clothes in a backpack. She wasn't sure if she would ever come back and see her mother again. All she knew was that life here had become so bleak and loveless that she had to get away, somewhere she could be alone and lick her wounds.

Her journey hadn't taken her very far: just across the river and over to the east, but it felt like a different world, full of strange faces. She'd spent a couple of nights wandering, once walking through the night and once kipping down in a park, and she'd been OK but had known her luck wouldn't hold out. There was only so long a young girl could roam without being molested in some way. One evening, sheltering in a pub and using one of the last tenners she'd nicked from Michelle's purse to get herself a drink and a hot meal, she'd got talking to a crowd of people, hippy types who were squatting in a deserted house, and they'd taken her back to theirs. That had been all right – she'd been given a few cushions and a sleeping bag in the corner of one of the rooms, and had spent a while in the house. But the novelty had worn thin: the other inhabitants were constantly smoking weed, rolling joints or making up bongs, and they talked without stopping, about things Chanelle didn't understand. They were into art and politics, always off protesting about something. Besides, she had to earn some money; she couldn't sign on without a proper address, and she had no idea what she was going to do. She couldn't live off shared tins of beans and bowls of plain pasta.

She'd been away from home for about four months when she'd met Blanche at a pub lock-in. They'd got talking and hit it off, and Blanche had suggested the job at the club and found Chanelle a flat to stay in. It seemed so obvious, she wondered why she hadn't thought of it before. One thing she could do was dance, after all. At first it had seemed like salvation: a source of money, the shared flat in Whitechapel, the steady employment, but she knew that she'd have to get out before too long, if she ever wanted to make something better of herself. She felt dimly that she owed it to Jamal and the love he'd had for her not to spend her life writhing round a pole for other men's amusement.

For now, though, she had a new name, Coco, and a new look, with her white hair. And she'd learned skills in every direction.

Blanche didn't do hand jobs or blow jobs for the punters like some girls did.

'I got class,' she said frankly, 'and sucking some bloke off in the back room ain't classy.'

Class for Blanche meant being a call girl. She would never walk the streets or let men touch her when she danced, but she would pay home visits if the price was right, and she was happy to add extras when they were asked for nicely. 'Men, women, couples,' she said with a shrug and a smile to Coco, when she'd explained what she sometimes did after hours. 'A little bit of bondage, a bit of pain games – not mine, theirs. But only on my terms, you see.'

Coco had not been particularly shocked by Blanche's extra-curricular activities. Nothing much shocked her, especially now. Ever since she'd left Peckham, she'd felt very little – unless it was anger and hatred, usually directed at the men she performed for. Besides, there was a world of difference between what Blanche was doing, and what those poor foreign women were forced to do. Coco had seen them brought in, Eastern Europeans mostly, usually in a terrible state, obviously kept oppressed and terrified; mentally, if not physically, beaten up. Their minders would demand jobs for the girls, but it wasn't Sam's policy to have them in his club. He didn't want pimps and controllers involved on his turf so he'd turn them away, but there were plenty of places that did have them. Coco knew the girls were little more than slaves, forced to work in massage parlours, or improvised brothels, or in lap-dancing clubs or even just made to walk the streets, getting into cars with strangers and handing the cash over to their guardians afterwards. It was a scandal but no one seemed to give a shit. Nothing ever happened to change it anyway.

Life's fucking tough, Coco thought. *You got to look after yourself or someone will fuck you over, and that's all there is to it.*

One night Blanche had told her that a visitor to the club had liked their double-act so much that he'd invited them back to his apartment to give him a private show.

'What do you think?' she had said, laughing. 'I think he's kosher. He's got a nice suit on. Looks loaded. He lives in Spitalfields so he's just up the road. He's offering us five hundred each.'

Five hundred. For maybe an hour of her time. Coco had never done anything like that before but maybe it was worth trying it out. God only knew she needed money.

'You know . . . you know that a private show is a bit different to what we do here,' Blanche had said lightly. 'There'll be other stuff, yeah? And if a guy wants two girls, well . . .' She'd come up close to Coco and touched her arm lightly. 'You don't have to be scared if you haven't done it before,' she murmured. Her eyes were dark and chocolatey, and her lips seemed tender. 'I have. I know what I'm doing. You might even like it.'

Coco stared back at her, and for a moment felt as though she was staring into Jamal's eyes. She felt a stab of desperate pain at the same time as an awful yearning possessed her. She longed for Jamal so badly, she thought she might collapse right there. She swallowed, somehow managing it despite her dry throat.

'Well?' pressed Blanche.

'OK,' Coco had replied. 'OK. I'll do it.'

The night had taken on a dream-like quality after that. It was two in the morning before their shift was over and they took a taxi up to Spitalfields, each wrapped up in a coat but with only underwear beneath. The man had been waiting for them in his apartment, a converted loft-style warehouse, with exposed brick and industrial pipework. He was middle-aged but fit and stylish, with a stubbly grey beard and grey hair in a fashionable cut. He'd called them 'ladies' and offered them real champagne. Then he'd cut lines of coke. Blanche and the man had snorted them, Coco had turned it down. They'd mellowed out for a while over the booze. Coco had liked it, despite the prickling bubbles that made her want to sneeze, and she'd necked hers quickly, hoping it would both anaesthetise her and give her courage.

'Hey, that's vintage Bollinger,' the man had laughed. 'Don't drink it too quickly.' But he'd topped up her glass anyway.

After a while Blanche had asked for music and started to dance lightly about the room. Then she slid her fur coat from her shoulders and began to dance more sensuously, writhing and twisting so that she showed off her magnificent body to the man sitting on the sofa. He watched, a half smile on his lips, his glass of champagne close to his face so that he could take a sip every few moments.

Blanche danced over to Coco and held out her hand, helping her to her feet. Coco started to move, finding her rhythm after a few moments and slipping easily into some of the routines the girls danced on stage, but bringing it down a notch or two. The high theatricality and exaggerated movements of the club did not seem suited to the intimate atmosphere of this man's sitting room. She began to enjoy moving to the music, the warmth and luxury of the apartment, the sensation of being lightly, pleasantly drunk and getting drunker.

Blanche moved close to her, swaying and twisting to the beat. When she was so close that her breasts were almost touching Coco, she smiled and leaned forward, stooping a little so that she could reach the other girl's mouth, and kissed her. There was a murmur of appreciation from the man on the sofa, and Blanche increased the pressure of her kiss, running her hands over Coco's arms and back.

It was a pleasant sensation, Coco found, the touch of soft full lips on hers, and when Blanche prodded open her mouth with the tip of her tongue, it felt like the most natural thing in the world to open to her. This was different from the cold, mechanical dancing she did for the men at the club, where it was all about them and not about her in the slightest. She felt that Blanche wanted to make her feel good, that the man watching them wanted to see them enjoy themselves. In that moment, she relaxed and decided to go with it and let it happen.

Now she remembered that night, she recalled being naked on the floor with Blanche, letting the other girl do whatever she wanted. She remembered the man leading them both through to his bedroom where he joined them in his huge satin-sheeted bed. She remembered the shudders of pleasure that had rocked her

178

body when, finally, she'd been pushed over the brink by the man's cock thrusting deep inside her, as Blanche's fingers and tongue were busy on her.

It had been her first sexual experience since Jamal, and she'd felt simultaneously treacherous and relieved. The orgasm had been a great release but it was nice simply to feel loved, to forget her pain for a moment, and to have the ceaseless longing for Jamal lifted for just a brief while.

'So?' asked Blanche now, as she began to coat her eyelashes in layer after layer of mascara. 'What's your answer?'

'I dunno.' Coco came over and sat beside her at the rackety dressing table all the girls used. She ran her fingers through her snow-white hair and picked up a hairbrush.

'You must be feeling flush right now if you can turn down five hundred quid,' observed Blanche.

'No, I ain't flush or anything. I need the money actually. I just don't think I want to.'

'Come on, love. Bit of champagne? Free coke – well, I know you don't touch it, but I do – and some loving in a nice warm bed? What's the big deal?' Blanche turned her head to look Coco in the eye. 'You and me are a good partnership too. Don't you think?'

It was another reason why Coco wasn't sure if she should. Lots of the girls in the dancing world were gay or bisexual and Coco didn't know if Blanche was or not, but she had the uneasy feeling that the other woman was fond of her and getting fonder. It wouldn't be right to lead her on. *I don't mind girls, but I'm not gay. I don't want a girlfriend.* Blanche had tried to kiss her one night when the shift was over, stroking Coco's lips with the tip of her tongue and running a hand lightly over her breast, and Coco had pulled away with a smile and a quick joke to diffuse any awkwardness.

'Not tonight,' she said at last. 'I got stuff to do in the flat. Maybe another time.'

'You're crazy, turning down a gig like this,' Blanche said, shaking her head. She peered into the mirror again, twisting out a lipstick. 'I guess I could ask Kandy if she'd be interested but it won't be the same. That bloke liked you lots, I could tell.'

Just then Roberto came in and struck a pose, hands on hips and smiling. 'Girls!' he declared dramatically. 'I've got a very exciting opportunity for you ladies. One that doesn't involve you two doing any girl-on-girl either!' He stood between them and put an arm around each girl's shoulders. 'I tell you – you are going to *love* me for this. Seriously – you will owe me big time. So . . . Wanna hear what it is?'

22

The receptionist looked up at the girl standing at the desk. 'Yes? Can I help you?' Her accent held a strong Bristol twang.

'I'm Daphne Fraser,' said the girl. She had black hair cut in a short bob, her brown eyes blinked nervously behind a pair of dark-framed glasses, and she was dressed smartly in a dark pencil skirt and a ruffled top. 'I'm here to see Mr Armstrong.'

The receptionist sighed and picked up the phone to call him. Daphne Fraser looked about: the lobby of the small hotel was neat enough but its touches of grandeur – the grandfather clock, brass chandeliers and an oil painting – had an air of shabbiness.

Replacing the handset, the receptionist said, 'He's ready for you now. He's in the office. Go down the corridor, first on your left.'

'Thank you.'

Daphne followed the directions and knocked on the door labelled 'General Manager'. A voice behind it called her to come in, so she opened it, revealing a messy office scattered with paperwork and files and dominated by a large wooden desk. Behind it, a man of about thirty-five was striding about, a phone receiver clamped to his ear. He wore baggy cord trousers and a thick cotton shirt with the sleeves rolled up to his elbows, and as he moved he was gradually wrapping himself in the telephone cord. He looked over at her and mouthed, 'Yes?'

'I'm Daphne Fraser, Mr Armstrong. You're expecting me?'

'Oh, am I?' Armstrong looked at her, his light brown eyes startled. 'Oh, yes, just wait a moment, please. No, not you,' he said into the phone. 'I wasn't talking to you. Sit down, please. No, not you!' he said to the person on the end of the phone. He looked at Daphne. 'You. Sit down.' In the phone he said, 'All right, you'll get your payment by the end of the week. I'll see to it personally. Yes. Well, we all make mistakes. We're only human, aren't we?' He laughed expansively and then stopped suddenly, his expression serious. 'No, of course it's unacceptable. Yes. By tomorrow. Absolutely. Apologies again. Goodbye.' Armstrong put the phone down and sighed heavily. Then he looked over at Daphne as though seeing her for the first time. He frowned. He had brown hair the same colour as his eyes, in soft short curls all round a large bald crown, and looked simultaneously boyish and middle-aged.

'Sorry,' he said, 'but who are you again?'

'D . . . Daphne Fraser.' She had ventured into the office and was loitering by a chair, not sure if she should sit or not.

Armstrong went to sit down and realised that he was tangled up in the telephone cord. 'Oh . . . crikey Moses! What's going on here?' He started to turn back

182

and forth, trying to unreel himself from the cord. Daphne had to stifle a giggle as he finally freed himself and sat down. She sat down herself, perching carefully on the edge of the seat.

'Right!' He rubbed his hands. 'Let's get on with the interview. Right.' He scrabbled under a pile of paper, found a sheet and scrutinised it. 'Here's your CV.' Daphne's fingers tightened around the straps of her handbag but he seemed perfectly happy with what he read there. 'Yes . . . yes . . . Well, it all looks jolly good.' He looked up at her, his face friendly. 'To be honest, you're rather over-qualified for this job, with your advanced diploma. You do realise this is starting right at the bottom, don't you? You'll be chambermaiding. It's not well paid.' He looked solemn. 'To be honest, that's why most of our employees are immigrants, though we do get the odd student. The hours are long and the money's terrible. Why do you want to work here, out of interest?'

'I'm passionate about the hospitality business, that's why I did my diploma in it. I'm happy to start at the bottom to get my foot in the door.'

Armstrong looked down again at her CV, frowning. 'Yes, but you've studied all aspects of international hotel management from finance and cashiering to staff management. It's not what I usually require from the chambermaids!' He snuffled with laughter for a moment. 'You could probably go in at a higher level in a much grander hotel. Why do you want to come to the Excalibur?'

Daphne smiled. 'To be honest, it's because I want to work near my mother. She's not well. It's all about location really.'

'All right. Well, I'm not going to look a gift horse in the mouth. I expect you'll be off in five minutes when you find something better, but in the meantime, it'll be an advantage to have someone whose first language is English.' Then he added hastily, 'Not that I'm being racist, you understand. Most of the girls are incredibly hard workers. I just find the language barrier a bit tiresome sometimes. The other two I've seen today were particularly bad. Now . . . salary . . . It's minimum wage.' He looked apologetic. 'Not much I can do about it, it's head office, you see. You know we're owned by a much bigger group . . .'

'Are you?' She gazed at him innocently.

'Yes.' He assumed an exaggerated expression of pain, then smiled. 'Capitalist bastards further up the chain. Keep us on a tight leash. But you do get some benefits – health care, pension contributions, holiday and sick pay . . .' He leaned forward and examined her a bit more closely, squinting a little. 'Sorry,' he said as he lifted his head the better to stare down his nose through scrunched eyes. 'I left my glasses at home today. Well, here are the terms and conditions –' he passed another sheet of paper across the desk towards her '– and the job's yours if you want it.'

Daphne blinked in surprise. 'Oh! So quickly? Well, that's great.'

'I always need good help, to be honest. In fact, if you could possibly start today, that would be great.'

Daphne thought for an instant and then smiled. 'Why not?'

Armstrong looked delighted. 'Super. I'll find you a uniform and you can get stuck right in. I'll need you to fill out this form with your bank details and National Insurance number, and then we're off.'

Daphne Fraser put down her handbag. 'Let's get started.'

An hour later, dressed in a black dress and apron, Daphne was scrubbing out a first-floor bathroom. The guests had been late checking out and they'd left a hell of a mess. In the bathroom, every towel was sopping wet, a couple covered in unidentifiable brown substances; the floor was flooded with water, and the lavatory was such a foul mess that she had to hold back a retch more than once as she tackled it.

She caught a glimpse of the large mirror over the counter top and looked startled to see herself. Then she stopped to gaze at her reflection and laughed softly. She removed her glasses and blinked her eyes as though they were feeling dry and uncomfortable. Then she ran her fingers through her hair.

'Well, well, Daisy,' she said to her reflection. 'I don't think even your father would recognise you now.' She glanced down at the cleaning cloth she was clutching in one hand. Her cheeks were pink from the exertion of scrubbing out the lavatory. 'And he wouldn't believe it even if he did.'

She wondered if he'd ever thought about her since that day over two years before when she had left the house. It was still vivid in her imagination and she could relive it almost moment by moment if she chose to – though she rarely did. Today, though, she felt impelled to recall what had happened, now that she had taken the first, vital step towards the place she was determined to reach.

After that final confrontation, she had walked out of Daddy's study in a state of stunned bewilderment. Did he really mean that she was banished? Where on earth would she go? What would she do? The first thoughts that flew into her mind were ridiculous: *Will I still be able to go travelling with Lucy? What's going to happen with my university place? Will I still be going to the States? What about my shoe business?*

Then it began to sink in. Everything had changed. Anything certain in her world had just been whipped away from her. She didn't even know who she was.

Daisy had begun to walk up the stairs towards her room in a state of frozen shock, not really aware of where she was going or what she intended to do when she got there. Then she'd heard the study door shutting, footsteps crossing the hall and a voice.

'Daisy?'

She'd turned, still moving like someone in a trance, and seen Margaret at the bottom of the stairs. Her father's assistant was staring up at her with blank, emotionless eyes. If she felt anything for the girl whose life had just imploded, she did not show it in her face. She simply said, 'You'd better come and join me in my office. We need to discuss a few things.'

Margaret's basement office was like her: muted, impersonal and absolutely tidy. There was nothing out of place, and every diary, notebook and folder was in black or grey leather. A sleek black computer took pride of place on the glass desk. A black Cartier pen lay perfectly in the centre of an ebony lacquered rectangular dish.

Margaret went to sit in the black leather chair behind her desk, gesturing to Daisy to have a seat.

She sank down, gazing at Margaret with imploring eyes. As the older woman took out a large notebook, opened it and picked up her pen, Daisy said, 'Margaret . . . he didn't really mean what he said, did he? He's going to calm down, get over this . . . I mean – it's not my fault!'

Margaret lifted one perfectly arched brow. 'I'm very much afraid he did mean it. Every word. You see, the test cannot be mistaken. You are not a Dangerfield. No one knows whose child you are, but it's absolutely certain that you are not Mr Dangerfield's.'

The words hit her like punches. 'But . . . he's the only father I've ever known! He's loved me all my life. Can he really just switch that off? Surely there's more to being a father than just DNA.' Daisy's voice shook. She felt another torrent of tears threatening, brought on by the overwhelming sense of hurt and rejection sweeping over her. It was taking all her strength to keep it at bay.

'Not as far as Mr Dangerfield is concerned. He feels that your mother perpetrated a fraud on him. Obviously you appear to be unaware of this con trick, but I'm afraid that your f— Mr Dangerfield feels that you are implicated. However, whether or not you are a victim of this fraud, the fact remains that you are not related to Mr Dangerfield and he no longer has any reason or desire to support you. You have profited for many years from your association with this family. I'm afraid that has now come to an end.'

Daisy gasped. How could she describe the situation in this cold, horrible language? Didn't she have any human emotion? Perhaps Daisy had imagined the look

187

of pity she had thought she'd glimpsed in Margaret's eyes earlier in the study. How could anyone describe a child growing up with a man she loved as her father as 'profiting by association'? It was ridiculous! Cruel. Inhuman.

Rage began to swirl inside Daisy, along with the shock and the grief. She let it grow – it helped to keep the sadness under control. *Fuck you*, she thought, the fury building. *Fuck you all.* 'All right,' she said in as cool a voice as she could muster. 'You'd better explain the situation then.'

Margaret had explained the situation very clearly indeed. Daisy had no right to any part of the Dangerfield fortune. That included living in the family properties, eating their food, or being funded by Dangerfield money. A lawyer, Margaret said, might advise Daisy differently, but that lawyer would be wrong, and would simply be hoping to make money from a long, complex court case that she would certainly lose. No one wanted that. No one wanted the scandal.

Margaret set out Daisy's position: she was to leave Dangerfield property, and everything she owned would revert to the family. She could take some of her personal possessions – some clothes, books and things she might need – but anything of value must be returned. 'Your car, of course, and any large items of significant worth must remain here.'

Daisy's credit cards were to be stopped immediately.

Money! Daisy was suddenly terrified. *How on earth will I cope?* She'd never had to think about money. She didn't even have a bank account. She'd only ever needed her Coutts platinum credit card – it bought her anything she wanted, and delivered notes from machines in the wall whenever she required cash.

Margaret was staring at her as though able to read her mind. 'That of course leads me to money,' she said smoothly. 'There are certain conditions that we require you to fulfil. There will be a document for you to sign, and the estate will make you a one-off payment to give you a start in your new life. A goodwill gesture.' She looked sternly at Daisy over her glasses. 'There is absolutely no legal requirement for us to make this payment. You will acknowledge as much when you sign the contract.'

'What if I don't sign it?' demanded Daisy defiantly.

'Oh, I think you will.' Margaret's lips curved into a tight, joyless smile. 'It would be remarkably foolish to do anything else.' She leaned towards Daisy, fixing her with a stern look. 'I say this entirely for your own good. You have nothing to gain from fighting Mr Dangerfield, and a very great deal to lose. I strongly advise that you accept the payment and its terms.' She took some sheets of paper from inside a black folder and pushed them across the desk towards Daisy. 'Here is the contract for you to read. You will see that the sum is generous, considering. It will be enough for you to make a fresh start.'

Daisy looked down at the typed pages. So this little plan had been in motion for a while, if the contract that would cut her off forever from her life had already been prepared. She gave a bitter laugh. 'And what will Daddy say has happened to me?'

'You are going away to study and on an extended holiday.' Margaret shrugged. 'People will soon learn not to ask questions but at some point it will be understood that there has been a break between you and Mr Dangerfield. An irreparable break.'

'I suppose that with Daddy's track record, that will be pretty believable,' Daisy said. She gathered up the contract and stood up. 'I'll take this away to read.'

'You have until tomorrow morning to leave. Mr Dangerfield was unhappy about your staying under his roof for another night, but I persuaded him it was only fair.'

'Tell him he doesn't have to worry,' Daisy shot back. 'I'm not about to stay where I'm not wanted. I'll call you when I've read this.' She turned to leave and then looked back over her shoulder. 'I take it that I won't really be studying. My place at Brown University—'

'Is cancelled,' Margaret finished for her. 'The authorities have been informed that funding for your place has been withdrawn. You're welcome to reapply under your own auspices.' She smiled her small, mean-looking smile again.

'Yeah, right,' said Daisy. Then she marched to the door and let herself out without a backward look.

In the safety of her room, she was attacked by a fit of trembling. Her legs gave way and she collapsed into a chair, hunched over and shook violently. It was thirty minutes before she could gain control of herself, but she managed it by an effort of will. *You don't have much time*, she told herself. *You've got to make a plan.*

She had never felt so alone.

Spreading the contract out on the table, she began to read, forcing herself to concentrate. The terms were fairly straightforward. She was to cut off all communication with the Dangerfield family forthwith. She would be permitted her birth certificate and passport, and a bank account had been opened in her name, on the understanding that she would change her surname within one year. There was no need to advise the Dangerfield lawyers of what her new identity was. By signing and accepting the terms, she would agree never to disclose publicly what had gone on, or to reveal any details of the Dangerfield fortune or lifestyle. If she did so, the sum of money she was to receive would instantly be repayable. She could leave with agreed chattels and personal possessions but no single item over a value of one thousand pounds.

In return, £50,000 would be deposited in the bank account for her use.

Fifty thousand! She bit her lip. Her dress allowance was £15,000 a month. How long would she be able to live on £50,000? How much did things cost in the real world?

There was a knock on the door. At her call, the door opened and a footman came in carrying two empty suitcases. They were plain navy blue leather.

Not the usual Louis Vuitton trunks then, she noted.

'Thank you,' she said, as he deposited the cases and left. *Do the staff know? I bet they do. They probably knew before I did.*

Now she had to decide what to take, what clothes she would need, what shoes, what books, what mementoes of the life she was saying farewell to for ever . . .

As she thought this, she was overcome with horror

191

and sadness at her situation, put her hands to her face and wept, sobbing as if her heart were broken.

Eight hours later, as the clock ticked towards ten, Daisy went to Margaret's office. The assistant was waiting for her, looking exactly as she had that morning.

'I'm ready to sign,' Daisy said defiantly. 'But I have a couple of conditions of my own.'

Margaret looked enquiring. 'Yes?'

'I want to keep my mobile phone, with the contract paid until the end of the year.'

Margaret nodded. 'Very well.'

'And I want this.' She produced a large silver photograph frame containing the beautiful black-and-white shot of her mother, the one that had been used on the funeral order of service.

'I don't think Mr Dangerfield requires that any more,' Margaret replied coolly.

'And . . .' Daisy lifted her chin. '. . . I want a hundred grand, not fifty.'

There was a pause and then Margaret said smoothly, 'Very well. I shall make the arrangements. Now, if you've packed, I'm afraid I shall need to inspect your luggage before you go. To be sure you are not taking goods that don't belong to you.'

'Of course.' Daisy stared the other woman straight in the eye. Margaret had agreed too fast to the sum of money she had suggested. *She would have agreed to more. I should have negotiated harder.* But the cold hard object tucked into the cup of her bra pressed against her breast and reminded her that she was still getting away with something.

'Then if we are agreed, I'll call a witness and we

192

can get the signing over with immediately.' Margaret had looked pleased, as though she'd been anticipating a great deal more trouble than this, and was glad to have been proved wrong.

Twenty minutes later, Daisy was signing away all rights to her Dangerfield heritage. Thirty minutes after that, she had left her father's house forever.

23

'Ladies, ladies!' Roberto clapped his hands, the sound echoing about the dance studio. The girls stopped moving and turned to look at him. He shook his head in exasperation.

'Not like that!' he said. 'Look, watch me again, I'll show you.'

He went through a quick series of moves, ending with a high kick and arms spread wide. 'Then you have to smile,' he said. 'Now, come on, one more time. You need to look like those Hollywood girls – the Busby Berkeley girls. Beautiful, glamorous, perfect.'

Coco stopped, panting with the exertion but feeling exhilarated. She could hear one of the other girls moaning under her breath about having to do the routine again, but she didn't mind. If she had her way, they'd be dancing all the time. It was such a wonderful feeling, the only time she felt as though the drabness and horribleness of her life dropped away. She only hoped that Roberto wasn't too concerned that she wasn't a properly trained dancer like the others. She'd stopped her lessons years ago, and had only done her dancing at the club since then. It made her feel second best. Blanche had already dropped out, unable to put up with Roberto's constant criticism and the discipline of learning a complex routine. 'Besides,' she'd told Coco with a shrug, 'I look like a giant next to you little girls. I don't fit in the line at all.'

She was right and Coco suspected that was why Roberto was glad to see Blanche go. He had given the girls the chance of some excitement and a bit of money away from the club because he liked them – there were plenty of other dancers who needed the work, after all. He only worked at the club himself to make some extra cash on top of his job at the studio as a dance teacher and choreographer.

The line might look neater without Blanche, but it had been a shame to lose a friend because the other girls were less than friendly. They thought they were so wonderful because they were proper dancers, or training to be proper dancers, and word had spread that Coco worked in a lap-dancing club. That was why they avoided her, gave her sneery looks and didn't speak to her. But they also knew that she was a good friend of Roberto's, so they were careful to keep their scorn hidden.

I don't care, Coco thought, as she got back into position to start the routine from the top. The others might be properly trained but she was catching up with them quickly. She was muscular and strong from her pole-dancing routine, and she had the legacy of her ballet and modern-dance lessons. When the music began, she felt that wonderful feeling of freedom and pleasure as she danced the rehearsed steps in perfect time with the others. She loved the way they all moved together, and when the routine went smoothly, it was a joy. Her tap dancing was rusty and she practised at home in the tiny kitchen, tapping away and trying to perfect the heel-toe shuffle. It was hugely important that she got it right – they now only had three weeks until the performance, and it was a one-night event. Roberto had done her a favour, asking her to be in the line-up, knowing she needed the generous pay the gig offered, and she didn't want to let him down.

'You're crazy to work this hard,' Blanche would say, when Coco arrived at work already exhausted from an afternoon's rehearsal. 'You could make the same money in one night with me! And no need to practise either.'

'Yeah, I know, I must be crazy,' Coco would grin back, but besides Roberto, there was another reason why she was working so hard.

She knew she wanted to get out of the clubs and away from this life, and maybe dancing was the way to do it. She didn't mind hard work – in fact, she preferred it to the sleaziness of the club and the way she was just a piece of meat to the punters. Maybe, after this, she could get into a proper dance troupe. She'd heard some of the other girls talking during their breaks. None of them hung out with her, of course, but while they sipped on their skinny lattes and smoked endless cigarettes, they would talk loudly about auditions and jobs they were going for. There seemed to be a lot of work in the dance world: some of the girls were auditioning to be in pop videos or in films, which paid well. One had even boasted that she might be considered as a professional dance partner on one of the celebrity ballroom dancing television shows.

It had made Coco think, and work even harder at the routines they were learning. She practised and practised until she was dancing them in her sleep.

Roberto turned off the CD player. 'OK, girls,' he said, his voice echoing around the studio. 'That's enough for today. You can go home. Come early tomorrow, we've got a costume fitting. You've each got three outfits for the show. OK? *Ciao,* ladies, *ciao!*'

The girls dispersed to where they'd left their things, chattering and stretching as they got dressed, put on their coats and headed out.

'Coco?'

'Yes?' She looked round from pulling her jeans up over her leotard to see Roberto behind her.

'Wanna go get a coffee or something?'

'Sure.'

They wandered out of the dance studio together, and headed down the back streets of Covent Garden to a café that Roberto knew. It had a little patio garden where they could smoke.

'You know, this gig could be a big deal,' he confided as they went along.

'You think so?' Coco was guarded. She hadn't revealed her ambitions to him. After all, he worked at the club, even if it was just to supplement his income from the studio, and he might tell Sam that Coco had ideas above her station. Sam wouldn't be too pleased to see a girl like her leaving. She was good, reliable and popular with the punters. And she didn't do drugs.

Roberto nodded. 'Yeah, you should definitely make

the most of it. You might not get another opportunity like this.'

'What do you mean? It's just a party, innit?'

'Well . . . yeah.' They reached the café, went in and ordered mugs of tea, then took them out the back so they could smoke in peace.

'So?' Coco prodded, interested. She shook out her white-blonde hair as she expelled a stream of smoke. 'You told me this was some bloke's party and he wants a dance routine at it. Some glamour girls doing a bit of old-time Hollywood dancing. And there's a singer, in't there?'

'Yeah, Haley. She's a Rita Hayworth-style glamour puss with one of those sexy deep voices.'

'Rita who?' Coco asked, frowning. She hated stumbling on yet another area of her ignorance.

'A famous redheaded Hollywood star from the forties and fifties.' Roberto frowned and waved his cigarette to show that it didn't matter. 'But the point is, it's not just any old party. Have you heard the name Dangerfield?'

Coco shook her head and took a sip of the tea. It was made the way she liked it: strong with lots of milk.

Roberto gave her a meaningful look. 'The Dangerfields are really rich – I mean, rolling in it. Super-rich. I don't know how they got their money, but they got plenty of it. And this party, well, it's the old man's birthday. He's sixty or something.'

'Yeah, well . . .' Coco took another drag of her cigarette. 'I guessed it had to be something like that. I mean, we're being bussed down to his place, ain't we, and put up at a hotel? I guessed it was someone with money.' She was already curious to see how rich people like that lived. It was a universe away from her own experience, and the shared flat in a nasty area of Whitechapel.

'Yeah.' Roberto leaned in confidingly. 'But the point is, there are going to be a lot of other successful people there. Rich men. In their sixties. Maybe getting a bit bored of the wife and ready to trade her in for a new model.'

'Ah. I get you.' Coco laughed. 'You think I should go on the hunt for a sugar daddy, do ya?'

'Why not, babe? You're a good-looking girl, you're really sexy, and you're young and exciting. You're dancing like a fuckin' angel, if you don't mind me saying. I mean it – really. You've got talent. Lots of those blokes would be panting to get their hands on you. I'm serious.' He put his head on one side and gave her a sympathetic look. 'You and I both know that you can't stay in the club for ever. You wanna think about your future.'

'I do. I do think about it.' Coco stared down at the shiny metal surface of their table. Her reflection, blurred and distorted, gazed back. 'I was thinking I might make a go of being a dancer . . . if . . . well, if I'm good enough?'

'Babe, of course you're good enough! What did I just say? But, honey, the world is full of wannabe dancers!' Roberto rolled his eyes and pouted theatrically. 'It's a fucking hard life and, like Jesus sainted Christ, you're finished at thirty-three! Much easier marrying some security, yeah? I fuckin' would, if any rich bloke would have me. So, I'm just saying. When you get to this party, you better think about it. You're not going to be in a roomful of millionaires any time soon after that, are you?'

Coco laughed and tapped her ash on to the ground. It floated downwards, tiny grey fragments disintegrating as they fell. 'Yeah. You're right. Thanks, Roberto. I'll think about it. Promise.'

'How are you off for cash?' he asked.

Coco shrugged. 'All right, I guess. I had a couple of good nights last week.'

'Then get yourself a proper haircut, something glamorous. See if you can get some extensions put in. You've got a great figure, but you wanna look your best.'

'Thanks a lot!' Coco put a hand to her shaggy white crop. 'I think it looks good.'

Roberto pouted again. ''Course it does, darling. But you could look twice as good with a bit of care, though, yeah?'

She laughed. 'Lucky for you we're such good friends, babe.'

'I say it 'cos I love you.'

'Yeah. I know.'

24

The alarm clock on the bedside table rang shrilly. Daisy woke up blearily and put out one hand to turn it off. Shaking off sleep, she climbed out of bed. It was just after five and she had to be at the Excalibur at six, ready to start her duties.

She picked up her towel, let herself out of her tiny bedsit and padded down the hall to the shared bathroom. It was aged but kept fairly clean, though the shower curtain hanging over the old bath was mottled and stained. The shower head stuck out from cracked tiling over the bath. Daisy climbed in and turned it on. The plumbing banged and shrieked as the water made its way through the old pipes and out in a warm gentle shower. She put her head underneath the soft stream.

It was only now that she was beginning to understand the world she'd been born to – and ejected from – and to comprehend her father's enormous power, and his arrogance. He really believed that it was possible to make her vanish from his life, erasing her like a dictator doctored photographs to remove those who had fallen from favour.

Daisy finished her shower and climbed out of the bath to dry herself. *But if he thinks that I'm going to disappear from his life for ever . . . well . . . he's going to get one hell of a surprise.*

The plan had come to her, floating into her head fully formed a week after she had left the London house. She had gone to the only place she could think of. Lucy had been amazed when Daisy had turned up on the doorstep of her family's Notting Hill townhouse at going on midnight.

'Of course you can stay here, honey!' she'd cried when Daisy had explained that she had nowhere to go. 'Mummy's away skiing anyway, and Daddy's at some conference in Switzerland. Come in, come in. But I don't understand. How can you have nowhere to go?'

The girls had gone into the cosy sitting room in the basement and curled up on the big red sofas, clutching mugs of tea, while Daisy told Lucy the whole story. It had been a relief to spill it out, and she'd been unable to stem the tears as she talked. Lucy had listened in appalled fascination, occasionally leaning over to hug her friend or hold Daisy's hand. At the end of the tale, she looked incredulous.

'But, Daisy, he must be mad! He'll change his mind surely. All he has to do is adopt you and everything will be like it was.'

Daisy shook her head sadly. 'No. You don't understand. Blood really is thicker than water for him. He's obsessed by it. I'm not his daughter, so as far as he's concerned, that's that. I'm on my own.'

Lucy had been unable to believe it, telling Daisy over and over that when he'd had time to calm down, Daddy would take her back. Daisy did not argue. She didn't even tell Lucy the truth, which was that she wasn't even sure she wanted him to take her back, not now. How could they ever go back to what they'd had before? She'd adored him, despite everything. Despite the anger, the rages, the demands that her world revolve entirely around him . . . despite the way he'd treated her mother and despite the way he'd alienated Will and Sarah . . . despite the high standards he'd insisted she meet, and the lack of choice she'd been given in her life . . . despite all that, she'd loved him unconditionally. And he'd thrown that back in her face.

Would she go back to him now and let him treat her like that again? She knew the answer to that. *Never*. Her heart had hardened and something inside her had died.

For the next two days she stayed at Lucy's, trying to sort her head out. She lay for hours in one of the guest bedrooms, thinking over everything that had happened, gathering her strength and making her plans. Sometimes she just lay there and sobbed, frightened and desperate to call her father and beg him to take her back, but she managed to stop herself. At other times, she paced about, ranting and raging, telling him all the things she was desperate to say, just for the relief of getting them off her chest. She was tormented by wondering who her father really was and why her mother had kept it a secret.

Then she thought about survival. She and Lucy discussed what she should do, but they both came up blank. Neither girl had a clue how much things cost.

'Can I buy a house with a hundred grand?' Daisy wondered.

'Maybe a small one,' Lucy said doubtfully, but a few minutes on a property website made them realise that there was very little a hundred grand was going to buy in London, and certainly not in Notting Hill or Kensington.

'I've been an idiot,' Daisy said solemnly. 'Daddy could have easily paid me off with a million. I've taken nothing.'

'How could he be so *mean*?' Lucy breathed, round-eyed. The full implication of what had happened to her friend was only just beginning to sink in. Without the soft cushion of money, life was going to be rocky in ways they'd never once considered. Losing a dress allowance and access to the family estates was the least of it. Managing to house and feed herself would be Daisy's main priority.

'I'll get a job,' Daisy said firmly. 'I've got experience after all.'

'Have you?' Lucy blinked with admiration.

'Yes – I helped to run the shoe boutiques and I've listened to Daddy talking about business. I've looked at profit and loss sheets. I'm sure I can do something with all that.'

'Won't you need qualifications?' Lucy asked in a small voice. 'I mean, I know we've got our A-levels but . . . your father was going to send you to uni, and then to business school. I think you need that kind of education to do that sort of job.'

Lucy was right, Daisy knew that. She paced about even more, thinking hard about how best to use her resources. The important thing was not to spend them, but to invest them so that the money would pay dividends and help her achieve her ends.

That evening she was watching television when Lucy came into the den looking worried.

'What is it, Lu?' Daisy said, reaching for the remote and clicking off the programme.

'I don't understand it.' Lucy looked pale and rather ill. 'It's . . . Dad's just been on the phone. He asked if you were staying here. I don't know why he would – I never mentioned to him that you were here. When I said yes, he said I had to ask you to leave immediately. And he's flying home to make sure.'

'Oh.' Daisy felt her stomach flip over with a nasty sickly sensation. *I should have been expecting something like this.* She put out a hand to her friend. 'It's OK. Really. I expect Daddy's been making sure I can't hang around causing trouble. He will be working his way through my address book, ensuring that I can't expect help from my old crowd.'

Lucy looked dismayed. 'But I don't understand why my father has to do what he wants!'

'It's all about power and influence. My father is incredibly influential. He can find a way to make anyone do anything. He won't be above making threats either.'

'I'm so sorry.' Tears filled Lucy's brown eyes and her lip trembled. 'I can't believe this. You're supposed to be able to rely on me.'

'Don't be silly. It's time I struck out on my own anyway. That's the way it's going to be from now on, right?' Daisy smiled at her friend.

'Are you going to stay with Antonia?' Lucy asked in a small, miserable voice.

Daisy shook her head. 'There's no point. I don't want to drag other people into this. Daddy wants me off his patch, so I'm going to make his life easy. For now.'

'If you need any help, or any money . . . you know you can contact me, right?' Lucy's eyes were even damper as she gazed earnestly at her friend.

'Of course – and I really appreciate it. I will have some favours to ask you, I'm sure. You're going to be the only one I'll keep in touch with for now.' Daisy stood up, her face grim. 'I expected something like this.'

'I'll do whatever I can, you know that. But . . . Daisy, what are you going to do? Where are you going to go?'

'I have my plans,' she said. 'That's all I'm going to say at the moment. But don't worry about me. I'll be fine. I promise.'

If Daddy wants me to disappear, then I will. And I've got to assume that he's going to be on my trail for a little while longer.

But the truth was that she didn't really have a clue what to do.

Leaving Lucy's house was her first real experience of life beyond her own pampered upbringing. The only place she could think to go was the Dangerfield Florey but that would be madness: she would be recognised at once. So instead she got into a taxi with her cases and asked the driver to take her to Claridge's. As she was booking in and handing over the bank card that Margaret had given her before she'd left, she thought to ask what the cost of a room was. On being told that it was nearly £700 a night, she felt like she might pass out. *I can't afford that kind of money,* she thought, aghast. It would not take long before she'd burned through her cash entirely.

'I . . . I . . . I've changed my mind,' she stuttered, and went back outside with her bags, trying to ignore the receptionist's pitying look.

Where can I go? she wondered, panicked. Then she tried to get a grip. *Come on – there have to be cheaper hotels than this.* But she had no idea where they were or how she might find one. She hailed a taxi and asked the driver to take her somewhere reasonable. He'd laughed knowingly, raising his eyebrows at the famous Claridge's frontage, and then taken her to a small but clean and welcoming hotel in South London, not far from the Oval cricket ground. 'You'll be all right here,' he said, dropping her off. 'Tell the lady Dave sent you. She'll look after you.'

He was right, the landlady had been welcoming, but even at £85 a night, Daisy knew that she couldn't stay there indefinitely. Besides, she had to decide what to do next. The problem was, she felt in such a daze. The emotional fallout of what had happened was crippling her: she was permanently exhausted and on the brink of tears. She could think of only one thing to do.

The next day, she took a train from London out to the village near Thornside, and then walked from the station to the churchyard. There was her mother's grave, still fresh from the funeral service only weeks before. It felt strange and almost dangerous to be so close to her old home, but it had been a compulsion to come. Daisy kneeled down by the damp earth and stared at the newly carved headstone.

'Why didn't you tell me that he wasn't my father?'

she whispered. Sorrow as heavy as a stone felt as though it was weighting her down. 'Why weren't we closer, Mummy? Was it because he kept us apart?' She tried to think back over the past but it was all so difficult. 'I wish you could help me now. I wish you could tell me who I am.'

She reached out and traced a finger around the letters of her mother's name. Julia Dangerfield. Poor Mummy was linked eternally to that name. She'd never be anything other than Daddy's wife now.

That was when the idea had come to Daisy. She would show him how wrong he was to treat her the way he had, discarding her like an unwanted toy. It would take time, planning and determination. But as she'd sat by her mother's grave, her fists clenched from the force of her decision, she'd resolved there and then to do whatever it took. That had been the first step on the road to her ultimate revenge.

Once she'd come up with her plan, she set the whole thing in motion. She'd stayed a few weeks in the hotel in the Oval, negotiating a special rate with the owner, so that she could do all the research she needed. In the day she would travel up to the British Library where she sat and worked, sometimes online and sometimes from books and journals. She had bought herself a laptop, having left her old one behind. She stopped using her old Daisy Dangerfield email account, though she logged in to monitor it, and set up a new one. That was when she'd decided on her new name: Daphne Fraser. She'd always liked the name Daphne, thinking it rather stylish in an old-fashioned way, and had picked Fraser at random from a bookshelf. It had appealed to her for some reason. Daphne Fraser she would be from now on.

She had searched out the best courses in the country for Hotel Management diplomas, and had settled on St Prudence's College just outside Brighton. There was no problem in being accepted: once she had paid her deposit, she was registered on the two-year course starting in September. As soon as that was confirmed, she made the move to Brighton. Renting a place was not easy. She still had no bank statements and no permanent address for the bank to send them to, but she managed to find a small furnished apartment where putting down three months' rent in advance and speaking in her most refined voice was enough to get her in. The landlord didn't ask too many questions after he established that she was going to St Prudence's. The fact that she had paid for her course seemed to vouch for her intentions to stay.

She'd had to apply to the college as Daisy Dangerfield – her examination certificates were in that name for one thing, so she couldn't get a place without them – but she told them that she preferred to be called Daphne, and after the first six months, she explained she was changing her surname to Fraser because her parents had divorced and she was taking her mother's name. That way, her graduation certificate would be issued to Daphne Fraser and she'd be able to apply for jobs under her new identity. She'd also changed the name on her bank account and applied for a passport in her new name. It took many hours of admin, and she feared that she would still be traceable if her father ever decided to track her down but there was nothing else she could do. It wasn't possible to change her birth certificate and she wasn't about to start doing anything illegal, like buying an identity or forging documents.

Then she'd had to become Daphne Fraser. She'd bought a box of black hair dye. A few hours later, the bath was grubby with grey streaks and her fair hair was gone. She'd had it cut into a blunt bob. A visit to the optician, and she had brown-tinted contact lenses and some black frames filled with clear glass. She acquired a new wardrobe from high street stores, places she had never visited before, wondering where her beautiful Birkin was now as she bought a cheap fake-leather lookalike.

Burned probably. Or shut in an attic somewhere. Oh well, it doesn't matter now anyway. Daphne Fraser is not the sort of girl to have a £10,000 handbag, let's face it.

But she rather enjoyed finding her new look, inventing Daphne's character with cheap but cheerful outfits with a touch of sass. She bought bright floral dresses, colourful cropped cardigans and wide belts, giving herself a fifties prom-style look.

It was, she discovered, easier to change her name and looks than it was to change her attitudes. Daisy Dangerfield might not live in cosseted luxury any more, but Daphne Fraser knew nothing of the world outside. She had fallen to earth with a bump, and even by the standards of students, she was spectacularly un-house-trained. Cleaning was not something that came naturally to her; in fact, she'd had absolutely no idea how to do a thing for herself. She'd barely picked her own clothes up in the whole of her life. From her earliest childhood Nanny had done everything for her, from combing her hair to sorting out her underwear. She hadn't even cleaned her own teeth until she was eight years old and told Nanny that she wanted to do it herself. The nursery had been cleaned by an invisible troop of maids who scurried in and did everything while Daisy wasn't there. Meals arrived from the kitchen in their finished state. It had barely even occurred to her that toast was bread that had been grilled, because she'd never considered the process of how to make toast.

With no idea how to cook, she left burned pans and revolting disasters in her wake whenever she attempted it, and she'd really had no clue that she would have to clean the flat herself. After a few weeks, the place was messy and dirty, and Daisy felt increasingly miserable surrounded by chaos. At college she was learning the importance of high standards of hygiene and the orderliness that had to reign in any successful institution while at home she was wading through unwashed clothes and abandoned dishes. Realising she would have to retrain herself, she got a book on housework, stocked up on products and began to learn how to look after herself properly, though there were certain things she couldn't bear to get to grips with: it made inroads into her precious savings, but she used a private laundry service that collected her washing once a week and returned it, clean and pressed, the following day. She told herself it was worth it.

Learning to clean was not her only problem: she also had no sense of what things were worth. Lights were left burning and heaters on without Daisy having any idea that running them cost money, until the bills came in and she gasped with horror. She tried to pay

211

for loaves of bread or pints of milk with a credit card, and looked blankly at change as though it was foreign money. She nervously watched her bank account, appalled by how quickly the money drained out of it even though she was trying to be frugal. Her idea of frugal was not everyone's, however – she'd decided that learning to cook on top of everything else was a bit much, especially when there were so many delicious ready-made things that could be delivered by boutique catering companies, so she'd mastered only a few basics.

Daisy had rented her own place so that she could have privacy, and she steered clear of the other students whenever possible. Being alone was the price she was going to have to pay for now. She was too frightened to make friends in case she inadvertently gave away the truth about her previous life. She soon had a reputation for being horribly stuck up, as she'd known she might, and everyone ignored her as thoroughly as she had hoped they would.

Being lonely hurt, she discovered, and there was no one to turn to. The day she made her great plan, she had also come to a momentous decision: she would break with all her friends except Lucy. It was heartbreaking but she told herself that there was no other way. A horrible little voice whispered to her that now she was no longer Daisy Dangerfield, with access to millions and enjoying a glittering lifestyle, perhaps many of them would no longer want to be her friend anyway. She sent round a chatty email saying she was going travelling alone in a last-minute change of plan and would be off the radar for some time. That, she hoped, would be enough to keep them happy, and after a while they'd become absorbed in their own lives and forget about her. She closed her Twitter account and shut down her Facebook page. She allowed herself to visit her old email once a week, watching as the messages there diminished too. Without her input, her friends began to drift away.

The final message was one to Freddie, who'd been her on-off boyfriend since those happy, carefree days before her mother had died. She sent him a breezy email explaining her plans to go travelling – a spur-of-the-moment thing with no fixed return date – and that they'd be better off as friends for now. He sent back a sweet message saying to keep in touch and to look him up if they were ever in the same country and signed off with lots of kisses.

She was surprised by how much it hurt. She knew he wasn't the one, but even so she would miss him and all the fun they'd had. He belonged to a different life, though, and she was certain that he couldn't come with her into this new one. His world was of travelling round the globe, going to parties and having fun. He would never dream of dating a girl like Daphne Fraser.

I never realised how much my money made my choices for me – or how many doors would close when it disappeared.

When all was ready, she made her plans for the next move. She needed to find a particular hotel in a particular place, where she would slip unnoticed into the workforce and start her campaign.

25

The costumes were stunning. Coco didn't think she'd ever worn anything so beautiful in her life, ever. She turned in front of the mirror at the studio, admiring her sequined gown as it shimmered and glittered under the lights. Each girl had a different-coloured dress but in identical styles: traditional Hollywood glamour. The dresses were strapless and figure-hugging, but slit up to the thigh so that the girls could dance.

Mine is the best, Coco thought with satisfaction. There was gold, silver, blue, green, pink and purple, but none had quite the same impact as her fire-engine red dress, especially when teamed with her white hair. She had taken Roberto's advice and gone to a hair-dresser who'd freshened her dry peroxide white into a sparkling silver, cut out some of the shaggiest bits and attached shoulder-length extensions. Now she could see how she would look with her hair styled and her stage make-up on, her legs endless in stilettos. *Maybe Roberto's right – I should be on the lookout for a rich bloke.*

Each girl had three different outfits: a sexy little military number for their dance to a medley of hits from the forties – Coco's favourite was 'Boogie Woogie Bugle Boy From Company B' with its irresistible bounce. Their next routine was tap dancing to songs from golden-age Hollywood musicals, their costumes a take on the classic tuxedo, with the girls wearing fishnet tights, black satin hot-pants, a close-fitting tail-coat over a white silk corset, and a top hat at a jaunty angle. They also carried canes for some of the dance. It was the finale that was going to blow the audience's socks off, though, as each girl appeared in her sex-bomb sequined dress for the delicious, sexy last number that began with Haley, the singer, cooing out 'Fever', segued into a smoky 'Do Right', and ended with a big bump-and-grind routine with Haley belting out 'Diamonds are a Girl's Best Friend'.

Coco couldn't take her eyes off the reflection of the dress in the big mirror opposite, and the way it made her look. *This is real glamour,* she thought. Forget thongs and cheap silver material, forget the kind of look they wanted in the club. *This* was what she wanted. A touch of class. Was this stunner in the mirror really little Chanelle Hughes from the Peckham estate? The girl whose uniform was always shabby, who couldn't afford her dancing lessons? She could hear Jamal's voice buzzing in her ear, telling her she looked fantastic, that she was beautiful and he loved her.

A stab of pain made her almost moan aloud. She tried never to think of Jamal. Over the last two years she'd done her best to shut all the memories of him out of her life. It hadn't been that difficult: her body had obliged her by remaining in that numb, emotionless state that had descended on her the night he'd been killed.

'Girls, girls!' Roberto came in, clapping his hands and followed by a pretty but stony-faced girl with elfin looks and cropped black hair. 'This is Haley, our singer. She's come for a run-through.'

Coco looked at her, interested. So far they'd only danced to a tape of Haley singing. Here was the real thing. Haley nodded curtly at the assembled dancers, glancing coolly at their sequins. She turned to Roberto. 'Where's my outfit?'

'Over there, babes. You've got the best – the black – of course.'

She looked a little mollified and went to change. The dancers got themselves into position as Haley came back, wiggling along in her dress and platform heels. Roberto set the music playing, counted them in and off they went, Haley singing over the top and sounding a little reedy without a microphone. Coco went into the routine, loving the way the tight dress subtly changed her movements: her bottom wiggled just a little bit more, her breasts jiggled enticingly and she couldn't help smiling when she caught a glimpse of her red sparkling dress in the mirror. The song moved into 'Do Right', and without thinking, Coco began to sing along. She'd learned all the words during rehearsals and had often sung them when she was practising in the dressing room at work. Blanche said she sounded good, too, but Coco had protested she was definitely no singer.

She didn't even realise that Haley had stopped singing and was staring daggers at her; in fact, she hadn't realised that she was now singing loudly against

216

the music, her voice rising pure and clear over the recorded track, until her concentration was broken by a wild shriek.

'What the *fuck* do you think you're doing?'

Coco came to an abrupt halt, gazing round her, confused. Everyone stopped and Roberto switched the music off. Haley stood by the mirror, her eyes blazing. She pointed at Coco, then turned to Roberto, screaming, 'She's singing, Roberto! That little cow is *singing!*'

Coco blinked at them, still puzzled. Had she been singing? She must have. One of the girls next to her shot her a look of sympathy while another muttered crossly. 'Oh. I didn't realise. Sorry.'

'Er, Coco . . .' Roberto said sheepishly. 'I'm afraid Haley's the singer, so . . .'

'Oh, it's Coco, is it?' Haley put her hands on her hips. 'I've heard about you. The *lap* dancer. Roberto – keep her out of my sight as much as possible, do you understand?' She tossed her head. 'Now, shall we start again?'

Coco stared at Haley, her cheeks burning with shame and fury.

'Forget it,' muttered the girl next to her, one of the nicer ones. 'She's a stupid cow. You sound better than she does anyway.'

'OK, from the top!' called Roberto.

Coco fought down her fury so she could start again, but the joy had gone out of it.

She's going to be sorry, she thought grimly.

26

'Morning, Daphne!' called Mr Armstrong, sticking his head out of his office door as Daisy walked through the back corridor of the Excalibur.

'Oh.' She blinked at him, still dazed with tiredness after her early start and the journey across town on the bus. She'd already worn herself out dealing with the first linen delivery of the day. 'Morning.'

'Would you come into my office for a moment?' His head disappeared back inside the office. Daisy went in to where Mr Armstrong was already standing behind his desk. He looked to be in a state of chaos as usual, his office piled high with boxes and the desk top scattered with so much paper that the computer was almost entirely buried in it.

'What is it, Mr Armstrong? Can I get you anything?'

'Alan.' He put his hand to the back of his head and rubbed away at his curls distractedly as he stared at the boxes all around him.

'Sorry?'

'You can call me Alan. I won't know who you mean if you keep calling me Mr Armstrong. Now, a cup of coffee would be nice. Pop to the kitchen and ask Chef, would you? My mug is marked Alan, so you'll know it's mine.'

She went off obediently, remembering with wry amusement the way that she'd been fawned over whenever she'd visited Dangerfield's plush head-quarters. That splendid building was a world away from this dingy, badly lit office, and the idea of her fetching coffee for anyone there would have been extraordinary.

'Hey, Pete! Coffee for the boss,' she called as she marched into the kitchen.

Pete looked up from where he was going through stock lists, and grunted in the direction of a large pot of freshly brewed coffee. 'You all right?' he asked, as she went to pour a mugful.

Daisy nodded. She'd been here for four weeks now and was beginning to get to know the other staff; they were mostly a friendly lot, resigned to working in a state of constant chaos. They were all fond of the boss but knew he was exceedingly disorganised, making their jobs difficult when supplies ran out or bills were left unpaid. Only last week, the laundry contractors hadn't turned up in protest at the outstanding invoices still sitting in a pile on Mr Armstrong's desk. Daisy had asked Muriel, the head receptionist and unofficial deputy manager, to sort it out for them or there would be no clean linen for any guests that day, but Muriel, in a flat spin of panic, had scrabbled about, achieving nothing. In the end, Daisy had got on the phone herself, arranged for a temporary replacement service to deliver that morning, and then had forced Muriel to go into the boss's office, find the invoice and get the money transferred by wire that afternoon. Normal service was resumed the following day, and when the clean linen was delivered, the other maids had given Daisy a round of applause.

'You're doing well,' Pete said gruffly, which was high praise as he was usually hard to please and very critical. 'We like having you around. Don't let anyone frighten you off, you hear?'

Daisy smiled. 'I won't.' She took the mug of coffee back along the corridor to Alan's office, where he was absorbed in something he was doing on the computer. 'Here you are,' she said, putting it down.

'Oh, thank you, Daphne,' he said absent-mindedly, not looking up. She went to leave but he said, 'Sit down a mo, will you?'

She did as he said, wondering what he might want. When he finally looked up, he said, 'You still here?'

'You asked me to sit down.'

'So I did. But why?' He frowned, thinking hard, then his face cleared. 'Yes, I remember. I've got some people coming in later, from head office. And I'm aware that this is a bit of pigsty. Won't really do to have them see the place like this. When you've finished upstairs, can you come and give me a hand?'

'Of course.'

'Good, good. I'll see you later then.'

Daisy went about the usual chambermaiding duties, pushing her trolley from room to room so that she could strip and remake beds, replace towels, clean and replenish the supplies. As she went, she marvelled at the way people could leave the rooms in such different states. Some you would never know had been slept in. Others looked as though a pitched battle had taken place in them. Some people clearly prepared elaborate meals in theirs, others scattered food and drink cartons everywhere. Some were scattered with used condoms and twisted up tissues, others were picked clean as a bone, every sachet of sugar gone. Each room had to be returned to the same standard of cleanliness for whoever would be arriving that day. It was dull, repetitive and tiring, and she could still hardly believe she had taken this job, especially when she'd slogged her guts out getting her diploma in hotel management.

But, she reminded herself as she pushed her trolley along the corridor, getting her passkey from her belt ready for the next door, *this was the best way to get inside without being noticed. The Excalibur is exactly the right hotel, I know that. They wouldn't have had a vacancy for someone of my qualifications. It had to be like this.*

The work might be sheer drudgery but Daisy was surprised by how much satisfaction she got from it. Annunciata, one of the older maids, had shown her exactly how to clean the rooms, laughing with disbelief at Daisy's lack of skill.

'You never seen a cleaning cloth?' she shrieked in her Brazilian accent. 'Look at this! It's not clean, dear, it's covered in smears. You never cleaned a sink? C'mon, you can do it.'

She'd never believe that I hadn't seen a bottle of cleaner until two years ago, Daisy thought wryly. *Or even changed a pillow case.*

Under Annunciata's guidance, she'd learned how to make taps and mirrors shine, and how to whisk

221

through the rooms like an efficient tornado, stripping out dirty linen and making crisp new beds, each day trying to improve on her time for the day before.

But I won't be sorry when this particular part of my plan is over, she thought as she bent over to smooth out the twentieth sheet of the day. *In fact, it can't come too soon.*

Two hours later, Daisy knocked at the office door.

'Yes?' came Alan's voice from inside.

She went in. 'You wanted me to help clear the office. I've finished the rooms so I can give you a hand now.'

'Excellent, excellent.' Alan rubbed his hands together, smiling. 'Let's get stuck in. Filing is not my forte, I'm afraid.'

'No.' Daisy eyed the boxes of paper and the piles on the desk. 'You need an assistant.'

He guffawed. 'No money for that! I tried to get Muriel to help but she said unless she's paid more, she's not lifting a finger. You can see her point. Wages are rubbish in this outfit, hours are long. Why should she?'

Daisy began to shuffle through a stack of unpaid invoices. 'I could help you,' she said innocently. 'I've got a bit of admin experience from my diploma course.'

Alan stopped what he was doing and regarded her carefully. 'Yes, that's always been a bit of a puzzle about you, Daphne. What's a girl like you doing as a chambermaid? I'm sure you don't need to. The others now, they're bright ladies but they don't have many options because of their lack of English. You, on the other hand . . .' He studied her even more quizzically.

'And if you don't mind my saying, you don't sound like a girl from the wrong side of the tracks. It's not a criticism,' he added hastily, 'just an observation.'

'I suppose it seems odd,' Daisy said carefully, 'but I want to climb the ladder. I don't intend to be a chambermaid all my life, of course not. But I think it helps to know a business inside out, from the bottom up.' She held up a piece of paper with a red 'Urgent' stamped across it. 'Alan, you'd better see to this one immediately, or Pete's not going to get his vegetable supply tomorrow.'

'Ah, yes, well spotted,' he said, successfully diverted. 'I'll deal with it now.'

An hour later, the office was looking much tidier, with a pile of paperwork for Alan to deal with immediately and a stack of filing that Daisy said she didn't mind doing, if he wanted her to.

'That would be most helpful, if you're sure,' he said, frowning. 'I can't promise more money.'

'I'm happy to help.' Daisy smiled.

The phone on Alan's desk rang. He picked it up. 'Thank you, Muriel. Yes, show them in.' He put the receiver down, grinning at Daisy. 'Just in time. The big bods are here.'

She stood up to straighten her skirt, and a moment later Muriel had knocked on the door and then stood back to allow two men to enter, both in smart suits, one silver-haired and middle-aged, the other dark and much younger but stony-faced.

'Good day, gentlemen,' Alan said heartily, coming forward to shake the visitors' hands, looking quite shabby and down-at-heel compared to them. 'Can I offer you tea or coffee?'

'No thank you,' said the older man, a little stiffly, 'we'll just get on if that's all right.'

The younger one shot a glance at Daisy, his brown eyes cold. 'And, if you don't mind, miss, this meeting is private.'

Daisy stared back at him, interested. What were these head office guys about to say to Alan? Their body language was not good, although Alan didn't seem to have noticed. 'I'm just leaving, actually,' she said sweetly.

'Yes,' Alan put in. '*Pas devant*, eh? I understand. That's all, thanks, Daphne. You can skip off home if you like.'

'Thanks, Alan,' she said, gave the visitors a beaming smile and let herself out.

She'd have liked to stay and listen – but all in good time.

27

The party was on the Saturday night, and the girls were taken down to Surrey in a bus first thing that morning so that they could do a run-through and full rehearsal during the day. There would be a lot going on, Roberto had warned them. The place would be swarming with caterers, decorators, electricians and all the rest. They would have to work hard to make sure that everything ran smoothly and they were familiar with the venue.

'Yes, yes,' said one of the other girls with a sigh. 'We are professionals, Roberto, we know what we're doing!'

I don't, Coco thought. She knew she was the least experienced of them all. She'd only danced the routines in the studio or in her bedroom and had no idea if she'd be able to do them somewhere else. She'd never danced in front of an audience either. The punters in the club didn't count; they wouldn't care if she had two left feet and did hopscotch for them, so long as she did it with her tits out. The people at the party would be properly posh, used to the best.

She felt sick every time she thought about the performance. She feared being the one to forget the steps, or fall over and wreck the whole thing.

Sam had let her have two days off, but grudgingly. Blanche had teased her: 'We won't be good enough for you any more when you get back here! You'll get a taste for the high life and we'll never see you again.'

'Don't be stupid, you'll see me here Monday night just like usual,' Coco had said, though in her heart she wondered if something was going to happen.

The coach picked them up at Marble Arch at what felt like the crack of dawn. It was very luxurious, with reclining seats, air con, little televisions in the back of each seat, and a very nice lavatory as well. Coco chose a seat at the back where she could sit on her own and keep quiet, and was relieved to see that Haley wasn't part of the party. She must be going down under her own steam.

The coach pulled off and they moved smoothly out into the road and past Hyde Park. *I can't believe I'm twenty*, Coco thought, *and this is my first-ever trip out of London. Properly out of London.* Then she remembered. *Today's my birthday. I'm twenty-one today.* There didn't seem much pointing telling anyone. Who would care? Maybe Michelle had remembered but it had been ages since Coco had been back to see her, and her mum didn't even know her address. *Maybe I'll get a glass of champagne or something later. I can toast my birthday then.*

The journey took only a couple of hours. The other girls chatted, read magazines or watched the programmes on their mini-television screens while Coco gazed curiously out of the coach windows as they drove through towns, villages and stretches of countryside. It was certainly beautiful – rolling green fields, dark patches of woodland, neat hedgerows and banks of wild grasses and flowers everywhere – but also very strange. Where were all the shops and houses? Where was all the traffic? Where were the *people?*

The coach rumbled along country roads and then they were going along the high brow of a hill, the land sweeping away below them to where villages nestled in valleys.

'That's it, I think!' cried Roberto, pointing, and they all craned their necks to see. Coco pressed her nose against the glass to get a proper look. Beneath them, near a small picture-book-pretty village dominated by a church, was a huge house, but what drew the eye were the two enormous white marquees in the grounds, shining in the sunlight. And in the field next to them, three helicopters were parked, also glinting in the morning sun.

'Oh my God!' Coco breathed, hardly knowing she was speaking aloud. 'Fuck's sake, look at that! Bleedin' 'ell.' She knew people lived in places like this – she'd seen the pictures in celebrity magazines, the big mansions where pop stars, soap actors and footballers dwelled – but it was hard to imagine it. Now she was going to see what life in that world was really like. She felt excited, but also awed. Surely someone was going to notice that she didn't belong.

As long as I keep my mouth shut, I'll be fine, she thought. *No one will guess what I really am.*

The dancers were not shown into the house. Instead they were taken into the largest marquee where workmen and technicians were working furiously. Coco was disappointed. It looked a bloody mess, with wires everywhere, tables and chairs stacked over most of the floor, along with lights, air-conditioning units, and boxes and boxes of glasses and booze. A team of florists was in one corner, arranging huge stems of lilies in enormous glass vases, and one of them was throwing a tantrum because she hadn't received a delivery of something vital. People swarmed everywhere, going about their many different kinds of work, while harassed party planners dashed about with clipboards, shouting at people and barking questions.

'Dunno how they're going to get this sorted by tonight,' Roberto whispered. 'It looks like a task from *The Apprentice* or something.'

'Are you the dancers?' cried an anxious-looking woman in black, a clipboard in her hands. She brushed her dark brown hair out of her face as she scanned it. She was wearing a headset with a small microphone bent round her jawline towards her mouth. 'Please say you are! Or else say you're the vodka-shot girls!'

'We're the dancers,' Roberto said.

'Oh, fantastic! Huge load off.' She ticked her clipboard theatrically. 'I'm Polly. Over there is Sophie, and that's Taggie over talking to the barman.'

Coco stared at her in astonishment. She'd never heard a voice like it. So that was what they meant by a plum in the mouth. *How does she do it? It sounds like really hard work, talking posh like that. But she can't half dish it out.*

Polly was talking rapidly as she led them towards the back of the marquee where a stage was being constructed. At one side, workmen were stringing up glittery streamers and putting up a black backcloth while technicians were loading a lighting bar with spotlights. At the other was a discreet passageway that led to a backstage area.

'I'm afraid you'll be sharing this with the catering staff,' Polly said as they all trooped after her. 'Their mobile kitchens are parked just over there and the waiters will be using this as the way in out of the main part. You'll need to keep well out of their way when dinner is in full flow.' She suddenly seemed to focus elsewhere, and a moment later spoke into her headset. 'Roger that, Miranda. Dancers are here. Just showing them the backstage area now.'

She took the small party to show them their quarters – a makeshift dressing room with a table, mirrors and a rail for costumes.

'Show run-through at eleven-thirty,' said Polly. 'Lunch laid on afterwards, OK? Thanks so much. Grab me if you have a problem.' Then she dashed off.

Coco felt anxious as she put her things down, and helped Roberto unpack the costumes and hang them on the rail by the changing area. They were wrapped in plastic and a label attached to each hanger named the dancer who would be wearing that outfit. This wasn't how she'd imagined it. It was chaos out there. How could it ever be ready in time? How on earth were they supposed to have a rehearsal in that bloody mess?

But at eleven-thirty the stage had been constructed and an area in front cleared so that the dancers had room to do their routine. Coco was keen to start dancing. She limbered up in the shadows as catering staff dashed around her, but the preparations seemed never-ending, most of it focused on the lights and the sound technician. There were long, tedious stretches of time where nothing happened. Haley had arrived separately, and now stood at her mic stand where every now and then she sang a few notes, and then they all waited while levels were changed or connections checked.

Coco passed the time watching the tables being set out and the florists manoeuvring their vast displays on to plinths around the marquee. *All this for one bloke! One bloke's birthday.* She wondered how much it was all costing. There had to be a hundred people rushing about, and she'd once seen a bunch of white roses that cost thirty quid, and there were dozens and dozens of them here, long luxuriant stems mixed with lilies. *It must be hundreds. Thousands, probably. Who the fuck has that kind of money?*

Rich famous people she understood – Hollywood stars, singers . . . but ordinary people no one had heard of? How did they do it? She suddenly became aware of the limits of her own world, how small her experience of life beyond it was. *I know fuck all about stuff like this.* She realised that she could either reject it and return to her life in London, determined to shut out things that awed and frightened her. Or she could accept it and try to understand it. She was too interested to ignore it, though, and she might never get a chance like this again . . .

At last they were able to rehearse, the music sounding muffled through the huge speakers, Haley's voice not quite carrying properly. The routine didn't fit the space available, and Roberto made some hasty improvisations. Immediately Coco felt nervous and upset. She knew the routines back to front. How was she supposed to relearn them now? If she forgot to count three instead of four, she could ruin everything . . . With the stress, she managed to make several mistakes and one of the girls swore under her breath at her, and called her fucking clumsy.

Coco wanted to punch her in the mouth but she held back. She was miserable and scowling when they were finally led to a trestle table in the marquee where sandwiches, fruit and cake were laid out for them.

'Cheer up, love,' Roberto whispered. She tried to smile as she loaded her plate with chicken sandwiches but inside she was furious at the way things were turning out. It was going to be a disaster, that was certain, and she was terrified she was going to mess it up.

In the afternoon, the dancers were banned from the main marquees. The workmen had finished and now the decorators and caterers had moved in in force. The girls were allowed to go for a walk and Coco went off on her own, trying to get on top of her frustration.

'Fucking hell,' she whispered to herself, her hands stuffed deep into her pockets as she walked across the cool green grass of the lawn. The only sounds were birdsong from the trees and the distant buzz of a tractor or something, working away in a field nearby. It was beautiful in a way she'd never seen before, and yet she was miserable.

I've got to get on top of this before tonight, she told herself sternly. *I've got to sparkle tonight. I don't know why. I just do.*

* * *

231

They had to be out of sight by seven o'clock. At the front of the house, valets were preparing to take the guests' cars as they arrived. The waiters and waitresses, immaculate in their black-and-white uniforms, were in position, ready to carry out their duties. Jugs of cocktails were mixed and champagne was on ice.

On her way backstage Coco saw a woman walking around, clearly checking everything was in place and as it should be. The party planners were following behind in a nervous cluster, like chickens following a mother hen. The woman, in a plain dark suit, was regarding everything with an eagle eye and giving orders for things she wanted changed, but so quietly and calmly that it was obvious she had to be important.

Birthday boy's wife? Coco wondered, interested. She'd imagined someone a bit flashier, with more diamonds and better shoes.

Then she heard the woman say, 'I don't have to tell you that this has to be perfect. Mr Dangerfield expects nothing less, do you understand? Failure will not be tolerated.'

Sounds like a charming bloke, thought Coco, then Roberto called them all backstage and she decided to start on her make-up. They weren't due on until ten or so. The dancers were the after-dinner entertainment, to be enjoyed while the guests were eating their pudding, so there was plenty of time to do her face and hair, although space in front of the mirror was at premium and Haley was claiming most of it as her right. Coco tried to put her hair in curlers so that she could create glossy forties-style waves, but Haley shooed her out of the mirror space.

'I'm doing my eyelashes!' she declared grandly, and shot a nasty look at Coco. 'People aren't going to be bothered about you, but they *will* be looking at the singer!'

'Really?' Coco said coolly, rolling a platinum lock around a Velcro curler. 'Don't be too sure, love. You must be thirty if you're a day, and you look it.'

Haley looked outraged but, before she could think of a reply, Coco had deftly tucked her curler up and walked off, displaying her excellent figure to its best advantage in her skimpy bra and knickers. She'd already almost caused waiters to drop their trays by wandering about in her underwear, totally unselfconscious.

'Hey, you're not in the club now,' Roberto muttered, grabbing her by the elbow and steering her back to the dressing area. 'Some people ain't used to it. And what's this about you upsetting Haley?'

'She's a silly bitch. Thinks she's a superstar.' Coco scowled.

'Yeah, well . . . she is the singer so let's give her a break.'

'She can give *me* a fuckin' break,' Coco said indignantly. 'She's been in front of that mirror for hours and we all have to share. Stuck-up cow.'

'Coco,' Roberto said warningly, 'no fireworks tonight. Promise?'

She eyed him sulkily. The bad mood that had been building all day was threatening to explode. She bit her tongue. 'OK.'

'Good. Now go and put some clothes on, for Christ's sake.'

* * *

She heard the buzz of voices as the guests arrived. They would spend an hour or two in the first marquee, champagne, canapés and cocktails served as they mingled. No doubt the hosts were there, greeting their guests, moving among them, accepting birthday greetings and compliments on the lavish party. Coco peeked through the passageway and caught glimpses of men in dinner suits and bow ties, and women in long gowns, jewels sparkling at their throats. Then she was flapped away by party planners who were now running the operation out of sight, flitting around and whispering frantically into their headsets.

At eight-thirty, the noise grew louder as dinner was announced and the throng made its way into the main marquee. Coco's nerves were coming back to life with a vengeance. She felt unable to eat anything from the table laid with food for the girls, and longed for a cigarette to calm her anxiety. Her fingers felt shaky and her stomach churned with apprehension and fear. She went back to the mirrors and reapplied her red lipstick. She was in her sexy soldier-girl's uniform – a short khaki shirtdress with military-style pockets and a peaked cap, along with towering black platform heels.

'Christ,' she muttered to her reflection. 'I'd better pull this off.'

The buzz from the dining room grew louder as the meal progressed, helped along by numerous bottles of wine. Coco watched the waiters take out trays laden with plates of exquisite food. When the dirty plates began coming back from the dining room in huge stacks on the waiters' arms, Coco began to feel truly sick. In a moment, pudding would start going out, and then it would almost be time. Everyone looked nervous. Even Haley looked pale and had beads of sweat breaking out across her upper lip and forehead, which she had to keep blotting away.

Then suddenly Roberto was there, herding them all towards the stage, reminding them where the costume changes and props were, and running through the new steps they'd all agreed.

The noise in the dining room subsided as someone stood up and began to make a speech. The audience roared with appreciative laughter at his jokes, and clapped enthusiastically when he made a good point. The girls fell into line for the first dance. The speaker announced, 'And now . . . a very special, very spicy surprise! I'm telling you – these girls are amazing! Ladies and gentlemen – enjoy the show.'

The opening bars of the music sounded, loud and clear over the sound system. Coco took a deep breath, smiled broadly and followed the others as they ran out on stage to take their places and begin.

It went so amazingly quickly. At the same time as she was remembering her steps and concentrating on what she had to do, she was also taking in the room and the people in it. The marquee had been totally transformed from the chaos of the morning. Glittering chandeliers hung from the ruched ceiling and vast candelabras glowed softly on the tables where there was fine linen, china and candlelight glinting off silver and crystal. Waiting staff lined the walls. A cocktail bar glowed at the back of the marquee. Around the tables sat sleek and glossy men and women, well fed and watered, leaning back to enjoy the show.

What a load of old men! Coco thought to herself as she noted grey head after grey head, and paunch after paunch. They seemed to be paying close attention to the long legs and billowing bosoms on display. *They're the same everywhere – rich and poor. It's not so different from the club – except these guys have a million times more cash than my usual audience.*

But who knew who was out there, watching?

She put even more effort into her shimmies and her smile. The routine came naturally and she remembered all the changes without a hitch. Her confidence began to grow and she started to enjoy herself.

'Well done!' hissed Roberto as they came backstage to do their quick change into the tuxedos. 'Keep it up, ladies!'

Haley was crooning through her solo as the girls changed. They were barely into their hot pants and tailcoats and were still picking up their canes when the music changed and it was time to dash back out again to the area in front of the stage, to pull off their fast-moving tap routine. It was hard to see much of the audience with the bright spotlights in her eyes, but Coco did her best. The men she could see were appreciative of the girls, but some of the women looked distinctly stony-faced.

Who cares? We're gorgeous and young. They've had their chance. Now it's our turn. And she put even more bounce into her dancing, flashing her long slim legs as sexily as she dared. *If they only knew where I usually display my thighs . . .* she thought, laughing inwardly. *Wonder if any of these old gits want to shove a tenner down my pants?*

236

Then she was heading off stage again, ready to change for the finale. Haley was there too, just sliding into her black dress for the final number.

'You! How long have we got?' she demanded as Coco came up to get her dress.

'Dunno. Three minutes? It's the instrumental now,' Coco said with a shrug, wriggling out of her hot pants. This was the moment she'd been looking forward to. The other girls were doing their own quick changes, each lost in her own world.

'God, I've got to have a piss!' said Haley, her small pointed face worried below the dark pixie haircut.

'There's the toilet,' Coco said. 'Just behind that curtain. Go now. You've got time.'

'Do you think so?'

'Yeah, if you go right now. I'll help you.' Coco lifted the curtain and went over to the door of the temporary lavatory and opened it for her. As she did so, a wicked thought occurred to her. *Could I? It's pretty nasty but fucking hell, she's asked for it . . . Besides, I'll never get another chance like this.* She beckoned to the other girl to duck behind the curtain after her. Haley hesitated. 'Hurry up! If you're quick, you'll have plenty of time.'

Haley dashed forward into the cubicle and Coco pushed the door closed behind her. It took her barely half a second to decide she was going to do it. She grabbed the fire extinguisher from next to the cubicle, dragged it down and wedged it so that the door could not be pushed open. Satisfied it would not move, she ducked back under the curtain and pulled it shut. It would muffle any noise from the toilet, she was sure of that.

Then she pulled on the beautiful red dress, zipping up the side as she marched up to Roberto. 'Haley's sick. She's throwing up. She can't go on.'

His mouth dropped open in horror and he stared at her, speechless.

'Don't worry. I'll do it. I know the words, I know Haley's moves. It won't matter if there's one dancer less on the floor.'

'B-b-b-but – can you sing? I mean, properly?'

Coco flashed him a smile, tossed her head so that her platinum hair swished over her bare shoulders and said, 'We'll find out, won't we?'

There wasn't time to be frightened. Before she was really aware of what was happening, she was up on the stage, striking a pose in her shimmering sequins. She knew that she must look amazing in the spotlights, her full breasts pillowing out above her low-cut bodice, her white hair glowing and one long thigh emerging from the split skirt.

Good thing I watched how Haley did it, she thought. But she had also listened to Roberto and had made it her business to watch some Rita Hayworth movies. In one, there had been a spectacular routine where Rita had wowed an audience of glamorous nightclub goers while she danced and sang up a sexy storm. *That's me. I'm Rita tonight. I'm Marilyn. I'm Madonna. I'm all of them.* She knew she could do it.

The music started up. Exhilaration coursed through her. She threw open her arms, jiggled her hips, opened her mouth and began to sing.

28

'Oh, God, it's going to be a disaster, a horrible disaster,' groaned Alan, his head in his hands. They were sitting at his coffee table surrounded by paper covered with the hotel's financial details. 'Why the hell do they put me through this? The last directors' meeting was so terrible, I'm still having nightmares about it. I was sure they were going to fire me.'

Daisy put a comforting hand on his arm. 'Come on, Alan, it'll be fine. I'm here to help you. Besides, things are looking much better than they were.'

'You're right.' He looked up but still appeared gloomy. 'We've you to thank for that, Daphne, I know. You've tidied things up wonderfully and there's no doubt that the figures are better than they used to be.' He leaned over and picked up one of the spreadsheets. 'But bookings are down. There's no other way to look at it. And if they don't decide to sack me, they might close the hotel anyway and put us all out of work.'

'Is that likely?' said Daisy, aghast at the idea. 'I thought we did good business? We're in a prime location in the city centre, we always seem to be well booked.'

Alan looked even more miserable. 'There's so much competition. And we don't get enough tourist trade, or enough business trade either. We're too quiet in the week. We've not had the function business lately either, with everyone cutting back in the recession. Doom – doom and despair, Daffers, I'm afraid that's the only conclusion.'

Daisy laughed. 'Don't be so pessimistic. I'm sure that by the time the directors come in next week, we'll have a couple of surprises up our sleeve.'

She had been at the Excalibur for six months now, and had gradually made herself indispensable. It had started with volunteering to help Alan after her chambermaiding duties were over. He didn't seem to think it odd that she didn't want to be paid for the extra work, but he was that sort of man: he didn't examine anything too deeply. Daisy had become his right-hand woman, much to the relief of Muriel who was no good at dealing with Alan's muddle and hated being asked. Slowly, the office became tidier and more organised. Systems were put into place so that invoices were dealt with properly, and Daisy used everything her diploma had taught her about cost control, purchasing, cashiering and financial management to make everything flow better and more efficiently. She overhauled staff rotas and worked out that if she got rid of a couple of extraneous – and unreliable – members of staff, she could give a rise to those who remained. This made her very popular. They all knew that life at the Excalibur had improved since she'd arrived. There weren't quite so many crises, or irate guests, or stopped deliveries, and it was down to her.

Alan was overjoyed. Within a couple of months, he'd decided that she could drop her chambermaiding altogether (which had been Daisy's intention, especially when she reorganised the rotas, freeing herself up from the back-breaking and boring work of cleaning the rooms) and work full-time in his office, with a pay rise that she was able to fund from the savings they were making.

'Well done, Daphne!' he'd say. 'What a magnificent team we are!'

Daisy would laugh and agree. Alan's state of constant chaos was often frustrating but she knew that having him as a boss was a gift – his incompetence meant that she was able to learn a tremendous amount on the job.

And often, when Alan had gone home, she would stay on in the empty office, accessing his computer and roaming through the company system, discovering all she could about the Excalibur and her owners, a property company called Craven Dalziel & Co.

When she wasn't researching the hotel and the company that owned it in the quiet of the deserted office, she was at home, with business books she'd borrowed from the local library, finding out how to decipher what she'd learned and how to apply her new knowledge. It helped that Daddy had given her a solid grounding in the language of business: she understood profits, losses, turnover and net gains. She had a grasp of cash-flow projections and break-even analyses – but it was all theoretical. She had never had to apply her loosely gained knowledge, and that was

241

why she was working as hard as possible to understand how to turn theory into reality.

'Listen, Alan,' she said now, feeling that the moment was ripe to start revealing some of her plans. 'I've had a few ideas for what we can do to impress the directors. Would you like to hear them?'

He sat up eagerly, clasping his hands together as if in supplication. 'Of course I would! I knew you'd come through for me – I bet you're going to save my bacon. It was my lucky day when you walked through the door, Daphne, it really was. Fire away – I'm all ears.'

Daisy didn't get home until after nine o'clock, letting herself in wearily at the front door and going through the mail on the hall table to see if anything had arrived for her. Nothing had.

She was just about to climb the stairs to her bedsit when the bloke from the ground-floor flat popped out. 'Hi, Daphne,' he said. 'You're late back.'

'Oh hi, Nathan. How are you?' She smiled at him, though her heart sank. He was nice enough – a pale, eager-eyed graduate student with thinning fair hair – and he wanted to be friends with her. He probably even hoped for something more, but he was on a hiding to nothing – he was not her type.

'Fine. Do you want to go to the pub for a drink?'

'That's sweet of you, Nathan, but—'

His face fell. 'Just a quick one at the Admiral?'

Daisy realised she was starving and remembered that the Admiral did food. On impulse, she said, 'You know what? All right. But only quickly. I'm exhausted. And Nathan . . .'

'Yes?' He had cheered up at her sudden change of mind and was grinning broadly.

'This isn't a date, OK?' she said sternly but with a smile. 'Just as friends.'

'Yeah, yeah. Of course. I'll get my coat.'

As she and Nathan walked down the road to the pub, she thought about her old social life. Once upon a time, it was playboys ringing her up to ask if she wanted to drink Cristal champagne and vodka cocktails at the hottest clubs in town, or taking her out for dinner at the trendiest new restaurants. Her old favourite, Le Gavroche, practically had a table on permanent reservation for her. The old Daisy would no more have imagined wandering to a grotty local on the outskirts of Bristol with a poverty-stricken student than flying to the moon. Instead, she had wafted through her constant round of parties and lunches, shopping and beautifying, working when it suited her but on projects where someone else did the actual graft, and popping off on endless holidays whenever she felt like it.

Nathan chatted away as they walked along the dark, litter-strewn streets, but she wasn't listening.

Did I really once have access to a private jet? A fully staffed yacht at my disposal? She could hardly believe it now – the impulse trips to the Med, where she and her girlfriends recovered from their hectic lives of pleasure by sunning themselves in designer bikinis on Daddy's yacht. And then there was her lavish coming-out ball. She remembered that crazy night at the Crillon, which had ended up with Freddie making love to her in the four-poster bed of the Leonard Bernstein Suite. He'd opened a bottle of vintage Dom

Perignon from the minibar, joking that this might be the most expensive bottle of champagne he'd ever popped – he could have bought a small car for the same amount. They'd frolicked in bed and afterwards sat on the terrace, Freddie smoking, as they watched the sun coming up and touching the Arc de Triomphe with its first orange rays.

It was a world away from having a burger and chips at the Admiral with Nathan. But Daisy's eyes were open now. She was learning about other lives, the millions of other existences parallel to those of the pampered few. As she and Nathan settled at a table and ordered their food, she realised that some aspects of her previous life now made her feel vaguely ashamed.

All the more reason to succeed in what I'm doing, she told herself firmly. *I'm going to show everyone that I'm not afraid of work, and that I can earn success – not just inherit it.*

She returned to her bedsit two hours later and got ready for bed. The trip to the pub had unexpectedly been fun, and she'd enjoyed listening to Nathan talking about his course. It reminded her how lonely she had been over the last few years, only the odd chat with Lucy providing any outlet. Her job had taken up most of her time, and what was left she devoted to furthering her plan.

Sometimes black depression settled on Daisy, but she refused to give in to it. If she did, it meant that bastard was winning and she wasn't about to let that happen. She would damn' well cope. Every day that went by, she was getting better at looking after herself, managing her money and letting go of everything the past had meant to her. All except one thing: getting even with Daddy.

She went over to her computer to check her emails before she turned in. She clicked on to the Dangerfield Florey web page, and scrolled through it, gazing at the photographs of the familiar hallways, the restaurants and ballroom. She made it her business frequently to inspect the sites of the most important Dangerfield assets. The Florey's page hadn't changed since the last time she'd looked, though the link to her shoe boutique had long since disappeared, of course. That business had been dismantled not long after she'd left the family. It was waste, but it could hardly continue without her. She went to the main Dangerfield site, looking at the upcoming projects and the company's usual marketing spiel about how fantastic it was.

Then she noticed a new link: The Dangerfield Foundation. That had definitely not been there last time she'd looked. She clicked on it. 'Page under construction', it said. 'News to follow shortly'.

I wonder what that can be. What the hell is Daddy up to now? I'll have to keep an eye on this.

That night, she had the usual nightmare. She was in a huge house which started off as Thornside Manor, but it rapidly became clear that this place was much bigger than her old house. Each door she opened seemed to lead to another, new part that she'd never known had existed. She was looking for someone but wasn't sure who, just that it was someone she needed to find but who was always tantalisingly just out of sight. Then, just as she was sure she'd got close, she would open a door and behind it was Daddy. When he saw her, he went red in the face and began to scream and shake his fist at her. Then she was running back through the unfamiliar corridors and passageways, but wherever she went he was close behind her, or just in front, or waiting around the next corner, determined to find her and punish her. Then she woke up, her heart pounding, a sick feeling in her stomach, and fear coursing through her.

Daisy felt the familiar nausea as she blinked and panted in the blackness. She hastily turned on the light and lay down again, trying to calm and reassure herself.

I never want to feel afraid of him again, she thought to herself. *I don't see why he should go on making my life a misery. Besides, if anyone should be afraid, it's him.*

246

29

'I know, baby, I know,' purred Coco seductively down the telephone. She tried to shut out the reality of her shabby bare room in the shared flat and pretend that she was lying on silk sheets. 'You know what – I'm naked right now.' She was actually wearing jeans and tee-shirt, but her feet were bare, perhaps that counted. 'I'm lying on the bed, thinking about you.' It was true she was lying on the bed, with its sagging mattress and broken headboard, but she was staring up at the wood-chip-papered ceiling, idly wondering how many little tiny bumps there were in it while she talked.

'You're naked?' said the voice on the other end, a rasping gruff voice. 'Christ, don't do that to me, Coco.'

She ran her hands across her chest. 'I'm feeling my tits. God, they're gorgeous. My nipples are going hard, they're like little bullets. They want you to suck them, baby. I'm getting wet thinking about it . . .'

She could hear heavy breathing down the line. She waited, making only a soft, longing, sighing noise to keep him ticking over.

When he spoke again, his voice was thick with lust.

She could just imagine him sitting in his swanky office behind his desk, trying to deal with the raging hard-on that was bursting to be free from his pin-stripe trousers. 'How soon can you get to Charles Street?'

'I guess . . . an hour or so.'

'Fine. Meet me there in an hour.' He put the phone down abruptly.

She laughed lightly to herself. She had him in the palm of her hand. Exactly where she wanted him.

Maybe this is my way out, she thought. It was an opportunity, she knew that, and she was keen to seize it.

Coco arrived at the flat in Charles Street exactly an hour later. She'd changed into a tight dress and high heels, with some of her sexiest underwear beneath. He liked the works – didn't they all? – the suspenders, stockings, wispy lace panties, a bra that pushed her tits up into a balcony. She'd decided against the leopard-skin coat; she would look like an old-fashioned tart in that. No. A discreet black belted trench, a pair of shades and her white hair drawn back into a chic ponytail. New-school tart, maybe.

The flat was located at the west end of Charles Street in Mayfair, where it narrowed and darkened and became a little bit more secretive. Just on the bend was a tall, narrow Georgian house divided into four flats. Coco pressed the buzzer of the one on the fourth floor and waited. She examined the brickwork, blackened by its coating of two centuries of London soot, then a voice came from the intercom. 'Come up.'

The buzzer sounded and she pushed against the door to open it. The next moment she was in an elegant, if neutral hallway. She closed the door behind her and began to climb the curving staircase. She had never yet seen anyone else in these flats. Perhaps they were all used as places for secret assignations by businessmen keen to keep their activities private, lying empty except for a few frantic hours. It seemed a waste.

Reaching the fourth floor, she knocked on the door of Flat D. A moment later it opened and he was standing there, almost quivering with anticipation, his belly seeming to judder under his waistcoat. Without a word, she strode forward and pressed her lips to his, licking them with the tip of her tongue. She went past him, undoing her coat.

She turned and faced him, smiling as she let the coat drop to the floor. Then she reached under one arm and began to unzip her dress. 'Well,' she murmured. 'Shall we?'

He didn't need much encouragement. An instant later he was on her, running his hands all over her and grunting with pleasure as they half stumbled into the small bedroom and on to the bed. He was a forceful kisser, thrusting his tongue into her mouth, his own jaws wide open as though he wanted to swallow her. She thought she caught the faint tang of tooth decay but tried to ignore it. His hands were not tender: he liked to pinch and squeeze and pummel her breasts and bottom, twisting her nipples just to the point of pain. And he liked her to scratch and pinch him in return, running her red talons over his slightly scaly back (*He needs a back scrub or something. A good oily massage,* she would think, trying not to imagine flakes of skin gathering under her nails) and seizing the hairy flesh on his buttocks.

Now he was well primed and eager, his cock stiff and twitching the moment he released it from his trousers. He wanted to fuck her, and quickly; she had suspected as much, and made sure to lubricate herself in advance. She never got aroused while they had sex and the lube helped.

'Condom, babe,' she reminded him, and he fumbled for one in the drawer of the bedside table. She took it from him and deftly ripped the packet open with her teeth, plucked out the small saucer of rubber and, with a smooth movement, rolled it down over his prick. He was still dressed but he seemed to find that exciting – the rushed, lustful nature of it. Swiftly he pushed her knees apart with one hand while with the other he held his cock, pushing it towards her entrance.

I never realised that pubes went grey, Coco thought, catching a glimpse of the stiff shaft inside its latex covering where it emerged from a nest of greying hair. *I suppose it makes sense.* After all, the hairs in his nostrils were grey too, and his eyebrows. Why not pubes? *Concentrate, Coco.*

He was in now, panting when he wasn't kissing her, rushing forward to his climax. When she wanted to speed him up, she simply pushed a finger quickly and sharply up his ass, and that would make him gasp with pleasure, shudder and rush to orgasm, but she didn't need to do it this time. He was tensing and bucking within a few minutes of entering her.

'Christ, Coco,' he said, rolling off her with a sigh. 'You do things to me . . .'

'You do things to *me*, hon,' she purred.

'But . . . you didn't come . . .' he said, smiling as

250

though they shared a special secret. He kissed her complacently, as though it was understood that Coco didn't really need satisfaction, she was simply there to provide it. She smiled back. She was happy with that arrangement. She couldn't bear to think of getting off with this guy.

She turned on to her side so that she was facing him, and undid his tie. 'Don't worry about that. That was just the starter. When we get to the main course . . .' She began to pull the tie out from round his collar.

He frowned and made a rueful noise. 'I can't, Coco. I have to get back to work. It was madness sneaking out as it was. I've got an important meeting at five, and then drinks with more clients, and a charity dinner at eight-thirty . . .'

'Shall I wait until you get back?' she asked winsomely.

'Well . . . I don't think there's any point. I've no idea if I'll have time . . .'

'You know, hon, I've been thinking.' She pouted at him and smiled, gazing up at him from under her lashes. 'Wouldn't it make sense if I was here for you all the time? I mean, you've got this place – it's empty most of the time, right? Why don't I stay here for a while and you can see what's it like to have me at your beck and call any time you want . . . but without the hassle of me having to get here?'

He considered this, obviously attracted by the idea of having Coco in constant attendance and tickled by the thought that he could dash in at any time to have her. 'But . . .'

'But what?

'Well, this is a company flat, in theory. It ought to

251

be available for visiting clients if we need to find them accommodation.'

'But you're the boss, ain't ya?' she said quickly, slipping into the South London accent she tried to tone down for her lover. 'Why not just put 'em up at a hotel? And how often do you use it anyway?'

He laughed. 'True. I can't remember when we last did. But sod's law says that if you move in, it'll be required immediately.'

She pouted at him again and whispered, 'Come on, darling, imagine it . . . our own little love nest . . .'

He gazed back, his eyes darkening with lust again. She took his hand and pushed on to her mound so that he could feel the small strip of hair and the puffy lips of her pussy.

'This would be yours . . . *any time.*'

'Ahhh, Coco . . .' He tickled her with a finger, then pushed it into the entrance. She let her legs fall open and sighed as though with pleasure.

'*Baby* . . .' She licked her lips and closed her eyes.

'Listen, I'll see what I can do, all right?'

Coco was confident of getting what she wanted in the end. After all, she had her lover wrapped around her little finger, and was determined he would help her escape life in the poky shared flat in Whitechapel and evenings spent dancing in the club.

That night of the birthday party, when she'd taken to the stage, had been magnificent. Shafting Haley like that had definitely been worth it, even if it was cruel. The moment when Coco had burst into song had been fantastic. The other girls had stared at her in astonishment as they'd realised she was belting out

Haley's number, but they were pros and had carried on the routine as rehearsed, only with one less dancer. It had raised the roof as well: by the end, the audience had been on their feet clapping and cheering, yelling for an encore, so they'd done the whole song again, and this time Coco had really gone for it and had a ball. After the show, some of the girls stayed backstage to comfort Haley, who had been released from the loo by some waiter and was now screaming and crying. She'd rushed at Coco, looking like she wanted to scratch her eyes out, but Roberto had held her back. Coco ignored her, got changed into a slinky black number, refreshed her lipstick and went out to join the party. It had been great: men watching her, sidling up to congratulate her and have a quick chat while their wives shot nervous looks in her direction.

She'd been approached by a stiff-looking woman in a plain black evening dress who'd said that Mr Dangerfield wanted to meet her, and had led her over to the table of honour. Coco looked at him with interest – so this was the birthday boy. He was a tanned man with a dodgy dye job on his hair, and he'd given her a glass of champagne and complimented her on the routine.

'Wonderful,' he'd said, staring at her from a pair of dark brown eyes with a particularly penetrating gaze. She couldn't help noticing his bushy black brows and his jowly features. 'You're very talented.'

'Thank you,' Coco had returned with her best smile. 'And a happy birthday to you. It's a funny coincidence actually, 'cos it's my birthday today too.'

He'd reacted to this quite oddly – visibly jumping,

his eyes widening – but only for a moment. A second later he said smoothly, 'That is indeed amusing. Margaret will see to it that you get a birthday present from me, as a token of my appreciation.'

She'd been hoping to be asked to join him and perhaps be treated to some more of the champagne cooling in a bucket on the table, but another old man in a dinner suit came up to greet Mr Dangerfield in a booming voice, and she was led away by Margaret. She took Coco's details and then Coco was free to roam the party. That was where she struck gold. From the first moment he came up to talk her, she'd known what Matthew had in mind. There was a wedding ring on his finger but his wife, he told her, was not at the party. Would she like to dance? After several dances and heavy flirtation over cocktails, she knew then that she'd landed the big fat fish she'd been looking for.

She'd played the game carefully, not putting out right away but reeling him in with teasing and promises until he was putty in her hands. The night she'd finally slept with him, he'd nearly blown a fuse with excitement. She'd fucked him three times in succession, and by the end he was practically her slave. She'd been careful to ask for nothing so far and now, she was sure, he was on the brink of doing what she wanted, getting her out of her drab old existence and into a glittering new one.

She'd been surprised when the birthday present from Mr Dangerfield had duly arrived: she'd forgotten all about it. It was a cheque for £100 issued by his private bank inside a signed card. She couldn't bank the money without an account so she threw away the card and kept the cheque tucked in her purse as though its presence tied her to that magical world of limitless money and pleasure.

Besides, it was the only present she'd received.

30

The directors from Craven Dalziel & Co. were shown into Alan's office at eleven o'clock precisely. It was the same two as before, both in dark business suits, one man middle-aged and balding and with an air of authority. But Daisy's eyes instantly went to the younger man. He was around thirty, she guessed, with a full head of dark hair and chocolatey brown eyes under strong straight brows. She watched him as he returned Alan's handshake, said hello and took his place. There was an intensity about him that was underlined by his fine bone structure and rather aquiline nose.

'Gentlemen, hello,' Alan said nervously, as everyone sat down. He was looking very smart, at least by his standards, in a well-worn brown suit, mustard yellow shirt and green checked tie. Daisy privately thought that he looked better in his usual battered get up, but he'd obviously made an effort. 'I hope the trip here wasn't too dreadful. Please sit down.'

Daisy became aware that she was staring at the young director when he looked over at her, frowning, and said, 'So, Alan, who is this?'

He jumped and looked at her as though he had no idea who she was, then his face cleared. 'Oh yes, sorry – this is my assistant Daphne. She's new here but an absolute godsend. She's taking minutes today. Now, Daffy, this is John Montgomery, division managing director –' Alan indicated the older man, who nodded at Daisy but couldn't be bothered to speak to her '– and Christopher Cellan-Jones, who is deputy MD. A notch down, you might say, Christopher.' Alan laughed a little, then added, 'But I'm sure you're on your way up!'

'It's *Christophe*, actually,' the other man said lightly. 'Not Christopher.'

'Oh! Sorry. Christophe.' Alan laughed again. 'What happened, did your father spell it wrong on the birth certificate? Did the registrar spill his tea on the "r" by mistake?'

Daisy looked over at him imploringly. He was nervous and that was making him clumsy. If only he would shut up and stop trying to be funny. Alan caught her eye and stopped laughing at once, trying to turn it into a cough instead.

'No. It's Christophe, the French version of Christopher,' the young man said. 'And my surname is Welsh, pronounced *Kethlan*. Confusing, I know. Blame my parents for the ethnic mix.' Then he smiled at Alan, and instantly became dazzlingly handsome. Daisy felt something inside her melt and her head whirled with a strange dizziness. She dropped her gaze to the table in case he saw in her eyes that she had just been so strongly affected by him. 'But please, don't worry about it,' he went on, oblivious to the effect he'd had on her. 'I'm used to being called Christopher. Shall we get on?'

'Of course,' Alan said, solemn and business-like now. 'Right, gentlemen. I'll start by giving you an overview of how things have improved.' He picked up the speech that Daphne had prepared for him and began to read it out. It outlined how the hotel had performed over the last six months and the efficiencies that had been made to reduce costs and overheads. Alan stuck to the script just as she'd told him to and, when he finished, cast a quick look at her as though asking for approval. Daisy gave him an encouraging smile and raised her eyebrows at a couple of neatly bound folders. 'Oh, yes,' Alan said quickly. 'Here is a printed version along with the necessary figures and graphs.' He handed them over to the two directors.

'I see,' John Montgomery said, taking his copy. 'Well, Alan, I'm rather impressed by this.' He shot a look at his deputy and added, 'To be honest, we thought we were about to hear the familiar litany of problems compounded by the usual chaos, and I wasn't really prepared to let things continue in that vein for much longer. But you seem to have halted the decline. How have you managed it?'

'Gentlemen,' Alan said importantly, 'it's been relatively simple. I've instigated some new systems such as an invoice . . . er . . . . payment process that . . . er . . .' He looked over at Daisy for help. 'What was it, Daffy?'

'A fairly straightforward cashiering system, some cuts in staffing numbers, longer lines of credit with suppliers, some renegotiations of terms,' she prompted.

'Oh, yes –' Alan nodded '– what she said. Anyway, that's helped the bottom line quite a bit – you'll see some better results coming in the next few months.

And we've worked on promotions as well as . . . er
. . . what else did we do, Daffs?'

This is it. This is the moment. Daisy breathed in and
then said in a calm but authoritative voice, 'Alan,
would you mind if I just outline for the directors a
few of the improvements we've put in place?'

'Oh.' He looked startled. 'N-n-no. Go ahead.'

'Thank you.' She rose smoothly to her feet and
fixed the two men with a clear, candid gaze. 'Gentlemen,
for the last five months, we've been on a serious drive
to streamline our systems and overhaul every part of
the operation. This has seen significant improvement
in our outgoings. But, as you'll see from the figures,
we do also need to improve visitor numbers.' On cue,
the overhead projector hummed smoothly into life,
thanks to the plug extension she'd put by her foot
and now pressed down to connect, and she brought
the laptop on the table next to her into life with a
movement of the mouse. Then, with clarity and focus
and aided by her on-screen visuals, she outlined what
the local competition was like and how the Excalibur
could target more of the market.

'This place looks old and feels tired. We're up
against the new ranges of budget hotels that have
sophisticated systems of room bookings – offering
cheap rates when rooms are empty, higher when
there's more demand – and have a strong internet
presence and loyalty schemes. They also don't look
cheap. They've got a simple, clean, stylish feel that's
a world away from this place. Alan and I feel that
we need to look hard at our promotion and
marketing strategy, and invest in the look and feel
of the hotel. To be honest, it's only our location

that's keeping us going. We could be doing so much more.'

When she'd finished and sat down, there was a pause that carried the weight of approval from the directors, while Alan looked astonished.

John Montgomery nodded his head with quiet satisfaction. He tapped his pen on the table. 'Well, Alan, I must say that is very impressive. A huge turn-around. Some excellent planning there, and good creative thinking. You're really taking on your role as manager here. I was worried that this was beyond you. Well done.'

'Oh, er . . . thank you,' Alan said, nodding importantly. 'Yes, I like to think that the Excalibur has turned a corner under my direction.'

Daisy stared over at her boss, hurt by his refusal to acknowledge her input, but Alan was studiously avoiding looking at her. *Surely he's going to say something!* she thought indignantly.

'Actually . . .' A cool voice cut into her thoughts and she turned to see Christophe Cellan-Jones had spoken. He had fixed Alan with his intense brown stare. 'Actually, Mr Armstrong, would you mind telling me when your assistant started?'

Alan glanced over at him, a little ruffled. 'Certainly, certainly . . . let me see . . . Daphne's been here four months now.'

'Six,' Daisy said in a quiet but clear voice.

'Six, is it? Goodness, are you sure?' Alan laughed and leaned back in his chair. 'Time does go fast. She's a good sort. Learns quickly. I called her Daffy. You know, like the duck – quack, quack!'

'Then it's rather a coincidence, isn't it?' Christophe

continued. He looked over at Daisy, something like kindness glimmering in his eyes. 'Previously your situation was pretty hopeless and your position among our managers about as low as it could be . . . and then Miss Fraser starts work and, hey presto, everything starts improving in ways you've never dreamed of implementing before.'

Alan began to turn dark red. 'Well . . . she has *helped*, that can't be denied.'

'Helped?' Christophe stared at him unblinkingly.

'Yes,' spluttered Alan. 'Credit where it's due. She's been a great help.'

'Then I assume you'll be rewarding her – say, with some sort of bonus?'

'Of course. I was just about to say that when you *interrupted*.'

'Hmm.' A glimmer of amusement twitched at the corners of Christophe's lips. 'I'm glad to hear it.' He looked over at Daisy. She couldn't stop herself from smiling back, as though the two of them were part of a special conspiracy.

I don't even know him. But he saw through Alan. He knew it was me. A delicious tingle ran over her skin and she wanted to shiver.

John Montgomery pushed back his chair and made to stand up. 'Well, we'll go through the figures and projections in more detail this afternoon, but I think we should break for lunch and a tour.'

'Excellent, excellent,' Alan said, also standing up. 'We'll go through to the restaurant. Daffy's arranged a very nice menu so the chef can really display his skills. I think you'll like it.'

As they all headed out of the office, Christophe

261

lingered for a moment so that he was next to Daisy. 'You've worked a miracle here,' he said quietly as they walked into the corridor. 'I'm very impressed. And don't worry, I'll make sure you get the credit.'

'Thank you,' she said, smiling at him. 'To be fair, Alan and I worked on this together.'

He raised an eyebrow. 'Alan could never have done this in a million years. He was going to be sacked today. You've just saved his bacon in a big way. He owes you, believe me.'

31

Coco sat on her suitcase to make it shut over her pile of stuff. She hadn't thought she owned all that much, but it turned out to be quite a lot. It was mostly clothes and shoes, along with a ton of make-up and hair products: irons, tongs, curlers, straighteners, and all the rest. She still had the teddy her mother had given for Christmas ages ago, and a few photos and ornaments, but nothing else to show for her twenty-one years.

That's all gonna change. I'm gonna hit the big time, I just know it. I'm on my way, properly.

She managed to close the case, and fastened it shut. Then she stood up and looked around at the empty room. It was smaller somehow now that it was bare: a couple of metres square, with a window that looked over the back of a Chinese restaurant, and full of the constant reek of fat, sizzling meat and soy sauce.

As she stared at it, she took a vow.

I fuckin' swear that I ain't never coming back here. This is it. I'm not coming back. I'd rather die trying than come back to this place.

Then she hauled her cases out to where the minicab was waiting, and left.

Her next stop was at the club. She left the driver outside waiting for her while she went in. The place always looked grim during the day, before the lights had been turned down. In the daylight, you could see how shitty all the furniture was, how scuffed the floor and how grimy and cheap all the fittings. Without pounding music, make-up and spotlights, girls in their underwear just looked oddly underdressed, skinny and rather cold.

'Hiya, Sam,' Coco sang out as she walked in. She was wearing tight jeans, a plunging top that showed off her cleavage, sunglasses and very high heels. *I'm a glamorous woman, and I'm on the up,* she thought, pleased with the reflection she glimpsed in the mirror.

'Oh, it's you,' he growled, emerging from the door behind the bar. 'What do you want?'

'I've come in for my last pay packet, innit?' she said, putting her white leather handbag down on the bar. 'You got it?'

'I ought to give you fuckin' nothing, you ungrateful bitch!' Sam glowered at her.

'Ah, come on. You've had my best years, mate! I've been nothing but reliable, and brought you in plenty of dough, too. Give us a break and be happy for us, yeah? And hurry up, I've got a cab waiting.'

Sam harrumphed and went back into the darkness of the office. Roberto appeared from the stage, shrieking with delight when he saw Coco standing at the counter.

'Babe! You come in to say goodbye?'

'Yep.' She took off her sunglasses and smiled at him. 'I'm moving up West today.'

'Ah, honey!' Roberto came up and enveloped her in a hug. 'You take care, you hear? Shit, I'm gonna miss you!'

'Yeah, me too,' she said, hugging him back, sad at the thought that she might not see him again. After all, she'd known him for a long time now. He'd been a friend to her.

'But you done *real* good.' Roberto stood back, grinning, his eyes admiring. 'I might have known that you'd pull something like this out of the bag.' He shook his head. 'I should have been *furious* with you when you locked Haley in the bog and took her spot, but you were fuckin' amazing – and I obviously wasn't the only one who thought so, eh? Well done, babe. You enjoy it, that's all.'

'Thanks.'

'So . . .' He took her hand. 'When are you going?'

'Right now, soon as Sam gets my dosh.'

'Now?' Roberto looked surprised. 'Aren't you gonna stay and say goodbye to Blanche? She'll be in soon. And what about your mum? You been to see her?'

Coco tensed. 'Nah,' she said briefly. She wasn't in the business of goodbyes. She'd never have come back here at all if she hadn't had some wages to collect. When something was over, it was over. She travelled alone, that was how it was.

'Oh. OK. Well, stay in touch, yeah? Let me know how it goes. Come back and see us.'

'Yeah.' She grinned at him. 'When I make it big, we'll do something, yeah? Remember the dream!'

Between them they'd planned a fantasy future,

where they owned a string of dance studios. Sometimes Coco was a famous dancer, sometimes a mega-successful businesswoman with Roberto helping to run her empire, but the basic premise of the fantasy was the same: money, security and some fun.

'You betcha, babe!' Roberto said, laughing, as Sam came back through with a brown envelope for her.

She was itching to be gone. It felt as though her future was waiting for her just beyond the club door, the taxi with its engine still running eager to take her there. She took the proffered envelope and said, 'Thanks. See ya later.' Then she put on her sunglasses and began to stride for the door, her heels clicking on the wooden floor.

'Bye!' Roberto called after her as she headed towards the sunlight outside.

She didn't look back but raised one hand in farewell, then she was gone.

32

Sitting in Alan's office, Daisy scrolled down the website until she found the link. Yes, there it was. The Dangerfield Foundation. She clicked on it and was taken to a page. Instantly she felt sick. There was a photograph of her father staring out at her. It had been airbrushed to the point of ridiculousness – Daddy's skin was almost wrinkle-free, which seemed absurd in a man of his age. And he was definitely thinner too, the jowls hanging loosely like a turkey gizzard around his neck.

What the hell is this Dangerfield Foundation? she wondered. *What's it all about?*

She read on. The Foundation must still be in its early stages: there were just two short paragraphs that did not give away much, but from what she could glean, it had been set up by Daddy to investigate aspects of health, youth and vitality.

'We are living longer,' proclaimed the text, 'and we want to live WELL. That means we must eliminate the physical problems that can occur as we progress through our lives. The human body has a built-in obsolescence that we must begin to tackle if we are to enjoy our later years. The Dangerfield Foundation is dedicated to scientific progress in this area.'

This sounds kind of weird, she thought. *Daddy was never interested in this stuff before. It was money, money and more money with him.*

The phone on the desk buzzed, making her jump. She picked it up. Muriel was calling her.

'There's a visitor here for you and Alan, from Head Office. Shall I show him in?'

'Oh. Yes, please, Muriel.'

Daisy barely had time to close the website down, erase the browsing history and stand up before Muriel was showing in the visitor. Daisy's heart skipped a beat. It was the very handsome Christophe Cellan-Jones, currently smiling at her in the friendliest manner she'd yet seen from him. It was only a week since the directors' last visit. What did he want?

'Hello,' he said as he came in. He looked impressive in a well-cut suit and a dark blue silk tie with a fat Windsor knot. 'Sorry to surprise you.'

Daisy got to her feet. 'I'm afraid Alan's not here,' she said, feeling her cheeks get warmer. *Get a grip, Daisy,* she told herself. *This is one of the directors you're supposed to be trying to impress.*

'I know.' Christophe smiled again. 'I wanted to talk to you actually. I've come to take you out to lunch. Unless you have some other plans . . . ?'

'No . . . no, of course not,' Daisy said, puzzled. 'I know somewhere nearby we can go. I'll just let Muriel know I'm going out.'

They headed out to a small café across the road and settled themselves at a table. When they'd ordered,

Christophe, who looked rather out of place there in his smart suit, said, 'Right. I expect you're wondering why I'm here.'

'I was a bit,' Daisy admitted. 'I just hope it's not bad news.' She looked at him anxiously. 'I thought the presentation went well.'

'It did, yes. And as I told you at the time, you saved Alan's job for him.'

'Yes. I'm pleased about that. I know he's a muddler but he's a decent man and tries his best. He just needs a bit of direction.'

Christophe nodded, his dark brown eyes serious. He had a delicious olive complexion and the intensity in his eyes was distracting Daisy every time he looked at her. She sternly told herself to concentrate. During the hotel tour last week, Christophe had paid no attention to her at all, and had said nothing more to her directly either. The last thing she'd been expecting was a personal visit.

He leaned back and looked thoughtful. 'It's not ideal when the manager needs a bit of direction. Especially when it's one of the maids who's doing it.'

'Oh.' Daisy flushed again, her heart sinking. It was going to be bad news after all.

'After I left last week, I decided to do a little research. You see, Alan doesn't officially have an assistant, so it was rather strange to find you there. Then I discovered that you started as a chambermaid over six months ago, and now here you are, virtually running the place. I found your emailed CV on the system.' He leaned towards her again, his expression quizzical. 'And you've got a diploma from St Prudence's in International Hotel Management.'

'Ah.' Daisy knew she was blushing even harder. 'Well . . . you see—'

Christophe interrupted, holding up a hand to quieten her. 'I don't need you to explain. I just consider Alan bloody lucky to have found you. And it's clear now how you knew what systems to implement. It's no wonder you've been able to sort out his messes so effectively. He was on borrowed time, as you know. But it can't be allowed to go on like this, it's completely mad.'

'Oh no!' cried Daisy. 'You're not going to sack him after all, are you?' She gazed at him imploringly. That would be disastrous. As it was, her own job was probably on the line.

Christophe sighed. 'No. There are reasons why we won't, even though I personally think it would be much the best option. But things can't go on in this topsy-turvy manner, especially as I sense that you've got some interesting ideas for the future of the hotel. So I recommended to John that you be promoted to joint manager, alongside Alan, with immediate effect. I don't like the fact that you're still on the payroll as a maid, and that you're not getting a proper wage.'

Daisy gasped, a surge of delight rushing through her. 'Really?' She clapped her hands with pleasure. 'That's wonderful! But . . .' her face fell '. . . how will Alan take it?'

'He'll smile nicely and be grateful, if he's got any sense,' said Christophe. He smiled at her. 'I'm pleased you're pleased. Now where's our food? I'm starving.'

Over lunch, they talked about the hotel and how everything worked there. Christophe told her that Craven Dalziel had hotel holdings all over the west of

England, and they in turn were owned by a larger hotel and property company. Daisy had to pretend she didn't know anything about this, and used her supposed ignorance to ask as many questions as she could about how Craven Dalziel worked and was run.

Eventually, when they'd finished eating and were lingering over coffee, Christophe looked at his watch regretfully. 'I'm afraid I've got to be going. I've some other meetings this afternoon. It's a shame. I'd like to carry on chatting.'

'Me too,' Daisy said, trying to sound normal and not as though she'd like to spend all afternoon with him if she could. He was charming, intelligent and funny – and extremely attractive.

'I'm actually staying in Bristol tonight. I thought . . .' Christophe looked a little bashful but only for a second and then he was smoothly charming as usual. 'I thought it might be nice to go out and celebrate your promotion. I know a good place we could have dinner . . . if you'd like to, that is? You may have other plans.'

'Oh, no,' she said hastily. 'I love to.'

'Good.' He smiled. 'I'll collect you from the hotel at eight.'

By the time he came to collect her, Daisy was a bag of nerves. She hadn't been able to do a thing in the afternoon, and had even forgotten the excitement of her promotion in the anticipation of her evening with Christophe. Instead, she'd slipped out to Princes Street and bought herself a clinging red jersey dress that flattered her slender figure.

This is ridiculous, she told herself firmly as she

hurried back clutching her shopping bag. I hardly know him. And, what's more, he's my boss. If I'm a joint manager, I'm going to have deal directly with him all the time. Getting involved is a terrible idea, even if he were interested. Which he isn't.

Despite her little lectures to herself, she went home, showered, changed, and got ready carefully. Putting her dark lenses back in, she wished she'd never bothered with them in the first place, but she could hardly stop wearing them now. Even Alan might notice if his previously brown-eyed assistant – sorry, joint manager – walked in one day with blue ones instead. She assessed her reflection. Her dark bob was softened with an enamelled hair clip, and the new dress was elegant and quietly sexy. It was just right.

'But nothing's going to happen,' she told her reflection. 'You'll see.'

The champagne cork flew out of the bottle with a satisfying pop, followed by a spume of white froth.

'Quick, a glass!' urged Christophe, laughing, holding the bottle up.

'Here!' Daisy pushed a champagne flute towards him and he tipped the bottle so that the foam fell into the glass like whipped egg whites, then topped it up with the honey-coloured liquid. He filled another flute the same way, and shoved the bottle back into its ice bucket.

Christophe lifted the glass, smiled and said, 'A toast to you, Daphne. To your success. Congratulations.'

She laughed. 'Thank you. I'm so excited, I don't know what to say.'

'You deserve it. And I'm sure it's just the start.'

They both sipped their champagne. The bubbles exploded pleasurably over Daisy's tongue. Christophe had arrived, looking handsomer than ever in a dark coat, and they'd taken a cab to this elegant, discreet restaurant in Clifton. It was the first time she'd done something like this since she'd left home, and it was lovely to feel spoiled again. She ordered the oysters, and black cod to follow. While they waited for their food, Daisy said, 'Where do you live, Christophe?'

He picked up a bread roll and broke a piece off. His cufflinks glittered in the candlelight. 'I have a small flat in Cheltenham where I live during the week so I can be close to the office. At weekends I escape to my house in Wales. It's beautiful there. The countryside is amazing.'

'Do you live by yourself?' she asked innocently, and then blushed at the implication.

'Yes, by myself,' he said, without appearing to notice. 'I love the solitude actually. Nothing better than arriving home on Friday evening, turning on the heating and getting a fire going, then cooking myself a bit of supper, opening a bottle of wine and relaxing with a book or a film.'

Daisy nodded. She understood the kind of comfort that could be derived from one's own company. She'd grown up with it.

'Of course, I'm not always on my own,' he then added gravely.

'No? Who are you with?' she said, just a touch too quickly.

'A very beautiful lady called Sasha. You should see her. Gorgeous brown eyes with extraordinary eyelashes. And boundless energy.'

'Oh,' Daisy said, trying not to feel too disappointed.

'Yes, she's wonderful. Just a bit *licky*. You know – she does like to climb up me and lick me all over if she can.'

Daisy stared at him, astonished, then realisation dawned and she burst out laughing. 'Sasha's a dog!'

'Of course. What did you think?' he said with a mischievous grin. 'She won't forgive me if I go to Nant-y-Pren without her.'

The oysters arrived and Daisy dived in happily, dousing each one in shallot vinegar before shucking it down, savouring the salty taste. 'Yum,' she said, reaching for another, then stopped as she realised Christophe was staring at her. 'What?'

'Nothing.' There was curiosity in his brown eyes. He'd looked at her the same way when she'd scanned the wine list earlier and excitedly recommended a particular vintage. 'You intrigue me, that's all. You're a bit of a mystery. Tell me more about yourself – where are you from?'

'There's not much to tell,' Daisy said lightly, trying to quell her uneasiness at being scrutinised.

'Really?' He lifted his eyebrows. 'Come on. Everyone has a story to tell.'

'Well, mine's very dull. Just a boring little girl from a suburban backwater, with a good convent education and a desire to get on.'

'Brothers and sisters?'

'Only child,' she said lightly, moving chips of ice about on the oyster plate with her fingertip. She looked up at him from under her lashes. 'And what about you?'

'Me?' He shrugged. 'I'm like you. Perfectly normal. Just your average French Welshman.'

They both laughed.

'So how did you end up at Craven Dalziel?'

'Well, it wasn't my boyhood dream, I admit that. I trained as a pilot actually, and flew professionally for some years. I was a contract pilot, going wherever the work was. Then something happened and . . .' His face darkened and he frowned, gazing down at the table. Daisy went still, sensing he might be about to reveal something about himself, but the moment passed. When he looked up, his usual good humour was restored. 'Anyway, I gave that up. It wasn't right for me. I had a friend who worked at Craven Dalziel and she recommended me for a position there. I got it, not intending to stay very long, and of course I'm still there. But I enjoy it – and it suits me. It's close enough for me to get back to Nant-y-Pren as often as I need to.' Christophe smiled, showing a row of fine white teeth. He buttered some of his bread roll but didn't eat it, putting the pieces back on his plate.

'And . . . the friend?' Daisy asked shyly. 'Is she still at the company?'

'No. She left a while ago. And we're still . . . just friends.' He shot her a look. 'And you? A boyfriend?'

'Me?' She burst out laughing. 'I don't think so!'

'Why not?'

She stared at him, not knowing what to say. How could she have a boyfriend? After all, how could she tell anyone new the truth about herself? And she felt so strange, living in virtual disguise, having to dye her roots dark every few weeks and keep her horrible contact lenses in. 'Well . . .'

'It seems to me you need to have a bit more confidence. You hide away behind those glasses – but I can see that there's a lovely girl underneath. Now,' he said, swiftly changing the subject before Daisy could feel embarrassed, 'let's have a little bit more champagne and discuss how I'm going to break the news of your promotion to Alan.'

The evening came to an end far too soon. Daisy felt on a high, the happiest she'd been for a very long time. Christophe was handsome, funny and interesting, and there was clearly a spark between them. He leaned close to her, gazing at her seriously with those melting brown eyes. Everything about him was delicious and she yearned to be close to him. She longed suddenly to be held, embraced, kissed . . . at the thought, a wave of dizziness swept over her but she managed to hide it and appear normal. By the end of the meal, though, as they sipped their coffee, she could hardly think of anything else but how much she would like him to kiss her.

But how can I? I mean, he's virtually my boss. That didn't seem to matter now they were alone, though. She knew hardly anything about him, but they were so comfortable together – except for that undeniable frisson of electricity that flowed between them, sparking and crackling whenever they got close.

As they left the restaurant, he helped her put her coat around her shoulders and said, 'Come on, I'll walk you home.'

'That would be lovely.' A delicious, quivering sensation stirred in her at his nearness. They began to stroll together through the dark streets, saying very little, both aware of how a couple walking together in the night was usually a romantic occasion.

Outside Daisy's building, they lingered on the pavement to say goodbye.

'You do realise we'll be seeing a lot of each other, don't you?' Christophe said. 'You'll have to report to me every month.'

Daisy nodded, unable to think about anything other than how much she wanted him to envelop her in his arms and put those soft-looking lips on hers. She wondered if she should ask him to come upstairs but she couldn't form the words.

He was staring at her and she was certain she could see desire glimmering in his eyes. She waited, hoping he would do something, step towards her, put out his hand, anything . . . But he turned suddenly and abruptly away. 'Good night, Daphne,' he called back over his shoulder as he strode away. 'Sleep well.'

'Goodnight!' she called after him, and then sighed heavily, shaking off her excitement. As she let herself into the dark hallway, she was overcome suddenly by a terrible sense of loneliness.

But it's for the best. I've got to do this on my own. I knew that when I started.

33

I reckon I could get used to this, Coco thought as she pulled the door of her flat shut and went downstairs. In the hall, she passed the rather grand, white-haired lady who lived on the ground floor, and who came in and out several times a day to walk her ridiculous Pomeranian ball of fluff – sorry, dog – in Green Park. The lady was always immaculate, with coiffed snowy hair, wearing smart jackets with glittering brooches on the lapels, dark trousers and flat shoes with velvet bows on them. Whenever she saw Coco, she stiffened and her coral-lipsticked mouth tightened with disapproval.

'Wotcher, missus,' Coco sang out as she headed for the door. 'Lovely day, innit?'

The old lady said nothing but looked huffier than ever.

Coco giggled as she went out of the front door. It brightened her day a little to piss off her stuck-up neighbour, who was no doubt scandalised by the presence of someone from the wrong side of the tracks. And it didn't take a genius to work out the nature of the arrangement between Coco and Matthew.

Who gives a fuck? she thought defiantly. *Her life's nearly over and she probably had everything given to her on a plate. I've got to work to get anywhere I want to go.*

She pulled her fake-fur coat round her shoulders and walked jauntily on stiletto heels towards Bond Street. So far, the new set-up was suiting her very well: it had been eight weeks since Matthew had installed her in his company flat and she was adjusting to Mayfair life just fine. She loved being away from the noise and dirt and litter of Whitechapel, and the sense of chaos and desperation that pervaded the streets there. Here, she was surrounded by money, and money seemed to keep streets clean, iron railings gleaming, brass polished and everything neat and attractive. Behind the smart Mayfair doors were expensive flats and even more expensive houses, or else they were private clubs, important institutions or discreet businesses – bespoke property consultants, private banks, investment companies, and God only knew what else.

Who gets to have all this? she wondered. *And how do I get it too?*

She wasn't doing too badly though. Matthew had sorted her out a credit card and all the bills were taken care of. She was practically a lady of leisure and was enjoying the unusual sensation of having nothing to do. Soon she'd start putting her plan into action – Matthew would need to be tapped for even more money, but why not? He could afford it and was getting a very nice service in return, coming round virtually every afternoon and quite a few evenings too for plentiful sex, just the way he liked it.

That was the trade-off, of course. She was literally a call girl. When he called, she had to be there, all ready to welcome him in. That was fine for now. After all, what else did she have to offer? What other options were there? She wasn't like the girls she saw all around her in Mayfair: smart girls in black suits with clean neat hair and clever faces, heading off to work every day. They had qualifications, training and, no doubt, loving parents who'd supported them through school and college and made sure their little darlings had the right start in life. Well . . . that hadn't happened for Coco, so no one had better criticise her for trying to get ahead in the only way she could.

She found herself on a smart side street between her place and the shopping Mecca of Bond Street. It was lined with the kind of shops she was becoming familiar with: boutiques and shoe shops with names in chic lettering above the windows. She stopped in front of one and gazed at the dress on the mannequin, suddenly entranced. It was beautiful, an asymmetric, one shouldered style that clung to the body and skimmed the model's plastic thighs. It was covered in hundreds of burnished gold square sequins so that it looked almost like a piece of armour, protection against enemy arrows. Coco stared. She loved it. She wanted it. *And I can have whatever I want, right? I reckon I've earned it.*

She stepped out fifteen minutes later, the dress neatly folded inside the stiff paper carrier bag, and her credit card lighter by four thousand pounds. To celebrate, she went to have a cigarette in Berkeley Square. She was sitting on one of the benches watching people passing by as she smoked when a voice interrupted her.

'Coco? It's you, isn't it?'

She turned to look, instantly on her guard. To her surprise, it was one of the girls who'd danced that night at the Dangerfield party. Sheridan was one of the nicer ones, a sweet-natured girl from Peterborough.

'Yeah, it's me.' Coco wasn't sure if she was glad to see her but managed a smile. 'Hiya. How's it going?'

'Good. I've got a job in a West End show at the moment. It's great. Mind if I join you?'

'Oh. Sure. If you like.' Coco tried to quell a pang of jealousy. Sheridan was doing something she herself would love to do. She glanced down at the bag containing her new dress. She'd give up the credit card and the dress and whatever else in a heartbeat if it meant having a proper dancing career, one with a future. Her life had seemed such fun a moment ago. Now, suddenly, she felt hollow inside.

Sheridan sat down next to her and smiled encouragingly. She was a normal-looking girl, her brown hair pulled back into a pony tail, and unremarkable enough in her shorts, tights and jacket, a bag slung across her front. Coco knew though that once Sheridan was in costume with her hair and make-up done, she could be a smoky femme fatale, or a rosy-cheeked girl-next-door, or whatever she wanted.

'So,' Sheridan said, 'I haven't seen you since that birthday party when you pulled that blinder by locking Haley in the loo.' She laughed. 'God, it was hilarious!'

Coco softened and smiled back. 'I thought you all hated me for it? Haley certainly did.'

'Oh, God, no. Couldn't stand Haley. She totally deserved it, the cow. So . . . what are you doing? Are you going for jobs?'

'Nah. No point.' Coco took a drag on her cigarette and blew out a steady stream of smoke. 'I'm not a trained dancer. No one would hire me.'

Sheridan looked astonished. 'Are you crazy? You were great at the party! We were all knocked out by your performance. You really had *it*.'

Coco looked at her suspiciously to see if she was taking the piss but Sheridan gazed frankly back. So she shrugged. 'Well, I wouldn't know where to start.'

'That's negative thinking,' Sheridan replied wisely. 'Just start by going to some auditions. Buy the *Stage* and turn up. You probably already know most of what you need.' Then she added, 'It's funny I should bump into you like this. I was at the studio yesterday. Roberto's looking for you. Have you changed your number?'

Coco felt a stab of apprehension. 'Yes. I got a new phone. What does he want?'

'I don't know. But he's quite keen to find you. Here, take his number in case you've lost it.' Sheridan reached into her bag and pulled out a scrap of paper and a pen. She scrawled a number and handed it to Coco. 'He'd love to see you.' She stood up. 'Listen, I've got to go. But good luck, OK?'

Coco looked at the paper, then squinted up at the other girl. 'Yeah, thanks. You too.'

Then Sheridan was gone, heading across the square and off to wherever she was going.

Coco stared at Roberto's number. Why on earth would he want to contact her? She was instantly back in the club, back in her old life and everything it meant. She felt her heart start pounding, and her eyes stung as though she was on the point of weeping. She realised that she was afraid to ring Roberto in case he was somehow going to demand she return to the club, to the dingy flat, to everything she was trying to escape.

'I'm not going back to that,' she said to herself through clenched teeth, digging her nails into her palms. 'I can't!'

34

Alan was in the most almighty sulk for the first couple of weeks after Daisy's promotion but he couldn't sustain it for long. He was essentially a good man and part of him must have guessed she had actually saved his job. Before long they were working together well and the hotel was running smoothly. Daisy had more time now to think about something other than work, and one of the first things she did with her pay rise was to move out of her bedsit and into a one-bedroomed flat. She also hired a cleaner, relieved to rid herself of the business of household chores, which she'd never really taken to despite her best efforts.

Nathan had been very depressed to see her go, but had still helped her move, loading up the little second-hand Fiat, which she had recently bought (pushing thoughts of her pink BMW firmly from her mind), with her crates and boxes to make the short journey to the new place, an airy apartment on the first floor of an elegant Regency townhouse in a smart part of Bristol. For the first time in years Daisy was reminded of her old way of life. The area was full of chichi shops, expensive delis and coffee houses. Wealthy girls, students probably, dressed in expensive jeans, deceptively simple tops, boots and sunglasses, were wandering about, racking up credit-card bills in the boutiques or zooming around in sports cars with good-looking men.

That would have been me, Daisy thought, almost with surprise, as she passed them in the street at the weekends. *Carefree. Nothing to do but enjoy myself. No idea of the lives going on all around me.* It seemed almost unbelievable to her now. There was so much to do. When she wasn't in the office, she was working at home. She was concentrating now on the long-term strategy of the Excalibur, and increasing its revenue. The hotel had some excellent facilities that weren't being taken advantage of, and every possible avenue had to be explored and exploited. She had also taken on the entire human resources aspect, managing the payroll, staffing levels and internal disputes. People had quickly grown used to going to her instead of Alan with their problems, forgetting Daisy's relative youth and relieved to find that she had a quick grasp of what they told her and common-sense ways of finding resolutions.

When she wasn't working, Daisy went running (cheaper than a gym membership), occasionally went shopping – although these days she found she preferred vintage and flea-market finds – or went off to the movies on her own. That was when she wasn't poring over business books, reading the *Financial Times* or accessing the foreign newspapers online. Thank goodness she had fluent French, some basic German and Italian, and a decent grasp of Mandarin. Her expensive education was something not even Daddy could take away from her.

The phone on her desk rang and she picked up the receiver with a brisk: 'Hello, Daphne Fraser.'

'Daphne . . . Christophe.'

Her heart sped up and her stomach did a pleasantly lazy flip. 'Hi . . . hi, Christophe.' He was often in contact with her, though it was most often by email, and it was obvious that they were closer than they should be considering that they were business colleagues – and he was her boss. But they were both helpless to resist the attraction between them that grew stronger and stronger every time they met. The atmosphere between them was tense with the suppressed electricity.

'How are you?' he asked.

'Fine . . . and you?'

'I'm well, thanks . . . actually, that's not true. I'm not so good.'

She felt a furry of fear. 'What's wrong?'

'Nothing life-threatening, but I've given my ankle an exceptionally bad twist and I can't drive – or walk very well, come to that. It was a stupid accident while I was at Nant-y-Pren and I've been stuck here ever since. My neighbour got me to the hospital and back, but I can't drive for another week or so. I'm working at home. The thing is – we're due to have a meeting this week.'

'Oh, yes, we are,' she said, unable to hide the disappointment in her voice. She would probably have to meet John Montgomery instead, and miss Christophe for another month. How depressing. In that moment, she realised that her meetings with him were the only bright spots in her life, the only thing she had to look forward to and the only contact with another human that meant anything to her. She felt as though she could cry.

'So I had an idea.' He hesitated. 'Now, feel free to shoot this down if you want to but . . . I wondered if you'd like to come up to Nant-y-Pren and have the meeting here? It's beautiful, I'd love you to see it. You might enjoy the change of scene and . . .' He stopped there, leaving whatever else he was thinking of tantalisingly unspoken.

'That sounds wonderful,' said Daisy, delighted. He'd often spoken of his home in North Wales and it sounded idyllic. 'But . . . when were you thinking?'

'It's a long way to come for an afternoon,' he said, his tone happy. 'Our meeting was scheduled for Friday. Why don't you come up then and stay over till Saturday – or even Sunday if you want to. I'd be glad of the company.'

There was a long pause. Thoughts whirled around Daisy's brain. *I ought to say no. I ought to – I know where this will go, it's bound to but . . . I don't think I can resist* . . . The idea of a weekend with him, just the two of them together, far from where they could be spied on or made the subject of gossip, was too much.

'Yes,' she said in a voice so low it was almost a whisper.

'Good,' he said. 'I'll email you the directions. See you on Friday.'

The little Fiat bumped and jerked along the driveway to Nant-y-Pren House. *It's not made for this kind of terrain,* Daisy thought, glad that the drive was no steeper and that it had not been raining. As the little car made its way around the curve of the road, she saw the house appear. It was very pretty, a two-storey farmhouse with a pitched roof and scallop-edged gables, old brick chimneys leaning slightly off kilter. Its render was painted a soft greeny blue that made it seem to melt into the hills beyond, and it was surrounded by gently decrepit old grey stone walls, overgrown lawns and an orchard with lichen-speckled trees.

It's beautiful, she thought as she drove closer and pulled the car to a halt by the house. Instantly a golden lolloping dog came bounding out, barking. Daisy got out of the car and the dog was beside her, wagging its tail furiously, panting and barking. She stroked it and fondled its soft ears. 'Good girl, you must be Sasha. Hello, Sasha.'

'Hi!'

She looked up to see Christophe come hobbling out of the house towards her, supporting his bandaged ankle with the help of a walking stick.

'Hello, how are you?'

He lifted his stick. 'Still one of the walking wounded, I'm afraid. I see you've met Sasha.'

'Yes, she's lovely.' Daisy stroked the dog's head again.

'She likes you.' Christophe came level with her and leaned over to kiss her cheek, which tingled under the touch of his lips. He looked different here, she thought. Younger and less serious. Happier. 'How was your journey? Give me your bag – no, it's fine, I can carry it, don't worry – come on, come inside.'

He grabbed her overnight bag, hoisting it easily on his shoulder, and they walked together back to the house, Daisy telling him about the journey. She felt

instantly at ease and relaxed, as though a lovely
serenity had descended on her. The farmhouse was
very isolated – there was not another dwelling to be
seen, just a few broken-down outhouses and old farm
buildings – and surrounded by the rolling Welsh hills.
Inside, it was distinctly shabby.

'I need to spend a few months doing the place up,'
he said apologetically as they went into the hall. 'But
there never seems to be the time, and there's no one
here but me.'

'I think it's lovely as it is,' she said, not seeing the
chipped paintwork or the cobwebs in the high corners,
but rather the homeliness of the vintage Welsh rug
on the flagstones and the coats and boots piled
haphazardly beside an old dresser.

'Come through, let's have a cup of tea.' He hobbled
ahead of her, leading the way down a corridor and
through a door that opened into a large light kitchen.
A shiny black range gave out a welcoming warmth
and a plate of scones sat on the large farmhouse table
that dominated the room. 'Sit down.'

He put a copper kettle on the range to heat up.

'It's wonderful here,' Daisy said, her face bright.
The whole house seemed overflowing with comfortable calmness and peace.

'I'm glad you like it,' he said with a smile. 'I just
wish I didn't have this blasted stick, then we could go
for a proper walk.'

'How did you do it?'

'I was down on the old railway line. We've got some
abandoned track in the grounds from when the railway
came across the land years ago. It's quite a nature
reserve down there, and very pretty. Anyway, I tripped

on a bit of old track hidden in the undergrowth and wrenched my ankle. It took me hours to get back to the house.' He grimaced. 'One of the hazards of living alone in a place like this.'

'Thank goodness you managed to get back. You might have died all on your own like that . . .'

'Yes, well, I didn't. So it's all right.' Christophe smiled over at her. He was looking quite different from his usual business-like self, in jeans and a thick dark grey jumper, faded shirt collar poking out from underneath. He looked gorgeous, in fact. She wondered what it would be like to rest her cheek on that jumper and run her hands over him, and inhale his scent, perhaps reach up and nuzzle his neck with her lips . . .

She flushed at her own thoughts and felt suddenly awkward. 'Um . . . right, well, I've brought my report if you want to get started.'

He raised his eyebrows in surprise. 'That's dedicated. Shall we have our tea first? And I don't know about you, but I rather fancy one of those scones with jam. I got them delivered by the postman this morning – he often drops off my supplies.'

'Yes, yes, of course,' Daisy said, feeling more disconcerted than ever. 'Let's do that. Absolutely.'

He laughed and turned back to the kettle just as it was coming to a whistling boil.

They had tea and the delicious scones while they talked, Christophe telling her how he and his sister had inherited the house from their parents, but that his sister now lived in France and came over only once a year or so with her children to visit the old place. Then he took her outside and they walked slowly around the orchard, Christophe limping as little as he could, and he pointed out the places where he used to play as a boy, and where the roof was slipping a little and needed replacing. Daisy was enchanted by everything. The dilapidation added to the beauty as far as she was concerned. Growing up, she had only lived in houses that were kept immaculate, according to Daddy's high standards. Every flower border, every blade of grass, had been perfect. Anything chipped or broken had been thrown away immediately. There had been no sense of history or the gentle passage of time. Daisy couldn't help but find Nant-Y-Pren charming.

'If this were mine,' she said fervently, 'I would never leave it.'

He looked at her intently. 'You really like it?'

'I love it.'

Daisy gazed up at him, smiling. Then, in that instant, the mood changed and she caught her breath. A breeze stirred a strand of her hair and blew it over her face. Christophe leaned over and brushed it away, and she was staring straight into his eyes, which were burning with a strange intensity.

'Daphne,' he said, his voice low.

She couldn't say anything. She could hardly breathe and her throat felt dry. All she could think was that it was here, the moment, it was about to happen whether she wanted it or not . . . *but I do want it, I do.*

Then the most delicious feeling she had ever known swept over her as his lips touched hers. They were cool and dry and soft. Her eyes closed and she instinctively put her head back, returning his kiss, unable to do anything but lose herself in

291

the unbearable sweetness. Her mouth opened under his and then they were tasting each other, as Christophe's arm slid around her back, pulling her close to him. He leaned against the orchard wall so that he could embrace her fully, and she found she was standing on tiptoe, snaking her arms round his neck to make the kiss even deeper. Everything inside her was whirling and she felt amazingly, beautifully alive.

At last, he pulled away and stared into her eyes, looking astonished but happy.

'Oh, dear,' he said ruefully, 'that wasn't supposed to happen. Not here anyway. I had a big seduction routine planned for this evening. Dinner . . . candles . . . soft music . . .'

Daisy laughed. 'But the spontaneous moments are best of all, aren't they?'

'Yes, they certainly are.' Then he kissed her again, slowly and deliciously. He tasted sweet and honeyish and his skin smelled wonderful. When they pulled apart again, he murmured, 'I don't know how long I'm going to be able to wait.'

'Let's not wait,' she breathed. Her insides were so liquid with longing, she wasn't sure how long she'd be able to stand if she weren't able to lean on Christophe.

'Then let's go inside.'

If it hadn't been so romantic, it might have been a little ridiculous, Christophe hobbling with his stick and his bad ankle, the pair of them stopping every few moments to kiss again. It must have taken twenty minutes to get inside and another ten to climb the stairs to Christophe's room, but Daisy didn't mind. As far as she was concerned, it simply heightened the delicious anticipation and the fizzing excitement that was coursing through her body. It was so long since she'd done anything like this, and she was half afraid of it, but the desire overcame everything else and she surrendered to it entirely.

By the time they reached his room, things had grown more intense and serious. They'd stopped giggling and started gasping with pleasure as they became more aware of one another's body and their mutual desire. In the bedroom, they fell together on the large mahogany sleigh bed and immediately Christophe's ankle was forgotten. Now they could concentrate properly and begin to enjoy each other. She helped him pull his jumper over his head and slipped her hands inside his shirt to feel his hard muscular chest, while he caressed her arms and back, and delicately brushed her breasts.

She couldn't think of anything but the delight of being close to him and the wonderful sensation of feeling his warm solid flesh against hers. The sun had moved round the house and the shadows were growing long. Christophe's shoulders were touched with gold and his dark hair glinted when the last rays of sunshine caught it. He moaned softly when Daisy's shirt was unbuttoned, revealing her white silk bra and the soft mounds of her breasts rising from it. He touched them reverently, telling her how beautiful she was. Within a few moments, lying on the rough Welsh blanket, they were both naked in the diminishing afternoon light.

She wanted nothing more than to feel him inside

her and when at last he entered her, she was more than ready, pulling him to her with an elemental hunger. It felt perfect, as though he was made for her and she for him.

'Don't stop,' she begged him. There couldn't be anything better than this, their bodies joined together and moving in harmony, knowing how much pleasure they were giving each other, reading in one another's eyes the astonished wonder and happiness at how right it felt.

Daisy had never known that it could feel like this: she was utterly relaxed with him. He was confident and sure, but alert to every movement and the things that made her sigh with pleasure. She lost all sense of self-consciousness and abandoned herself joyfully to the sensations he was giving her: the rush of bliss she felt when he moved very deep within her, and the excitement that grew greater along with their need for each other.

She almost didn't want the climax that built up inexorably for both of them, it would mean an end to this heavenly moment, but eventually she couldn't resist any longer, and when it came, lifting her up and whirling inside her like a tornado of pleasure, she dug her fingers into his back and surrendered to it with a cry, just as he tensed and came with her.

Afterwards, they lay languidly in each other's arms, enjoying the satisfied pleasure of being together. He was so beautiful, Daisy thought. More beautiful without his clothes than she could have guessed before she'd seen him. How was she going to manage at work now, knowing exactly what lay beneath his suit? And that reminded her . . .

'I suppose I'll have to give you my report later,' she said, her voice replete with fulfilment.

Christophe laughed and dropped a kiss on the top of her head. 'No one can fault your dedication, darling. But how about we wait until we're dressed before you take me through the figures?'

35

'Yes, yes, yes, yes . . . ooooh! Oooooh, right there, babe, yes, keep going . . . please!' Coco began to whimper and shriek. It was quite an effort. 'Yeah, yeah!'

As she'd hoped, her lover began the familiar grunting sound of his approaching climax, thrust furiously into her three times and then collapsed on her with a yelp.

Thank God that's over, she thought, as she stroked his back.

He rolled off her, still panting, plucked some tissues from the box next to the bed and wiped himself. He didn't offer one to her. Part of the new arrangement had included Coco going on the pill and both of them having blood tests. After that, it was unprotected sex.

'Did you have a good time, honey?' Coco asked, stroking his hairy chest.

'Yeah, yeah.' He wasn't meeting her eye properly, seemingly still absorbed by wiping his penis.

'So – are we going out tonight? Didn't you say you were going to take me somewhere nice?'

'Well, actually, Coco, there's been a change of plan.' Matthew scrunched up the tissue and threw it on to the floor. He got up and began to pull on his clothes.

'What?'

'Well . . .'

He was getting dressed at quite a rate, she noticed, pulling on his trousers and shirt as fast as he could. He sat down on the bed for a moment and looked at her. She pulled the sheet up around her bare breasts, feeling suddenly cold.

'I've got some bad news,' he said, his voice brisk and business-like.

'Yeah?'

'I'm afraid our little arrangement has to come to an end.' He had assumed a sorrowful expression that was also furtive, as though he were keen for this to be over so he could get away. 'You're going to have to move out.'

She felt as though a blast of icy air had just engulfed her. Her skin prickled. 'What?' she said, disbelieving.

'It's all over between us, Coco. My company has found out you're living here. One of the neighbours wrote to them to complain. I managed to explain it away but there's no way round it. You've got to go.'

'But . . . but . . .' She sat up straight, panic rushing through her. 'Why don't you just buy another place? Or rent one or something?'

He laughed, and she winced. His face looked suddenly unaccountably ugly, with its close-together eyes, coarse dry skin and a nose reddened by years of company dinners and fine wine. His grey hair was wiry and sparse. 'That's a lovely idea, my sweet, but it's not really practical, for a lot of reasons. Besides, this was

297

never going to last forever, was it? We've had a lovely few weeks, but that's that. Let's end it now while we've still got fond memories of each other.'

She gaped at him, the fear turning to fury. 'What the fuck are you talking about? You think you can just cast me aside like this? You came here knowing you were going to say this, but you fuck me first before you tell me to get back to whatever hole I crawled out of? Fuck that!'

'Come on, Coco, don't be like this . . .' He put out a placatory hand towards her.

'Easy for you to fuckin' say!' she shouted. 'Easy for you, going back to your cushy life and your pathetic wife and your money. What the fuck have I got?'

He looked offended. 'I thought you'd enjoyed yourself,' he said in an injured tone. 'Lots of girls would love a holiday like you've just had.'

She sprang to her feet, her eyes flashing, not caring that she was standing naked before him. 'You fucking prick, is that what you think this is? And I'll just go nice and quiet back to my old life, feeling *grateful*?' She put her hands on her hips, and stared at him. 'Well, I'm not going to. You want me to go, you're going to have to make it worth my while. I want money, or I'm going to tell whoever would be interested about our little arrangement.'

Matthew stood up as well with a stern expression on his face, though he could not quite hide the flicker of admiration in his eyes on seeing her naked form. 'That's blackmail, Coco. It's illegal.'

She snorted. 'So let's go to the fucking police then! You and me together, now! We'll tell them all about it, shall we?'

Pulling on his jacket, he stared at her, his face hard. 'All right. Five grand. I'll give you five grand and it's finished. OK?'

'Ten,' she snapped back.

'Five,' he said in an emphatic tone. 'I'll put five on the credit card. When you get to the end of that, it's finished.' He picked up his briefcase. 'And you have to be out of here by the end of tomorrow. Thanks, Coco, it's been nice. Good luck.'

'Fuck you!' she called after him as he walked to the door. As he disappeared through it, she shouted, 'And you're going to regret treating me like this, you prick!'

36

That weekend at Nant-y-Pren had been idyllic; Daisy wished it would never end. This was surely perfect happiness: the cosy old farmhouse, the dog slumbering on the rug before the fire as she and Christophe lay wrapped in one another's arms. He had made them a delicious dinner and then they'd gone back to bed, this time taking their time, glorying in each other's bodies, the touch of skin on skin, the delicious rightness of their joining together. Daisy had never known anything like it. She felt as though with every second she was blossoming, opening out like a sunflower, and could hardly bear not to be touching him, as though she was drawing strength from his proximity.

On Sunday, after Christophe had cooked them garlicky roast lamb scented with pungent woody rosemary, they had discussed the Excalibur and Daisy's report.

'How's Alan been treating you lately?' Christophe asked. 'Has he forgiven you?'

'Yes.' She grinned. 'Just about. He thinks he's a

tiger but he's really a pussy cat.' Unbidden, an image of Daddy floated into her mind. That was a man she had been truly afraid of all her life, she knew that now. Realising that not all men were as powerful and controlling as her father had been had made her able to reconsider her relationship with him and her role of slavish adoration. *Of course I loved him. I was terrified of what would happen if I didn't! It wasn't healthy. And what did his love count for in the end? When I wasn't what he wanted, he tossed me aside like a piece of rubbish.*

The bitterness she felt when she thought this was so strong, and her determination to get back at him so overpowering, she tried not to think about it too often. It would send surges of adrenaline racing through her, making her fingers tremble and her breath ragged. It was better to shut it out.

After discussing the month's figures, Daisy had confided her plan to request money from Craven Dalziel for an overhaul of the hotel's fabric. 'No matter how good our service is, we look a bit shoddy and nothing can change that. The bathrooms are spotless, the towels clean, but cracked tiles and stained grouting look bad – that's all there is to it. We need a bit of a makeover.'

'I agree,' Christophe said, nodding. 'I think we'd be very interested in seeing what you come up with and looking at some figures. And I like the way your function bookings are up.' He lifted her hand to his lips and kissed it idly as he continued scanning the results. 'It was our lucky day when you came to the Excalibur.'

'Mine too,' she said softly, 'mine too.'

* * *

Back at work on Monday, people seemed to notice that she had a spring in her step and a flush on her cheeks. Someone asked her if she'd been on holiday, and another if she'd been on a sunbed. One of the receptionists said slyly that Daisy looked as though she was in love, and Daisy had flushed violently as they all cackled with laughter at her discomfort.

Am I in love? she wondered. If she wasn't, then it was something very like it. She felt full of unaccustomed happiness and sometimes experienced a delightful jolt as she recalled some moment of blissful ecstasy with Christophe. He sent her an email on Monday and called her that evening. They didn't talk about the business once.

This must be a relationship, she thought giddily. *A proper one.* He was so different from Freddie – a man, not a boy – and that made being with him more serious than anything she'd ever known before. Besides, she couldn't stop craving him, feeling a need to be physically close to him that was like a desperate thirst or rabid hunger.

It was gorgeous and glorious and yet dangerous as well. After all, Christophe thought he was involved with Daphne Fraser, the little nobody from Bristol. He had no idea of Daisy Dangerfield's existence.

They soon fell into a routine: on Friday night she would climb into her little Fiat and zoom northwards, towards the green and brown mountains of North Wales, arriving nearly four hours later when night had fallen and the farmhouse windows glowed like golden beacons against the black shadows of the hills beyond. Once his ankle had healed and he'd returned to Cheltenham, Christophe tried to leave early on Fridays so that he could be at the house before her, with supper cooking and the fire warm and bright by the time she arrived.

Those weekends were heaven. When they weren't in bed, they were striding out across the hills, with Sasha bounding along beside them, and the landscape turned from its bright spring colours to the deeper, richer hues of summer. Where once they went out in coats, boots and warm jumpers, now they were walking in tee-shirts and sunglasses, carrying bottles of water.

But Daisy couldn't help being aware of the dark secret at the heart of their relationship. It might seem perfect but she knew that it was based on a lie – one that kept growing bigger the longer they knew each other and the more Christophe wanted to know about her. His idle questions about her childhood and family led her to spin a story of a life she had never had, and she was terrified in case she forgot something she had told him and said something different next time. She bought a little notebook that she kept with her to record in it all the things she said to him: the names of her fictional parents, their jobs, where they lived. She even had to record the names of her made-up school teachers and best friends from her schooldays. Sometimes, at night, lying in Christophe's arms and listening to the slow rise and fall of his breathing, she would stare in to the blackness wishing with all her heart that she hadn't started wading into this morass of lies, but she had no idea how to retreat from it. If only she'd said that her parents were dead, but before she and Christophe had got together, she'd told him that her father was a retired headmaster and that her parents lived in a comfortable house in Hampshire

303

where he played golf while her mother gardened. It had seemed like a perfectly safe explanation at the time, but lately he had been dropping hints about meeting them and asking if Daisy had told them about him.

'Yes, yes,' she'd said irritably. 'But they're miles away. I don't want to share you with anyone right now. Can we just drop it?'

Christophe had looked surprised at her sharp tone. 'OK, sweetheart, whatever you say. There's no rush.' He leaned in to kiss her. 'I don't want to share you with anyone either, truth be told. Let's keep the outside world at bay for just a little longer.'

As time wore on and autumn arrived, she knew she wouldn't be able to keep the lie going forever and wild ideas began to take shape: could she kill them off? Pretend they'd both been killed in a car crash? But . . . a funeral . . . how on earth could she arrange that? And anyway, she couldn't manufacture that kind of grief and suffering, it would be a terrible thing to do. She wondered if she could hire a couple of actors to play her parents and stage an afternoon with Christophe that would get him off her back for a while, but she could see that would lead to more problems. She'd have to hire the same people over and over whenever it was necessary to have them on the scene. No, she would just have to put him off for as long as possible – and then, when she was sure that they were going to last, she would tell him the truth.

It was difficult to imagine sharing her secret with anyone but perhaps it would be a relief. Maybe he would even be able to help her. The idea of actually being able to talk about everything she had been through seemed at first frightening and then appealing. She would do it soon, she decided. If she and Christophe lasted a year, then she would find a way to confess. And meanwhile, she had to continue her deceptions, writing down her lies in her little notebook so that she didn't forget them.

37

Coco found a small hotel in Victoria where there were lots of places offering cheap rates to tourists, travellers and backpackers. Her room was cramped and noisy, enormous coaches rumbling past her window every few minutes and the chatter of tourist parties on the pavement below, but she didn't care. She didn't intend to stay very long if she could help it.

After all, she only had five grand. She had to get going or she'd run out of money in no time.

The first day she spent fuming, cursing Matthew's name and planning various revenges, before calming down and telling herself not to waste her time. The main thing now was how she was going to get on. Matthew was history, over. She would cut him out of her life and not give him another thought – just as she had always done when something caused her pain. Besides, she'd been using him as much as he'd been using her, she knew that much. She had to shrug her shoulders and think of something else to be getting on with.

On the second day, she took a walk around some

of the dancing joints in the area, but every time she went to ask if they needed an experienced girl, something would prevent her and she'd stop short in front of the entrance, staring at the pictures of the girls in their sparkling bikinis and heavy make-up, before eventually turning away and walking off. That was a life she never wanted to go back to.

She was sitting in a café, nursing a coffee and searching for a lighter so she could have a fag, when she found a scrunched-up piece of paper in her pocket. She opened it and saw Sheridan's handwriting. It was Roberto's mobile number. She blinked at it for a moment. She had decided not to call him right away and then forgotten about him. Was he still looking for her? And why?

She pulled her mobile out of her pocket. No harm in finding out. He answered at once.

'Roberto – it's me. Coco.'

'Coco! Babes! I can't believe it, where the hell have you been?' He sounded ecstatic that she'd called.

It was nice to hear his voice again. She'd put him out of her mind when she was living her swanky life in Mayfair but now she realised that she'd missed him. 'I've heard you've been trying to get in touch.'

'Honey, I've been spreading the word through every club and dance studio for weeks, once I realised your old mobile number was no good. Absolute blank. You vanished, darling.'

'But why the hell do you want to see me so much?' Coco asked. She'd guessed that he wanted to tempt her back to the club – but had she really been that valuable a girl to them? There were plenty like her, surely.

'I don't want to say over the phone,' he said mysteriously. 'Let's meet. Where are you?'

She walked into the pub in Waterloo, looking about for her old friend and then saw him perched on a high stool with a pint of lager on the bar next to him. He'd shaved his head to a dark fuzz over his scalp and was wearing a Gucci jacket and white jeans.

'You look exactly like a dancing queen,' she said jokily as she came over. 'Anyone given you your own reality show yet?'

'Teaser!' he said, jumping up to give her two big kisses. He stood back to look at her, his blue eyes bright. 'You look fab, darling, *of course*. Mayfair obviously suits you. Now, let's get you a drink and we'll go out to the terrace.'

When they were settled in the pub's back yard, bordered on one side by rows of huge metal beer barrels and on the other by a rickety wooden fence, Coco asked again why he'd wanted to find her.

'It's not me so much, hon, though it's a pleasure to see you, of course.' He gave her a saucy look over the rim of his glass as he took a sip, clearly relishing the suspense. 'It's *them*.'

'Them? Who's them?'

Roberto pulled the expression of one who knows a really juicy bit of gossip. '*They*, my darling, are the people who want to find you . . .'

'We're going round in circles here,' she said curtly, wanting him to get to the point.

'Baby,' Roberto declared, throwing out one hand theatrically, 'your ship might just have come in. I know you're busy living it up with your lover boy, but you might want to think again when I tell you about this little gig.'

She snorted contemptuously. 'Forget that piece of shit! He's off the scene now.'

'Oh.' Roberto looked sympathetic. 'Sorry to hear that, babe. But maybe that's all for the best because . . .' He raised his eyebrows tantalisingly, obviously enjoying keeping her on tenterhooks.

'Spit it out,' Coco said warningly, 'or else . . .'

'Remember that party – your great *pièce de résistance* when you took Haley's place?'

'Of course.'

'Well, it wasn't just your man in the West End who liked your act.'

'No?'

'Nope.' Roberto smiled broadly. 'Guess who?'

'I'm not in the mood for playing games, Roberto. Just tell me or I'll get up and go.'

'You wouldn't do that. You're too interested, and I don't blame you because it was only . . .' Roberto paused for effect and then, when he could see that Coco was on the verge of losing her temper, said with a flourish: 'It was only birthday boy himself!'

'Oh.' Coco was taken aback. She thought back to the night of the party, remembering her brief intro-duction to the man whose party it was. He had seemed rather taken with her, and then sent her that birthday card and the money. She recalled him: a solid man, with a tan-and-dye job to conceal his age. Perhaps he'd once been attractive, a long time ago, but it was hard to see it now; eyes that might once have been fiercely handsome were now deep-set in pouches of skin, the eyebrows above overgrown. But . . . there had been the unmistakable aura of power around him. 'What does he want?' she said at last.

'Who knows? But he's probably not after a chat about the state of the commodities market. Anyway, he wants to see you pretty bad. His assistant has been calling virtually every day to see if I've found you. They couldn't reach you on your old number so they called me.'

Coco frowned. She hunched over slightly, running her fingers through her peroxide hair which was now in need of a good touch up at the roots. 'But I don't understand. He could find any girl if that's all he's after.'

Roberto leaned in to her so that she could see every dark grain of stubble on his face. 'He doesn't want any girl, does he? He wants the girl in the red sequins who sang like a screen siren and shook her booty like Beyoncé, don't he? You're the girl of his dreams and he's not going to give up until he's got you.' He leaned back, smirking. 'And that, babe, has got to be worth a lot of money. Congratulations! You've hit the jackpot, love. Just remember your old friend Roberto when you're dripping in diamonds, that's all!'

Coco laughed. 'Yeah, right,' she said. But despite her outward insouciance, she felt a flicker of excitement. When one door closes, another one opens . . . Maybe this was fate stepping in to give her a helping hand. 'Wanna go and have a fag? I'm bloody desperate.'

38

'Can you talk?' Christophe's voice came crackling down the line. Daisy was out of the hotel for once, walking through town on her way back from visiting wholesale fabric merchants. She'd submitted her ideas for the redesign of the Excalibur to the Craven Dalziel directors, and while they considered the overall concept, she was working on the details. She'd recruited a designer to help her but had got involved in every aspect, down to sourcing fabrics and negotiating a massive discount for buying in bulk. Every penny she saved would make her proposal more attractive, after all. The larger the return in proportion to the investment, the better. Daisy was confident that her new look would be a hit with customers, particularly business people, who wanted cleanliness, a decent level of comfort, and plain modern styling along with good Wi-fi and media access.

'Yes,' Daisy said. Her fingers felt chilled just holding her mobile to her ear. The temperature had taken a sudden dive and the grey skies were heavy with the promise of snow. Shop windows were festooned in

Christmas decorations and people were muffled in scarves and hats. 'What's up?'

'I've got some good news. I won't tell you now, though. Listen, it's the directors' Christmas dinner tonight. Would you come as my guest? I can tell you then.'

Daisy didn't know what to say for a moment, then she ventured, 'But they'll all know we're together.'

'They'll have to sooner or later, won't they? Besides, you'll understand more later.'

'All right. Yes, I'd love to.' Daisy's eye was caught by a boutique with a sweeping evening dress displayed in the window. 'You could have given me a bit more notice! Goodness knows what I'll wear. I'd better take the afternoon off and go shopping.'

The dinner was held in a stunning Cotswolds hotel in a village outside Cheltenham. It had once been a Tudor manor house but was now a sumptuous place to stay.

'This is wonderful,' Daisy said, eyeing up the luxurious country-house style with its rich fabrics, beautiful antiques and immaculate finish. 'I love what they've done here.'

'Yes,' Christophe said, walking beside her as they went through the foyer and into the library where pre-dinner drinks were being served. 'This is one of ours, actually. We've just acquired it from the previous owner. He had three hotels, all beautifully done like this one, but hasn't been able to make them work. We're very hopeful, though.' He smiled at her. 'I'm glad you like it.'

Christophe looked amazingly handsome in his

dinner suit and black tie. Daisy felt a shiver of lust just looking at him, and when he leaned closer and murmured how gorgeous she looked tonight, the buzz of his voice in her ear sent waves of electricity over her skin.

'Thank you. I wanted to look my best for you.' She'd bought a midnight blue velvet cocktail dress that showed off her slim but voluptuous figure. She'd also splashed out on a pair of black heels, fifties-style, with a hidden platform and a black glittering buckle on the front.

'This is beautiful,' Christophe said, looking admiringly at the jewellery she'd pinned to her dress, at the neckline between her breasts. 'Is it real?'

'Oh, no!' she said airily, and glanced down at it. 'Just a piece of paste I found in a junk shop.' *Perhaps lying to Christophe has become second nature,* she thought wistfully. The brooch was anything but fake, although she could hardly admit that. A girl like Daphne Fraser would be unlikely to own a vintage Van Cleef & Arpels design set with a small fortune in diamonds. She'd thought hard before taking it out of the box where she kept it, but tonight had seemed the right occasion. It sparkled on the dark blue velvet, sending out glints of multi-coloured light; the one thing of real value she'd taken from her old life.

In the library, a roaring fire gave the room a comforting glow and the swags of ivy and holly wreaths, along with a sparkling Christmas tree in the corner, made everything very festive. The Craven Dalziel directors and their guests stood about, talking and sipping glasses of hot rum punch, mulled wine or egg nog. As soon as he spotted Daisy and Christophe, John

Montgomery came over, looking distinguished in his dinner jacket.

'Daphne, hello. How lovely to see you. Happy Christmas.'

'Thank you, John,' she said rather shyly. She hadn't seen much of him since his last visit to the Excalibur and was aware that he must be clocking the fact that she and Christophe were now a couple.

'You've done some excellent work lately, we've all been delighted with the way you've turned things round at the Excalibur.' He smiled encouragingly at her. 'Has Christophe told you the good news?'

Christophe grinned. 'Not yet. Why don't you, John?' He turned to Daisy, his eyes bright with happiness.

Daisy looked at John, who smiled again.

'Young lady, we like your plans for the Excalibur very much. In fact, we don't see any point in refurbishing just one of our hotels in the way you suggest. We've decided to roll your vision out across all our town-centre and airport hotels.'

Daisy gasped, hardly able to believe it. What an incredible vote of confidence in her ideas. 'Oh, that's marvellous!'

'And that's not all. We'd also like you to take charge of the project. But that will mean a promotion and leaving the Excalibur. You'll need to think about it. We wouldn't need you to start till after Christmas in any case.'

'I'm sure I'll want to do it,' Daisy put in hastily, elated at the news.

'I like your enthusiasm. Come in and see me in the New Year and we'll discuss it then.' John raised his glass to her. 'Here's to you, Daphne, and a very Happy

Christmas. Now I must mingle, but no doubt I'll see you later. And Christophe . . . it's good to see you with a guest at last.'

As he left, Daisy, pink-cheeked but delighted, turned to Christophe almost accusingly. 'You knew! And you didn't tell me!'

'I wanted it to be as official as possible,' he protested, laughing. 'So you didn't think it was just me who considers you extremely talented. Congratulations, darling,' he said, putting his arm around her and dropping a kiss on her cheek. 'You totally deserve it.'

After the dinner, a lavish four-course affair in the hotel's private dining room, there was dancing to a band. On the dance floor they clung together, their desire for one another growing stronger the longer they stayed. Christophe ran his hands along the smooth velvet of her gown, taking in the curves of her waist and hips, while Daisy put her arms around him, slipping them under his jacket so that she could feel the warmth of his skin through his shirt. They danced staring up into one another's eyes, each seeing the promise within, until Christophe said, 'Let's go outside and get some air.'

They took their wine glasses out to the terrace where it was icy cold but refreshing after the humidity inside. They kissed for a while, laughing about the general drunkenness inside and the comical displays of dancing.

'What a fabulous evening,' Daisy said, feeling a little tipsy after several glasses of very good wine. She was filled with happiness. Her promotion meant that every-thing was proceeding perfectly. And now she had

Christophe too. He hadn't been part of the plan but he was the most marvellous bit of it all. 'Thank you for bringing me.' She studied his handsome face. He looked rather brooding in the half light. 'What did John mean earlier when he talked about you bringing a guest?'

'Oh. That.' Christophe frowned, his expression solemn. 'I thought you might ask – and I decided that if you did, I would tell you. Do you remember I said once that I was a pilot? Well, the reason I stopped was because . . .' His face darkened and he looked choked. There was a long pause and then he continued. 'There was a terrible accident when I was at the controls. I had my own plane then, a small four-seater, and I was flying home for Christmas when I suffered from something called spatial disorientation.'

Daisy stayed silent, realising that he was confiding something very significant to her.

He looked away again, staring out into the night. 'I was travelling in darkness and I had no sense of the external horizon. Without that, the senses can become very confused. You don't know if you are turning left or right, or even if you're upside down. I was reading my instruments, of course, but it happened so fast, and I had no clue . . .' His voice broke on the word. Daisy put a hand on his arm to offer what comfort she could. 'I couldn't believe what I was reading, I was convinced I was at a safe altitude. I wasn't. We hit a forest in Normandy at speed and . . . and Hélène, my girlfriend, was killed.' He drew in a deep breath and released it. 'I was taken out of the wreckage unconscious and with severe injuries. It took me a long while to recover from them, but I haven't ever

316

recovered from what happened to Hélène. I blamed myself, of course, and I've never flown again. I've never been able to open up to anyone about it.' He turned back to look at her. 'Until now.'

'Oh, Christophe,' she said in a low voice. 'Oh, darling. You've suffered so much. I'm so sorry. What happened to Hélène was tragic, but it was an accident.' She put her arms around his neck, and kissed him. 'I love you,' she whispered.

He returned her kiss, slowly at first and then more passionately. In unspoken agreement, they left the party and went upstairs to Daisy's room, stopping along the way to kiss intensely while she pulled off his bow tie and began to unbutton his dinner shirt. The power of Christophe's story had heightened their desire, each feeling desperate for the other as soon as possible, needing the connection and the passion at once. They stumbled into the dimly lit hotel room, slamming the door behind them and falling on the bed, so eager for each other they could hardly wait. Christophe was hard already, his cock pressing against his trousers and eager to be free. He pushed Daisy's dress up and made an appreciative noise at the sight of her thighs with their lacy stocking tops. She was wearing hold-ups with no knickers.

'God, I'm glad you didn't tell me that you didn't have any underwear on,' he said in a voice that rasped with lust. 'I don't think I could have lasted through dinner.'

She laughed and tried to pull him to her, but he said, 'Wait. You look delicious.'

He sank down and began to cover her mound with kisses. She pulled in a sharp breath. The touch of his

317

lips was electric and she couldn't help her knees from falling slightly apart to allow him greater access. She could feel every nerve responding to him as the blood rushed to her pussy and made her feel as if her very heart was beating there. He began to explore her with his tongue as he ran his hands along her legs and up to the curve of her waist. She gasped again as he licked the hard bud of her clitoris, making her stomach contract with pleasure and waves of sensation flood out along her body. He began to tease it with his tongue, until he was making her shudder with delight and longing. She half wanted him to stop and half feared he might, but when he pulled away from her and began to kiss her mouth, devouring her with need, she knew that was what she wanted too.

He pulled down the zipper of her dress and slid it down her body so that she was only wearing her black lacy bra and the hold-ups. Unable to take his eyes off her, he quickly stripped off the rest of his evening clothes and returned to her soft belly and the inviting mounds of her breasts with a murmur of pleasure. She reached down to touch his cock: it was ramrod stiff and, at the touch of her fingers, he moaned. She grasped it, feeling the heat emanating from it, and stroked it. She loved it, it felt almost as much hers as his, theirs to share.

'I can't wait,' Christophe murmured in her ear. He nibbled her earlobe. 'You're too tempting . . .'

She kissed him hard and guided him towards her. He moved between her thighs and hesitated for just a moment, the head of his cock pressing tantalisingly at her entrance. She sighed with longing, and wrapped her arms around his strong back. He pressed in, pushing up deep inside her and making her throw back her head with the pleasure of feeling him fill her up. 'Christophe,' she said, her voice caressing his name as she said it.

'My darling . . .' He kissed her neck and shoulders and lips as he moved slowly inside her.

I don't want this ever to stop, she thought, high on the sensations he was producing within her. She wanted to make love to him all night long. After all, they had no need to hurry. There were hours to spend luxuriating in each other's body and the pleasure they could give one another, just the two of them, sighing and moving as one in the darkness.

39

'Welcome, Miss Hughes. This way, please.'

Coco followed the maid across the marble-floored hallway and down a flight of stairs carpeted in thick beige wool pile. This house was incredible. She might be a Londoner but she certainly didn't know this part of town, where terraces of huge white stucco mansions overlooked private gardens. She could tell it took a great deal of money to live in a place like this.

The maid showed her to a seat outside a closed door. 'Could you wait here, please? Miss Anderson will see you soon. Can I get you something? Tea, coffee, water?'

'Nah, I'm fine.' Coco sat down and fidgeted nervously as she looked about her. It was all done expensively: the deep, well-cushioned chair, the gilt-legged side table, the paintings in gilded frames on the walls. Spotlights glowed discreetly in the ceiling while small table lamps cast a warmer light over side tables.

Five minutes later, the door beside Coco opened and a woman stepped out. She was in her late-forties, by the look of it, with dark hair pulled neatly back, a striking white streak at the front and ribbons of silver visible amid the black. She was wearing a navy suit with a smart white silk shirt and flat pumps. Her face seemed curiously unlined, as though years of showing no expression had left her unusually youthful. Coco recognised her as the woman she had met at the party, the one who had taken her details. 'Miss Hughes? How nice to see you again. I'm Miss Anderson. This way, please.'

Coco stood up and followed her into the office. Her nerves flickered into life again and she felt a little sick. The room beyond was incredibly neat and minimalist. There was little to be seen on the polished black shelves or the perfectly tidy desk. Miss Anderson gestured her to sit down while she took her own place in the chair behind the desk. When they were both settled, she folded her hands together and stared at Coco with a faint smile.

'So, Miss Hughes. At last we've found you.' Her voice was low and almost musical but like her face, it had no expression.

'Yeah. Here I am!' Coco said brightly.

'I suppose you're wondering why you're here.'

'Oh, I've got a fair idea.'

The other woman raised her eyebrows. 'You have?'

'Yeah.' Coco nodded, jiggling one of her knees. She'd already worked it all out for herself. Well, it didn't exactly take a genius. So she'd dressed carefully for the part, in a skin-tight black leather mini-skirt, a gauzy, leopard-print top over a black bra, and some high boots that laced up to her knees. She'd hoped she'd covered all the bases: sexy with a hint of some possible bondage or mild S&M, if that was what he liked.

'Do tell,' Miss Anderson pressed.

'Well – it's obvious, innit? Your boss saw me at the party and he fancies a bit.' She shrugged. 'Fair enough. But if you're handling arrangements, then I have to say that I've been fucked over before and I want to make sure it's all clear beforehand. I don't want to be kicked back into the gutter again, all right?'

'Ah, I see.' Miss Anderson smiled a small joyless smile. 'You have made the assumption that my employer wants you as a personal plaything. A toy, an indulgence, a *maîtresse*. You are hoping, perhaps, for the traditional trappings that come with such a position, such as fur coats, jewellery and silk pyjamas. I'm very sorry, but I'm afraid you're going to have put that right out of your mind.'

'Oh.' Coco stared at her, puzzled. *Why does she talk like that? A mattress? Bloody hell, what's she on about?*

'In a short while, I will take you to meet my employer, Mr Dangerfield, but first there are a few things I must explain to you.' Miss Anderson leaned towards her, her blue eyes suddenly flashing a warning. 'What I'm about to tell you is a secret. It must remain entirely confidential, do you understand? I have here a letter that you must sign – it is a confidentiality agreement. Any sign that you have broken this agreement and . . . well, you will regret it. I'll say no more than that.'

'Uh-huh.' Coco nodded, though inside she was scornful. *What does this bitch know about anything? I've heard some threats in my time and I ain't scared of much.* But she was curious now. If she wasn't being asked to provide sex for that gruesome old man, then what did they want from her? And why were they about to entrust her with some secret?

Miss Anderson produced the letter and Coco signed it, scanning it first though she didn't understand much as it was written in long words and legal-sounding language.

'Good,' Miss Anderson said, filing it away in her desk drawer. 'Now. A few things you have to know before you meet Mr Dangerfield. He is a complicated man, but brilliant. A genius in his way. He is the son of Josef Dangerfield, who founded a very successful property and hotel business, beginning by buying bomb-sites in the south of London and building on them. That business is now a world-wide property empire and Mr Dangerfield oversees it. Such responsibility is a great burden for any man, though my employer carries it magnificently. However, he demands certain things from everyone in his life: utter loyalty is the main one. He needs total understanding too. Is that clear?'

'Yeah.' Coco shrugged. Who cared what the old bastard needed? It wasn't her problem.

Miss Anderson stood up and began to pace about the room as she talked. 'Mr Dangerfield has two children, a son and a daughter. Years ago, he fell out badly with both of them because of their unreasonable behaviour. There has been little, if any, contact since, although he has made it his business to be aware of what they are doing. His daughter, Sarah, is following a blameless enough path. She has married – and broken her father's heart by not inviting him to the wedding – and now lives in the country as a wife and mother. His son Will, however, is a different matter altogether. Will is a devious character. He has made sure that his movements are not so easy to follow. But we know where he lives and what he does – and, much like his father, he has shown marked talent in the arena of business. He has founded his own company and appears to be enjoying some success. But word has come to us that Will has certain plans. He has written letters to family lawyers that have caused us concern, and my employer feels it is important that we learn more about his motives and way of thinking.'

Miss Anderson stopped her pacing by the large window that looked over the garden in the square outside and stared out for a few moments.

Coco watched her and then said slowly, 'So it's not him, is it? It's not the old bloke. You want me to get to know his son.'

Miss Anderson turned back to her. 'Yes. You're quick. That's a good sign, I suppose. I'll speak frankly, Miss Hughes. I don't approve of this arrangement. I think we could hire a professional to undertake this job. But my employer has decided on you, and so you it must be, no matter how difficult that makes matters. I warn you that once you meet Mr Dangerfield, you will not be able to back out of this arrangement, so think carefully before you consent to see him.'

Oh, speak English, can't you? Coco thought irritably. 'Yeah, all right. I get it. You'd better tell me what you have in mind then, hadn't you?'

She listened as Miss Anderson began to outline the whole, extraordinary scheme.

Thirty minutes later, she was upstairs being shown into a grand study, plush with damask curtains, walnut lowboys, bronze busts, oil paintings and brass fittings. Her eye was caught by three stuffed fox heads over the fireplace, their sharp white teeth bared and their glass eyes staring at her. They were creepy, all right, but she didn't look at them for long. Behind a giant Victorian desk sat the old man Coco had seen at the party, his artificially black hair glinting in the lamplight. He looked different from how she remembered him, slimmer and with fewer wrinkles. The pouches that had surrounded his eyes had disappeared and the skin around them was unusually tight-looking and several shades lighter than the rest of his walnut-coloured face, creating a panda-like effect. His forehead was smooth and shiny, reflecting the lamplight with its tautness. He stood up as she came in, a welcoming smile on his face and a look of relief in his eyes. Miss Anderson urged her forward and then lingered at the door, watching.

'My dear,' he said warmly, coming out from behind his desk. His suit was baggy on him, as though he had only recently lost weight. He reached out a hand covered in thick ropey blue veins, and Coco took it. He shook hands with her vigorously. 'Yes! You're the one. The very girl. That magical, talented, beautiful girl. What an honour.'

Maybe he's not so bad after all, Coco thought, smiling back at him. 'Hiya.'

'Has Margaret explained what we require from you? Are you happy to do this job for me? It is very important, you know.' He looked at her seriously but kindly, as a parent might at a child.

'Yeah, she's told me all about it.'

'Do you think you can do it?' he asked anxiously.

For that money, I'd climb Mount Bloody Everest in the fuckin' buff. 'Yeah. Sure. No problem.' She smiled at him, giving him the full treatment. 'You bet. Honestly, it'll be straightforward. Easy as pie.'

He thumped the desk, frightening her for a moment until she saw that he was smiling gleefully. 'I knew it! I *knew* you were the girl! You've been on my mind ever since that night . . . the night of my wonderful party. Something told me you were going to reappear in my life and play an important part. And you and I share the same birthday too – I was struck by the coincidence. Excellent! Wonderful. Let's celebrate. Margaret – tell Finola to bring in a bottle of champagne, the best vintage we've got. We need to toast the future and everything that this splendid girl is going to do for us.'

He grinned at Coco, who returned another shining smile. *Roberto was right. This is a real stroke of luck. A few weeks of doing whatever, and then I'll be a free agent, and doshed up too. Perfect.*

40

Daisy was determined that Christmas at Nant-y-Pren was going to be the best ever. She had spent the last few Christmases by herself, trying not to think about how alone in the world she was. She'd coped by ignoring it as much as she could, treating it like a normal day, resolutely walking past carol singers and shutting out decorations and lights. Perhaps that was why, this time, she went a bit overboard, wanting to make the perfect Christmas. She'd taken all the arrangements in hand, from ordering the huge tree for the hallway of Christophe's house, to arranging for hampers of luxurious food. It was a little taste of the old days as she made sure there was foie gras, champagne, Belgian chocolates, cheeses and charcoal biscuits, the finest Christmas cake, a pudding, melting mince pies, and a whole side of smoked salmon. That was on top of the turkey she'd ordered, though she asked Christophe if he would be able to cook a Christmas meal.

'Yes, of course. Why, can't you?'

'Hadn't you noticed?' she said jokily.

'Well . . .' He frowned. 'Now you come to mention it, I suppose you don't cook very much.'

'No. I can't,' she said lightly. 'Nothing complicated anyway.'

'Didn't your mother teach you? Didn't you learn anything at school?'

'No. Now can we drop it, please?'

So they agreed that Christophe would cook all the food if Daisy arranged the delivery of whatever was needed. She consulted all the festive features in newspapers and magazines to make sure that nothing was forgotten. She also spent some happy hours browsing shops and websites for gifts for Christophe, ordering him cashmere gloves and walking socks, a pair of extremely expensive binoculars that she knew he would love, a pile of books, music, and gold cufflinks engraved with his initials. It was a little extravagant, she knew that, but she couldn't resist. And besides, for once she was using her own money. Her promotion at Craven Dalziel, which she fully intended to accept when she visited John Montgomery in the new year, would surely mean another pay rise, and she was living well within her means now. It was a source of enormous pride that all the money she was spending she had earned, not a handout or an allowance but the proper reward for her efforts.

The excitement began when she arrived on Christmas Eve, the car stuffed with goodies including a box of tree decorations she'd bought that afternoon. It was pitch black by the time she reached the house, but Christophe had the fires lit, the radio piping out carols from King's College, and wine mulling on the range. It was like something from a dream, she thought, as they festooned the huge pine tree with baubles and glittering fairy lights, stopping every now and then to sip hot spiced wine or to nibble a mince pie. Then the presents went under the tree – lots more for Christophe than he had for her, but Daisy didn't mind. She'd wrapped a few little treats for herself anyway: some Trevellyan Moroccan rose bath oil and a gorgeous printed silk scarf she'd ordered online from Noble's department store in London.

'I'm so excited!' she cried, eyes shining as she stood back and looked at the wonderful tree. She clapped her hands with delight.

'I can tell.' He came over and hugged her. 'You're like a little girl. It's really sweet.'

'Not such a little girl,' she said, kissing him. 'I'm just happy. I love Christmas when it's done properly.'

'How about sharing a little Christmas present right now, huh?' he murmured, kissing her neck gently.

'Mmm . . . I'd love it . . .' she said huskily.

He led her through to the sitting room, toasty warm from the fire and with two red stockings hanging up beneath a merry garland of holly on the mantelpiece, and made slow and delicious love to her on the soft rug by the hearth.

The next day Daisy woke early, feeling excited, and switched on the light. 'Merry Christmas, darling!' She reached down for the stocking she'd brought up and filled the night before. 'Here's your stocking!'

'What time is it?' groaned Christophe, opening one bleary brown eye. 'I shouldn't have had Father Christmas's whisky last night.'

'Don't tell me that,' she said, shoving him lightly, 'you'll spoil the magic. Here – now, where's mine?'

He leaned over and passed her the stocking he'd filled for her, and they spent a happy half hour opening small gifts, then Christophe went back to sleep while Daisy happily munched on chocolate coins and read the book he'd given her. After she'd showered, she put on a smart black silk shirt dress belted at the waist, then opened the little jewellery box she'd brought with her and took out her brooch. She examined it for a moment, wondering whether to wear it. She always felt a connection with her mother when she did because it had been meant for her; that was why she had taken the risk of smuggling it out in her bra all those years ago. And it was her insurance. If all her money went, she would still have this as her bulwark against disaster. Although she hoped it would never come to that.

It's Christmas – I'll wear it, she thought. Taking it out of the box, she pinned it on the breast of her dress, below the collar. It glittered there, its many diamonds shimmering in the filigree setting. She looked at her reflection. She'd let her severe bob grow out a little recently, though it was still dyed dark and the fringe still covered her forehead. She put her glasses on. They were so familiar now that she felt undressed without them, and even forgot that she didn't need them. Sometimes, when she wasn't wearing them, she felt as if her vision was blurred. *Funny, the power of the mind,* she thought.

She went downstairs. When Christophe came down a little later, she was already preparing scrambled eggs for breakfast.

He came to give her a kiss. 'Hello, gorgeous.' His attention was grabbed by the brooch sparkling on her dress. 'That really is very pretty. Are you sure it's fake? It's a jolly good one if it is.'

'Yes. It was a present from my parents,' she answered, kissing him back as she stirred. 'They definitely couldn't afford real diamonds.'

Christophe frowned. 'I thought you said you'd bought it in a junk shop?'

'Well . . . yes . . . with my parents. They paid for it. Now – these eggs are nearly ready. Can you get some toast on?' She turned back to the pot, cursing herself for not getting her story right. She'd let her guard down lately.

Christophe set about slicing bread. 'Do your parents mind your being away from them at Christmas?' he asked.

'No. And I'll see them at New Year while you're with your sister in France,' she said lightly, taking the saucepan over to the table where the plates were waiting. 'It's fine. They don't mind.'

Christophe turned round, grinning. 'So did you notice?'

'Notice what?' She looked about to see if anything had changed but nothing had as far as she could tell.

'The flowers!' He nodded at the table where there was a vase full of small, pink, star-shaped flowers with thick green leaves. She'd noticed a strong sweet smell in the room on first entering and realised now where it had come from.

'Oh. Yes – they're lovely. Very pretty.'

'But don't you recognise them?'

She gazed blankly at the flowers. 'No.'

'They're daphnes! I had a hell of a time getting hold of them. I had to ring every florist in the country. Honestly – don't you recognise your own flower when you see it?'

'Oh! Oh, yes, of course!' Daisy felt a warm flush spreading over her cheeks. 'Yes – they're daphnes. Yes.'

He shook his head, frowning and laughing gently, while she bent her head and wondered how she could change the subject.

The faux-pas over the flowers was forgotten soon enough, and instead they dedicated themselves to a day of eating and indulgence. As soon as breakfast was over, Daisy insisted they open their presents, then she wanted to try out the new walking boots that Christophe had given her, along with a cosy cashmere scarf, some beautiful silver earrings and a stack of books. Sasha needed to go out anyway, so they wrapped up and went for a hike through the bitter wind while the turkey roasted in the oven, filling the house with a delicious aroma.

They got back in time for Christophe to put the vegetables in to roast, then it was time for more champagne and lazing for Daisy in front of the fire while Christophe put the final touches to lunch. Then they sat down to eat.

'Oh, that was amazing,' she said with satisfaction as she tucked away the last scrap of Christmas pudding. 'I don't think I'll eat anything for a week.'

'Don't you believe it,' Christophe said wisely. He looked rather funny with his red paper hat on. He'd clearly forgotten about it, and it was falling down towards one eye. 'You'll be starving by suppertime. That's the weird thing about Christmas. You get hungrier and hungrier, no matter how much you eat.'

'Well, that was wonderful, darling, thank you so much. I'll definitely wash up.'

'I rather like this china, actually, so I'll wash. But you can dry.'

'Rotter.' She tossed her napkin at him. 'Now, how about coffee and some games?'

'Games?' Christophe raised a quizzical eyebrow.

'Of course. It's not Christmas without games. How about . . . something with words?'

'I've got Boggle. Someone left it here once, I haven't played it since.'

'Yes, let's play Boggle. We'll need some paper. There's a notebook in my bag, I'll get it. Where's the Boggle set?'

'It's in the dresser in the hall.' Christophe stood up and started clearing the table. 'You get it while I clear here and get the coffee on.'

'OK.' She jumped up and went out to the hall. It was much colder there than in the toasty dining room. The old dresser was almost black with age and sticky with layers of wax and dust. She kneeled down and opened one of the cupboard doors. It was full of boxes and odds and ends, and on the bottom shelf she saw a pile of old games: Monopoly, Scrabble, Trivial Pursuit, Ludo, Snakes and Ladders, and a jumble of strange-looking pastimes she'd never heard of, their boxes faded and weak at the corners with age and use. She spent a happy few minutes shuffling through them all, then located the Boggle box, pulled it out and headed back for the dining room. Christophe wasn't there, so she wandered back to the kitchen, clutching the box.

'I've found it!' she called as she went in. 'Is the coffee ready? Shall we open those Belgian truffles? I think I could possibly squeeze one in, can you believe—' She stopped abruptly as Christophe turned round and she saw the expression on his face for the first time. He was deathly white, his features suddenly haggard, and he was holding out a notebook towards her. Her black notebook.

'Your book,' he said, his voice sounding broken.

'I didn't mean that one!' she cried, her own voice rising with panic. 'I meant the work one, the one with the blank pages! Why did you get that one? Why? I said I would get it!' She began to sound angry, when really she was plunged into horrible, stomach-churning fear.

'And I can see why,' he said in a low voice. He opened the book. 'I guess you didn't want me to see this.'

'Why did you read it?' yelled Daisy. She wanted to curse herself for not hiding it better. She usually moved it from her handbag and kept it hidden among her clothes, but she'd forgotten in the excitement of Christmas.

There was a long and awful silence. Then Christophe said in a strange, strained voice, 'Who are you exactly?'

'You know who I am!'

'No, I don't. Are you Daphne Fraser? Do you have parents who live blamelessly in Hampshire? Because, according to this, you need to have a written reminder of their names and birthdays and every time we've ever talked about them! Look.' He flicked through the pages and stopped randomly on some. 'You've listed virtually every conversation we've ever had. You've marked it all down. Look . . . *things to remember . . . new facts . . . friends from school* – and a list of names. It goes on and on.' He shook his head disbelievingly. 'What is this, Daphne?'

'I . . . I can't tell you. But, please believe me, it has nothing to do with us!'

'What? How can it have nothing to do with us? This has *everything* to do with us!'

'It doesn't,' Daisy said obstinately. 'Just forget it!'

He stared at her, shaking his head, bewilderment in his eyes. 'There have been so many mysteries about you . . . the way you appeared from nowhere, with no family, no attachments. The girl with no past. And you don't even recognise your own flower. Why haven't you rung your parents today to say Happy Christmas to them? You know what – why don't we do it now?' He stalked over to the telephone and picked it up, holding the receiver out towards her. 'Come on, call them. Put me on the line, I want to wish them season's greetings too.'

She stared at him in anguish. Why had he meddled? She was going to tell him everything at some point, when she was sure it was right. But she couldn't do it now, not when he was so angry, standing there with his eyes flashing at her. 'No. I can't call them.'

'Why not?'

'Because . . . because I can't. Because they're dead.' Tears sprang to her eyes and she sniffed.

'Dead?' He looked puzzled again. 'Then why have you pretended they're alive?'

'I don't know! I didn't want to tell you.'

'But my parents are dead. I understand what it's like. Why couldn't you tell me, of all people? Why did you tell such an awful lie?'

She stared at the floor, wishing this could all just go away so they could be back in their perfect Christmas Day with its happy, loving, cosy atmosphere.

'Daphne . . . please.' He walked towards her. 'Please tell me why you kept something like that from me?'

'I don't know,' she said lamely, longing for him to take her in his arms. 'I just don't.'

'Can't you see that it makes me question everything about you? About *us?*'

'Yes,' she whispered in a small voice.

'I don't know how I can trust you. This book . . .' He held it out again, wafting the pages back and forth. 'It's got so much in it. I don't know what to make of it except that you've been spinning me some enormous story and I've fallen for every bit of it. But I don't understand *why.*'

'I can't tell you.' Her voice was loaded with the misery she was feeling. 'Please, you have to trust me . . .'

'But don't you see?' He sounded hard and angry again. 'I can't. That's the last thing I can do, until you explain exactly what this is.'

The day was finished for them. There was no cosy fireside game of Boggle while munching on chocolates. Christophe put on his coat and boots, pointedly leaving behind his new gloves, and took Sasha out for a long walk. Daisy sat by the fire, alternately weeping and staring into the flames, feeling furious. She considered telling him the whole story but she didn't dare. What if he somehow stood in the way of her plans?

What if he decided to tell everyone the truth? What if Daddy found out about her and where she was and what she was doing? The very thought made her shudder with fear. And it wasn't just her. She would bring Christophe to his attention too, and that could ruin his life as well. No. She couldn't risk it. There was no way she could tell him the truth, even if it meant losing him.

Damn that notebook, and damn my own stupidity for leaving it in my bag!

But it was too late. What was done, was done. There was no closing Pandora's box now.

Part Three

Part Three

41

Once she had agreed to the scheme put to her by Margaret Anderson, Coco found that her life was taken out of her own hands.

Back in the pristine office, Margaret had opened out an extensive contract. Coco hadn't bothered reading much of it except to check how much they'd be paying her and when, and what she had to do in return. The money clause seemed pretty straightforward: £50,000 for the job, half now and half on completion. *Fifty grand! With that I might be able to get started, think about investing in a dance studio. Roberto and I can go into business together maybe . . .* The obligation clause was a little less clear, just saying she had to supply such information as was in her power according to the requirements of blah-blah-blah. She'd got bored with that bit, and skipped to the end and signed it.

'Good,' Miss Anderson had said. 'Now, I'll need your bank details to make the first payment.'

'Don't have a bank account,' returned Coco. 'Cash, please.'

'No bank account?' The other woman had looked

astonished. 'Very well, cash if you want it. I'll give you a small advance now – say five hundred – and arrange for the rest. But I do advise you to get an account, your money will be much safer that way. You'll only need a passport and a utility bill with your address on it.'

Coco sighed sulkily, running her fingers through her white hair. 'No passport, no address – OK?'

Margaret Anderson frowned, pursing her thin lips. 'No passport? We'll certainly have to remedy that. Do you have a birth certificate?'

'My mum probably has it.'

'Then you'll have to get it from her at some point. It's not urgent. Perhaps when you see her at Christmas. But we will need it.'

Coco hadn't been intending to see her mother at Christmas, or at any other time come to that, but she supposed she might be able to stand the prospect if it was the only way of getting the rest of her dough.

As soon as Coco had signed the contract, it was as though this Margaret woman thought she owned her. She went with her back to the Victoria hotel and checked her out at once, settled the bill and hailed a taxi. Within a short time they were bowling up to a house in Kensington, one of those wedding-cake white-iced ones with pillars at the front.

Margaret led her up the stairs to the third floor, talking as she went. 'Luckily, Mr Dangerfield has a property vacant that you can use while this business is going on. I will take care of the admin, but you'll be registered here as the tenant. That will give you a permanent address and then we can see about getting you a bank account and whatever else you might need.'

When they got inside, Coco looked about, pleased. The flat was small all right, and felt like the kind of place where no one stayed for long: a stop gap or a holiday home. But it was very comfortably arranged, with everything necessary for one person to be quite snug. The front room had a big broad sofa flanked by lamps and facing a flat-screen telly. In one corner, by the French windows that gave out on to a miniscule terrace, was a round table with two chairs. In the other was a U-shaped kitchen area, neatly done so that all the appliances were stowed under the blond-wood surfaces, behind pale blue cupboards. At the rear of the flat was a bathroom, prettily decorated in white and sandy seaside beige with touches of red, and a cream-painted bedroom with a built-in wardrobe, dressing table and neat double bed.

'Yeah, this is nice,' Coco said, nodding as she looked about.

'You're lucky to be getting it free of charge,' Margaret observed, closing the wardrobe door she'd opened to show the space inside.

'Mmm. Well, I might get something like this myself one day,' Coco said carelessly. 'I like this area.' The bedroom window looked down over a neat garden, and the back of the house on the neighbouring street. Everything was clean and fresh.

'If you've got the best part of a million pounds to spare, I'd certainly advise it,' Margaret said tartly, leading her back towards the little hallway.

'A million pounds for this?' gasped Coco.

'Close on. You're in South Kensington, my dear, not the back of beyond.' She gestured to Coco to sit down on the sofa. 'Now, a few things to be sorted out.

What Mr Dangerfield hasn't exactly realised is that you're not really in a suitable state to be introduced to his son.'

'What's wrong with me?' demanded Coco, wondering if she could spark up a cigarette. She considered asking Margaret and then decided she would wait until she'd gone. In the meantime, Margaret was looking her up and down with a steely light in her eyes.

'What's *wrong* with you? I hate to say this, my dear –' she always said 'my dear' as though she could not bring herself to say the word 'Coco' '– but there is very little that's right. Poor dear Mr Dangerfield is under the impression that you are a very good-looking girl and obviously spirited, so all you'll need are a few nice new dresses and then you'll be quite ready to introduce into polite society. But, as Professor Higgins knew only too well, it's simply not that easy.'

'Professor who?' Coco was instantly suspicious.

'Never mind. What I'm saying is that you'll need some lessons before I'll feel confident sending you off to do this very particular job.' Margaret caught a glimpse of Coco's face. 'Now don't worry. We won't do anything until after Christmas, so if I were you I would take a few days to calm down and get used to what you're going to be doing. I'll send round some reading material for you to study. Here are your keys. Do you have a mobile? Give me the number. Oh goodness, look at that – what a state it's in. You must look after your things, my dear, particularly when we start to acquire some decent ones for you.' Margaret shook her head and clicked her tongue disapprovingly but looked more energised by the challenge ahead than daunted. 'Right, then. I think that's all. I'll call later to check on you. Goodbye.'

When Margaret had gone, Coco danced around the flat, whooping and cheering. She was still stunned by everything that had happened but realised that she had fallen spectacularly on her feet. Her own flat in South Ken, cash in her hand, some people taking an interest in her and looking out for her and – best of all – she hadn't had to sleep with anyone to get it.

Well, not yet, anyhow.

She hadn't gone to her mum's on Christmas Day. She'd known only too well what that would be like. Her mum might not even recognise her. But two days later, when the hangover was probably nearly gone and Michelle might be able to cope, Coco found herself on the doorstep of her mother's old house.

Shit, I don't know if she even lives here any more.

She looked about. It hadn't changed: the estate was still tatty, down-at-heel, unkempt. Gloom weighed down her shoulders as she stood there on the doorstep. The whole place seemed full of memories, most of them miserable. The only good thing in her life – Jamal – had been ripped away from her here. There was nothing to remember with pleasure.

Once I get away again, I'm never coming back. Never. This is the last time.

But before she could truly be free, there was business to be done. Coco took a deep breath and knocked on the door. It was a long time before she heard any sound from inside, but eventually she heard a slow shuffle approaching the door and it opened a crack.

'Yeah?' said a deep voice roughered by thousands

of smoked cigarettes. A bleary eye blinked behind the edge of the door.

'Mum. It's me.'

The door opened a little more, revealing Michelle's ravaged face. It was heavily lined and mazed with broken veins. Puffy dark bags sat under her eyes. Her stringy hair hung around sunken cheeks. There was a tube going into each nostril and vanishing around the back of her head. 'Chanelle?' she said in a wondering tone.

'Yeah. Let me in.' She was impatient to be inside away from any prying eyes that might have spotted her.

Looking astonished, her mother stood back to let her into the hallway. 'What you doin' here? You never said you was coming! You should've let me know.' She peered harder at Coco. 'What you done to your hair?'

'Anyone else here?' she asked, going into the sitting room. It was a tip, as usual, with overflowing ashtrays and half-drunk mugs of tea everywhere. There were some pathetic attempts at Christmas decorations as well: scraps of tinsel, some crêpe-paper chains and a wispy plastic tree in the corner.

'Nah, nah, I'm on my own now. Bill fucked off, didn't he?' Her mother followed her, shuffling along in her pink slippers, perking up as she realised that Chanelle had come to visit her. 'Well, this is a turn up, my girl. I didn't know if you was alive or dead!'

'Now you know.' Coco found a place to sit on the sofa. 'How are you?'

Michelle shook her head. She looked aged well beyond her years, more like an old woman than someone in her early-fifties. 'Not so good, love. It's this emphysema. They've given me oxygen and all but they don't reckon it's going to get much better.' She looked mournful. 'Don't know how long I got now, love, and that's a fact.'

'Mum, I need something, that's why I'm here,' Coco said, swiftly changing the subject. She didn't want a long, self-pitying monologue from her mother. If she hadn't wanted emphysema, she should have given up the fags, shouldn't she? 'It's my birth certificate.'

Her mother stiffened. 'Why do you want that?' she asked after a moment.

'I need it.'

'Why? Why do you need it all of a sudden?'

Coco snorted. 'Why do you think? Everyone needs their birth certificate, don't they? I wanna get a passport.'

'Oh. Going somewhere nice, are we?' Michelle lowered herself into an armchair and then puffed and wheezed painfully with the effort. 'Wish I could afford a holiday, I'm sure!'

'Gotta travel for work and I need a passport. I can't get one without a birth certificate. So have you got it or not?'

There was a long pause as Michelle breathed noisily, whistling and wheezing. 'Yeah, I got it. But you'll have to fetch it. I can't.'

Coco was surprised. She realised that she'd been expecting her mother not to have the certificate, to make excuses, to be as useless as she'd always been. But here she was, saying that she did have it after all. 'Where is it?'

'Upstairs. Under my bed. There's a shoe box. Inside there's a big brown envelope. It's got Birth Certificate written on it. It's in there. But . . .' Her mother held out a hand, her eyes anxious. 'There's other stuff in there. Promise me you won't go through it? It's private.'

Coco rolled her eyes. ''Course I won't. Think I'm interested in your life? I ain't.'

She stood up and went up the stairs to her mother's room. So Michelle was alone now. Well, it didn't look like she was up to much in the sack any more, and she'd never been any good at looking after anyone: she couldn't cook and didn't clean. No wonder the men had vanished now that she was just a sick old lady with nothing to offer. Coco felt a stab of pity for her mother – what did she have to live for? It was a miserable existence by the looks of things. She felt a pang of fear that Michelle might try and drag her back to this house, to share this excuse for a life. *No way,* Coco thought grimly. *I can't do it. I just can't.* The bedroom was full of a dense, musty smell, as though it needed a good airing. A couple of oxygen cylinders and some bits of equipment stood by the bedside, where her mum had to hook herself up each night before she went to sleep.

Coco bent down to look under the bed. Just the sight of it made her want to sneeze; it was thick with dust and full of detritus: odd shoes, abandoned pairs of tights, old cotton wool balls and other rubbish. There was also a large box. Coco reached under and pulled it out, brushing off the fluff and dust on top. She lifted the lid. Inside there was a collection of letters, cards and photographs, but she had no interest in them, pushing them aside and catching only brief glimpses of her mother in a few of them – Michelle

348

in younger days, with long fair hair and a fresh complexion, always holding a cigarette between her fingers. There was the manila envelope.

Coco took it out and stared at it for a moment. Then she lifted the flap and pulled out the certificate inside. So there it was. Her name, her date of birth, the address. Michelle's name was there as the mother. And the father's name was . . . unknown. Of course. A small smile tugged at one corner of Coco's mouth. Unknown. She'd known he was unknown. It was one of the things she *did* know. And her mother wouldn't have let her up here if there had been anything really secret to discover. She'd always told herself that Michelle didn't have a clue who her father was; after all, she'd been a junkie back then, no doubt sleeping with anyone who'd help her score. But an inner voice had whispered of other possibilities to her. There was another candidate, and she'd been half expecting to find his name on the certificate. But it wasn't there.

Unless she didn't want to name him. Didn't want him to know maybe.

There was no point in dwelling on it. She pushed the certificate back into its envelope, kicked the box back under the bed and hurried down the stairs.

'OK, Mum, I got it!' Coco called. 'See ya.'

'You ain't goin', are ya?' cried Michelle weakly.

'Well, I'm in a bit of a hurry actually . . .'

'Ah, come on, it's Christmas! Stay and have a cup of tea with me, won't you? Don't know when I'll see you again, do I?'

Coco stood in the hall. The front door was tantalisingly close and, beyond it, freedom. But then . . . the state of her mum. It was obvious she didn't have all

349

that much time left. *But knowing her, she'll hang on for bloody years.*

'Chanelle?' The voice was pitiable, crackling and strained, the breath to speak fought for.

'Yeah. All right. One cup of tea, OK? Then I'm gone.' She turned away from the door and towards the sitting room. 'I'll make it. Just as long as you've got some bloody milk.'

42

Daisy found leaving the Excalibur in January an emotional experience. There were lots of tears at her leaving party, her own and other people's, as various maids, receptionists, sous-chefs and waitresses sobbed on her shoulder and said how much they were going to miss her. Even Alan looked as if he might be going to weep, but probably because he was afraid of what might happen now that he wouldn't have Daisy to rely on.

'We're certainly going to miss you, Daffy,' he said in a tone of immense bravery. 'You've been a breath of fresh air here, and it's no wonder that they want you at the big HQ. You're off to work your magic elsewhere in the company, so I hear?'

'Yes, but I'll always be rooting for the Excalibur!' she said, blinking away more tears. 'I'll come back and visit, I promise.'

'We'll have a room on permanent standby!' declared Alan. They gave her a leaving present of a framed sketch of the hotel and a card signed by everyone, then they toasted her future success.

She cried all the way home, but not just because she was leaving. Her emotions had been in turmoil for almost a month, ever since the events of Christmas.

On Christmas night, Christophe had slept in the spare room. The next day he'd told her frankly that if she couldn't explain herself to him, tell him why she'd told those lies, then it was over. Daisy had wept but told him that she couldn't say anything more than she had. He had to accept her as she was, or not at all.

Not at all then, he'd said, and she was sure he too was on the brink of tears. She'd got into her car that afternoon.

'I can't believe you're doing this,' he'd said, his eyes desperate as she prepared to drive away.

'I can't believe *you're* doing this,' she'd retorted, and they'd stared at each other in frustrated anguish before she started the engine and drove away, fighting the tears that threatened to cloud her vision all the way back to Bristol.

They hadn't spoken since. She'd known Christophe was going to France for the New Year and that she would miss him horribly but she couldn't have anticipated how painful it would be, standing at the window of her flat, watching fireworks pop in the sky as revellers roared and danced in the streets below, feeling more alone and grief-stricken than she had since the first night she'd left home. There was no one to turn to. Even Lucy was away for New Year, and anyway she'd never met Christophe. She wouldn't understand.

On Daisy's first day at the Craven Dalziel headquarters, a modern office building on the outskirts of Cheltenham, she sat at her new desk in her plainly furnished office and tried to read through the company literature John had left there for her, while she waited for IT to come and log her into the system. The words swam in front of her eyes, and her attention wandered.

Concentrate, Daisy, concentrate, she said firmly to herself, and turned back to the monthly reports on the company's performance. It wasn't exactly gripping, but she had to absorb it all. *I need a break. Some water.* The commute from Bristol had taken longer than she'd expected. Perhaps she ought to think about giving up her flat there and moving closer. She felt a pang of sadness as she remembered wondering if Christophe would invite her to move in with him, and how much she'd looked forward to being with him all the time. *Don't think about it.*

But she couldn't help it. All she could think about was the fact that he was in this very building, right now.

She got up and went down to the water cooler at the end of the hall. She'd just filled her glass when she looked up and saw Christophe walking towards her, a bunch of files clutched to his chest. He was staring at her and yet looking through her, his eyes intense and his mouth stern. She felt her insides spin with something that was both fear and excitement, and she began to shake. What would he say to her? For a moment she had a wonderful vision of their being reunited, falling into one another's arms. She missed him so much and had almost called him a hundred times, but held herself back.

But as he came close, he simply nodded once and said, 'Daphne.'

'Hello, Christophe,' she said, though it came out weakly and not at all the way she'd expected.

He stared past her and continued to walk by without looking back. Misery washed over her. This was awful. But what could she do?

John called her into his office later that day to go through her new role in detail. As well as overseeing the implementation of her suggestions in the group's town centre and airport hotels, he wanted her to take on another special project.

'We have a group of eight hotels in the Cotswolds area, each completely different. They belong to us but are lived in and managed by the previous owners. I'd like you to take a look at them and come up with some ideas for their future development. It may be that it's best simply to bail out and sell them if you don't think there's potential. Here's all the information I have on them, and no doubt you'll need to make some field trips.'

Daisy nodded. 'No problem.' She picked up the files. 'It sounds fascinating. I can't wait to get stuck in.' She turned to go, only to be stopped by John.

'Daphne – I can't help noticing that you and Christophe don't seem to be on very friendly terms today. Is everything all right?'

'Yes, fine,' she said miserably. 'It's all fine.' She walked out, knowing that John was watching her and hoping he wouldn't see the sadness that had engulfed her.

The following week was agony. Christophe ignored her in meetings, in the staff café and in the corridor, except for an expressionless greeting with eyes that never met hers. Being around the man she loved and not able to touch him, talk to him or laugh with him was torture, but she had no choice. She'd made her decision and couldn't go back on it now, much as she wanted to. There was no way she could risk everything by getting involved with him again, even if he wanted her, which she doubted. He would have to know the truth – and she'd vowed that no one could know that. Besides, she couldn't expose him to any danger. No. It had to be this way.

On Friday, John Montgomery called her to his office. When she arrived, his assistant nodded her straight in. John was standing at his office window looking stern-faced.

'Ah, Daphne. Come in. Sit down.' He indicated the sofa by his coffee table. She went over, feeling a little anxious.

'Is everything all right?'

'Yes. But . . . I thought I should let you know. I've just had a visit from Christophe.'

'Oh?' She felt weak at the sound of his name, full of longing. She pushed it down.

'Yes.' John came over and sat down opposite, his expression serious. 'I'm afraid he's handed in his resignation. He wants to leave immediately as well, if it can be arranged. I thought I'd better let you know.'

She averted her eyes, her shoulders drooping. 'I see.'

'Yes. It's been plain for the last few days that he's in a terrible state. He's been a wreck since the holidays. I take it something happened between you? I don't mean to pry, but you seemed so happy at the firm's dinner.'

'We were,' she said in a small voice. 'But, yes, we

broke up over Christmas. It's been hard . . . for both of us.'

'Obviously you couldn't go on working here together like this, and it seems Christophe has taken the decision to leave.'

'Do you know where he's going?'

John sighed. 'Oh, you young people, making life so miserable for yourselves. He's going abroad. To France.'

She flinched. He was leaving Nant-y-Pren. That was how much he hated her now. He'd rather go to another country entirely than be near her. Tears threatened to well up but she bit her lip hard to stop herself. She couldn't cry in front of John, she had to be strong. She couldn't speak for the effort of controlling herself.

'I'm sorry it's come to this, and I'm very sorry to lose Christophe. But we've got you, Daphne, and the talent you've shown so far. You're a real asset to us.'

'Is he . . . is he going today?'

John nodded. 'I said that he didn't need to work out his notice under the circumstances. He's going to finish up any last bits and pieces from home.'

Daisy stood up shakily, smoothing down her skirt, desperate to get out of John's office now. She had to be alone. 'I'd better get back to work. Thanks for telling me about Christophe. And you needn't worry – I won't let this interfere with my performance.'

She was grateful to be out in the corridor. As soon as she'd closed the door behind her, she ran for her own office and to the window that overlooked the car park. There he was, walking towards his car, a box of possessions in his arms. She watched as he opened the boot, stowed the box and went round to the driver's door. A moment later, the little Audi had reversed and then roared out of the car park. It disappeared at the roundabout as Christophe headed away from Craven Dalziel for good.

'I won't cry,' said Daisy in a shaky voice. 'It's better this way. I have to do this alone. There's no other way.'

She went back to her desk and forced herself to pick up the file and start reading. She ignored the hot splashes that hit the pages, and stayed in her office till very late.

43

Coco hadn't liked being in school much, and sometimes this reminded her of that – but without the noise, chaos and the frustration of never being able to hear anything the teacher said. In fact, if school had been more like this, perhaps she would have enjoyed it. She had plenty of lessons to get through, that was for sure, but the focus was entirely on her.

Margaret – as Coco now called her – had arranged it all: the timetable of lessons, the afternoons out, the visits to hairdressers and stylists.

'It's a little like running my own finishing school with a pupil of one,' she said wryly. 'But it's amusing, in its own way. If you're going to be accepted into certain social circles, you have to know how to behave.'

Coco found some of it hilarious and some of it infuriating. She couldn't see why it mattered. Table manners drove her wild. On three mornings a week, a prissy woman called Lady Arthur Rewsham came to instruct her in matters of etiquette, and table manners were the first thing she tackled. Lady Arthur was an immaculately turned out woman, with short blonde hair, blue mascara and pink lipstick. She wore three strands of pearls to match her earrings, plain or stripy blouses with navy skirts and low-heeled smart shoes, and always white tights and sensible cashmere cardigans. On her little finger she sported a huge gold signet ring with a crest engraved deep on its surface.

'Not being funny, but why's your name *Arthur*?' asked Coco, hardly able to believe it when the woman told her to address her as Lady Arthur.

'My name is actually Shirley,' the woman said loftily, 'but my title is Lady Arthur.'

Coco giggled.

Lady Arthur sighed. 'I see you have a lamentable ignorance of the peerage. It's very simple. A child of four could understand it. It simply means that I acquired my title through my marriage to Lord Arthur Rewsham, younger son of the Duke of Haslemere. I cannot be Lady Shirley – that would mean I was born the daughter of a duke, marquess or earl myself. If I were Lady Rewsham, that would mean I was married to Lord Rewsham – who would be the holder of a main title, or the heir to one and holding the heir's courtesy title – *or* that I was married to Sir Arthur Rewsham. Do you see?'

Coco made a face and shook her head. 'Er . . . no.'

Lady Arthur warmed to her theme. 'That's why it infuriates me when they call some women "Lady" incorrectly.' She tutted with irritation. 'They do it all the time, even the *Telegraph*. One would expect better.'

Coco put up her hand.

'Yes?'

'Don't it get confusing at home, with both of you being called Arthur?'

Lady Arthur turned her eyes to heaven. 'Silly girl! My husband and friends call me Shirley of course! And anyway . . .' she sniffed '. . . we're divorced, as it happens. It was a rather brief marriage. Now, on with the lesson.'

Lady Arthur had brought with her a canteen of silver cutlery, plates, napkins and a selection of glassware. She carefully laid two place settings which looked to Coco like some kind of weapons display. Why did anyone need so much cutlery to eat one meal? Lady Arthur began to instruct her in how to recognise and use all the different knives, spoons and forks. It seemed like a never-ending task. The first thing she got wrong was the most basic – how she held her knife and fork.

'No!' screeched Lady Arthur, appalled. 'That is the most *terrible* giveaway. You mustn't hold your knife like a pen, you must hold it like this.' She demonstrated how the handle fitted into the palm and the index finger stretched along its length. Coco couldn't see why it mattered, but the woman wouldn't let up until she'd mastered holding both knife and fork correctly. The rules seemed endless.

'No, no, Coco! You use your soup spoon by pushing away from you, not towards! You simply mustn't cut your bread roll, it isn't done. You must pick it up and tear it gently like this. And don't butter the whole thing at once. Remember – *dainty, dainty* movements.'

There was different-sized cutlery for different courses, different-sized glasses for different wines, there were times to put a napkin on and times to take it off, and accepted places to leave it. There were finger bowls here, and condiments there, and conversation on your left for one course and conversation on your right for another.

Coco thought it was all stupid and a massive waste of time, but Lady Arthur persisted and before long she was beginning to hold her knife and fork in the required way without even thinking about it. When they weren't at the table, practising how to eat asparagus or how to take fish neatly off the bone, they were on the sofa, learning to get and up and sit down elegantly, or walking across the room to improve Coco's posture – 'You have a good strong back, my dear,' Lady Arthur said admiringly, 'do you dance?' – or taking afternoon tea, learning the correct way to pour it out into porcelain cups, add the milk, sit and drink it. And how not to gobble all the little delicacies that came with it.

'If you can,' advised Lady Arthur, 'always eat something before you go out. It is much more elegant to eat very little at tea or a cocktail party than to wolf down everything you see. Besides, accidents with canapés are so easy – very difficult to eat them while holding a drink and an evening bag. I knew one woman whose poached quail's egg slid off her foie gras and broke on the carpet – at Buckingham Palace! Can you imagine?'

Coco laughed. The longer she knew Lady Arthur, the more she enjoyed her company and all the hilarious stories she told to illustrate her points, as if doing the right thing at a party were a matter of life and death. Coco enjoyed the cocktail lessons the best, when she learned to mix martinis, G&Ts and Bloody Marys, and how to spoon caviar on to crème-fraiche-covered blinis, even though her teacher told her firmly that no lady ever, but ever, got drunk at a cocktail party. Or anywhere else, come to that.

'One gin fizz or two glasses of champagne or one of white wine,' Lady Arthur said firmly. 'Any more than that is *forbidden*. It's frightfully common for women to get drunk.'

No wonder the posh bitches are so obsessed by their knives and forks, thought Coco. *They're not allowed to get pissed and let their hair down.*

Etiquette was boring and repetitive. Coco much preferred some of the other aspects of her new education. There was, for instance, Leanne, a stylist at Noble's department store, who was tasked with changing the way Coco dressed.

'To be frank,' Margaret said, taking her into the grand old store with its beautiful Art Nouveau interior, 'you need to stop dressing like a prostitute and more like a woman of style.'

Coco loved these afternoons in the private shopping area where she had her own dressing room with velvet armchairs, a wall of mirrors and small leaded windows looking down on the busy London street below. Leanne would bring her piles of clothes to try on, along with mountains of shoes and bags, and instruct her in the art of looking fashionable. At first, Coco couldn't see any difference between designer jeans and the ones she'd got in Whitechapel market, except for a few hundred pounds, but she soon began to learn the subtle differences in cut and quality.

'Besides,' said Leanne, shaking out a Vivienne Westwood dress, 'half of it is what you buy and the pleasure of wearing it, and the other half is people recognising the

362

brand and respecting your style knowledge and choices. It's all about telling people: I know what's chic and I've already gone out and bought it, and mixed it with this fab Alexander Wang top and a scarf by this new designer who's about to be massive. See?'

'Yeah,' Coco said, fired up by her new understanding. 'I get it. I really do.'

'And you're lucky, you've got a great figure,' Leanne said admiringly. 'You look terrific in expensive clothes.'

'My bust's too big,' Coco remarked, inspecting herself in a mirror and adjusting her floaty top so that it hung over her boobs a bit better.

'Maybe for a model it's too big. But believe me . . .' Leanne gave her look '. . . a lot of women would kill for legs like yours and that bra size as well. They all go to surgeons to get it, and you've got it naturally.'

'Yeah,' Coco said cheerfully. 'A boob job is one thing I've never had to worry about.'

Each week a few more items were purchased – Coco had no idea how they were paid for, they were simply wrapped in tissue, put into boxes and bags and handed to her – and each week she transformed herself further from the person who'd arrived in the little flat in South Ken just before Christmas. Her hair was growing and Margaret had insisted on a colour change. It had meant hours in a hairdresser's chair, but now her hair was a warm, caramel blonde, glittering with lights. She had to go back once a week for treatments to restore its health after so much heavy dying, and each time she came out her hair was a little smoother and glossier. At the salons, long facials were mitigating the effects of years of late nights, booze and countless cigarettes. 'Your epidermis is severely dehydrated,' she was told firmly by the white-coated facialist, 'and you need to work hard to restore it right away. You're lucky you're young and that you've naturally good skin.'

Coco was put on a course of supplements and provided with a vast array of bottles and tubes and strict instructions on how to apply them and when. Each morning, she was expected to anoint herself with serums, boosters and moisturisers, eye creams, sun screens, lip salves and hand creams. Each evening, she had to do a whole different routine with exfoliators, polishes, washes, more serums, more creams, more eye treatments, and goodness knows what else. At the dentist, her teeth were cleaned and assessed, and three weeks later she was fitted with a clear invisible brace like a mouth guard, which she had to wear at all times except when eating or drinking, and was renewed every three weeks. Its purpose was to push a couple of her teeth into perfect alignment, then they would be whitened. Coco hadn't been aware there was anything wrong with her teeth, but she submitted. Why not? What bit of her were they going to leave alone, after all?

When she wasn't being groomed, she was being educated in different ways. She had a tutor, a shy young man called Charles, who took her to galleries and exhibitions and gave her stuttering, low-voiced lectures on everything she was seeing. She'd thought it would be boring but she became interested despite herself.

'I didn't realise all this was here,' she said, as they wandered out of the National Gallery, having spent an hour or two inspecting the works of Goya.

'Oh, yes,' said Charles, 'and all free. Our nation's

heritage. And there's much, much more . . . We have the V&A, the British Museum, the Natural History Museum, the Science Museum, the National Portrait Gallery . . .' And on it went.

He took her to all sorts of plays as well, which she was surprised to find she loved: Oscar Wilde, Chekhov, Rattigan, Shakespeare – she found something to enjoy in all of them, even when she didn't quite follow what was going on.

He gave her a reading list and a stack of books to work her way through. This wasn't such a success. Reading was too much like hard work and Coco didn't fancy it. She had no idea of when she was supposed to read, and sitting down with a book in the day felt odd. Eventually she got tired of Charles asking her what she was reading and blurted out that she fucking hated it, it was weird, and she couldn't sit down and relax. After that, Charles gave her audio books on her iPod and she listened to novels and poetry while she was on the treadmill at the gym that Margaret had insisted she join. That was much better, and she got quite into the stories after that. She liked Charles Dickens, though the stories went on forever, and she liked more modern stuff too. But she adored P. G. Wodehouse, to Charles's surprise, because he made her laugh.

'It's that man from the telly reading them,' Coco explained. 'And he just does it funny. I really like it.'

The last of her instructors was a large woman called Penny, a lady who spoke with a rich theatrical alto voice and whose job was to sort out Coco's flat London accent and bad grammar.

These lessons really were Coco's least favourite. It

was hard work to try and change her voice and the way she talked. Every time she opened her mouth, Penny was stopping her or cutting in with the right word. And every time she said 'innit' or 'sort of like' or 'yeah', Penny jumped on it. 'Bad habits, bad habits!' she'd cry. 'We must stop these pointless fillers, mustn't we? Speak clearly, enunciate and lose the bad habits!'

Coco wasn't allowed to say 'you was' or 'he don't' any more and the effort of changing was driving her mad. There was more than one tantrum when she stormed out and was found in a rage on the balcony or in the street below, smoking and tapping her feet with rage. But gradually, with everyone correcting her – Lady Arthur, Charles, Penny and Margaret – and with the constant murmur of approved literature in her ears from her audio books, she began to lose her old way of talking and slip into a new, posher way of expressing herself. Her accent started to change subtly as her mouth narrowed when she spoke and her vowels became rounder. She would never have the drawl of the girl who was born to it, or the barely noticeable giveaways in certain words that marked out someone from a privileged background. But she didn't sound like Coco from the estate any more either.

One day, six months after the experiment had started, Coco looked in the mirror. The peroxide blonde with her vaguely unhealthy look, her too-tight clothes and cheap shoes, had gone. In her place was a healthy, glowing young woman, with artfully applied barely there make-up that brought out the colour in her eyes and added shimmer to her cheeks, lids and lips. This woman had glossy, caramel-blonde hair, and wore Chloé trousers with a Prada top cinched in with

366

a skinny belt, and Balenciaga stacked shoes, and held herself with poise and confidence. She could still hear the strains of *The Magic Flute* in her ears from last night's trip to the Royal Opera House, and that afternoon Margaret was taking her to one of the Dangerfield hotels for tea to test all her newly acquired scone-buttering skills, followed by dinner at Le Gavroche.

'Fuck,' she said out loud, amazed. 'Look at me! I've been fuckin' Cinderella-ed!'

She could tell she was nearly ready for whatever plan it was they had prepared for. She tried not to think about what would happen when the clock struck midnight.

44

The heels of her black patent Jimmy Choos tapped on the black-and-white marble floor as she walked across it. The sound was so familiar but Daisy had thought she'd never hear it again – not in this particular place, anyway.

It was a bizarre feeling to be back. Even though she'd often looked at the website, it was nothing to the experience of actually being here.

Inside the Florey! Imagine. What would Daddy do if he knew I were here? Daisy's skin prickled at the thought of it, although whether with fear or excitement she couldn't quite tell. She was confident that she wouldn't be recognised – after all, she was a world away from the girl who used to waft about this place as though she owned it. Then she'd been dressed in skin-tight Hervé Léger or Gucci, her fair hair in deceptively casual-looking waves, a Prada bag on her arm as she tottered about in her sky-high heels. Now she was an elegantly dressed businesswoman with a sharp black bob and, while she looked successful, there was no way she could be mistaken for a spoiled trust-fund princess. Surely no one would ever connect the two very different people . . . but now was the time to put that to the test.

She walked into the hotel brasserie and looked about. Quickly locating her lunch date, she went straight to the table. 'Hello.'

The woman sitting there looked up from her paper and gazed at her blankly. 'Yes?'

'Lucy – it's me. Daisy.'

Lucy gasped, her eyes widening with astonishment. 'Daisy! Is it really you?' She leaped to her feet and hugged her friend. When she stood back to examine her again, there were tears in her eyes. 'I can't believe it! You look so different. I simply wouldn't have recognised you.'

'That's the idea.' Daisy sat down, putting her bag under the table. 'I could hardly stride in here looking like I used to.'

'But it's been four years,' Lucy ventured. 'Is it really still dangerous?'

'I think it always will be. Oh, I'm sure the staff have changed and there are plenty here who've got no idea I ever existed. But imagine if I ran into Daddy . . .' Daisy shuddered. 'It's not worth the risk.'

The waiter came up to give them menus. As he left them, Lucy gazed at her friend, grinning broadly now that she'd got over her shock. 'Honestly, I would never have recognised you. That black hair and those glasses – you're completely transformed!'

'You're just the same,' Daisy said warmly. It was a thrill to see her old friend and she realised how much she'd missed her. 'Actually you look even better.' Which was true – Lucy had acquired a sophisticated gloss, the result of plenty of leisure and fun. She reached out and put her hand over her friend's. 'It's so great to see you, Luce, it really is. Talking on the phone and emailing is fine but . . .'

'I know what you mean.' Lucy smiled back fondly. They'd been in touch once a month or so since Daisy's departure but usually by email. They hadn't spoken for a while. 'There's masses to catch up on.'

'And you said you've got something to tell me . . .'

'We'll get to that,' Lucy said, putting her snowy white napkin on her lap. 'Let's order and have a catch up, then tackle the other stuff.'

They both ordered crayfish salad and ate them while they sipped large glasses of bone-dry Reisling. Lucy, city-smart in a white silk top and beige high-waisted Céline trousers, chattered away, telling Daisy all the gossip, and she drank it in, revelling in this taste of her old life, lunching in her favourite hotel as though she didn't have a care in the world.

'It's so funny to see you,' Lucy said, 'because I was thinking about you only last weekend when I was at a wedding. You remember Freddie Umbers, don't you?'

Daisy had an instant flashback to Freddie's golden good looks and wicked way with her. She saw the two of them rolling around the vast canopied double bed in the Crillon. 'Oh, yes. What's happened to old Freddie?'

'It was his wedding. He got married.'

'Married?' Daisy blinked in surprise. Marriage still seemed to be aeons off for her generation – another five years at least. And it was hard to imagine Freddie settling down with one woman for the rest of his life. 'Who did he marry?'

370

'You'll never guess – only Keira Bond!'

There was a brief astonished pause from Daisy and then she burst out laughing, Lucy joining in. 'Do you think it will last?' she said, when she'd managed to draw breath. She realised to her relief that it didn't matter to her that Freddie was married, even if it was to the dreadful Keira.

'Who knows? They both looked blissful. It's a good starter marriage, anyhow. Antonia asked after you. I said I hadn't heard from you for ages but apparently you were doing very well, living in a village in the hidden depths of Patagonia.' Lucy shrugged. 'She seemed happy enough with that.' She gave Daisy a quizzical look. 'But how long is this going to go on for? How long before they have to be told the truth – that you're not who you used to be any longer?'

Daisy put down her fork and examined her plate for a moment before she answered. 'I don't know. My plan is progressing as well as I could have hoped. It shouldn't be too long before all is revealed.'

'I'd better have you turn into a missionary or something then,' Lucy said with a laugh. 'Anything to keep you away for a few more years. Although to be honest, people don't care about much beyond themselves. They all seemed perfectly content with the idea that you're in a mud hut somewhere.' She leaned in towards Daisy. 'The only thing is – I'm worried that someone might be on to you.'

A flicker of anxiety ran through Daisy. 'Really? Why?' A waitress walked past, apparently oblivious, but there was no sense in being reckless. She leaned closer as well so that they could speak without being overheard.

'I had a call, asking if I knew where you were, from someone who wouldn't say who they were.'

'Was it a woman?' Daisy asked swiftly, thinking immediately of Margaret.

Lucy shook her head. 'A man. With an American accent.'

'What did he say exactly?'

'He asked if I knew the whereabouts of Daisy Dangerfield and when I'd last had any contact with you. I didn't give anything away, of course. I just asked who was on the line and why they wanted to know.'

'And . . . ?'

'He tried to imply he was a friend of yours, but I told him I didn't buy it and that I wasn't going to talk about anything to a stranger. He asked if he could come to see me and I said no.' Lucy looked worried. 'That's it. Not much, but I thought you should know.'

'Thanks.' Daisy bit her lip and frowned, feeling edgy and uncertain. 'I wonder if it was safe even for us to meet up. What if you're being followed?'

At once, they both instinctively looked about as though for someone lurking suspiciously in a corner.

'I'm sure I'm not,' Lucy said cheerfully. 'They'd have had to spend a jolly long time in Fenwick's bra department, anyhow!'

They both laughed, and Daisy felt her fear subside a little.

The lunch came to an end all too soon, and the two friends kissed one another's cheeks fondly and promised to keep in touch.

'I'm travelling a bit for my job,' Daisy explained. 'So I'm sure I can get away more often.'

'Your mysterious job!' Lucy said, looking curious. 'Aren't you going to tell me what it is?'

'Uh-huh. Best you don't know. Then they can't torture it out of you.' She grinned to show she was joking.

Lucy went but Daisy lingered a little, reluctant to leave the luxurious comfort of the beautiful old hotel. She wandered out of the brasserie and into the atrium, where afternoon tea was already being served. A piano tinkled gently over the murmur of voices and the chink of china. This felt like home to her, she realised. She'd grown up believing that the Florey would be hers one day. That was pretty much impossible now, even if her plan was successful. This might be all the connection she ever had to it.

It was hard to drag herself away from a place that felt like a refuge from the pain and heartbreak she'd been suffering since Christmas. Sometimes she missed Christophe so much, it felt as if there was a gaping hole in her centre. But she'd heard nothing from him and had to respect his apparent desire never to see her again.

She walked towards the hotel entrance, catching a glimpse of herself as she passed the great gilt mirror in the foyer: a slim figure in a belted Moschino suit. She was so absorbed in her thoughts as she exited through the revolving doors that she hardly noticed the long black Rolls-Royce gliding to a halt in front of her. A moment later, as the doorman opened the car door, a woman stepped out on to the pavement, and Daisy drew in a horrified breath as she recognised her.

Oh my God, it's Margaret! And if she's here, that means only one thing . . .

Daisy dropped her head, resisting an impulse to veer away violently and run. That would only draw attention to herself. Instead she fought for calm despite her pounding heart and kept moving easily forwards, watching from beneath her lowered fringe as Margaret turned and waited for the other person inside the car.

Was he there? Was Daddy inside? She looked for that imposing figure with its bulky stomach straining under a waistcoat. But there was nobody like that in the car. Instead, a slender honey-blonde climbed out, holding tight to a crocodile-skin handbag as she put one elegant Gina-shod foot to the pavement and then another.

Daisy had to keep moving. She turned to her left and started walking west, risking one backward look. The elegant young woman, surely no older than herself, was following Margaret into the hotel entrance.

Who is that? Daisy was still shaking with adrenaline, but the question thudded relentlessly through her mind: *Who the HELL is that?*

374

45

In the cinema room of the Belgravia house, the only light came from the movie flickering away on the screen. It showed a small red-headed boy riding his bike. He was freckled, knobbly-kneed, and a big gap between his front teeth flashed black as he grinned into the camera. Near him, a smaller girl was running about chasing a puppy, a serious expression on her face. The children were playing in the grounds of a large house that Coco recognised as the one where she had performed at the party. A woman's voice in the background was urging them on.

'That's the children's mother, Elizabeth.' Margaret's voice floated over from the back of the room. 'I apologise for the quality. The technology wasn't up to much in the early eighties.'

The movie cut to another time: it was Christmas Day and they were opening their presents. The boy, older now and even more gappy where he didn't have huge grown-up teeth descending from his gums, was clearly delighted with the vast Lego set he'd received, while the girl, her fair hair in pigtails, was cooing over a doll in a perfectly scaled Silver Cross pram.

Then the scene changed to a birthday party: a lavish affair by the looks of things, with merry-go-rounds, helter-skelters, dodgems, candy floss and popcorn stalls. Clowns, stilt walkers and magicians were wandering through the crowds of children in their party best, some holding on to the hands of their parents and evidently overawed by the spectacle. The boy zoomed into range of the camera, older now and getting gangly, and then raced out of sight, appearing again by the dodgem cars where he hopped about, eager for a ride. The girl came into focus, standing by an enormous birthday cake and smiling and waving at the camera. Then the camera panned left to a glamorous-looking woman in a blue dress, who was holding a baby, a girl by the look of her sprigged dress. The woman made the baby wave at the camera, lifting one fat arm and waggling it.

'Who's that?' asked Coco, interested.

'No one who matters,' came Margaret's reply. 'A family friend.'

But the girl featured in the next snippet as well, this time as an unsteady toddler waddling across the lawn, her nappy jutting out behind her. The older boy was watching her with a curious expression on his face, as though he was interested in observing this strange creature but set apart from her. Then the glamorous woman from the last scene came running across the lawn, laughing. She picked up the toddler and swung her upwards before hugging her to her chest and covering the little girl's face in kisses.

The film was switched off abruptly.

'Is that it?' Coco said, surprised.

'Mr Dangerfield says that William refused to take part in any films after that age. But he appears in the family photo albums. Come along. We'll go and look at them now.'

Margaret led her out of the basement and upstairs to a library where the books didn't look as though anyone ever read them. On a gleaming walnut table were laid out large photo albums bound in green, navy and burgundy leather, each stamped in gold with a crest and a year. Margaret opened one and flicked through the pages.

'The old-fashioned way of storing photographs,' she remarked with a tight smile. Before Coco could see any of the pictures inside, Margaret suddenly closed the albums and said, 'You know, I think we should look at the file I've prepared for you. It's probably more use than these old things.'

'All right,' Coco said, though she was sorry not to be looking in the albums. She liked looking into the past and examining these people's childhoods. Their experience was so different from her own, it was hard to believe they had grown up in the same country. She'd seen these kids on horseback, on skis, riding miniature sports cars, swimming in their own pool, relaxing on the deck of their own yacht. It was a life she couldn't imagine, a universe away from the estate and everything that had gone on there.

Margaret led her over to the armchairs by the fire-place and they sat down. She handed Coco a black folder. 'Everything you'll need to know is in there. When you've read it, we'll discuss it. It's important you understand exactly what we want.'

'So – let me get this straight. This William has written letters to the family lawyers, and that's what made everyone upset?' Coco frowned as she flicked the pages of the folder back and forth, glimpsing more up-to-date photographs of the red-headed boy.

Margaret nodded. 'There are several trusts that were set up by Josef Dangerfield to protect the family fortune and ensure that the next generation's inheritance would be kept intact. William is alleging mismanagement of the trusts by his father – quite untrue, of course – and he's threatening legal action to uncover the trusts' actions if his questions are not answered. We need to discover first exactly what he wants to know and why – and whether there is anything in his own behaviour that is less than . . . shall we say . . . proper.'

'Oh, right. You want to get the dirty on him, so if he tries anything you can threaten him?'

'I'm not sure if I'd put it quite like that,' Margaret said in a tight voice, 'but knowledge is power.' She stood up. 'Spend an hour or so reading that file. Then tonight we're going out. There's one last tutor I want you to meet.'

Coco groaned. 'Not another tutor! What else do I have to learn?'

'Oh, I think you'll like this one,' Margaret said. 'We're going for dinner at Scott's. Wear something nice and don't forget everything you've been taught.' She went out.

Margaret returned an hour later and asked if Coco had enjoyed reading the file.

'Yeah,' she said honestly. She'd been drawn into the

details of this person's life and become immersed in his story. 'Interesting.'

'Good. I hope it will all prove useful to you. Now, you'd better get ready. We're due at Scott's in two hours. I'll have the driver take you back to South Kensington. Leave the file here, please. The car will be back to pick you up at seven-thirty precisely.'

Later that evening, Coco watched London sliding past the car window as the Rolls took her to the restaurant. She felt wonderful in the gorgeous dress she was wearing. She'd been yearning to wear it for ages, and maybe it was a little too dressy for dinner but . . . she didn't care. It was an Alexander McQueen black crêpe dress with built-up samurai armoured shoulders that were strong enough to make a statement but subtle enough not to interfere with the overall elegance. It was short, showing off legs that were looking their best since the salon had spray-tanned her an even apricot gold all over, and she'd teamed it with a punky black clutch bag with a crystal skull catch, and high strappy sandals. Now she was on her way to one of the most fashionable restaurants in the city.

Coco laughed to herself. It was incredible how quickly she'd become entirely used to her new lifestyle, almost as though this was the way she should have been living all along but there had been a slight administrative error that had at last been put right. She still could not believe that old man Dangerfield and Margaret were prepared to go to such lengths, and for what? She was not even entirely clear yet what exactly was expected of her, though she was sure it would be made plain in due course.

This boy William – well, man now, she supposed – had been brave simply to walk out on his privileged life, although there was the safety net of the family trusts to take into account, she reminded herself. It wasn't exactly like heading off to live on the streets. Even so, his achievements couldn't be discounted. It took guts and vision to set up a company like he had, one that made millions for him in his own right. She wondered what he was like. *Well, in a few weeks, I'll know for real. But first I've got to meet this new tutor, whoever the hell he is. I can't believe I've still got stuff to learn. What is it now? Do I need my face surgically altered or something?*

When the car arrived at Scott's in Mayfair, she felt nervous. She didn't usually have to walk into posh restaurants alone, but this was a good chance to rehearse what she'd need to put into practice soon enough – having self-confidence and believing in the person who had been created by Margaret's teachers. She could now walk into any restaurant – even in France or Italy – and understand the menu, and how to eat what arrived, and what wine to drink with it. She didn't need to be afraid any more. She belonged. She wasn't sure if she truly believed that, but it was what she had to tell herself in order to get through.

The maître d' greeted her at the door and showed her to the table where Margaret was already waiting. She was talking to someone seated with her. It must be the new tutor. Margaret moved and Coco saw that it was a man who, as soon as he saw her approaching, leaped to his feet with a glowing smile. He was strikingly handsome, tall and slim with high cheekbones, blond hair, dark blue eyes and a charming lopsided way of grinning.

'Ah, Coco,' Margaret said, also rising to her feet, 'may I introduce Alexander McCorquodale?'

'Please,' said the young man, 'call me Xander. Everyone else does.'

'Hi,' Coco said. She warmed to him at once. Charm seemed to spill out and fall about him in pools of sparkling light. *But what,* she wondered, *is he going to teach me?*

As if in answer to her thoughts, Margaret said, 'Xander is going to be your passport into the world we are eager for you to enter. Now, shall we sit down and decide what to order? Then we can discuss business.'

46

Later that evening, in the study of the Belgravia house, Daddy Dangerfield sat in the green leather chair behind his vast desk, one elbow resting on the top. Margaret stood close beside him, rolling her employer's shirtsleeve up his arm and tucking it back neatly so that an expanse of tanned flesh was revealed. The skin, covered in thick dark hair, hung a little loosely as though it had only recently lost a padding of fat from beneath. Margaret swabbed a patch of it lightly, then picked up a small syringe filled with clear liquid. In a practised move she held it up, squirted out a stream of the liquid, then jabbed it quickly into the uncovered arm.

Daddy pulled in a sharp breath but said nothing as he watched Margaret press down on the syringe, sending the fluid into his veins.

'There,' she said with satisfaction as she withdrew the needle, swabbed the skin again and rolled down the shirtsleeve. 'All done.'

'Thank you, Margaret.' Daddy smiled at her, though rather wanly. 'I think I rather needed that today.'

'You'll feel the benefits at once, sir, I'm sure.' Margaret cleared up the equipment briskly, packing the syringe away into a neat little metal case. 'The professor tells me that this is the very latest version of the serum, and that its effectiveness is greater than ever.'

'Good, good.' Daddy absent-mindedly rubbed his arm where Margaret had injected it.

She bent down a little closer to him, her thin lips curved into a smile. 'You look in the prime of health, if I may say so. You seem younger and more vibrant than ever.'

'Do I?' His brown eyes, the eyeballs tinged slightly yellow, turned to her hopefully.

'Absolutely.' Margaret closed a small case containing two rows of vials, each filled with a clear serum, and locked it carefully. She tucked the key into her pocket and frowned. 'But, sir, I'm afraid there's a certain matter we must discuss. The one I raised with you earlier.'

Daddy's eyes seemed to dim again and his shoulders slumped a little. 'Ah, yes. I remember.'

'I'm afraid we can't avoid it. The situation must be dealt with. The lawyers received another letter today, this time formally requesting information. And they've mentioned the fact of the girl's whereabouts. Besides, I was reminded today by the films I showed Coco in preparation for her trip. Naturally she asked who the other person was in them. I think I fobbed her off easily enough but it wasn't possible to show her the albums. It would have been too obvious. She would have asked questions. It made me realise we need to finalise this matter once and for all.' Margaret regarded her employer with a serious expression. 'Don't you agree with me, sir?'

The old man's face had turned down until his chin was pressed to his chest and she could not make out what was in his eyes. 'What? Oh, yes. Yes.' He raised his eyes to meet hers. 'Of course. You're right. We must finish off what we started. We have a plan in hand, don't we?'

'Yes, sir. We're simply waiting for word from you and it'll be done.'

Dangerfield stood up slowly, as though deeply fatigued. 'Well then, arrange it immediately. The sooner, the better. I don't know what we've been waiting for.'

Margaret nodded in a deferential manner. 'Yes, sir. Just as you say. It may take a little while to get everything we need to sort out the . . . well, you know . . . but wheels will be set in motion at once.'

The old man sighed. 'It must be finished, I suppose.' He seemed bowed down by the weight of his decision. Then his dark eyes flickered with a different light as he said, 'And what of young Coco? How is my protégée?'

'Doing marvellously. I must say, I've been quite astounded by her progress. You'll remember I was not convinced that she was the right person for the job—'

'I knew she was,' cut in Daddy. 'I sensed it from the start. She has the spirit we need, the background . . .'

'Quite.' Margaret smiled. 'I feel that she has become very comfortable in the new life you've provided for her. I'm quite certain she will not wish to jeopardise it for any reason. What else has she got after all? My investigations into her background have shown that she's exactly the rootless, unanchored person we require.'

'Good. Good. Then we're close to being ready?'

'Absolutely. Tonight, I produced our joker. The McCorquodale boy.'

'I wondered when we were going to get the help we expect from that quarter.'

'The chips are being cashed as we speak.'

'Excellent. You've done a splendid job, Margaret. I won't forget it.'

She gave a slight bow, her expression pleased. 'Thank you, sir. Just as long as it delivers results, then I'll be satisfied.'

47

I deserve this, Daisy told herself as she lay on the comfortable massage table in the dimly lit spa area of Minot's Hall, a well-established country house hotel that was providing her with lots of ideas for what she wanted for the Craven hotels. An expert young masseuse was rubbing a deliciously scented oil into her back, smoothing away all the tensions and cares of the last few weeks. She'd already enjoyed soaking in a warm perfumed bath and then a facial with more scented oils, and the finishing touch was this luxurious massage.

Bliss . . .

Life had become extremely busy for her lately. She was overseeing the redesign of the town-centre and airport hotels, which was time-consuming but basically a management job. Her heart really lay in the redevelopment of the eight Cotswolds properties, now reduced to six. At her suggestion, Craven Dalziel had sold off two of the less attractive ones to help fund the redesign of the others. At a board meeting two weeks ago, she'd also scored her greatest triumph. At her suggestion, the company had changed its name from Craven Dalziel to the Craven Hotel Group. It had been nerve-wracking making the suggestion in front of the entire Craven board, especially as the grandson of old Mr Dalziel was there and hadn't exactly looked happy about it, but in the end they'd seen her point: Dalziel was a hard word to pronounce and the new name had a much stronger sense of identity. It had given her an amazing thrill when they'd agreed to adopt the name she'd suggested. At last she was making her mark in a way that meant she was truly achieving what she'd set out to do.

Since then she had been working frantically, visiting each of the properties, consulting with architects and recruiting the extraordinary Tomasz, who was overseeing the interiors. Daisy herself was involved with every stage of the new look, from the fabrics to the light fittings, to the menus. What she wanted was high comfort with a strong brand identity that was absolutely reliable and trustworthy: customers had to be certain they would get unvarying standards of food, service and rooms. But it meant dragging the managers of the hotels with her, kicking and screaming. They wanted to resist at every step and she was losing patience with some of them. She'd spent that morning with Genevieve and Mike Holland, owners of the Grey House, listening to them complain about builders, about dust, about Tomasz and his plans . . . and just about everything else they could.

'I've explained the vision for the Grey House,' Daisy had said wearily, while Genevieve sat opposite looking outraged, jaw tight over her regulation string of pearls and large bosom. 'You know that it has to be in line with the other Craven hotels, and that's all there is to it.'

If Genevieve carried on being so obstructive, Daisy would have to see about replacing her, which would be a shame considering that she'd received good reports from the secret guests for her warmth and kindness. *It's just me she's such a monster to.*

But it was all worth it to see her vision being realised. It was incredibly exciting to see the hotels materialising from blueprints and mood boards, from swatches and photographs, to the actual real places where guests would soon be staying. Daisy enjoyed thinking up quirky touches: the alcoholic ginger beer and heritage gins in the mini-bars; the vintage school desks that opened up to reveal a PC system; the curious hand-selected titles in the Edwardian bookcases.

She knew that if her little group of six country hotels was a success, she would have truly made her mark. She would have justified the investment that the company had made in her. The next part of her scheme could open up.

She found that work also kept her mind off thoughts of Christophe. When she felt tired or lonely, she longed with all her heart to be going back to Nant-y-Pren for one of their wonderful weekends, full of walks, good food and romance. But that was impossible. She wondered where he was now – somewhere in France perhaps, staying with his sister. Maybe even starting a new life with someone else. The thought made her feel so sick, she shut it out at once.

I'll concentrate on this fantastic massage, she thought as the masseuse pummelled and then smoothed her skin. She'd come straight here from the Grey House, desperate to get away from the mud and dust, and this break was exactly what she needed.

Although, of course, it's work. She smiled to herself as the masseuse pressed intensely along her spine and then followed up with a long strong rub. *I suppose there are benefits to this job.*

The massage was a professional bonus, allowing her to experience the lotions and essences that Minot's Hall used in its spa.

Daisy closed her eyes and let all the stress flow out of her, wishing this delicious feeling could go on for ever.

'So, how was it?' The glamorous blonde by the window, dressed in an Alberta Ferretti floaty chiffon dress with a Pringle ribbed cardigan and Manolo heels, stood up as Daisy came in. She was beautiful, with wide-set grey eyes and a full-lipped mouth. In her late twenties or early thirties, she carried herself with easy confidence.

Daisy went over, feeling just a touch dowdy in her own bronze, drop-waisted Burberry dress and Rupert Sanderson sandals, some of the things she had treated herself to when she'd been in London. It had been odd to walk about the places she'd once frequented, carelessly flashing her daddy's credit card and scooping up whatever she wanted without a second thought. Now she had to think carefully about what she purchased. Daisy shook the other woman's outstretched hand. 'The massage was lovely, thank you.'

'Shall we have a drink? What would you like?'

'Oh, just white wine, thanks.'

'Fine. I'll join you.' The blonde woman summoned a waiter with a lift of her eyebrow. 'Two glasses of the Puligny Montrachet, please.' Then she turned back to Daisy. 'The orange oil is fabulous, isn't it?'

'Amazing,' agreed Daisy with a smile.

'Part of our newest range.' Jemima Calthorpe returned the smile, showing perfect white teeth. 'So . . . would you like to see what I'm suggesting for your hotels?'

'Yes, please.' Daisy watched as Jemima lifted up a large Mulberry hold-all and started taking samples out of her bag. It had been a thrill to be contacted by one of the managing directors of Trevellyan, the famous perfume house. It had recently been inherited by three sisters, daughters of the founding family, and they were in the process of a massive revamp of the brand. No longer did it signify old ladies clutching lavender-scented handkerchiefs on their way to church; now it was getting a reputation for being the latest chic must-have brand, with scented candles and lotions to go with its traditional range of perfumes. And they had relaunched their signature scent, Tea Rose, with a sexy new campaign fronted by a top model. Jemima Calthorpe was in charge of developing the spa side of the business. When she'd heard that Craven was in the process of upgrading a small chain of hotels, she'd sent an introductory email, hoping to pitch for the contract to supply the toiletries and skin products. It had been her idea to treat Daisy to a pampering afternoon using the Trevellyan range, to see if they were the kind of products that would fit with the chain's revamp of their hotels.

Jemima took a range of samples out of her bag and

put them in a row in front of Daisy as the waiter brought over large wine glasses half full of honey-coloured wine. 'Here,' she said, indicating the pretty little plastic bottles, each with a small nude-pink gros-grain ribbon tied at the neck. 'We offer hand soaps, shower gels, shampoo, conditioner, body lotion. That's standard. For our more luxurious range, there's also a bath oil, facial cleanser with a miniature muslin cloth, and a moisturiser. We can do the basic range in our famous Tea Rose scent, or the Orange if you feel that Tea Rose is too feminine and you want a more unisex approach. We can also provide miniature scented candles for the rooms, bathrooms or as fare-well gifts. And, of course, if you have spas on site, then we have trade-sized supplies for facialists and masseurs.' She picked up her balloon wine glass and lifted it. 'Cheers.'

'Cheers.' Daisy lifted her own glass and took a sip of the dry yet rich white wine. It rippled over her tongue. 'Very impressive. The bottles look beautiful and they suit the level of luxury we're pitching for perfectly. And, of course, our customers will recognise the Trevellyan name.'

'One of the benefits of being around for well over a century and a half,' Jemima put in.

'Absolutely. The historical aspect of our hotels – the antiques, the prints, the evocation of an age of ease and comfort – that's all vital to our vision. Trevellyan fits well with that.' Daisy put her glass down. 'It all depends on price, really. If this goes ahead, I'll be offering a large contract to supply six hotels, with the possibility of future expansion. Can we do a deal that will satisfy us both?'

Jemima stared at her with a look of amusement mixed with respect. 'I'm sure we can,' she said slowly. 'I get the feeling we understand each other.'

Daisy felt a tremor of surprise. Jemima Calthorpe reminded her of girls at her old school: born to wealth and privilege, just as she herself had been, and endowed with that magical combination of beauty, brains and confidence. But there was the faintest trace of vulnerability about her, as though she had faced her own demons and was determined to beat them.

'Maybe we do,' she said slowly.

Jemima leaned forward. 'You're young, I can see that. How old are you? Twenty-five? Twenty-six? You're in charge of your own chain of hotels . . . and you didn't even inherit it from Daddy.'

Daisy's stomach flipped over but she tried to keep control of her face and not reveal any of her emotions.

'I respect that,' Jemima continued. 'Really. More than you can know. I'd love for us to be a part of your success story. Because I'll tell you now, women like you become successes. You don't rely on anyone else for your motivation – it comes from in here.' She tapped her chest. The next moment, she was leaning forward, concerned. 'Hey – are you OK?'

'Yes.' Daisy fought for composure, knowing that she was showing her emotions on her face: Jemima's words had struck home, creating an upsurge of sadness inside her. Was she really succeeding on her own? Was she really capable of making it? Sometimes she became so fixated on the final goal that she forgot she was achieving it all on her own merits. 'I'm fine, really.'

Jemima didn't say anything more but watched sympathetically as Daisy composed herself. She brushed away a couple of stray tears and then smiled at the other woman.

'I'm sorry, I don't know what happened. I just . . . something you said . . . I'm fine. It's been a long day.'

'Really, it's quite all right.' Jemima smiled at her. 'I guess I triggered something. I'm sorry. Shall we finish our wine and I'll tell you about our pricing options?'

'That would be great,' Daisy said, and opened her notebook.

48

Margaret had told Coco to spend as much time with Xander as she could before beginning her mission, and that, for Coco, wasn't exactly a hardship. He was easy to be with: amusing, good-natured, handsome and always at her disposal.

'So you don't have a job?' she asked him, when he'd spent the morning lounging about on her sofa, watching her finishing up some grammar homework for her coach.

'Nope!' Xander gave her one of his grins, and an almost rueful look. ''Fraid I'm not really very employable.'

'Why not? Did you drop out?'

'Mmm, not exactly. But I came down from Oxford with a third and haven't set the world alight.' He shrugged. 'I've done some bits and bobs. My pal James gave me a job in his hedge fund for a while, but that didn't really work out. Too boring and technical for me and I did a rather massive fuck-up one day, lost a ton of cash. James was not a happy bunny and he let me go after that. Then I was a porter in an auction house for a while, and had a go at growing willow to make cricket bats . . . but I lost interest after a bit.' He looked a little sheepish. 'I have lots of friends who don't really work, you see. It's not so odd in my experience.'

Coco nodded. She knew plenty of people who didn't work as well. Her mother had never had a job. 'So, are you on benefits?'

Xander laughed, looking slightly scandalised. 'Er, no! Best not to mention things like benefits when you're hanging out with Will's crowd. We don't do benefits. I've got an allowance from my dad – though it's pretty bloody small – and I stay at his house in Onslow Square sometimes. Or I hang out with friends. Or go home to Scotland.'

'Sounds like a pretty easy life, then.' Coco stared over at him. *Bloody hell, these kids have no idea.*

'It sounds all right, but, you know, it's stressful. I'm always short of cash. I never have quite enough.' His voice tailed off and he looked rather wistful.

'Is that why you're doing this? I take it Mr Dangerfield's paying you well to ease me into the inner circle.'

Xander flushed and dropped his gaze to his lap for a moment, twisting his hands. 'It sounds pretty crumby when you put it like that,' he said at last. 'But, yeah, it was a fairly irresistible offer. And I don't know Will all that well – he's not my best friend or anything. I mean, we weren't at school together. He was at Winchester. But I did know him at uni. We moved in the same circles, as they say. He might be surprised to hear from me, but not amazed. It's likely I'd look him up if we were in the same city.'

'And you know what his dad's got planned?'

Xander shrugged, frowning. 'Not a clue. Look, Will's a big boy and he can look after himself. I, for one, am pretty certain you're not going to get much out of him. He's not a big talker, he's a private kind of guy. That's why I thought it would be OK to take the dosh for facilitating a small introduction, you know? God, let's have a fag. Have you got any?'

Xander, Coco found, never liked to talk about anything serious for long. He was happier chatting away about trivialities and gossip, but it was useful for her. In his long streams of chatter, she picked up plenty of hints about the way his kind expressed themselves, and their interests. For all of Penny's best efforts, she couldn't teach Coco the slang and idiom that this circle of privileged youngsters used without thinking about it. Penny wanted her to talk in tightly perfect, grammatical sentences; she didn't realise that Coco would need to have a lazier, more natural style if she were really going to fit in. All of this Coco was quietly picking up from Xander, along with his attitudes. Actually, his careless, live-in-the-moment approach to money wasn't all that different from her own; they both shared the belief that something would turn up, and it always did.

There was also something else she could see about him almost from the first moment she'd laid eyes on him, but she said nothing about that. She wasn't the nosy type, and she was sure enough of her instincts.

'Hey,' Xander said one day, when they'd spent the afternoon smoking and drinking, coffee for Coco and pints for Xander, outside a pub in South Ken, 'I need some cash. I'm going to see my sister tonight, she usually helps out when I'm short. Do you want to come? She works at this amazingly smart nightclub, it'll be worth seeing.'

'Yeah, OK.' Coco perked up. A nightclub. That meant dancing. She realised that it was a long time since she'd danced and longed to lose herself in music again, find the wonderful escape she'd always loved so much. What would she wear? Something short and glittery for getting attention on the dance floor, and the highest heels in her wardrobe. She had a sparkly dress that Leanne had said would be good for smart poolside parties on warm nights. That was just the thing.

When she opened the front door to Xander later that evening in her shimmering dress and silver platforms, her hair a glossy curtain of golden caramel and her lips a shining red, she was surprised to see him in a jacket and tie, though his blond hair was typically dishevelled and he had a light growth of stubble over his chin.

'Ah,' he said, grinning, 'you look terrific. Like a big silver . . . Easter Egg.'

'Thanks a lot! That's not the look I'm going for,' Coco said crossly. 'Why are you wearing a tie? You don't wear a tie when you go clubbing!'

'Crossed wires,' he said apologetically. 'I should have said. It's not like going clubbing. Look, you'll be fine. Lots of the girls wear gorgeous dresses like that one. But the blokes wear ties, OK? Come on.'

It was ten o'clock when they arrived in Berkeley Square, Xander explaining that he wanted to get there early so he could see his sister without too many distractions as she got busier when the club filled up.

The square didn't look like the kind of place where you'd find a club, in Coco's opinion, and there was no queue, no sound of thudding music and no bouncers. There wasn't even a huddle of barely dressed smokers on the pavement indicating where the action was. Xander led her towards a grand Regency house with a tented awning at the front and to the side, a doorman in a smart navy uniform and peaked cap standing next to it.

'Evening, Harry,' Xander greeted him as they got close.

'Evening, Mr McCorquodale,' said the doorman with a smile of recognition.

'My sister's in tonight?'

'Oh, yes, sir.'

'Good, good.' He looked over his shoulder at Coco. 'Let's go down.'

They went under the awning and down a flight of stairs, and the next moment they were walking into a long, narrow hallway, through a pair of open saloon-style doors painted the same dull cream as the walls, past the cloakrooms and down underneath the great house above.

'This is Colette's,' Xander explained. 'Bit of an institution. It was started by my uncle David in the sixties, and my sister helps him run it now he's getting on a bit.' He greeted a man in a dark suit standing by a small reception-style window. 'Evening, Gennaro, I've got one guest tonight. Do I need to sign her in?'

'Good evening, sir. No, as it's you, that's fine,' the man returned in a smooth voice with a hint of an Italian accent. 'Lady Allegra is in the bar.'

Bloody hell, thought Coco, who'd been reduced to

awed silence. This was not what she'd been expecting. This place, with its atmosphere of louche luxury, was not her idea of a nightclub. *Lady Allegra? What the fuck?* 'You didn't say your sister was a lady,' she hissed, as they continued down towards the hall. 'What are you, a lord?'

'Nope, just an Honourable. Sorry. Anyway, it doesn't matter. It doesn't mean anything.'

He led the way into the bar area, a warm and comfortable place painted in pumpkin yellow and hung with all manner of paintings, mostly of racing, and framed vintage cartoons. Several people were sitting about, or leaning on the bar, or in a cosy seating area across the hall, where there were red velvet banquettes and silk cushions below a vaulted ceiling. Behind the bar, a large man in a grey jacket that strained at the buttons was mixing a cocktail, and an exquisite girl with a thick mane of blonde hair was watching him.

'Sinbad, it never ceases to amaze me how brilliantly you do that,' she was saying as Xander darted up and put his hands on her back where her halter-necked black dress had left it bare. She squealed and turned round. Immediately, Coco could see the resemblance to Xander in the girl's fine-featured face and her navy blue eyes with their frame of dark lashes. 'Xander!' she cried, her surprise melting into pleasure. 'What are you doing here? I didn't know you were coming in.'

'I wanted to see you.' He dropped a kiss on his sister's cheek. Her gaze moved over his shoulder to Coco and her eyebrows rose quizzically. Coco smiled back timidly, feeling out of her depth again.

Xander pulled away and indicated her with a movement of his hand. 'Allegra, this is my friend Coco. Coco, my sister Allegra.'

'Hi,' Coco said in a small voice. She had never felt this intimidated. This girl was gorgeous, and clearly strong and intelligent with it, and she was a goddamned lady. How lucky could one person be?

'Hi, Coco.' Allegra smiled in a friendly enough way, but there was a spark of suspicion in her eyes. 'Well, this is a nice surprise. Shall I get Sinbad to mix us all some drinks?'

The barman made house cocktails, then Allegra led them through to the banquettes in the seating area while she and Xander swapped family gossip and talked about how the club was doing. It was quiet, considering it was going on for ten-thirty, and Allegra talked wistfully about how she hoped to attract more young people into the club but wasn't sure how to go about it. Coco sipped her delicious drink – it had lemon in it, she was sure – and listened to Allegra and Xander talking. After a while, they went through to the back of the club, passing cosy sitting areas in small vaulted bays, then going through a darkly glamorous restaurant area where the pillars were covered in gleaming beaten brass panels, and a dance floor that twinkled with stars, although there weren't any dancers on it yet. Some boppy pop music played and Coco gazed wistfully at the dance floor as she passed. It wasn't exactly her favourite track but she still itched to get moving to the beat.

'It's such a bore having to come out here,' Allegra said, leading them out of a back door into a tiny area open to the night sky, 'but I suppose the ban is making us all smoke less!'

'You guys go ahead,' Xander said, 'I'll be back in mo'.'

He disappeared back inside, leaving Coco and Allegra alone together. Coco felt very ill at ease with the other girl as they lit up and puffed away. After a pause that seemed to be going on forever, Allegra blew out a long stream of smoke that looked white in the darkness and spoke.

'So,' she said, in a slightly cooler tone, 'are you Xander's new girlfriend?'

'Oh, no,' Coco said quickly, sensing the undercurrent of hostility. 'It's not like that. He's just a friend.' It was true. She thought Xander was very good-looking and he made her laugh, but he didn't do anything for her. There was no spark.

'Oh. A friend.' Allegra tapped her ash and tossed her blonde hair back over one shoulder. 'Right. OK. I hope you're a good friend, and not a bad one. You see, Xander has plenty of bad friends and he doesn't need any more . . . enablers.'

Coco said quickly, 'Don't worry, I'm a good influence. I promise.'

'Has he asked you for money?'

'No. Actually, he's going to ask you for some.' Coco gave her a little apologetic smile.

Allegra sighed. Her hostility softened. 'I know. He usually does. What can I do? I have to give it to him, though I'll make him work for it. I've got something he can do for me. I can't have him starving on the streets. But I do worry about him.'

'Why?' Coco asked. Her suspicions about Xander

appeared well grounded. 'He seems OK. Just a bit directionless.'

'Well . . .'

Just then Xander came back, taking a packet of cigarettes out of his jacket pocket. 'Panic's over, ladies. I'm back.' He lit up his cigarette. 'What've you been talking about?'

'You,' Allegra said pointedly.

'Ah. Is that my favourite topic? I can't quite decide. On second thoughts, it isn't. Tell me how things are getting on here. How's David?'

'Fine, fine.' Allegra seemed distracted now, Coco noticed. 'Listen, Xander, I've got something that needs doing. I want you to pay Jemima a visit. She's got some samples for me and I said I'd collect them but I'm tied up here. As she's family, I want to keep her sweet . . .'

'Ah, the deadly McCorquodale charm. Don't worry. I can do it.'

'Thanks, honey. There's a nice tip in it for you if you do.'

Xander smiled. 'Excellent. I'm getting a bit low, as a matter of fact. But I'm off on a trip quite soon – with Coco, as it happens.' Allegra threw her another look but said nothing. 'So I'd appreciate it if you can give me the money now and I'll squeeze in a duty call to Jemima before I go.'

'OK.' Allegra dropped her cigarette butt and ground it out with the sole of her elegant shoe. 'Let's go to the office and I'll get it for you.'

Coco and Xander left Colette's about an hour later, after he had returned from the office with Allegra.

402

He was looking happy and patting his pocket. 'All done, we can get out of here.'

But he hadn't wanted to go home. Instead he'd suggested a late-night drink in Soho.

'OK,' Coco said slowly. They were out in the dark London streets, taxis roaring past them and people wandering by on their way to stations and bus stops. She turned to face him. 'Xander, did you need money so you could go and score?'

He grinned at her sheepishly. 'Mmm. Maybe. Are you shocked?'

She stared at him. *If you only knew.* She thought back to Jamal, and the days of trading drugs all over South London. It was partly men like Xander who kept the whole sorry business going: the rich boys who had no idea of the misery and death their habits were dealing out to others with the misfortune to be born at the other end of the scale. 'No,' she said. 'I'm not shocked.'

'Good,' he said happily. 'Well, we can score together then, can't we?' He looked at her eagerly, obviously hoping she might be a partner in the undertaking.

Coco shook her head. 'I don't do drugs.'

'What, nothing?'

'Maybe a spliff. But nothing else.'

'Oh.' Xander looked cross suddenly, like a little boy who'd been caught being naughty. 'You're going to disapprove of me, aren't you?'

'No, man,' Coco said, slipping back into her old jargon. 'Your life is your life. You do what you like. I'm not judging anyone. Do what makes you happy.'

His face cleared. 'Good. Come on then, it won't take long.'

He hurried off along the pavement, eager to get to his dealer. Coco followed behind, shivering a little despite her coat. No wonder he'd needed money. And she'd been able to read the signs of a habit on his face – the subtle pointers were all there.

She understood now. It was the dark side of having everything.

49

The launch of the new chain was not so far off now. Daisy was spending most of her time racing between one hotel and another, solving problems as they arose and overseeing the work. The transformation was already remarkable: where there had been a motley collection of different styles, menus, decoration and service, there was now cohesion and a noticeable, but not overbearing, brand identity. The Craven Hotels logo, a grey oval with an elegant C and H inside, was discreetly present. The new membership cards had just arrived for those customers who wanted to join the loyalty scheme, and they were very smart: pale cream with the grey logo in the middle and nothing else. All the membership details were on the back instead of the front.

It was a relief to take a day off and go to London. Daisy had decided to ask Trevellyan to provide the hotel toiletries and was taking the contracts to Jemima herself so that they could celebrate their partnership. She had struck up an instant rapport with the other woman, despite the age difference of a few years between them, and was keen to see her again. Jemima felt like the first real friend she had made since she'd started life as Daphne Fraser, a proper girlfriend she wanted to confide in and laugh with and just be herself – well, as much herself as it was possible to be.

I don't really know who I am, Daisy thought, watching the countryside fly by outside the train window as it sped towards the capital. She remembered Christophe's expression as he'd pleaded with her to tell him who she was. *I don't even know myself.* She pushed away the question that continually fluttered on the edges of her mind, one she had resolutely ignored for years – who was her real father? If she wasn't a Dangerfield, then who was she? *I AM a Dangerfield!* she told herself furiously when that little voice in her head dared to ask the question. *That's how I was brought up. That's who I am. It doesn't matter what my bloodline is. Daddy was the only father I ever had.*

She felt the familiar bitterness of rejection in her throat. It was only by not thinking about it that she could stay strong. If she confronted it head on, she was afraid she would crumble entirely, her schemes would collapse, and she'd be left with nothing at all.

Jemima Calthorpe's house was in a smart part of Chelsea, off the Old Brompton Road, a rustic white-painted cottage hidden behind a high wall with a wrought-iron gate. It looked quite incongruous in the centre of London.

'Do you like it?' Jemima said cheerfully as she showed Daisy into the light hallway, decorated in fresh pale colours, with large black-and-white photographs of a fair-haired man and a grinning, chubby baby.

Jemima herself looked elegantly casual in jeans, a cashmere vest and a pale grey draped cardigan. Her blonde hair was screwed up into a loose ponytail and despite wearing no make-up she still looked stunning. 'It's new. I had a flat in Eaton Square a while back but it was sold and my husband and I bought this together. A fresh start. But to be honest, we spend most of our time at our place in the country. That's where Harry is at the moment, with my little terror there.' She nodded fondly at the photograph of the baby.

'He's adorable,' Daisy said. She wondered for a moment if she would ever have a family and a beautiful home like this. *Business first*, she told herself firmly.

'Mmm. But it is lovely to have a day or so without him every now and then. Running the company is an excellent way to spend a little me time. Come through, let's get a coffee.'

Daisy followed her into a beautiful room, the back open to the outside with folding glass doors, letting lots of light into the handmade kitchen painted in the softest pale grey. A black double Aga gleamed below cream Métro-style tiling. A vase of softly drooping peonies brightened up the scrubbed-pine kitchen table.

'Here it is,' Daisy said brightly, her mood lifted by the pretty room. She pulled the contract out of her bag. 'The deal.'

Jemima laughed happily and took it from her. 'Hurray! I'm so pleased.' She looked over at Daisy, warmth shining in her grey eyes. 'Not just because it's an excellent deal that is just the right thing for both of us, but because I'm glad we're going to be working together.'

Daisy smiled back. 'I'm delighted too.'

'Come on. Let's forget coffee and have some champagne.' Jemima opened the fridge and took out a bottle of Veuve Cliquot. 'This calls for a celebration.'

They popped the cork, poured out glasses of foaming champagne and toasted Trevellyan, Craven Hotels and their continuing partnership. Then Daisy, who'd been wondering, asked Jemima how she'd managed taking over the family business, and Jemima started explaining how she and her two sisters had inherited a broken-down company and built it up again. They were deep into conversation that was leading away from business and into the territory of their families and pasts – though Daisy was careful to be vague – when there was a knock at the door.

'Oh, God,' exclaimed Jemima, consulting her watch. 'I forgot. My cousin's coming round to pick up some bits and pieces that I've got for Allegra. Sorry. He won't be long, I promise.'

Daisy watched her hurry out of the kitchen, regretting that their cosy intimacy was being disturbed. She liked Jemima and was enjoying the simple pleasure of talking and sharing. A moment later Jemima returned, followed by a man whose handsomeness redeemed the fact that he was a touch too thin and hollow-cheeked to look entirely healthy. He had dark blue eyes and a coating of stubble over his chin and jaw, and he was swaying slightly as he walked behind Jemima, an evening newspaper tucked under one arm.

'Daphne, this is my cousin Xander. Xander, this is Daphne Fraser. Her company has just employed us to supply their hotels.'

'Ah!' Xander smiled, his mouth curling up in a lopsided grin. 'How fabulous. Congratulations to you both.' His eyes slid to the yellow-labelled bottle on the table. 'No wonder the dear old Widow Click is being served.'

'Would you like a glass, Xander?' Jemima went to fetch one, while Daisy observed this new arrival. He was charming but there was something about him that made her wary: a lack of control or tendency to danger . . . she wasn't sure what it was, but it was definitely there. 'I've got the box of samples for you upstairs,' Jemima said. 'Take it to Allegra, she might like the new Orange range for the club.'

Xander saluted. 'Aye, aye.'

They sat down at the kitchen table. 'So, what are you up to, Xander?' Jemima asked as she topped up the glasses.

Daisy listened, a little disgruntled that her chat with Jemima had been disturbed.

'I'm heading off abroad soon, actually. To LA.' Xander took a long gulp of his drink.

'Nice. Holiday?'

He shook his head as he swallowed a mouthful of bubbles. 'Work . . . sort of,' he said when he could speak again.

Jemima raised her eyebrows. 'Work! How out of character.'

'Very funny.' He made a face at her. 'OK, it's not exactly cleaning windows on a skyscraper, but it's not a holiday.'

'Well, what are you doing?'

He tapped his nose and grinned. 'Can't say a word. Sorry!'

'Oh, go on,' coaxed Jemima. 'We won't tell, will we, Daphne?'

'You've always been able to make me talk,' Xander said, laughing. He threw his newspaper on the table and sat back in his chair. 'But I really shouldn't. Not this time.' At that moment Daisy let out a cry. The others looked at her, startled.

'Are you all right?' Jemima asked. 'You're white as sheet.'

Daisy stretched out one shaking hand towards the paper. 'Wh-wh-what's that?' she said through dry lips.

Xander picked up the paper and looked at a small headline at the bottom of the page. 'Oh yes. Poor kid's been killed abroad. Terrible. I didn't know her, though I'm friends with her brother. Did you, Jemima? Daisy Dangerfield.'

Jemima shook her head as she craned over to get a look. 'No. I'd heard of her, of course. She was quite the socialite for a while some years ago, wasn't she? Then she went off the radar.' She read the headline aloud. '"Millionaire businessman's daughter in tragic accident abroad". The full story's on page four.' She turned to it, and Daisy saw to her horror that there was an old photograph of her, from the night of the Crillon Ball, looking carefree and glamorous in her gown, her diamond brooch glittering at her cleavage and Freddie looking distinguished in white tie beside her. There was her old face, with its wide innocent eyes, surrounded by soft fair hair. Would they recognise her? Surely there was no way they could. 'Scuba diving accident,' Jemima said mournfully, oblivious. 'Poor girl. She was way too young.'

Daisy's heart was pounding, an awful tornado of emotion possessing her. She felt sick, as though she might pass out.

'Yeah.' Xander shook his head. 'It's kind of a weird coincidence really, because—'

'May I read it?' interrupted Daisy in a trembling voice.

'Sure.' Jemima passed her the paper and watched sympathetically as she read the article. 'Did you know her? You're about her age, aren't you?'

'She . . . she was a friend of mine,' Daisy said faintly, the pounding in her head increasing and horror encompassing her in its nauseating grip.

'God, how awful, I'm so sorry,' Jemima said, reaching out a hand to her while Xander watched sympathetically, keeping quiet now.

Daisy somehow managed to get to her feet. 'I'm . . . I'm sorry. It's an awful shock. I have to go.' She picked up the paper. 'May I take this?'

'Of course,' Xander replied.

Jemima stood up, concerned. 'Are you sure? I think you should stay here for a bit. You look terrible. Stay and calm down, you've had a bad shock.'

'No. No.' All Daisy knew was that she had to get out of here as soon as possible. In a minute she was going to lose her composure and she couldn't be sure what would happen then or what she might say. 'Thanks, Jemima. Goodbye.'

'Goodbye, sweetie, call me later, OK?' Jemima reached out to kiss her cheek.

Daisy was hardly aware of it. A moment later, she found herself on the street, her breath coming in sobs. She turned and ran, hardly knowing where she was going, until she reached some kind of small park with a couple of benches, one with an old man sunning himself on it. She went and sat down, the tears pouring down her face. They dropped on to the newspaper as she bent again over the article.

According to the report, Daisy Dangerfield had died in a scuba-diving accident as a result of faulty equipment off the coast of Thailand: '. . . close to where the family has an estate. Miss Dangerfield had been travelling alone and living at the estate for some time after leaving school.' The family were said to be distraught and had asked for privacy at this most distressing time.

So this was what they'd planned all along. To wipe her finally from existence. Daisy Dangerfield could not be brought back now. She was dead – or someone else was. Who the hell it really was she could not guess. Whether they'd managed to acquire a body somehow, or had bribed officials to pretend there had been one, or whether they'd arranged a death – it was an awful thought but she could believe they'd be capable of it – they'd done what they'd always intended. No doubt the body would be cremated, to make sure that there was no way it could be exhumed.

'Oh my God,' she sobbed. 'Can they really get away with this?'

But she knew the answer to that. They could get away with anything they wanted. No doubt Margaret had handled it all very well over the last six years. And who, after all, was interested in Daisy now? She had never known her mother's family. Her siblings had always resented and disliked her for being Daddy's favourite. Even her friends from school would have forgotten her long ago, except Lucy.

The old man opposite watched her curiously as she cried and scrunched up the newspaper, bending over as though in terrible pain. She had not thought it could get worse. But she had never felt so entirely, horribly alone as she did now.

50

'Hey, there are worse jobs than this, aren't there?' Xander said cheerfully as he strapped himself into a first-class seat.

'I suppose so,' Coco said. She was feeling rather ill. She'd never been on a plane before and Margaret had forgotten to include that particular aspect of civilised life in her education. She ought to be excited, considering they were travelling in luxury and had been having a very pleasant couple of hours before-hand being pampered in the first-class lounge, but she was frightened. Was this great thing really going to be taking off and soaring up into the sky? Tons of metal weighed down by hundreds of people and mountains of luggage? Would someone like to take a second to explain how that worked?

'It's a shame old Dangerfield didn't send us in his private jet,' Xander was saying. 'That would have been travelling in style. I love private planes. But I guess he didn't want to connect us with him too overtly.' He peered a little closer at Coco. 'Hey – are you all right?'

'Yes . . . yes, I'm fine.'

'You look a bit pale. You'll be all right when we get going.' He looked about with satisfaction. 'Yeah, I'm going to enjoy this.'

There was certainly plenty of room. Their large seats were next to each other, Xander by the window, and they each had a television screen and a side table. The seats converted into beds, apparently, if they fancied a sleep.

Coco wished that they could just be on their way.

'Let's pretend we're on our honeymoon,' Xander whispered, leaning over, his blue eyes sparkling mischievously. 'We might get even more special treatment!'

'No way,' said Coco, leaning back. 'I don't have a wedding ring, and anyway no one would believe it. Us married? If we can get through this without me whacking you in the mouth for winding me up, it'll be a miracle.'

Xander laughed. Coco closed her eyes and tried to pretend she was somewhere else.

In the event, Xander was right. Take off was alarming: the great plane had roared beneath them as it gathered speed and the moment of lifting away from the earth had been extraordinary. But once they gained altitude and the nose of the plane lowered, she began to feel better. After twenty or so minutes spent without plummeting back to earth, Coco started to relax and trust that perhaps they were going to make it safely to their destination.

The cabin staff were attentive and pleasant, bringing them cocktails and menus to study.

'You can eat at a table or here at your seat,' said the stewardess, smiling.

'A table?' Coco said.

The stewardess nodded. 'In the first-class dining room.'

Coco was amazed that there was a dining room on board a plane.

'I want to eat here and watch a movie,' Xander announced, so it was decided they would eat in their seats.

After a sumptuous three-course meal and more wine, Coco was feeling exhausted. Xander had clamped on his headset and was lost in his movie, so she went to the bathroom, changed into the cotton pyjamas she'd been given, and meanwhile the stewardess transformed her seat into a bed, complete with sheets, pillows and a duvet. Coco slipped in, put a sleep mask over her eyes, and within a few minutes, lulled by the constant boom of the massive jet engines, had fallen asleep.

When she woke, they were only a few hours off landing time. She refreshed herself with the toiletries supplied in a limited-edition designer bag, got dressed and returned to her seat in time for breakfast. Xander was white-faced and somewhat slurry.

'Have you been watching movies and drinking the entire time?' Coco asked, incredulous, as she settled back down in her seat. She liked Xander, but sometimes she couldn't help thinking that he was just a useless waster. He was charming company, though, and entirely unjudgemental. She had grown closer to him over the last few weeks and even confided in him the truth about her background at the club, and he hadn't minded at all. His attitude to her hadn't changed a jot.

He looked at her solemnly, his eyes bloodshot. 'Darling, it is a frightful waste of free Bollinger if you don't drink it,' he said, 'so it was plainly my duty to do so. I feel a bit crap, though. Where's that breakfast?'

They landed to blue skies and a warm, balmy afternoon, Coco squeezing her eyes shut and gripping the armrest during the actual landing and then breathing out with relief when they taxied to a stop. They got through immigration without too much trouble; she had worried that Xander might be stopped for being drunk, but he was practised at hiding intoxication and their status as first-class passengers helped smooth the way. Their limousine was waiting for them and soon they were gliding through the wide streets of Beverly Hills towards the hotel.

'God, it's just like in the movies,' Coco said, watching as Spanish-style villa followed Spanish-style villa. It all looked immaculate, down to the perfectly positioned palm trees that lined the roads. Normal people here seemed to be glossier than they were on the streets in London: girls with stunning bodies were walking dogs or jogging along with iPods strapped to their arms. The gardeners tending the bougainvillaea were ripped, with muscled shoulders and arms and perfect tans. Even the old ladies in smart trouser suits and sunglasses looked glamorous, with perfectly coiffed hair and full make-up.

'Oh, wow,' Coco breathed, gazing at everything. The sky was a perfect cerulean blue, unmarred by a single cloud, and the sunlight had a golden liquid quality. She felt like she'd arrived on another planet. Was little Chanelle from the estate really being driven down the LA boulevards in a limo? 'This is amazing.'

'I guess if it's your first time, it is kind of impressive,' Xander said insouciantly. He clamped his shades over his eyes against the sun's glare. 'But it's also a bit samey.' He leaned his head back against the seat. 'Christ, I feel like shit.'

At the Ritz-Carlton, they had a two-bedroomed suite, comfortable, modern and luxurious, in shades of caramel, apricot and white. The windows gave a fabulous view over the city and out towards southern California. How long they would be staying depended entirely on what happened over the next few days, but Xander was confident that they wouldn't be here long. As soon as they were safely settled, he disappeared into his room to sleep, leaving Coco on her own. This was a great adventure, sure, and she was still pinching herself to see if it was all real, but she was too anxious to enjoy it properly. All this time that she'd been with Margaret, she'd never really given a thought to what would be required of her in return for what she was receiving. The endless lessons, the expensive wardrobe, the head-to-toe makeover . . . she knew that her teeth alone had cost four grand, and she must be carrying several times that in clothes and shoes. Tomorrow was going to be the moment of truth. She had to succeed. She dreaded to think what failure would mean for her.

Does Xander really grasp what all this is about? she wondered. She suspected not. He was a sweet boy, and smart too, but he was too fond of the booze and the drugs to think about much else. Once he was comfortable with Coco knowing about his habit, he made no secret of how much he enjoyed coke, and depended on it for a good time. He liked speed too, and said he smoked heroin from time to time. He'd taken Coco to a few parties where all the posh kids there had plainly been out of their skulls on either alcohol or drugs.

'It's just what we all do,' he'd said, with his customary lopsided smile and a little shrug. 'One day we'll grow up and be sensible. But not yet.'

Coco picked up the file she'd brought along with her and sat down to look at it again. She knew it off by heart but needed to reassure herself that she was totally familiar with it. She flicked through the pages: it was all there. Will Dangerfield's life story complete with photographs. Here he was a round-faced boy at pre-prep school, his hair bright ginger and his nose covered with freckles. There he was a skinny boy in a blazer, cap and long socks on his way to prep school, and then again in a white vest and shorts, proudly holding trophies and medals he'd won. She found his face in the rows of wide-eyed boys in his class photographs. Then he was leaving the safety of his prep school behind him and heading up to Winchester. He looked so young and serious, his curly red hair darkening a little and legs lengthening so that he was standing a head above his classmates. There weren't many pictures after that, but there were some of him at university – the matriculation photograph of his year standing in front of their college library in their gowns and black ties, bright-eyed and excited at the prospect of their three years at Oxford, and another of him rowing for his college. She peered closely. It

419

was hard to make him out in the crew of eight, and he was clearly concentrating on the job in hand, but he appeared to have left the gawky stage behind him: the muscles on his arms and thighs stood out with the effort he was making.

Quite a nice body, she thought as she scrutinised it. *But I don't know if I could ever fancy someone with ginger hair.*

Along with the photographs there was the text, setting out all the stages of Will's life. It appeared that even after he'd left his father's house, close tabs had been kept on him at all times. His addresses were listed meticulously, along with the progress of his career. How had he gone from that innocent-looking schoolboy to a millionaire in his own right? The answer was simple: computer games. In his early twenties, Will had moved to LA and started a gaming company, hiring all the brightest talent he could recruit. His firm had been in from the very start on the craze for avatar-based games with the life game called Utopia, in which people had the chance to build a society along the lines they thought best, to see if their theories would work, whether they were socialist communes or capitalist markets. Utopia sold all over the world, as had all of its follow ups, and a dark, violent, post-Apocalyptic version called Dystopia had done even better. Each year the company released something new to great fanfare and excitement in the world of computer games, and had remained at the forefront of development. There was always some incredible new feature or improved graphics to keep fans buying and playing, and to keep Will's company DeVision in a very healthy state indeed.

And now he seemed to be enjoying the fruits of his success. An aerial photograph showed the house that she would be visiting tomorrow, if all went as planned, and it looked like something a film star might live in, with the usual squares of turquoise and green indicating pools and tennis courts.

So why does he care what his dad is doing with the family money? It's not as if he needs any of it. Coco narrowed her eyes. *It'll be interesting to find out.*

That evening, when Xander had woken up, sobered up and showered, they took a taxi to Matsuhisa in Beverly Hills for mouth-watering sushi at an eye-watering price, but Xander casually put it on his credit card and Coco guessed he must have been given some money for expenses. The city looked stunning as they returned along West Olympic Boulevard, the soft blue night sky illuminated by the brightly lit skyscrapers and the endless streams of traffic. Los Angeles seemed to go on for miles.

When they got back to the hotel, Xander made the call while Coco sat on the sofa, her legs tucked up underneath her, listening anxiously.

'Hey, Will, guess who? . . . Yeah, it's Xander! Listen, it's been bloody ages, how are you, mate? . . . Yeah, I'm great too. Guess what? I'm in LA for a bit and I thought I might pop round and see you, if you're not up to anything . . . Tomorrow? Yeah. Sure. What's the address? . . . Uh-huh.' Xander scribbled on the desk pad. 'Listen, I've got a friend with me. Can I bring her along? . . . Cool. See you tomorrow then. 'Bye.'

He clicked off his phone and looked over at Coco, smiling triumphantly. 'There. It's done. We're in.'

51

There they all were, faces smiling out from the social network site.

Sitting in the kitchen of her Bristol flat all alone, Daisy scrolled through her school friends, older now but unmistakably the same. Their privacy settings meant that she couldn't access their profiles. She wondered if they were discussing her even now. She put her name into the search tool, just in case someone had set up a page to her memory, but no one had. There was another Daisy Dangerfield, but it wasn't her. She felt obscurely jealous of the person who was allowed to use her name quite openly and without fear.

She had run several internet searches a day on the death of Daisy Dangerfield ever since she'd seen that awful newspaper piece but had learned nothing new. The incident was reported identically by news agencies: an unfortunate accident due to faulty equipment, but it had been Daisy's own, and she'd been alone when it happened. There was no one to blame. Very sad, but nothing more to be said on the subject.

Daisy was chilled by the gruesomeness of investigating her own death. But what scared her more was the evidence of her father's continued ruthlessness.

He'd rather see me dead than ever have dealings with me again. She wondered for a moment if her scheme was going to bring her into deadly danger. How would he react when he discovered what she'd been doing all this time?

Fuck him, she thought. *Let him do his worst. I'm going to have my say, if it's the last thing I do.*

The next time she met Lucy it was not in the Dangerfield Florey. Things seemed to have taken a much more dangerous turn since their relatively carefree lunch there. Instead, Daisy came to London wearing shades and a concealing hat, despite the fact that her eyes were still brown and her hair a sharp black, and she looked nothing like the girl who had been in the papers for a brief moment the previous week. She wore an unremarkable black suit and low-heeled shoes. The last thing she wanted was any attention.

'Oh my God, Daisy!' hissed Lucy, looking white-faced and nervous as she sat down at the bistro table. 'This is bloody weird. What the hell is going on?'

Daisy glanced around before saying in a low voice, 'Did you call?'

'Yes.'

'What did they say?'

'No funeral. You were cremated in Thailand, apparently. Any donations in remembrance to be sent to the Dangerfield Foundation.' Lucy's eyes filled with tears and her lip quivered as she stared at her old friend. She put her hand out and grasped Daisy's. 'This is horrible . . . horrible! They say you're dead! How could they do such a thing?'

'It *is* horrible,' Daisy said grimly, keeping her voice low. 'They're ruthless.'

'I realise that now.' Lucy shook her head slowly. 'I honestly believed this would blow over. I really did. I couldn't understand how a father could treat his own child so badly. It's unbelievable . . .'

'What did they say about the Dangerfield Foundation?' interrupted Daisy, not wanting to dwell on the awfulness of her situation. She tried not to think about it – it curdled her insides when she did. Thank God for Lucy. Without her, Daisy worried that she might begin to think that she actually did not exist, and never had.

Lucy leaned forward, her eyes wide. 'I asked, like you said I should. But the woman on the phone told me to consult the website, that it was a wonderful force for good in the world and I should learn all about it. But when I looked, there was hardly anything there.'

'The site is still under construction. It has been for months.' Daisy frowned. 'It's very strange. Daddy always had things done quickly. I still can't learn much about this mysterious foundation of his.'

The waiter came up and they both ordered a coffee. When he'd gone, Daisy said, 'Luce, this is awful. It's gone beyond a game now. Last time I was at the Florey, I saw my father's PA Margaret arrive, and she had a glamorous young thing with her. A WAG type. Do you have any idea who she might be?'

Lucy shook her head, looking puzzled. 'None. Another assistant?'

Daisy laughed. 'I can really see Margaret wanting an assistant like that! The girl was done up to the nines.' She sat back in her chair, feeling confused and deflated. 'I can't work it out. The internet doesn't turn up anything. It's a mystery.'

'I'll keep my ears open and see what I can find out.' Lucy smiled at her then shook her head. 'This is a bit like having coffee with a ghost. All the girls have been phoning up to talk about you.'

'I wish I could have heard some of it, it might have cheered me up,' joked Daisy. 'I didn't warrant much news space, did I?'

'Yes, disappointing. Next time, remember to die when it's a slow news week,' returned Lucy, and the two of them laughed again, finding what humour they could in the situation.

'Just keep pushing,' said Daisy, 'remember what we talked about.'

'I will.' Lucy smiled bravely. 'You can count on me. I don't care what that old bastard tries on.'

Daisy smiled back and they clasped hands more tightly than ever.

52

Xander hired a car and they drove up to West Hollywood, to an area in the Santa Monica Mountains above Sunset Boulevard known as the Bird Streets. The sun shone in a clear blue sky and everything gleamed in the sunlight. Picturesque, tree-lined roads wound through the hills, lined with massive house after massive house, of all varieties and styles, from modern mansions to medieval-looking castles, but each one on a large scale. Coco stared wide-eyed, amazed by the sheer size of everything. What could these places be like inside? Behind gated entrances she glimpsed beautiful landscaped grounds, pools and tennis courts, and the astonishing houses. They stopped at a large pair of gates set in a high manicured hedge and Xander pressed the electric buzzer in the wall, then spoke into the little grille. 'It's Xander McCorquodale, for Will Dangerfield.'

There was a buzzing noise, the gates glided open and their car roared in, up a paved drive and round a small hill to the vast white-and-glass frontage of the house. Xander pulled the car to a stop and they got out.

'Wow!' Coco said, taking off her shades for a moment. She had dressed carefully in white jeans that showed off her long slim legs and an elegant pale blue top with a low, draping neckline. 'I had no idea it would be so big.'

'He can afford it,' Xander said with a grin. 'There's money in them there games consoles. Come on.'

They stood in front of an enormous blond-wood front door and Xander pressed the button on a panel built into the wall beside it. The door swung open. Coco caught her breath. This was it. Then she realised she was looking at a small Hispanic woman in a white uniform. Clearly not Will Dangerfield.

'Good morning. Please come in.' The woman stood back and when they had entered, closed the door. Coco looked about, blinking in the sudden dimness. They were in a vast hall area with doors to left and right. Huge works of modern art hung on the opposite walls. A large steel and glass staircase ascended to an upper level that also appeared to be constructed from glass and steel. The entire double-height back wall of the hall was made of glass, looking out over an immaculately tidy Japanese-style garden with long rectangular ponds stretching away beside miniature cherry trees. A wide glass-roofed corridor led from the hall alongside the garden to another whole wing of the house, and the maid took them down it, saying, 'Mr William is in his office right now.'

Coco's heart was pounding and she tried to concen-trate on breathing evenly. Any second now she was going to be put to the test. Would she be able to carry it off?

As they passed an open door, she glimpsed a vast minimalist kitchen glittering white, then as they turned left along another glass-roofed corridor, so that they were now looking into the exquisite Japanese garden from the back, the maid stopped and knocked at a door.

'Yeah?' said a voice from inside.

'Your guests, sir.'

'Coming.'

They waited for a few moments and then the door opened and Will Dangerfield was standing in front of them.

There was a world of difference, Coco realised at once, between looking at someone in a photograph and meeting them in real life. Part of her had almost been expecting a gap-toothed schoolboy or a gangly teenager to appear. But nothing could have prepared her for the impact of meeting Will Dangerfield in the flesh. She felt punched in the stomach, almost winded.

He was tall, much taller than she had realised. He had to be at least six foot four, maybe more, and was built to match his height. His broad shoulders and chest were firm-looking and well-muscled, she could tell that even under the tee-shirt he was wearing. His jeans – some brand she didn't recognise but obviously very cool – sat loosely on his hips. She hadn't been expecting his sheer physical presence or the way she felt instantly drawn to him. Her impulse was to reach out and touch him, to run her hands over the chest and firm biceps, to caress the neck and pull his face towards her.

428

The face . . . She'd thought she knew what Will Dangerfield looked like, but now she realised she'd had no idea. She'd been imagining a boy and this was a man: square-jawed, with a touch of sulkiness about the well-formed mouth, a straight nose and eyes she could hardly stop staring at. They were green and hazel and flecked with coppery autumnal tones, well-shaped, with dark brows and lashes. He was handsome, she realised. She was suddenly reminded of statues of beautiful Roman men she'd seen at the V&A: naked men fighting snakes or dragons, with ridiculously gorgeous bodies and the faces of angels.

She remembered how she'd told herself that she could never fancy a man with ginger hair. That felt as absurd now as saying she couldn't fancy a man with two arms. Besides, his hair was the most wonderful colour she'd ever seen: dark copper, the colour of late-autumn leaves, and curling softly at the back of his neck and just behind his ears, though it was cut short to hide the curl elsewhere. She wanted to run her fingers through it and marvel at it.

She felt dizzy, breathless, as though she'd just climbed off a particularly terrifying fairground ride and wasn't quite sure of her footing. There was a strange thumping in her loins that was both pleasant and almost painful.

And he was staring straight back at her, unblinking, his expression impossible to read.

It had taken no more than two seconds for Coco to experience the extraordinary effects of instant lust.

'Hey, Will mate!' said Xander, oblivious to her reaction. He stepped forward, taking his friend's hand, shaking it and clapping him on the arm at the same time. 'How are you, old guy? Been a long time.'

For a fraction of a second, Will continued staring at Coco, then he looked at Xander and a smile spread over his face.

'Hi, Xander. Welcome! Great to see you. Come into my office.' Will stood back so that they could both enter. It was large and light with another wall of glass, this time looking over a terrace and down towards a vast glittering swimming pool. A large U-shaped table ran around three walls of the room, loaded down with an extraordinary array of computer equipment – screens, speakers, editing suites, cables, drives and piles and piles of games. Power lights glowed red and green everywhere.

'Ah, the power hub,' Xander said, looking about. 'The throbbing heart of your empire.'

'This is just my home office,' Will replied. 'The real work goes on downtown where my team are slaving away right now.' He looked round at Coco who quickly looked away, hoping he hadn't noticed her staring at him. 'Aren't you going to introduce us?'

'Oh, yeah,' Xander said casually. He was giving it the full, laid-back LA vibe today, in his white trousers, baggy linen shirt and shades. 'This is Coco, a friend from London. We're travelling together.'

'Uh-huh.' Will nodded.

'Hi,' Coco said. Her voice came out unaccustomedly high and light, as though she still hadn't managed to get enough breath back into her body. *Is this really me?* she thought amazed. *Am I actually being shy?*

'Hi.' He gave her a fleeting smile and then his

expression reverted back to its default setting: inscrutable with a hint of bolshiness at the mouth. 'You guys want a drink or something?'

'Yeah. That'd be good,' Xander said. 'I could kill a beer.'

Will looked surprised. 'At eleven-thirty in the morning?'

'Any time is beer o'clock,' declared Xander with a grin. 'You've been out of London too long, mate. You've gone all healthy.'

'Yeah, maybe you're right.' Will shrugged. 'Have a beer if you want one. I'm gonna have iced coffee. Coco?'

'Iced coffee sounds great.' She was putting a lot of effort into maintaining her new accent. She mustn't let it slip now, but the distracting presence of Will was making it hard to concentrate.

He led them back along the hallway to the kitchen she had glimpsed earlier. It was dazzling in there, the Californian sun bouncing off all the clear white surfaces and making the bowl of oranges on the glass table look like a pile of molten gold. Will opened the biggest fridge Coco had ever seen and took out a beer for Xander and a jug of iced coffee for the two of them.

'Decaff,' he said, handing a glass of it to Coco with a smile. 'Can't be too wired up to work.'

Then he led them out on to the terrace where there were sun loungers and chairs amid sculptural stonework and pots of topiaried lavender. It was a relief to be out of the glare of the kitchen. Coco sat down and sipped at her iced coffee, feeling a little more in control. But she only had to glance at Will to feel her insides tighten and then somersault, and that weird lightheadedness invade her skull again.

'So, what brings you to LA?' Will asked, and Xander started out on the story they'd prepared to explain how they came to be here, at a complete loose end and keen to catch up with his old friend Will Dangerfield.

Coco sat quietly and listened, thinking the whole thing sounded ridiculously transparent, but Will seemed to accept it easily enough as he sat there, lazily hunched over in what was, to Coco, an incredibly sexy way.

This wasn't supposed to happen, she thought, suddenly frightened. *I wasn't supposed to fancy him. But . . . I do.*

She hadn't felt like this since Jamal. In fact, she couldn't remember ever feeling exactly like this – as though a huge, unknown part of her had suddenly come alive and begun to possess her.

'Where are you staying?' Will asked.

Xander told him about the hotel, playing up some minor irritations and then shrugging and saying, 'But, you know, it'll do. I mean, it's OK. We can always find another if we don't like it.'

'Don't be silly,' Will said, just as Xander had planned. 'You can come and stay here for a few days if you want. I've got loads of room.'

'Hey, we couldn't impose on you like that.'

'It's no problem, really. My girlfriend's away, it's just me here. You can treat the place as your own.'

Girlfriend? Coco thought with a downward swoop of her stomach. Then she heard 'it's just me here' and something else sparked inside her. 'That's so kind of you,' she said. 'We'd love it, wouldn't we, Xander? As long as you're sure?'

Will glanced over at her and smiled. 'Of course I'm sure. Come this afternoon.'

Holy crap, Coco thought, clutching her glass even more tightly, her groin fizzing in response to the smile. *This is about to get much more complicated than I expected.*

53

The new Craven Hotels were almost ready to be launched. Daisy had to put her anxieties to one side while she concentrated on getting everything in shape in exactly the way she wanted. The tours for John Montgomery and other Craven directors went very well; they were unanimous in their praise of what she'd done, and the excellent budgeting that had made the whole thing as sleek and streamlined as possible.

Daisy was most delighted that she had managed to snare a well-known model, convincing her to have her wedding day at Tilly's Hall, one of the chain's hotels, by offering everything at a substantial discount. The model had got a wonderful magazine deal too, and while she was probably going to be in profit by the end of her big day, Daisy was going to get acres of coverage for the hotel and the Craven name.

'Congratulations,' John said warmly when she'd finished telling him. They were in his office, going over the last details. 'You're a natural at this, Daphne.

Anyone would think you have hotels in your blood. Well done.'

'Thanks, John,' she said. 'Do you know yet who's coming to the launch party at the Grey House? Everyone from here is coming, along with our best clients and suppliers and so on, but I wondered . . .'

'If anyone was coming from HQ?' John finished, smiling. 'Of course. You want the big bosses to see the scope of your achievement. Perfectly understandable. In fact, I've just heard that two directors are coming – Karen O'Malley and Darley Ross. Ross is MD of the entire hotels and leisure division, so it's a real feather in your cap to get him.'

'That's great,' exclaimed Daisy, flushing with pleasure. 'I'm so pleased.'

'I'll make sure he knows the extent of your input,' John said, a knowing look in his eyes. 'I promise.'

Daisy stayed up late into the night, exploring as many avenues as she could find, going to wherever the internet was able to lead her.

Darley Ross was her main focus. He was definitely next in her sights. If she wanted to get to the very top, then he was the man she needed to help her get there. It was odd to think that she would simply have been catapulted in, probably as Ross's superior, if she'd stayed in her old life. She'd have emerged from university and business school with all her degrees and diplomas, and started at the top. But, she told herself, it was better this way. Now she truly knew how hotels worked from the inside out. She'd been a chambermaid, scrubbed lavatories and changed beds. She'd overseen one small place and learned all the pitfalls and dangers. No number of degrees could have given her that wealth of practical experience and the invaluable knowledge she'd gained from the Excalibur.

Ross's photograph was on the company website – the standard black-and-white shot of a director, three-quarters on, with a smile that wasn't too broad. He appeared ordinary enough, a man in his fifties with salt-and-pepper hair cut close to his skull. He wasn't fat but a meaty look around the shoulders showed he might be if he was not careful. His short bio contained nothing but the usual bland inform-ation, but Daisy was certain that he was the key.

'Let's see, Mr Ross,' she said, as she began to run various internet searches. 'Let's see what I can find out about you . . .'

A few hours later, she knew a great deal more about Mr Darley Ross than he could possibly have guessed – or wanted.

The Grey House looked wonderful, the perfect Cotswolds country retreat. Swags of late-flowering roses nodded around windows and doors, the grey stone walls were mellow and warm, and the salvaged antique fountain playing at the front looked as though it had been there for centuries. Outside, the gardens were in the last weeks of their summer display but they still looked fragrant and welcoming, lit by hundreds of small lanterns that would glow even more golden as the light diminished. Waiting staff moved smoothly among the guests, distributing champagne and canapés.

Daisy had dressed carefully for the occasion in a

short Oscar de la Renta cocktail dress in nude-coloured silk with a black silk crocheted overdress; it was important to make sure she looked just right for this. Young but not inexperienced or naive; smart and sophisticated but definitely not tarty or frivolous. She made sure the whole thing was demure with a pair of black heels that didn't demand too much attention. She mingled, spending plenty of time chatting to her suppliers and those she wished to keep sweet, but also keeping an eye out for the people who really mattered: the Dangerfield directors.

The dear little Excalibur hotel was one of the most minor items in Craven's portfolio – which was precisely why she had chosen it as her launchpad. And Craven was a small holding within the much greater Dangerfield property and leisure group.

All roads lead to Rome, Daisy thought to herself. *Ah, there's John – and he's talking to Karen O'Malley, if I remember her picture from the company site correctly. And that grey speckled head I can see must belong to Darley Ross . . .*

She excused herself from the small circle she was talking to and made her way through the crowd, smiling at people she knew but not stopping until she had reached John's side.

'Ah, Daphne, just the person,' he said jovially, waving his glass of wine in her direction as she approached. 'Come and meet the people from Dangerfield, they're very keen to make your acquaintance.' He gestured to the woman on his left, smart in a black dress and towering heels. She was in her forties, chic and youthful-looking with brown hair swept back off her face. 'Karen O'Malley.'

'Hello,' Daisy said.

Karen smiled. 'Good to meet you. John is clearly a big fan of yours.'

'And,' he went on, 'this is Darley Ross, the MD. We're delighted to have you here, Darley.'

Daisy inspected the director's face curiously as he replied, 'Not at all, John. Always good to see how things are developing.' He was pudgier in the face than she'd expected, and a little piggier about the eyes. *He doesn't look all that trustworthy,* she thought. *Surprise, surprise.* He glanced at her. 'So you're the bright young thing we've been hearing about?' He nodded over his shoulder towards the hotel. 'Most impressive. I like what you've done very much.'

'I'm so pleased,' she returned, hoping she was striking the right note of confidence mixed with modesty. 'I've loved every moment.' She gave him a beaming smile. He needed to like her. Trust her. It was time to turn on the charm.

Two and a half hours later, Darley Ross was very well oiled, having chucked back glass after glass of the champagne the waiters brought round. His voice had grown progressively louder as the evening went on, and the others had floated away from him, leaving Daisy to keep him company. Darley was explaining how well his division was doing and how brilliantly the Dangerfield group was performing overall, with its many worldwide projects and investments.

Daisy listened, smiling, agreeing, flattering and drawing him out as much as possible. She'd already noticed an appreciative look in Darley's increasingly bloodshot eyes and, while she tried to make sure that she wasn't in the least flirtatious, she hoped he wouldn't get the wrong idea. That could complicate things a little.

I think now could be the right time to set the ball rolling she thought, as Darley drained his latest glass. She smiled, put her head on one side and said innocently, 'But tell me about your Scottish leisure project. I hear it's going to be magnificent. A huge luxury golf resort in some amazing countryside. Wow.'

Darley paused for a moment, inspecting the interior of his glass, his face red from the effects of the champagne. 'Yes, that's right. One of our biggest and most exciting projects.'

'But . . . you've run into some problems, haven't you? With your land acquisition?'

Darley stiffened, then frowned. 'What do you know about that?'

'I read the plans and projections for it in the Craven files – John had been copied in.' She adopted a puzzled expression. 'But when I did a little further research, I discovered that you've got a proverbial spanner in the works. Your date for commencement of works has already passed, hasn't it?'

A succession of expressions flickered over Darley's face. Then he looked her directly in the eyes and said, 'Yes. It's true. I can't deny that I've been trying to keep the lid on this one. We're in a bit of a pickle, if I'm honest.'

'I believe you've got a particularly tenacious opponent.'

Darley sighed. 'You clearly already know, but yes . . . it's all down to some bloody fisherman. We've already got a huge tract of land and all the various permissions and what have you. Cost a fortune in greasing palms and buying up properties. We offered very generous purchase prices to all the residents and most of 'em snapped our hands off. Couldn't wait to take the Dangerfield dosh and fuck off out of there.' His tongue was obviously well loosened. Daisy had a feeling he would certainly not be telling her these things if he were sober. 'It's a bloody dump. Back of beyond. Nothing but sand dunes and seagulls and grass for miles on end. Beautiful, I suppose, if you like that kind of thing. But . . .'

Darley leaned in towards her to confide, his breath sour with alcohol, 'There's this one bastard who wants to fuck the whole thing up. He's got a cottage and a bit of land slap-bang in the middle of our plot, sitting between where the main hotel will be and access to the links. He's a birdwatcher or a nature lover or some such. And he won't sell. Damn him!'

Suddenly Darley leaned back and began to roar with laughter. 'I've half a mind just to go up there and shoot him, have it over with,' he spluttered. Then he stopped laughing abruptly, a fierce and furious expression on his face. 'Who the fuck does that fucker think he is?' he hissed. 'He's fucking me over so badly . . .' He shook his head, his face now crimson. 'He's ruining my whole fucking life, if you must know.' His lips tightened and he seemed to be trying to control himself. He glanced up at Daisy as if realising suddenly that she was listening intently. 'I shouldn't say all this,' he muttered, looking away.

'It sounds like you're in a big trouble,' she said soothingly. 'Perhaps I could help.'

Darley snorted. 'That's nice of you – but how?'

She gave him a long measured stare. 'I get the

feeling that this might be a little worse than you're actually letting on.'

He gaped at her.

'In fact, I think it might be a very great deal worse.' She smiled at him. Now she was ready to play her cards. 'Why don't I come and see you in London, and we can discuss it then?'

He continued to stare at her, astonished.

'Good. I'll be in touch and we can meet next week. Now, Darley, shall we go and join the others?'

54

Xander was cock-a-hoop after their easy success.

'What did I tell you?' he crowed as they drove back to the Ritz-Carlton to get their belongings. 'Easy as pie! This is going to be great. I'd forgotten how much I liked old Will.' He looked sober for a moment as he remembered that their purpose was to betray his friend, then said, 'He won't care what we're up to. He won't tell us anything useful anyway. It's not in his nature. We'll have a great time with him, report back that we couldn't get him to spill the beans, and *voilà*. Job done.'

'Yeah, I guess so,' Coco said, watching the wide boulevards slide past the car window. She was in turmoil and could only hope that she was managing to hide the fact successfully. Her reaction to Will had taken her completely by surprise, and now she was aware of a geyser of excitement building up inside her at the thought of being near him for the next few days at least. But she also knew that she was there for one reason only: to get information. She couldn't forget that for one second, or she wouldn't be receiving any of the money left on her contract with the Dangerfields.

They packed quickly. Coco fired up the tiny but powerful laptop she'd been given by Margaret, logged in to the hotel internet and sent off a quick email reporting what had happened so far. Then they checked out and headed back towards Will's mansion, this time to stay.

Will was shut away in his office when they returned, and the maid, Maria, explained that he would be working until the evening. He had left instructions that they were to be given anything they wanted, and the place was theirs to roam about as they wanted. Would they like to see their rooms?

Yes, they would. Maria led them out of the main house to a series of low, connected guest cottages that lined one side of the garden near the pool. They'd been assigned one each. Coco went into hers: it was delightfully cool inside and as stylishly modern as she'd expected. It was a kind of large bed-sitting room, fully equipped with TV and stereo equipment, and next to it was a bathroom almost as large as the main room itself. There was no kitchen or way of making coffee, though a fridge hidden in a white lacquer cabinet held water, fruit juice and Diet Coke.

'There is the phone,' Maria said, pointing to the handset resting by the bed. 'Anything you want, dial the kitchen and it will be brought out to you.'

'Thanks, Maria.' She flopped down on the bed as the maid led Xander next door to show him his quarters. This was wonderful: privacy, a place she could retreat to, though she felt a flicker of disappointment that she wasn't going to be in the main house with

Will. Did this mean he was keeping a distance between them?

Don't let your fucking imagination run away with you, she scolded herself. *He's only known you five minutes. What did you expect? And he's got a girlfriend.*

But had he felt the same crackle of electricity when they'd met? Was it possible for only one person to feel that kind of instant attraction, that almost irresistible pull towards someone else? Surely it had to work two ways, or what was the point of it? The world was full of people who left Coco cold, so when she met a guy who provoked that kind of reaction in her . . . well, it had to be that their chemicals matched, fired off one another or however it worked.

She shivered with pleasure, thinking about him. Those arms! That chest . . . that easy way he moved. He was so comfortable in his own skin. She just knew he would smell good, too. She imagined running her lips along his neck, kissing that warm skin lightly as she went.

Her hands went to her chest and almost unconsciously she ran them across her breasts, where her nipples were already hard and sensitive. A ripple of desire travelled down her belly to her groin and she felt herself twitch and grow warm there. She sighed. This was longing like she hadn't felt for a very long time. One hand dropped down her stomach to her mound and touched it gently. She hadn't used her fingers on herself for ages. It was as though that part of her had been hibernating, and now she'd been awakened and was buzzing with pent-up need. She slid one finger down inside her jeans and under the flimsy silk of her panties. She ran it across the small thatch and over the nub of her clit which was already standing proud. It tingled to the soft touch, eager for more. She stroked her fingertip across it again and thought about Will sitting on the terrace, bending forward so that the neck of his tee-shirt gaped open, giving a glimpse of his skin beneath . . .

'Oh,' she sighed quietly.

Just then, the door to her cottage burst open and Xander came in. Coco whipped her hand out of her jeans and said crossly, 'Can't you knock?'

He came over, oblivious to what she'd been up to. 'Sorry, sweetie, were you trying to sleep? What shall we do? Let's go for an explore. I want to see all the goodies on offer.'

'OK,' Coco said, getting up, shaking off her arousal. 'Let's have a look around.'

They wandered about the house and grounds, taking everything in. For Coco, the sheer scale of everything was what amazed her most. The rooms were so large. There was so much space everywhere. The garages were big enough for six cars with plenty of room to spare, as well as worktables and storage for bicycles and a stunning Harley Davidson motorbike.

'Look, a Porsche, a Lamborghini, a Maserati . . .' Xander wandered around Will's car collection, stroking them lovingly, while Coco headed back out to the sunshine. She wasn't very interested in cars, although even she could tell that these were beauties.

They found the games room, with its full-length pool table, its collection of eighties arcade video-game machines, bar and jukebox. They found a vast night-club-style dance floor with DJ decks and lights. In the house, they wandered through more large luxurious rooms: a dining table that sat at least twenty; a huge sitting room with pure white sofas and chairs, and a great fireplace Coco couldn't imagine ever needed a fire burning in it.

'Hey, look at this.' Xander had found another staircase leading under the house and he disappeared down it. A moment later, laughter floated up the stairs. 'Oh, wow, this is so cool! Coco, come and see.'

She went down after him into the darkness and then stopped, astonished. In front of her was the entrance to a cinema. Over it was a big red sign rimmed with sparkling lights with the words 'Picture Palace' in flowing dark script. On the walls were classic movie posters: *Casablanca*, *The Godfather*, *Raging Bull*, *Gone With the Wind* and *Pulp Fiction* among them. There were gum-ball machines and jelly-bean dispensers sitting brightly by the entrance, next to an old-fashioned ticket booth, where, to Coco's surprise, a woman in a candy-striped uniform and jaunty hat was sitting smiling at them from behind the glass. As Xander approached, the woman turned her head stiffly towards him and said, 'Hi, what movie do you want to see today?'

Xander laughed again. 'Fantastic. It's a dummy.'

Coco saw that he was right: the woman was a plastic model, programmed to respond to movement and sound.

'We'd like to see . . . *Star Wars*,' Xander announced.

'*Star Wars*,' the model repeated, lips moving slightly in the ever-beaming face. 'Your movie choice – *Star Wars* – will begin in five minutes.' Two tickets emerged from a slot in the counter. Xander picked them up and turned to Coco.

'Come on, we gotta see this.'

'Please collect your snacks and drinks on the way in,' said the ticket girl, then froze as her animation came to an end.

Coco followed Xander into the cinema lobby where there was an almost perfect replica of a snack counter, although she was glad to see there were no eerily realistic models to start shovelling popcorn or loading cheese on to nachos.

'This is crazy,' she murmured.

'Yeah – but fucking great,' Xander said, taking in the hotdog machine that was turning gently, keeping the hotdogs sizzling under the grill, the striped dispenser of popcorn and the stack of boxes next to it. A freezer held ice creams and popsicles, and a fridge a selection of cold drinks. Another stand held bags of sweets and chocolate bars. 'Come on,' he urged. 'Let's get something.'

'How long have those hotdogs been there?' Coco said suspiciously. This was all a bit too freaky for her tastes.

'Don't spoil the magic, Coco. Have the popcorn.' Xander shovelled some into two boxes and got them each a drink from the fridge. 'Come on, I bet the movie's about to start!'

A pair of red baize doors evidently marked the entrance to the cinema. Inside, there was a gently sloping floor and five tiers of red velvet seats facing a pair of crimson curtains. Each seat was larger and more cushioned than a usual cinema chair, with a drinks holder and a small fold-out table for snacks.

447

There was also a discreet control set in the seat handle so that the film could be paused, rewound or forwarded.

They'd just sat down in the middle of the centre row when the lights dimmed, the curtains went back to reveal the screen, and the 20th Century Fox music boomed out of the sound system, followed by the opening words of *Star Wars*, and the great fanfare that began the theme.

'Cooooool,' said Xander, stuffing a handful of popcorn in his mouth as he settled back and prepared to enjoy the movie, while Coco wondered what the hell they were doing in that crazy place, and unable to forget that somewhere above them was Will.

55

Daisy climbed out of the taxi, looking up at the tall imposing building. It was years since she'd seen it, but it still looked exactly the same. The wind blew her hair over her face as she looked up at the many storeys and the endless panes of glass. This place had meant so much to her when she was a girl: it had been a symbol of her father's might and success, a physical manifestation of his great importance in the world. She had been the pet and darling of everyone who worked here – although she wondered now if they had really liked her as much as they all pretended. And today she was back, all grown-up and sleek in her Prada suit and Louboutins.

The difference was that today she hadn't come prancing in holding her daddy's hand, to be worshipped and adored. She had worked her way up to this point. And now she thought she might have the key to unlock the door into the Dangerfield Group itself.

She felt nervous as she walked into the grand foyer, almost as though someone would stop her, grab her arm and say, 'Oi, we know who you really are!' and take her straight to Daddy.

Her imagination stopped short at what might happen next but images of firing squads kept floating through her mind.

After signing in and getting her badge, she rode the lift to the eighteenth floor. Just the ordinary lift this time, not the executive one she once used. Butterflies flew about in her stomach and her mouth felt dry with fear. What if she ran into Daddy? Would he recognise her? Here she was, in the lion's den. She'd been forbidden from ever having anything to do with the Dangerfield family, and now she was deep in their lair.

What the hell am I doing? she wondered, almost in disbelief. All this time, she had barely questioned what she was planning. She'd been driven on to do it, to prove to Daddy that he'd been wrong about her. That even though she might not be his biological daughter, she was good enough to be a Dangerfield and didn't deserve to be cast away like a piece of rubbish. But perhaps that had been a stupid idea which might cost her more than she had already paid. Was it really worth it?

Are you crazy? Daisy smoothed down her skirt, shook out her hair and straightened her shoulders as the lift doors opened. *Of course it is. There's no way I'm stopping now.*

'Darley, hello. Good to see you again.' She walked forward, hand outstretched and a welcoming smile on her face. *He has no idea. He really hasn't.*

'Ah, Miss Fraser.' Ross stood up and came round

his desk to shake her hand. His expression was not exactly friendly and the formal greeting did not bode well.

He's probably deeply regretting ever speaking to me, she thought as they sat down, Ross behind his desk. *Now that he's not well-oiled on champagne.* His posture and attitude seemed to indicate that he was going to pull rank on this little nobody from the Craven Group. After all, he was Managing Director of the entire division, wasn't he? Why was he sitting here with this chit of a girl, about to discuss confidential company business? She could see the irritation deep in his eyes.

'What can I do for you?' he said, with a forced smile that verged on the condescending.

Daisy smiled back at him, taking in his silk tie, handmade shirt and tailored suit. She wasn't nervous. *After all, I fired a main board member when I was fifteen years old.*

'Mr Ross,' she said in a light upbeat voice, 'it's very simple. I've come to tell you that you'll be giving me a job here at Dangerfield HQ.'

Ross continued smiling but his manner turned even chillier. 'Sorry – what did you say?'

'You are going to appoint me as your executive assistant. I promise you, you won't regret it. I'm going to get you out of all the difficulties you've got yourself into. Then, at some appropriate time, you'll go on extended sick leave, and I'll step into your shoes.' She poured herself a glass of water from the carafe on the desk, sipped it and put it back on the table.

The director seemed stupefied for a moment as he took this in, laughed, stopped, and frowned again. 'I'm sorry, I don't understand. Why on earth would I do that? I don't have an executive assistant. And I'm not sick.'

'Well, you're going to have one now. And I think you're going to be feeling considerably less well when I tell you what I have in my bag.'

'Is it a gun?' he said jokily. 'Look, young lady, I was under the impression we were going to have a serious conversation. You don't seem entirely with it. Why don't you go off and have a lie down somewhere and perhaps we can talk later. You see, I'm very busy—'

'I expect you are, Mr Ross. You've plenty to keep you busy, after all. I mean . . .' She raised her eyebrows. 'What about the fact that you're now propping up a seven-hundred-and-fifty-million-pound investment that can't even get off the ground? You're in serious trouble, aren't you? That little fisherman in Scotland is causing you all sorts of grief, but it seems you've been concealing the extent of the losses you're incurring every day that he stops the work beginning. In fact, the debts you've got could be called in by the lenders if they suspect that this project is never going to be completed . . . and that collapse could bring down the entire company, couldn't it?'

Darley had turned paper-white as she spoke. 'I don't know what you're talking about!' he blustered.

'I think you do,' Daisy replied calmly. She couldn't help enjoying playing with him, watching his mental processes firing as he made connections and tried to anticipate what she might say next. 'I've been doing some detective work and I've followed a couple of very interesting trails, ones you've done your best to conceal. And you've done well – no one is actually asking the important questions yet, are they? But you've mysteriously found funds to keep your division's hefty losses hidden. A five-million bonus appeared from nowhere at all. And you've made some fascinating purchases too . . . one of them in roubles.'

Darley looked frightened. He began to stutter. 'How . . . how . . . what . . . ?'

'I think you're beginning to understand now. I really do know what you've been up to.'

There was a long pause as Ross stared at her. He looked as though he was desperately trying to think of an explanation but couldn't. Then his face changed, fury contorting it. 'You don't understand!' he spat, banging his hands on the desk suddenly. 'The pressure here is extraordinary. I'm not allowed to fail, none of us are. My division was haemorrhaging money. I was terrified of the debts being called in. I had to do something.'

'So you've borrowed more money, haven't you? And it looks as though you've done it without authorisation.'

Ross drooped and nodded slowly. 'You seem to know all about it, God only knows how. I thought I'd covered my tracks very well.'

'Something like that will always be found out eventually,' Daisy said softly. She felt sorry for him in an obscure way. He was in a hole and had tried to get out of it. There were plenty of people who were so frightened of Daddy's wrath they'd have tried similar desperate measures. 'The paper trails are always there if people know what they're looking for.'

Ross put his head in his hands and groaned. 'I know, I know,' he said, his voice muffled. 'Do you think I don't know that? But I hoped that by then,

I might have worked something out, some kind of solution.'

'But you haven't. And I'd like to know what this Russian investment is all about. You've paid out a substantial sum there. What is it?'

Ross looked evasive. 'A hotel investment. I saw a wonderful opportunity to go into business with a man building a luxury hotel in an up-and-coming area, and so I decided it was something the Dangerfield Group ought to be a part of.'

'But you haven't put it to the board, have you?'

Ross shook his head.

'Why not?'

He didn't answer for a while. His jaw was set hard and his eyes were now burning with something like anger.

'Mr Ross, you might as well tell me. If you do, I'll think about other options. If you don't, I'm going to go to the board, and I wouldn't want to be in your shoes when that happens.'

'But,' he said icily, 'that's exactly what you claim you want. To be in my shoes.'

'Hmm.' She smiled at him. 'Actually, you're right. I do. I want you to appoint me, just as I've said.'

'But . . . why?' He looked puzzled. 'Why do you want to be here?'

'I want to work here, and fast. You're my way in. And I'll sort out this mess for you, how about that? You'll be able to resign with all of your benefits and your pension intact. You can go on a long, well-paid sick leave. Imagine all the golf! Come on, Mr Ross,' she urged, leaning forward. 'Remember all those nights you've lain awake, wondering how the hell

454

you're going to get out of this mess? I've just opened the perfect escape route for you. In a few months you'll be out of here and then you'll never have to think about it again.'

Ross stared down at his desk for a long while. When he finally looked up to meet Daisy's gaze, he said slowly, 'You know, maybe there's something in that. Very well, I'll tell you what you're so desperate to know. Maybe we can work something out.'

56

Coco stood by the pool in her red bikini, looking at the turquoise water flashing in the late-afternoon sun. The sky stretched away in its infinite blue, and beyond the palm trees bordering the terrace the city lay below her, its grey mass glittering in the sunlight. The pool was as immaculately kept as everything else she had seen here and spotless white cushions made the sun loungers very inviting. Not so much as a leaf was out of place. She watched the water ripple and glint for a while, then put a toe into it. It was warm and gently refreshing. Her red nail-polish looked distorted by the water. She pulled her foot out.

Will's office, she remembered, overlooked the pool. She wondered if he could see her, or if he was even looking out of the window. Thinking that made her suddenly self-conscious. How did she look? Was she sexy? Did she measure up to his girlfriend?

She laughed at herself. *I've danced in a bloody bikini every night in front of random blokes for half my life! What the hell am I nervous about now? I know I look all right. And who cares what he thinks anyway?*

With that, she went to a lounger and lay down to soak up the LA sun.

She must have dozed off because when she opened her eyes again, someone was sitting near her. She turned her head, blinking. 'Xander?' She hadn't seen him since they'd discovered the cinema.

'It's Will,' came the answer, just as her vision cleared and she saw that he was sitting on a nearby lounger, an open beer beside him. He smiled. 'So, feeling a bit more rested?'

'Oh, yes, thanks,' she said, blushing. Had she looked an idiot, asleep? 'It's fantastic here.'

'Yeah. I know. I'm lucky.' He smiled at her and lifted the bottle to his lips. She felt a tremor of lust travel through her and wished she were not so undressed. She worried that he might be able to see the way her skin was reacting to him, or the muscles in her stomach tense with desire.

'So, Coco . . .' He looked straight into her eyes, as though her soft brown breasts in the red bikini top, and her long legs, didn't interest him. 'How do you know Xander?'

'Oh . . .' They had this story planned out. 'We met in London. Through his sister Allegra. Do you know her?'

Will nodded.

'We just hit it off. He's such a funny guy. Anyway, I was coming to LA and Xander was planning a trip, so we thought – why not go together?'

'So you two aren't . . .'

'Oh, no. We're not. Just friends.' She smiled at him, wondering if she was transmitting her eagerness to be available to him without even realising she was doing it.

'I see.'

'We're in separate cottages,' she added.

He laughed. 'I would hope so, if you're not together. There's plenty of room. You only have to shack up if you want to.'

'And . . . your girlfriend is away?' she said.

'Megan. Yeah. She's an actress, away in New York doing a play.' He stared at his bottle of beer for a moment, and then took another swig from it.

'Don't you get lonely here, in this big house all by yourself?' she ventured.

'Lonely? Nah.' He shook his head. 'Actually when you came by yesterday, it was unusually quiet. There's almost always something going on, someone turning up. People drop by, just like you guys. In fact, there's a party tonight.'

'Really?'

'Uh-huh. We'll have some drinks, barbecue some steaks . . . people will swim, play some games, maybe dance.' He shrugged. 'The usual thing. You'll enjoy it.'

'Yeah,' Coco said. 'It sounds good.' *But*, she was thinking, *what about you? Will you enjoy it?* There was something closed off about Will, as though he was shut away somewhere in his own mind. How would she be able to reach him? It was hard to imagine ever being so intimate with him that he'd start telling her his private thoughts.

'Hey, guys!' It was Xander coming across the terrace towards them, loping easily, though he looked pale again. 'What are you up to?'

458

'I'm just telling Coco about our party tonight,' Will said, looking over at his friend with a smile.

'Party? Terrific.' Xander sat down on a lounger. 'That pool looks good. Who's up for a swim?'

Will stood up. 'Not me. Back to the office for a couple of hours. Then I'll be able to party with a clear conscience.'

Coco examined her reflection in the mirror of her cottage. She was sure all the LA girls were going to be super-glossy and amazingly trendy, but she was well equipped to hold her own against them. She was wearing wide-legged white trousers that fastened high at her waist, emphasising her hips and flat stomach. With them she wore a white cropped vest top and over that a gauzy printed poncho-style top with a giraffe-skin print all over it, the wide boat neck dropping off one brown shoulder.

She looked good, she knew that. *Good enough?* Well, that was another question.

While they were at the pool, Xander had told her that he thought Will liked her, but she wasn't so sure. Besides, she didn't want him to like her. She wanted him to *like* her. And what about this Megan, the actress? He hadn't smiled when he'd talked about her. Maybe he was cross with her for going off to New York and leaving him alone.

Coco headed out to join Xander at the pool.

The party started off tamely enough, with hip-looking young people arriving – most from the world of games designing and technology, some from the acting and movie world – all with tans, white smiles and plenty of smooth self-confidence. The girls wore shorts and cut-off tops, the boys slouchy tee-shirts and baggy jeans. Beers were cracked open, cigarettes lit and the barbecue started smoking away, producing masses of steaks and burgers, which were laid out next to huge bowls of juicy-looking salads.

Coco stuck close to Xander, who seemed to have no problem talking to complete strangers, and tried to keep track of all the different people she was introduced to. From the corner of her eye, she was always aware of Will, his tall figure easy to spot as he moved among the guests. When he talked too long to another girl she wanted to rush over to interrupt them, but as she reached tipping point he would move on and she would breathe out with relief.

Get a grip! she told herself fiercely. She'd never reacted to a guy like this before, but she couldn't fight it.

As the night went on the barbecue was eaten, more drinks consumed. The beers began to kick in and people relaxed. Soon they were swimming in the pool, playing mildly flirtatious games as boys tossed shrieking girls into the warm water, or amusing themselves in the games room. Someone had put music on and a few were bopping away on the terrace.

The alcohol flooding her veins had loosened Coco up, and also made her feel sexy as hell. A guy at the pool tried to flirt with her, and she enjoyed the frisson. He was nice-looking too, but she could only think about Will. As her blood heated, she grew keener to find him. She began to wander about, making a slow circuit of the pool, wandering casually into the games room then into the house, looking for him without drawing attention to the fact. She found him at last, lying on the sofa of the sitting room, his phone clamped to his ear. He looked cross as he spoke. 'To be honest, Megan, I don't know. Please don't keep hassling me. You know how it is and I'm pretty tired of this conversation . . . Yeah. OK. Talk to you tomorrow then.'

He put his phone down as Coco came up, holding a mojito cocktail that someone had mixed for her outside. The rum was mingling nicely with the beer and giving her courage.

'Hi,' she said. 'Everything OK?'

'Yeah.' He sighed and smiled ruefully. 'It's all good.'

'Girl trouble?'

'Well . . . sort of.' He stood up, so tall, and radiating that incredible attraction that almost pulled her towards him like iron filings to a magnet. 'Shall we go back to the party?' he asked softly.

Coco nodded and went to go ahead of him but tripped on her wedges and almost fell. As she stumbled, she felt a strong arm encircle her waist and hold her up as she righted herself, and she instinctively held on to it.

'Thanks,' she said breathlessly, as she looked back over her shoulder and found herself gazing directly into Will's green-copper eyes. Her back was almost touching his chest and his lips were close enough that if she had moved forward, just a little, she could have kissed him.

'You're welcome,' he said in a low voice.

They stood like that for an instant longer than necessary, then Coco let go of his arm and he released her.

461

'Dangerous things, shoes,' he said teasingly. 'They can lead you into all sorts of trouble.'

Then they went back to the terrace, Coco hiding her trembling hands as best she could.

57

Daisy looked out of the plane window at the miles and miles of taiga beneath her: the icy forest land that covered vast expanses of Siberia. She had heard of tundra, where the earth was permanently frozen hard and barren, but never before of this almost limitless, frosted, tree-covered landscape.

The helicopter blades whirred above them and the shadow of the aircraft floated over the pine peaks below. They had flown up from Moscow in a private airplane to the city of Komsomolsk-on-Amur, a large, bleak, industrial-looking city on the far eastern coast of Russia, in the federal Krai of Khabarovsk. The city's name, Darley told her, meant 'Communist-Youth-Party on the Amur', and from the looks of its grim, grey architecture, most of the place had been constructed to celebrate Stalinist ideals. But they hadn't stayed there for long. A helicopter had been waiting to take them further north, away from the river basin and the industrialised city towards the frozen wastes beyond.

'It's enormous,' breathed Daisy. The white

landscape, with its ice-pruned, stunted trees, stretched away as far as she could see.

Darley's voice came through her headset. 'Siberia is so big that even if it were an independent country, it would still be the largest country in the world. Makes you realise how vast Russia is.'

Daisy gave him a sideways glance. He was in the seat next to hers, wearing an insulated black jacket that puffed up comically around his seat belt. 'Are you going to be full of facts throughout this entire trip? You're like a walking guidebook.'

'I thought you might be interested,' he said with a shrug. 'I researched this area for a while.'

Daisy turned back to continue marvelling at the view below. Yes, this was certainly an interesting little situation, to say the least . . .

Darley Ross was a man of influence. When he'd agreed to appoint Daisy as his executive assistant, things moved quickly. He had cleared it with John Montgomery, who'd been sad to lose her but unable to do much about it. It was agreed that she would continue to administer the new chain of hotels from the Dangerfield HQ, though she would no longer be involved with the upgrading of the other Craven holdings, and the situation would be reviewed in six months.

Within a fortnight, Daisy had found herself a flat to rent and had moved from Bristol to London. Driving into the city, the removal truck somewhere behind her on the M4, was an extraordinary moment. After her years of planning, she was actually returning to the place where it had all begun. She could hardly believe it had worked out the way she'd planned.

And, to her incredulity, she actually had the means to bring the whole Dangerfield empire down. With a few words, she could expose the fraud that was sustaining the hotel division. Then the banks would call in loans and the whole delicately poised structure would collapse.

She imagined Daddy's face, the pleasure she would feel in the revenge, in the moment of his realising that the girl he'd cast aside, even had 'killed', had become his nemesis, destroying the thing he loved most in life – the precious company that his own father had built up.

But then, she loved it too.

Who knows what the hell I'm going to do? But the moment of reckoning is almost here.

On the day she arrived at Dangerfield HQ, she was given her office ID and an induction into the systems of the great building that included a short film with a honey-voiced narration explaining how the Dangerfield Group had been created, grown and prospered, and what a privilege it was to be part of the global team.

'With hotel, leisure and property interests all over the world,' enthused the voice, 'Dangerfield is the most exciting place possible to realise your career goals. This company needs your talents and can richly reward your efforts.'

Daisy had thought herself so entirely into Daphne's mindset that when Daddy suddenly flashed up on the screen, part of her almost wondered who the hell that fat man with the dyed hair was. He smiled into the camera and said, 'I'm delighted that you're joining

465

our team. We value every member. Remember, you're part of the Dangerfield family.'

Daisy wanted to laugh. So she was a Dangerfield again, was she? Hmm. She had a feeling it wasn't going to be quite that simple.

At first she'd been so frightened of meeting Daddy that she'd come in to work very early and left long after she thought he would have gone, but she realised within a day or two that her chances of meeting him were in fact extremely slim. He went directly to the penthouse offices in the executive lift and saw only the most important directors who reported to him in his office. Even so, the knowledge that he was sitting a few floors above her, oblivious of her presence, made her feel strange and nervous. She stayed in her office, burrowing deeper and deeper into the Dangerfield company, a tiny and unobserved mole slowly and surely working her way towards the heart of it. Soon she became certain of one thing.

All Daddy's employees hated and feared him with a passion.

At the end of the first week Darley took her out to a small wine bar in a back street, far from the usual hangouts of Dangerfield employees.

There, huddled over a small table with a candle burning in a Chianti bottle, he explained what his investment in Russia actually was.

'I met a businessman called Sergei Anatolski, and we had a very interesting talk. He has hotel interests in Russia, and was keen to get Dangerfield to invest in his new venture of high-spec luxury hotels in Moscow, St Petersburg and Kiev. I thought it sounded like an excellent idea. We don't have any Russian interests, after all, and it was a good prospect. We had an excellent dinner.' Darley seemed lost in memory for a moment.

'So you decided to invest?' prodded Daisy. 'That doesn't seem such a terrible secret. Why didn't you take this to the board?'

'Well . . .' Darley looked a little sheepish. 'It wasn't his hotels I invested in.'

'Oh?' Daisy looked at him askance.

'He's a very persuasive man. Very. He told me about a fantastic new business opportunity. He'd recently inherited a small patch of ground in Siberia, no more than a mile square, and it turned out he was sitting on several million tonnes of high-grade iron ore. Most of the iron-ore mines in Russia are owned by Russian steel companies, who've been buying up all the mines they can over the last few years to integrate their business and control the mineral supply. It's rare to find an independent one like this.'

'Iron ore.' Daisy frowned. 'Not my area of expertise, I'm afraid.'

Darley took a swig from his glass of Burgundy. 'Iron ore is needed for the production of cars, mobile phones, computers . . . just about everything we need for modern life. The Chinese are desperate to get hold of as much as they can and they're keen to sign an exclusive deal for the mine's ore.'

'OK,' Daisy said. 'Sounds like an excellent result for your Russian friend.'

'And it looked like it might be the answer to our losses on the Scottish links,' Darley added. 'Anatolski told me that the mine would make a fortune but that he needed some extra cash to fund getting the stuff out of the ground. A quick turnaround, he said. A cash injection and I'd double or triple my money in no time at all.'

Daisy began to see how it all fitted together. 'So you borrowed some money without authorisation to invest . . .'

'Yes,' Darley said unhappily, 'to plug the gap and make back the cost of the loan, and more.'

Daisy shook her head. 'Oh, dear. Honestly, Darley, borrowing money on behalf of the company without authorisation . . . you might as well pack your prison clothes right now. And such a huge amount. How did you hide the loan on the company balance sheet?'

He waved his hand in an impatient gesture. 'Oh, it can be done, believe me. Maybe not for ever, but in the short term, with a bit of clever accounting. Anatolski needed help fast because he'd used all his cash to buy his brother out just before the iron ore discovery was made and had no money to invest in getting the damn' stuff out.'

'Wouldn't the Chinese invest if they're so keen on iron ore?'

'They would – but at a price. They demanded joint ownership, and Sergei didn't want that. In fact, everyone who was prepared to buy in wanted co-ownership, and he wasn't prepared to give it because of his previous experience working with his brother. I was the only man who had cash, and didn't want in permanently. All I wanted was the repayment of my money and a doubling of my stake in the shortest possible time. So we shook on it.'

Daisy stared at him. The candlelight flickered on

Darley's full cheeks. The red wine had left a dark stain around his lips. The extent of his scheme was becoming clear now. It was clever, she had to give him that. Over-borrowing and looking for a quick return to get him out of a hole. Or, if it didn't work, incredibly stupid.

'You've met old Dangerfield, haven't you?' Darley said suddenly.

Daisy shook her head.

'He's a miserable bastard. He inherited everything he had, but acts like he's some kind of business genius. He isn't. This whole company is a tangled mess and if it makes money, it's more by accident than by design, or through the fact that some brilliant people are working here. Dangerfield believes in tyranny. He gets results through fear. He'll destroy a man's life and career on the flimsiest of pretexts.' Darley rolled the stem of his wine glass between his fingers so that the ruby liquid tipped and swirled in the bowl. 'He pays well. He offers good benefits. The company sucks you in, offers you home loans, helps with school fees and lots of tasty little treats. But after that, you're a possession, a thing, with no right to be heard and no thoughts of your own.' He looked up at Daisy dully. 'I'll be pleased to get out. And you're a brave woman if you want to stay in.'

Daisy blinked. It was strange to hear her father spoken of like this. The man she'd grown up worshipping and adoring and thinking could do no wrong was detested by everyone who worked for him. *And, of course, I know the truth of that too.* 'Can't he be got rid of?' she asked slowly. 'Can't someone depose him?'

Darley shook his head. 'He could resign. He could be voted off the board, but that would never happen. We might all be very lucky and he could die – that's what we're all hanging on for. Maybe his son Will might come in and take over. He's a successful businessman in the States. He can't be any worse than his father anyway.'

Daisy realised that she was biting her lip hard. People actually wished her father dead. What a terrible indictment of a man.

'My problem is that things haven't worked out as I'd hoped.' Darley looked unhappy. 'The mine isn't anywhere near ready to produce the ore. Anatolski gave me to understand that he was on the brink of extraction, but it's not happening. In fact, I'm flying out there next week to see what the situation is for myself. He's being very evasive, but has hinted he might need even more money. So I'm going to take a look.'

Daisy sat back to process all of this. 'In that case,' she said at last, 'I'd better come with you. I want to see this mine too. We'll need to find out the truth of the situation before we can make any decisions.'

'Come with me?' Darley looked disbelieving.

'Of course,' she replied coolly. 'I don't see any alternative if I'm going to help you. You'd better sort it out first thing tomorrow.'

Now, as the little helicopter took her inexorably north to the Siberian mine where Sergei Anatolski was waiting for them, Daisy wasn't so sure about her decision to come. This seemed like a hare-brained scheme that would probably result in the sack for both of them. She'd be lucky to get her old job as a chambermaid at the Excalibur after public disgrace like that. She tried not to think about it. It was a crazy throw of the dice, but if it worked, then it could prove the perfect way to implement everything she had planned and worked for.

58

Coco woke mid-morning and wandered out. The party had gone on late into the night, but Will had disappeared early and, once he'd left, her appetite for enjoying herself had died completely so she'd turned in as well. The pool area was tidy again, all signs of the gathering cleared away. She went into the kitchen where Maria waved her back outside, promising to bring breakfast out to her and appearing a few minutes later with a tray laden with cereal, yoghurt, fruit, coffee, juice and a basket of warm croissants. Coco sat at one of the tables by the pool to eat, and when Maria came back with milk, butter and honey, she asked where Will was.

'Gone to work today,' she said. 'He's in town. Might be back late. I never know.'

How on earth am I going to find anything out? Coco wondered. *I never see the guy. He's either shut away here or else at work.* She could see that this might take time. Would she and Xander be able to stay here for as long as it took, without arousing suspicion?

She finished her breakfast and settled down by the

pool until Xander emerged from his room, white-faced and rather ill-looking, just in time for lunch. He'd got mightily drunk with a pretty girl from the Valley and had fancied his chances, but she'd left at dawn with a few of the others.

'You're pretty footloose, aren't you, Xander?' Coco teased, pouring him a glass of chilled water, which he drank gratefully.

He shrugged. 'I guess so. It's just the way I am. One day I'll settle down, but I'm still young, you know. Still lots of partying to do before I get all sensible and dull.'

'And you think anyone's crazy enough to take you on?' Coco gazed at him through the lenses of her sunglasses. They gave Xander an almost healthy glow but when she peered over the top she could see the truth of his greyish skin and dark stubble.

'You'd be surprised,' he said, leaning back. 'Actually, there's a friend of my sister's. A really sweet girl. She's had a crush on me for ever.'

'Don't tell me you've used her and tossed her aside, please?'

'Well . . .' Xander looked a little sheepish.

'Xander! You didn't.'

'Just once. It was rather romantic, if you must know. The two of us, under the stars, making love in an orchard . . . It's an experience I remember with great happiness.' He took a great swig of water and then sighed. 'I'm no good for her really, but if I ever shape up – well, I can think of worse things than ending up with Imogen.'

'Oooh, lucky Imogen, whoever she is!' replied Coco caustically. 'With that attitude, she's in for a treat.'

Xander picked up a napkin, screwed it up and tossed it at her. 'Shut up. It's a figure of speech. What I mean is, if I get my act together, then maybe we'll fall properly in love. That's all, you bloody pedant.'

Coco was quiet. *Falling in love.* That was something she'd never imagined would happen to her again. After Jamal, she thought that was over for her. She gave herself a mental shake. *Fancying someone does not mean love,* she thought. But she couldn't dislodge the rather wistful feeling that came over her.

After lunch Xander wanted to go into town to see some of the sights. Will had lent them a car, and Xander persuaded her to go with him to Venice Beach. They drove down Sunset Boulevard, past the Sunset condos, the Beverly Hills Hotel, and then got on to the 405 south past the Getty Museum. The roads were so long and straight, and there were thousands of cars. The city ought to have been familiar from movies but somehow it wasn't: it was so big, and the blazing blue skies and the endless palm trees made it seem even more unreal. When they eventually arrived at Venice Beach, Coco didn't like it much. Some people might enjoy the carnival atmosphere and freak-show vibe, but she wasn't comfortable with the drugged-out weirdos, the outsized body builders, the hair plaiters, the tattoo artists and the crazies proclaiming their new-age religions. Xander seemed fascinated by it all: the roller-skating gurus, the cheap-looking models in miniscule bikinis sashaying around, trying to get noticed, the drag queens and the women who'd been plastic-surgeried into freaks.

'Let's go somewhere else,' Coco begged, but Xander wouldn't go anywhere until he'd sat down and shared a joint with a chilled-out Rasta guy, while Coco amused herself looking at tat on the nearby stalls. When Xander had finished his smoke, he said he wanted to go to a bar, although Coco thought he looked far too spacey to start drinking.

'Boy, strong stuff,' he said, looking white around the lips, as they walked down the street looking for somewhere to get a beer.

'Xander, are you OK? Are you going to be able to drive?'

'Yeah, sure,' he said, but Coco wasn't convinced. She felt nervous. They found a bar and settled down on stools at the counter. A football game was playing on a small television suspended above the bar and most people seemed fascinated by it, though it meant nothing to Coco.

Xander quickly sank a beer and ordered another while Coco watched him anxiously. 'You know, you shouldn't drink if you have to drive. They're pretty strict here, aren't they?'

'It doesn't matter,' he replied, staring up at the screen as though he knew what was going on. 'We'll leave the car here if we have to. Or you can drive.'

'I can't drive. I haven't got a licence for one thing.' Coco was cross with him for being so irresponsible. She ordered herself a Diet Coke and drank it slowly while she tried to think over the options. The only thing that occurred to her was to walk him round until he worked the beers and the skunk or whatever he'd smoked out of his system. She'd just resolved on this when he made a strange moaning sound.

'Are you OK?' she asked, reaching out to put a hand on his shoulder.

'I . . . feel . . .' Xander pulled in a breath. 'Not so good.' Suddenly, to her surprise, she saw his eyes behind his sunglasses roll back in his head, and the next moment, he'd slipped from his stool and fallen heavily to the floor.

'Xander!' she cried, getting down next to him and shaking him. He appeared to be out cold.

'Whass goin' on?' demanded the barman, peering over. A few other people stopped watching the game to observe the action. 'He need an ambulance?'

'No, no,' Coco said quickly, 'don't call anyone. He's just had a bit too much sun, that's all. He's English. Not used to it.' She shook Xander again, and he groaned. 'Wake up, wake up!'

He opened his eyes briefly, then shut them again and seemed to slump back to unconsciousness.

'Lady, you better get him up off the floor, or I'm gonna call an ambulance, or the police, or both,' said the barman, wiping off another glass.

'OK, OK.' She managed to pull Xander up to a sitting position, leaning him against the counter. She felt inside his jacket pocket and pulled out his phone. Scrolling through the address book, she found Will's number and pressed dial.

'Mate!' came Will's voice in a moment. 'What's up?'

'Will, it's Coco. Xander's been taken ill in a bar, can you help me?'

'Where are you?'

'I don't know – by Venice Beach somewhere.'

'Find out the name of the place and text it to me. I'm on my way.'

'Thanks so much,' she said, flooded with relief, but he had already hung up. She got the address from the barman, texted the address, and twenty minutes later, after Xander had come round and was moaning about his head and stomach, Will walked in. She was delighted to see him.

'Hey, trouble,' he said, putting a strong arm under Xander's shoulders. He smiled at Coco. 'Come on. Let's get you home.'

His black Porsche was parked outside and he pushed Xander into the narrow back seat, where he at once slumped down, then Coco climbed in the front as Will got behind the wheel. He flashed her a kind look. 'You did the right thing. I wasn't sure if you knew about Xander's propensity for getting himself into trouble, but I guess you do now.'

'Has he always been like this?'

Will threw a look over his shoulder at his friend, who seemed to have fallen asleep. 'This? This is nothing. You should have seen him at university. Always had a self-destructive streak, our Xander.'

Back in Beverly Hills they managed between them to get Xander out of the car, through the house and out to his cottage. Will slung him on the bed.

'Do you think he'll be OK?' Coco asked anxiously.

'Sure. He's just smoked some weed stronger than he's used to and now he wants to sleep it off.'

'He won't be sick?' she said. Xander had flopped out on the bed, one hollow-looking cheek turned upwards, his lashes curling down towards it. He looked about ten years old and very helpless.

'If he hasn't puked by now, I don't think he's going to.' Will glanced at her. 'What about you? Are you hungry?'

'I . . . yes, I am actually,' said Coco, realising that it was now a long time since lunch.

'Let's get some dinner then. Maria's gone home. I don't cook. Shall we go out?'

'I don't want to leave Xander here on his own,' she said doubtfully, although the idea of dinner out with Will was more tempting than she dared admit to herself.

He smiled at her. 'You're right. We'll order in. Do you like Chinese? Or Thai?'

An hour later, they were sitting cross-legged on the floor of Will's fancy sitting room, surrounded by a detritus of boxes, eating the most delicious Thai food Coco had ever tasted. Everything seemed fabulous, fresh and delicious: the salt-and-pepper squid, the chicken parcels, the red duck curry and fragrant jasmine rice. They wolfed it down, with bottles of ice-cold beer, while Will told her funny stories about Xander at university.

'So were you two really good friends then?' she asked. She felt amazingly alive when she was with Will. Perhaps it was the way her whole body tingled and reacted to his presence. Tonight, for the first time, he unbent a little and appeared relaxed, smiling and funny, and the effect on Coco was delicious. She knew that her eyes were sparkling and that she was laughing at everything he said. She was putting her head on one side to show him her long, slender neck and shaking out her hair so that it tumbled about her face, but she was barely aware that she was doing these things. All she knew was that she felt good and that all her nerve endings were coming to life, hoping to be useful to her later.

'Me and Xander?' Will shook his head, probing in the bottom of the pad-thai box for one last shrimp. 'Not really. We were in some clubs together, we had some mutual friends, but I wasn't into his crowd as much as he was. Some real wasters in there. I knew I wanted to be successful, and that meant working. His gang weren't really into that – most of them inherited their money and didn't have to think about working.'

'And you didn't inherit anything?' she asked innocently.

He stopped chewing for a moment, looked over at her, then carried on. When he'd finished, he said, 'Well, my dad had some money, it's true. But I didn't want any of that. I wanted to show him I could make my own.' He shrugged. 'And I have. So I'm not like those kids. I always wanted to prove myself.'

'What you've achieved is amazing,' Coco said sincerely.

'Mmm.' He looked reluctant to agree. 'There's still a way to go. I don't want to stop until I can show my old man exactly what I can do without him.'

'Don't you get on?' Coco paid close attention to picking up the jasmine rice and spooning the last bits into a bowl, hoping she seemed suitably casual and unconcerned about his answer.

'No,' Will said tersely. There was a pause and then he said, 'What about your dad? Do you get on with him?'

'Oh . . .' She was taken by surprise. She hadn't expected her own questions to be thrown back at her and she had no answer prepared for this one. 'My dad . . . yes . . . yes, we get on fine.'

'That's good. What does he do?'

'Er . . . nothing special . . . he's . . .' She thought of what her schoolfriends' dads had done, those who worked – builder, taxi driver, council worker – none of that was right for Coco, not any more. 'He's a . . . a stockbroker.'

'Oh, right.' Will nodded, accepting this. He put down the pad-thai box. 'Hey, shall we watch some TV?'

'Sure, sure,' Coco said, disappointed. She felt an important moment had been lost because she hadn't been prepared enough. *I'm going to have to learn to keep asking the questions and not get sidetracked.*

The phone rang. 'Hold on,' he said, getting up, 'I'll just get this.'

'OK.' Coco starting gathering the empty boxes together. She didn't want the rest of the rice now. She'd lost her appetite.

'Hi?' Will said down the phone from the other side of the room. 'I wasn't expecting to hear from you.' He went very quiet for a while and, when he spoke again, his voice was full of rage. 'This is fucking . . . fucking appalling! How low can he fucking go?' There was a pause while the person at the other end of the line talked. 'No. Look, I'll have to talk to Sarah, all right? I'll call you tomorrow. 'Bye.' He put the handset down and stood for a moment without moving, his shoulders bowed.

Coco got up and walked towards him. 'Are you OK?' she asked softly. Was there another chance here to make some discoveries? 'Can I help?'

He turned round and she saw tears in his eyes. 'Will!' she said, moved and concerned. She rushed over and put her hand on his arm. 'What is it?'

'I . . . I had some bad news a while ago,' he said, his voice harsh and choked. 'My sister has died recently in a diving accident.'

Coco stared at him, astonished. No one had said that Sarah was dead. When had this happened?

'Didn't Xander say anything?' Will said, noticing her expression.

She shook her head dumbly, trying to process this new information.

'He gave me his condolences when you two arrived. It happened a few weeks ago. The thing is, my fucking father didn't even think to tell us!' He pushed his hands to his eyes and took a deep breath. 'Poor, poor Daisy. She was only twenty-six.'

Coco gaped at him, trying to take this in. No one had mentioned another sister called Daisy. 'I didn't know,' she said without thinking, 'they didn't say.'

'What?' Will took his hands from his eyes. 'Who didn't say?'

She recovered quickly. 'Your father didn't say *anything* to you? That's weird, isn't it?'

He shook his head. 'We haven't spoken in years. But honestly – to say nothing! Daisy was my half-sister and I hadn't seen her for a long time, but even so . . . My sister Sarah found a report in the paper. I've got a representative in London trying to get more information. That was him on the phone just now, telling me that my father's side are clamming up about Daisy's death, refusing to give us any details. I was trying to track her down not long before the accident and they wouldn't help me then either.' He stared at her, hurt and vulnerability in his eyes. 'What kind of an evil bastard would do that, Coco? Not tell us our

481

own sister had died? Not even invite Sarah and me to the funeral?'

'I don't know,' she said truthfully. She was entirely confused by the death of a sister she'd never heard of. What was Margaret playing at, keeping something like that a secret from her? Then she pushed the thought out of her mind, concentrating only on the pain Will was obviously feeling. 'I'm so sorry. This must be an awful shock.'

His face contorted. 'I want to ring that shit and give him a piece of my mind!'

'Don't do that, you'll only regret it. It won't change anything and you'll wish you hadn't.' She went over, put her arms round him and hugged him. 'I'm so sorry, Will. It's terrible.'

She felt him relax into her embrace. The feeling of her arms around his strong body was divine. She closed her eyes and inhaled: just as she had anticipated, the scent of his skin was wonderful, like fresh sea air mixed with something sweet and warm. His shoulders shook as he let himself surrender to the emotion of the moment, then he was still, breathing deeply. She luxuriated in the sensation of holding him close, not wanting to let go or for the embrace to come to an end. Then, she realised that she could feel his mouth against her neck. He had stooped just a little and his lips were now touching her skin, which burned and tingled beneath his touch. Then he moved his head so that his lips slid lightly over her neck. Moving instinctively, she turned her head to meet his, and an instant later they were kissing. A rushing noise filled her head as her lips touched his, and she felt as though she was flying through the air, even though she hadn't moved at all. Then she was centred again, all her consciousness focused in the place where she and Will were joined together. The kiss was all-compassing, intoxicating and wonderful.

His arms were wrapped around her, the hard firmness of his body pressing against hers. She felt as though she would do anything just to stay close to him and carry on enjoying this delicious feeling.

Coco didn't know how long it was before he pulled away and blinked slowly at her.

'I . . . I didn't expect that,' he said wonderingly.

'Neither did I.' She smiled back.

'I . . . don't know what to say.' He closed his eyes, a bewildered expression crossing his face. Then he looked at her again and said, 'This has been a bit of a strange evening.'

'I just want to . . . be with you,' she said, touching his face softly.

'I want that too,' he said longingly. 'There's something about you, Coco. I felt it as soon as we met. There's something between us, isn't there?'

'I felt it too,' she breathed, excitement coursing through her again. 'It's like a power surge or something, whenever I come near you. It's crazy.' They both laughed.

'Yes, yes, that's just it. Like we can't resist it.' He nuzzled into her neck again, sending a thrill rushing over her skin. 'God, you smell amazing.'

'But . . . your girlfriend . . .'

Will lifted his head and gazed at her. 'I think that's over. I think it was before you arrived – on its last legs anyway.'

That was all she needed to hear. 'Then,' she

murmured, 'what are we waiting for?' She reached for his mouth again, unable to spend another moment not savouring the incredible intensity of his kiss.

They moved together to the sofa and sank down in one another's arms, utterly lost in each other, thinking of nothing else but the delicious sensation of their mouths meeting. She never wanted it to end.

Coco woke later, with Will's arms wrapped around her. She nuzzled into his chest and sighed softly, still half asleep. He was carrying her out to the cottage, pushing the door open with his feet. After hours of delicious kissing, they had fallen asleep together on the wide white sofa in the sitting room, she remembered that. They hadn't gone further: her tentative attempts to push things forward had been met with a tender but firm rebuff. Kissing and embracing was all he wanted. It had been intensely tantalising, leaving her burning with longing, but also wonderful. The sense that he wanted no more than to be close to her filled her with happiness. Now he was laying her tenderly on her bed, taking off her shoes and pulling the goose-down duvet over her.

'Good night, Coco,' he said softly, dropping a kiss on her cheek.

'Don't go,' she murmured, snuggling down into her bed.

'I'll see you in the morning,' he said. 'Get some sleep.'

She drifted off, feeling more content than she had in years.

59

It was cold. Very cold. The air hit Daisy with a fierce blast of ice the moment she climbed out of the helicopter. She was wearing a thick insulated snow jacket, a fur hat, fur-lined gloves and heavy thermal boots, and every piece of skin except for her face was covered up, and yet she felt chilled to the bone immediately.

A man she assumed to be Sergei Anatolski was waiting for them by the landing area, waving at them, his dark blond hair ruffled in the wash from the heli-copter blades. As they approached, he came forward to greet them. He had a weathered face, as if he spent a lot of time outdoors, and strong features: a jutting chin, a nose with the hint of a healed break at the bridge, and hooded blue eyes. He was a man of great presence. He could be any age between thirty and forty-five, but she had the feeling he was in his late-thirties.

'Ross, my friend,' he shouted, 'how wonderful to see you. Welcome, welcome!' His accent was strong with an acquired American twang.

'This is my colleague Daphne Fraser,' explained Darley as he shook the Russian's hand.

'Wonderful.' Sergei took Daisy's hand and shook it hard, revealing bright white teeth as he smiled. 'You are very welcome too. Any friend of Ross's is a friend of mine. Come, let's get inside.'

He led them over to a nearby hut. Inside, to Daisy's great relief, it was warm although she shivered for some moments before she could relax. If a few minutes in the Siberian air could do this, how could anyone bear to be outside for long spells?

'It is a little colder than usual for this time of year,' Sergei said, 'and the wind chill takes it down another ten degrees or so. But it's colder than this in the north, you know. Let's have some tea.'

While they warmed up and drank black tea from the samovar in the corner, served in glasses inside silver holders, he unfurled a map on the table and showed them that they were only a few kilometres from the mine. He explained why it was such a spectacular investment. Few people had been prospecting in this part of eastern Siberia lately, considering the thin, taiga-depleted soil to be low in mineral resources; the thinking was that the good stuff had already been taken, and what was left was not worth the cost and effort of getting it out and refining it to a high enough grade. Attention had turned to the area of the Kursk Magnetic Anomaly in the west, where sixty percent of Russia's iron ore resources were to be found, or to the Urals, where fifteen percent lay under the ground. Then, recently, a little further south and close to the Chinese border, some wonderful discoveries had been made: mines that contained millions of tons of iron ore. It would take a hundred years or more to extract, but it guaranteed prosperity both for the area around the mine, and for the Chinese who had appeared quickly on site to do a deal for the resources there.

'I tell you, my friends, they are going to pay us very good money, wonderful money!' chortled Sergei. 'Wonderful' was obviously one of his favourite words. 'This will make Korsilkoff very, very angry.'

'Korsilkoff?' asked Daisy, curious.

Sergei's eyes darkened. 'The company who are trying to sabotage the mine and all our efforts. They're spreading rumours that the iron ore is too low-grade to be of any use, and that the cost of extraction will be far too great. They're determined to win all the Chinese business for themselves.'

'But that's not true, is it?' Darley looked anxious. 'I mean, you've got high-grade ore there! We've got to get the Chinese deal . . .'

Sergei scoffed, 'Of course it's good stuff. And there should be enough business for all of us – but they fear that access to my supply is going to lower the price of their own. That's why they want to buy in. My brother works for them. He's furious that I bought him out before we discovered the iron ore, and wants me to sell a stake to his company, who will no doubt reward him handsomely for it. But I won't sell, of course.' He grinned broadly at Darley. 'Why do I need to when I have you!'

Darley looked a little uncomfortable.

'Now, let's go and visit the mine. I will drive you myself in the Land Rover.' He pointed proudly out of the window at the big black-and-silver vehicle outside.

'Not much else can get through round here,' he added. 'The ground is very uneven.'

Daisy did not want to leave the warmth of the hut, but all too soon the tea was drunk and it was time to be on their way.

'I'm seriously regretting this already,' she muttered to Darley as they pulled their hats and gloves on again to make the short trip to the Land Rover.

'You've got to respect these guys,' he replied. 'Makes London look pretty nice, doesn't it?'

Sergei held the door of the jeep open for them – Daisy got into the back while Darley sat up front – then climbed in to the driver's seat. The heating came on full blast as the Land Rover pulled away from the landing site and out on to an unmetalled road that ran along the edge of the pine forest. The trees that had looked tiny from the air now towered over them with spindly bare trunks and straggly branches, crowding up to the road's edge and stretching thickly away like a massive snow-capped army of birch and cedar. The Land Rover bumped and jolted along the track. Daisy, jerking about in the back, began to feel sick. Sergei was shouting information to Darley; she couldn't make out much of what he was saying over the engine noise but it sounded as if he was talking about the workforce, an influx of Chinese labourers.

It seemed like hours before they finally arrived at the site, an enormous stretch of ground where four or five bulldozers were hard at work removing the top soil. Around it builders were constructing fences and huts. Figures in thick outer garments and bright yellow hats swarmed everywhere, some on foot and some on huge wheeled buggies that negotiated the uneven territory with ease. At the edges of the site were trucks and yet more Land Rovers and four-wheel-drive jeeps.

'Here we are,' Sergei said with a smile as he pulled to a halt. 'Here's my baby. Come and meet her!'

Daisy steeled herself for the frozen air outside, then jumped out, stuffing her hands into her pockets.

'This way,' Sergei said, obviously keen to show off. They stopped at the newly constructed fence and looked down over the rough, torn-up ground. 'One and a half square miles,' he said happily. 'And full of treasure.'

Darley stared out over it, smiling too.

'And how do you reach it?' Daisy asked. She'd read up a little on iron-ore mining before the trip, but she'd studied Swedish and Brazilian projects where the mines were underground.

Sergei shrugged. 'The simple way. Shovels and trucks. Bulldozers. Look, over there. Once the top soil is removed, we start excavating the rock beneath. We drill and blast to break up the ground, then we take the rocks to the primary crusher, which is being constructed over there – about half a kilometre away. That breaks them down to rocks about nine hundred millimetres big. After that they go to the gyratory crusher, which breaks them down further to around a hundred and fifty millimetres. Then we will stockpile the crushed ore, ready to transport it to another unit for processing.'

'What happens in processing?' Daisy asked.

'More grinding,' replied Sergei. 'Until the product is between two and eight millimetres big. Then we can proceed to copper magnetic separation, where the iron is actually extracted from the rock. And we'll be left with a final magnetite concentrate that will contain more than seventy percent iron.' He smiled over at Darley. 'Money, my friend! Money, money, money . . .'

'When do you expect to start selling your first consignment?' she asked. The bitter wind was stinging her skin as though it had invisible barbed wire laced through it.

'Oh, not for months,' Sergei said. 'We need to finish the processing plants. That's really what I have to talk to you about.'

Daisy flashed a shocked glance at Darley. *Months? Was that what he was expecting?* But the thick fur-edged hood of his coat hid Darley's face from her.

'Let's go inside,' Sergei said, 'and we can talk about it.'

They stomped around the perimeter until they came to a large building with a corrugated roof, and Sergei led them inside where some builders were relaxing and drinking tea.

It was blissfully warm. They took off their hats, coats and gloves while Sergei gave rapid orders in Russian to one of the men. 'He's getting us some lunch,' he explained, leading them over to some chairs and a table arranged in front of a large wood-burning stove. 'We need to eat often and heartily here. Next door is the dining room – it serves a constant flow of hot meals to the workers. Their quarters are a mile away in the nearest village. That's where we'll be staying too.' He grinned at Daisy. 'I would put you up in the hotel except . . . there isn't one. I don't expect many tourists here, so it's not worth building one. You'll be in my house – just a holiday dacha, nothing fancy. I hope that's OK?'

'Of course,' she said. She could smell something delicious being prepared next door and could hardly think of anything else except how hungry she suddenly was.

Darley looked serious and preoccupied but said nothing until platefuls of steaming food had been put in front of them.

'It's called pel'meni, a kind of pasta filled with minced lamb,' Sergei explained. 'A speciality around here.'

It was delicious, Daisy thought, but perhaps that was something to do with how ravenous she was. She spooned down the warm, filling food, savouring every mouthful.

'Sergei,' began Darley in a careful tone, 'you say it's going to be months before you can start processing the ore?'

He nodded, shovelling the pel'meni into his mouth, his spoon looking spindly and small in his great paw.

'Why is that?'

'You see for yourself!' he said, indicating the site outside the window. 'The processing units aren't finished. They'll cost a lot of money to install, and they have to be of the highest specification to make sure we extract every milligram of iron we can. We need to be self-sufficient here, so that we can ship pellets to the Chinese that are ready for steel production. That's how we'll make the most money, I'm telling you.'

'And . . . have you got the money to proceed?' Darley asked in a reasonable tone.

Sergei frowned and took another mouthful of his food. When he'd finished it, he said, 'The money you

491

used to buy into my mine has started this process. But we'll need more to finish it.'

'How much more?'

Daisy leaned forward, eager to hear the answer.

Sergei said blithely, 'Millions, I guess.'

'*Millions?*' Darley looked shocked and appalled. 'Where are you going to get millions from?'

'From you, of course.' Sergei's expression indicated that he thought this was the most natural thing in the world.

Daisy's stomach plummeted. This was not what she had expected. Darley had led her to believe the mine was ready to begin producing iron ore, not that it was months off having the necessary processing equipment and in need of millions of pounds to get it finished.

Darley was spluttering. 'Where on earth do you think we're going to get millions from?'

'Come on,' Sergei said in an ominously low voice. 'I'm not a stupid man. You work for a powerful company. It has billions. Look at the assets. I studied Dangerfield very carefully before I decided to let you buy in.'

'I bought in as a private individual!' cried Darley, panic sparking in his eyes. Daisy watched him, the feeling of dread in her stomach intensifying.

'I don't think so,' Sergei said coolly. 'You don't have millions of pounds at your disposal. I've checked you as well, of course. It was obvious that you were buying in with your company money. And here – ' he looked over at Daisy '– is another executive from your company. I think the signals are quite plain. Your business wanted to make a quick buck from mine.

Fine. But you won't be able to do that unless you find me another tranche of money.'

There was a long pause. Sergei took another slurp of his food. Daisy put her spoon down carefully by her plate, her appetite suddenly gone.

'How much?' she said quietly.

Sergei glanced over at her, his blue eyes flinty, and shrugged. 'Twenty-five or thirty.'

'Million?'

'Of course. You think twenty-five dollars?' He shouted with laughter. 'Listen, the Kimkan mine south of here? Four hundred million investment to get their iron ore out of the ground! This is a fucking bargain!'

Daisy sensed danger in the way Sergei's voice was rising. She saw the door to the room beyond open and a dark head look round briefly and withdraw.

'OK, OK,' she said, putting out her hand in a placatory manner. 'Give us a chance to take this on board, Sergei, all right? We had no idea you still required that level of investment. But, as you say, we're a big company. We've certainly got that level of investment if we choose. Why don't you talk us through the project again? In detail this time.'

60

For the first time in her life, Coco was happy.

She'd thought she'd been happy with Jamal but could see now that was a pale shadow of happiness compared to this. When she thought back to that girl, walking around the estate on the arm of her gang-leader, drug-dealer boyfriend, she didn't feel the same yearning to be there again that she once had. Instead she felt pity for her old self. But then, that girl had no idea that a life like this could exist.

'What the fuck have you done to Will?' Xander asked her with amusement. 'He's a workaholic and I haven't seen him go into his office for days.'

Coco shrugged and smiled. What they were discovering about each other was all-engrossing. There wasn't really time for work or anything but fulfilling the desire they both felt to be together.

Coco had moved out of the cottage now. She was in the main house with Will and had been ever since the night after their first kiss. The following day had been strange: she'd woken wondering if she'd imagined what had happened the night before. She'd gone out to breakfast on the terrace, feeling awkward, but Will had come out, padded over to her, smiled a heartbreakingly beautiful smile, and kissed her on the lips. Then she'd known that it was going to be all right. Coco had stepped out of a dull grey world and into a new, vibrant one, full of sensuous pleasure. Her body buzzed with desire just from looking at his large, capable hands holding a coffee cup; she melted inside with hot longing at the sight of his long firm thigh inside his jeans, and the pressure of his calf against hers under the table. She was obsessed by staring at his mouth, wondering how long she would have to wait before she could take possession of it again.

There was no question of holding back that second night. By the end of an outwardly quiet day, lazing by the pool, both of them were bubbling pools of pent-up desire, desperate to get their hands on each other.

Xander had picked up the vibe during the day – it was impossible not to – his gaze sliding from one to the other, watching as they took any excuse to touch each other, brushing fingertips, rubbing arms, pressing legs together. After dinner, he'd given them a knowing smile and told them he'd leave them to it. He fancied an early night. Then, winking broadly at Coco, he'd headed back to his cottage. As soon as he was gone, they were in each other's arms, hungry to slake the lust that had built up all day.

He'd taken her upstairs to his massive bedroom suite. White blinds covered the wall of glass, hiding them from the garden below. His wide, low and extra-long Japanese-style bed waited for them, as inviting as a patch of virgin snow, and in a moment they were on it together, reluctant to separate long enough to take their clothes off. Will ripped his tee-shirt off over his head, revealing his tight, muscled abdomen, a trail of brown hair leading from his navel down beneath the waist of his jeans, while Coco fumbled with buttons, desperate to get her Balmain dress off. In moments they were in their underwear and the tempo changed: they began to luxuriate in the feeling of his hard flesh pressed against her softer, more yielding skin.

'Oh, Coco,' he whispered as he ran his hands over her soft breasts. 'Oh my God . . . you're so beautiful.'

She felt beautiful too, not just an assembly of tits, arse and pussy, all the bits those men in the clubs had wanted to see, but fully and entirely beautiful. She had the feeling that Will would marvel over her toes and fingertips, or the tiny spot behind her earlobe which made her shiver to the touch, as much as at her hard, rosy nipples or the curve of her bottom.

Eventually, when they could wait no longer, they removed, slowly and lingeringly, the last flimsy barriers between each other. Then he pushed inside her and Coco gasped: he was huge, his cock engorged to full thickness. He was deep inside, right in the heart of her, and at last they were joined together. The beauty of the sensation almost overcame her entirely, and tears leaked out of her eyes, even though she was ecstatic with the pleasure he was giving her.

They couldn't get enough of each other; it was as though she couldn't take him far enough but had to keep pressing and pushing for more. She made him lie on his back and straddled him, straightening her spine so that she could feel him as far inside as possible. She leaned back as she rode him, dragging her fingertips lightly over his thighs and to the soft sac below his rearing penis.

When he couldn't take any more, he pushed her over on to her back and began to move with harder, stronger thrusts, his desire for her overtaking him. She bit into his shoulder and neck, and ran her hands over his biceps, now bulging with the effort he was making. The pleasure was too much: the electricity radiating out from her groin was almost unbearable. She had to peak or go mad. Then, with glorious intensity, her climax took hold, scooping her up in its grip and whirling her round and round, into dark ecstasy.

Opening her eyes was like regaining consciousness. Will was beside her, panting, his cock still inside her. They stared into each other's sated eyes and laughed softly. They didn't need to say anything at all.

After that, they were together constantly, addicted to the sight, touch and smell of each other. Xander was clearly amused by their dazed, almost drunken state, like two bees intoxicated by a surfeit of nectar. Will was with them all the time now, and the hours drifted by pleasurably, the world kept out of sight and mind. In here, they had all they needed. Coco wanted to stay here forever and never, never come out.

As they lay together in the long hours of the night, awake at odd hours, or lazed in the pools of golden sunshine that fell on the bed when Will lifted the blinds just so, they talked. Will told her about his childhood and the stormy relationship he'd had with his bullying, controlling, disdainful father. As she saw the whole story through the eyes of that gap-toothed boy from the film, she began to understand it differently. This was not the bolshie, selfish, ungrateful son that Margaret had portrayed, a young man who had treated his father with unforgivable cruelty. He was a boy who'd cried out for love and understanding; who'd been bitterly wounded when his father divorced his mother and married again, bringing another woman into the house without so much as discussing it with his children. They'd been expected to get on with it, accept it – to like it even. And then, when the new baby had been born . . .

'It was so hard,' Will said in a low voice, lacing his fingers through Coco's as they lay together in his bed. 'He adored her in a way he'd never adored us. As soon as she was born, it was as though we didn't matter. I hated her for it . . . or, at least, I tried to. I treated Daisy badly, I can see that now, when it wasn't her fault. She couldn't help the way Daddy spoiled her, and she was a sweet little thing in her way. He had such high hopes for her. It must have destroyed him when she died. He would have given her the stars if he could. I feel terrible about the way I treated her now. But the truth is, I'd been looking for her just before she died. I'd hired some investigators to track her down. The word was she was travelling, but we couldn't find a trace of her in Thailand, or anywhere else come to that.' He shook his head. 'It was as though she'd simply vanished. I'd even sent letters to my father, demanding to know where she was, but of course there was no reply. Then she was gone.' Sadness crossed his face. 'I feel so guilty. If only I'd found her earlier, perhaps

I could have saved her. Prevented the accident somehow.'

Coco stroked his shoulder. 'You weren't to blame. It wasn't your fault. There's nothing you could have done.'

He smiled and kissed her, and the pain in his eyes went away.

Sometimes he asked her to tell him about her life and she spun a pleasant tale of a privileged upper-middle-class existence. She gave her imaginary family a large house in South Kensington; she described her father coming in late with his briefcase, her mother playing the piano while her brother practised his violin, the telly on and supper on the table. The life she'd always yearned for she now gave herself, along with the education she'd missed out on. She conjured up a career: a job waiting for her in London, and her last few months of freedom, travelling about with no ties and no obligations. Part of her knew that this was storing up trouble for the future, but she didn't care if it gave her what she needed right now: Will, and the hours and days to enjoy him. When an email came from Margaret, asking her when she could expect a report, Coco wrote a short reply fobbing her off and did not open her email account again.

One night, wrapped in each other's arms, Will told her the whole story of his campaign against his father. She listened, motionless, almost wanting to put her finger over his lips and stop him as it all came pouring out. She was afraid of knowing because it meant she would have to make a choice at some point. Owning the knowledge was dangerous. But she didn't stop him. Instead she listened as Will described the family trusts set up by his grandfather and his suspicions that the trustees were puppets of his father, who allowed him to remove great chunks of money for his own purposes – money that was meant to be passed on to future generations.

'I don't know where this money has gone, but I have an idea. He's set up some kooky thing called the Dangerfield Foundation and I suspect it's all being poured in there. I'm going to stop him,' Will said with determination. His face was stony in the half light that came from the poolside illumination. 'I'm setting the whole thing in motion: I'll take him to court if I have to, and Sarah will sue with me. He can't get away with treating us like we don't matter. Not any more. Maybe if Daisy had lived, she might have come in with us – that's why I was looking for her, to see if she knew what was going on – but I doubt it. She never could see that the idol she worshipped had feet of clay.'

'Do you think you can stop him?' Coco whispered. She felt, suddenly, like a spy. She never had before. Now she felt like a traitor.

'I'm going to bloody well try,' Will said grimly.

Coco stared into the darkness, wondering what she would do now. *I can't betray him. I won't.*

61

They spent the afternoon at the site going through the mine specifications, then Sergei drove them to the small village where the workers were billeted. The houses were not pretty – basic grey concrete structures with low pitched roofs – but they seemed remarkably attractive when the alternative was the freezing countryside.

Sergei had his own place along the main road, which had just a few shops and an inn. He took them there as night fell and the temperature swooped downwards.

'It's winter here for seven months of the year,' he said cheerfully as he led them inside. 'You get used to it after a while.'

Sergei's house was furnished in a sparse style, and everywhere were signs of the constant struggle to keep the cold out. Windows were shuttered and covered in thickly lined curtains and a huge stove dominated the sitting room, bulging out like a beehive from the corner. A small wooden bench ran around it so that it was possible to sit next to the heat within. The chairs and sofas were draped with throws, blankets and furs.

I'll never grumble about British cold again, thought Daisy. She tried to imagine a life where battling the weather played such an enormous role. It seemed tremendously hard work. Was it worth the effort? Could anyone really like living here?

'This life is not for everyone,' Sergei said, seeing her look around. 'But there is also freedom here, you know. The land belongs to us all. We can wander where we please, and so can the animals.' He took off his coat and hung it up by the door, then put out his hand for Daisy's and Darley's. 'In the woods, you'll see moose, elk, bears, even snow leopards. Near the coast, there are Amur tigers.'

'Tigers?' It sounded so exotic. Daisy handed him her coat and took off her hat. Life here seemed to consist of putting warm clothes on and then taking them off again. Darley looked more unhappy than ever as he unwound his scarf. Daisy wished she could tell him to try and look more cheerful. It was vital to keep Sergei on side.

He showed them to their rooms and Darley went to lie down for a while, saying he was tired. Daisy treated herself to a hot bath to get some heat back into her bones. When she emerged, dressed in warm trousers and two cashmere jumpers, she felt a little better.

Sergei was at the stove in the kitchen, preparing supper: elk casserole with garlicky flat bread. Daisy guessed that vegetarians did not have a particularly easy time of it around here. He looked round with a welcoming smile as she came in. When he wanted to be friendly, his face was quite charming, the blue eyes soft and kindly. But she had already seen the other side: when he set his face so that the strong chin seemed to jut even further outwards, and his eyes turned hard. She sensed he was a quick-tempered man, and wanted to make sure that neither she nor Darley did anything to antagonise him.

'Did you enjoy your bath?' he asked. 'The fire here supplies plenty of hot water, so take as many you like.'

'Thanks,' she said, coming to see what he was stirring. 'That smells great.'

'Just basic. But all food tastes good here . . . except maybe some of it.' He laughed. 'We have some influences that can produce very odd dishes: Chinese meets Mongol meets Russian. Very strange. Where is Darley?'

'Still resting, I think.' She went over to the table and sat down.

'There is vodka if you want a drink,' Sergei said, indicating a carved dresser with a shelf of glass tumblers.

'No, thanks, maybe later.' Daisy began to trace the pattern on the floral oilcloth with one finger. 'Sergei, the company you mentioned – Korsilkoff. How serious a threat are they?'

His face darkened. 'They are scoundrels. They've threatened me. Attempted to sabotage the mine. Spread rumours. I have to screen every worker to make sure he is not a spy.' He turned to look at her. 'That's why I need to get more investment, you see? Until the mine is finished, the deal with the Chinese signed and production has started, I am very vulnerable.'

'I see.' Daisy tried not to show her worry but the truth was she felt out of her depth here. She and Darley were miles away from home, with no one aware of where they were. She had blithely supposed that her BlackBerry would always be at her disposal, but she hadn't picked up a signal since they'd left Komsomolsk.

Sergei came over to the table and sat down opposite her. 'You know,' he said, 'it's not often that a young woman like you comes to a place like this. There aren't many of you in the mining business.' He smiled. 'I'm going to have to be careful. I can't have you distracting the men too much. They're there to work, after all.'

She smiled back, though she didn't much like the implication. 'I'm sure they'll cope,' she said lightly. 'Besides, we're going home tomorrow.'

'Oh, yes.' Sergei nodded. 'Home tomorrow.'

Darley emerged blearily from his room in time for the supper of elk and bread. Daisy thought it was very good, though Darley's appetite did not seem to be up to much.

Sergei entertained them with stories of life in the village: the extremes of weather, the adventures he'd undertaken in the frozen countryside, his hunting exploits. He had grown up in the city, he said, then moved to the US with his parents when he was a young boy. He and his brother had returned from the States with his father, a geologist who had taken up a position in a state mining company. When the Soviet regime began to weaken and crumble, his father had bought some land, instinctively sure that it was rich in iron ore but without the means to test his theory. Sergei had made his career in the hotel business, and he and his brother had inherited the mine in due course. Now his father had been proved right.

'So my hotel business can look after itself for a little while,' he said jovially, 'while I become a very rich mine owner, you see?'

With dinner over, he brought out the vodka and started pouring it for them, proposing toast after toast.

'To my blessed father, of beloved memory!' he cried, lifting his little glass to chink it against Daisy's and then Darley's.

Then: 'To the many millions I am going to make! You must help me plan how to spend it! Perhaps I'll buy a football team and a castle, huh?' Clink.

'To your health – may you live for ever and see your children's children's children!'

Daisy was only sipping a little of the vodka each time, but she was still light-headed. She could see that Darley was rather drunk, swigging back the little shot glasses as though he didn't realise what the cumulative effect would be.

At last, she felt she could interrupt Sergei's exuberance. She stood up. 'I must go to bed now. Darley, I think you should turn in too.'

'I'm not tired,' he slurred. 'I slept this afternoon.'

'Still,' she said firmly, pulling him up by the arm, 'I think you should.'

Once she'd deposited him in his room, she retired to her own. Sergei ought to have been out cold with the amount of vodka he'd put away, but she heard him go out to the sitting room and later some murmured Russian that indicated he was on the telephone.

She climbed under the covers in her bed and lay awake late, thinking of the many people who'd been exiled to Siberia and never returned.

I'm out of my depth here. And while Sergei seems very charming, he has an air of menace, as though he can turn in an instant into someone very frightening indeed. She moved her head to find a more comfortable place on the pillow. *At least I'm going home tomorrow.*

London had never seemed so far away.

62

There was another party planned for the following night – they happened every few days or so. Will allowed it because he liked seeing the house filled with people, and because he wanted to let his work-force and their friends let off steam every now and then. They spent so much of their lives in front of screens, simulating emotions. He wanted to make sure that they also remembered how to live.

And it didn't hurt to have a reputation as the best boss in town.

Coco had gone to bed early, partly in preparation for a late one the following night, and partly because she had a headache. The sun had been strong that day and she'd spent too long lying out on the sun lounger, turning her skin an even deeper shade of gold.

Will and Xander stayed up together, eating dinner and then watching a ball game on TV with a stack of beers, even though both of them were hazy on the rules of baseball.

'I just think of it as really skilled-up rounders,'

Xander said cheerfully as they lay spread out on a sofa each, a pile of cushions propped behind their heads.

Will laughed.

'Hey, mate, you got any whisky?' Xander asked.

'Sure.' Will indicated a large Indian cabinet inlaid with mother-of-pearl. Xander got up, trotted over and helped himself to a bottle of Jack Daniel's.

'Gotta be Tennessee,' he sang lightly as he poured himself a large measure and returned to his place.

'Where did you go last night?' Will asked, looking over briefly at his friend. Xander was looking more stubbly and sunken-cheeked than ever, and he felt a pang of guilt that he was so wrapped up in Coco now. He'd hardly given his friend any attention, and it couldn't be great sitting around like a gooseberry when a loved-up couple were all over each other. Xander had taken to heading out on his own or with some of the people he'd met at Will's parties to discover the night scene in downtown Hollywood.

'I went to Joseph's on Ivar and Yucca,' Xander said idly. 'I hooked up with some girls.'

'The place where all the celebs keep getting into trouble?' Will asked, frowning. He was not a great clubber himself and only heard about these cool nightspots.

'The very same. I had a great night. Got totally off my tits. American girls are very generous with their drugs, I must say.'

'Just don't get caught, Xander, OK?' Will said warningly. 'It's better not to fool around with that stuff at all. You'll forfeit any right to come back here if you're busted.'

'I know that.' Xander made a sad face. 'It's so mean.'

Will felt a sudden stab of irritation. He'd moved on and left those party days behind him. It seemed strange that here was Xander, still as up for getting out of his skull as ever. Was he ever going to grow up and settle down? Will had a sudden vision of Coco, lying upstairs in bed. He pictured her, naked under the sheets, her back turned to the window so that the light fell on her shoulder blades and caught her hair spread on the pillow. He felt a stirring in his groin as he imagined slipping under the sheet beside her, reaching out for her incredibly soft breasts, letting one sit heavy in the palm of his hand as the nipple hardened in response to his touch. He saw the curve of her hip under the white covering and the small breath of warmth that would sigh out from under the sheet as he lifted it to reveal her belly and the mound below. *Shit,* he thought. He'd never felt desire like this. The more he had her, the more he wanted – it was the reverse of most of his relationships.

'But you know the latest thing, don't you?' Xander smiled over at his friend, oblivious to the images passing through his mind. 'To reduce chances of being busted.'

'No.'

'Mate, if you're really upscale . . . you order in.'

As if on cue, the buzzer in the hall went.

'Who's that?' asked Will, surprised.

'You'll see,' Xander said, getting up and going out to the hall to answer it. Will watched him go then sprang to his feet and followed.

'Who's that?' he demanded.

'A friend. Or two.' Xander grinned again. A moment

later, there was the roar of a car coming up the driveway and halting in front of the house. There was the sound of laughing and then a banging on the front door. Xander went and opened it. 'Hello, *ladies.*'

On the doorstep were two California blondes with big breasts, probably fake, bursting out of their low-cut tops and long tanned legs emerging from mini-skirts. They had billowing dyed blonde hair and heavy make-up, their lids weighted down by false eyelashes. Giggling and squealing, they greeted Xander with eager kisses and great excitement.

'Xander . . .' said Will with a sigh. These were not the kind of people he usually invited in. The kids he partied with were pretty normal, not plastic wannabe starlets who never would be.

'Ah, come on, we're just going to do a little partying,' Xander said, slipping his arm round the waists of both girls. They pouted at Will and fluttered their eyelashes.

'You gonna join us?' breathed one, giving his body an appreciative look.

'I don't think so. Go out to the pool if you want to,' he said, and returned to the sitting room. He heard them go out the back and soon was aware of muffled shrieks and gales of laughter. He knew what they'd be doing – drinking his booze, doing some drugs probably. He tried to lose himself in the ball-game for a while and then switched over to a late-night movie, but somehow he couldn't shut out the sounds that drifted in from the terrace. He thought about going to bed but didn't want to leave Xander in sole charge. *For fuck's sake,* he thought, *we're having a party tomorrow night. Xander could have invited those bimbos then.*

510

After an hour or so, he could take no more, jumped to his feet and headed out to the poolside. Xander and one of the girls were cosied up on a lounger, kissing, her bikini top now on the floor. Drink and drug detritus were spread out across the table and Will hated seeing it. Most of the time at his parties, people were discreet if they were going to indulge. They didn't disrespect his house by openly flouting the law there. The other girl was swimming in the pool singing to herself.

'OK, that's enough!' Will said roughly. 'Time to go home, ladies.'

The girl and Xander pulled apart, surprised, and she said, 'Oooh! We're just getting started!' She gazed provocatively at Will and said, 'You're cute.'

'Sorry. Party's over for tonight.'

The girl in the pool swam slowly to the side and started to climb out.

'Hey, come on, Will,' protested Xander. His pupils were wildly dilated and he was working his jaw.

'I mean it. That's it. Come back tomorrow.' The girls didn't put up much of a fight but Xander seemed furious. Within a few minutes, Will had rounded up the girls, their clothes and shoes, phoned for a cab and, when it came, herded them out of the front door.

Xander stood inside the hall as Will shut the front door, his expression mulish and his mouth set sulkily. 'I think that was pretty bloody *crap*, if you don't mind my saying.' He was slurring slightly. 'Why's everybody allowed a good time except me? Huh?'

'We're partying tomorrow,' Will said shortly.

'Why'd you have to spoil my fun? I might not see those girls again. My one was really nice.'

'Come on, Xander,' Will said, 'they're just club girls. Dancers. They make their living jiggling their breasts in front of guys like you. You don't need them.'

Xander stared at him, his eyes glittering dangerously. Then he muttered something under his breath that Will couldn't hear.

'See you tomorrow, mate, I'm off to bed.' Will loped up the stairs, leaving his friend staring after him, his blue eyes glazed and discontented.

63

The next day Darley did not appear at breakfast. Too hung-over, Daisy suspected. Sergei served her hot coffee, rolls and salami. She'd have preferred some muesli but it would have been ungracious to mention it.

'I don't think you're going home today,' he announced without any preamble.

'What?' She was startled. 'Why not?'

'The weather is turning against us. You won't be able to take a helicopter ride to Komsomolsk.' He shook his head. 'No way. And even if you get there, probably the plane won't leave.' Sergei appeared quite unconcerned. 'You'll have to go tomorrow.'

'But . . . but . . . I must go home!' she insisted, pushing her half-eaten breakfast away from her.

'Here, there is no *must*,' he said with a smile. 'The weather speaks and we obey. If we don't, we die. It's not like your soft weather in England. It has a spirit, a character, and a desire to kill you if it can.'

Daisy's spirits swooped downwards as she stared at him. Even if she insisted, how on earth could she make him do anything? She and Darley were completely in his power, she could see that. *But why would he lie to me? If he says the weather is bad, then it's bad. I'll have to accept it.* 'OK,' she said, trying to sound as calm as possible, despite the ripples of panic she was feeling. 'Let me go and tell Darley he can sleep in if he wants.'

Darley did not answer her knock. She went in to find him groaning in his bed.

'Too much vodka?' she said with a smile as she ventured closer. It was a little strange seeing him in bed in his pyjamas. 'I thought you might regret it.'

'No, no,' rasped Darley, looking up at her wild-eyed. 'I'm sick . . . I'm sick!'

She looked more closely. He did look terrible: his skin was white and clammy and sweat stood out all over his brow and upper lip. His hands were shaking. 'Darley, you're right. You look awful.'

'I feel terrible . . . I'm hot, but I'm shivering.' His jaw started to chatter, his teeth knocking together with a horrible clicking sound.

Daisy called Sergei in. He examined Darley and then fetched a thermometer and stuck it under the sick man's tongue. When it beeped, he removed it, read it and frowned.

'He has a very high fever,' he said tersely.

'Can we fetch the doctor?' Daisy said anxiously. It looked as if Darley had been hit by a severe case of 'flu.

'Doctor – yes. But here is what the doctor will say: give him fluids, keep him warm or cool, give him medicine to fight the fever. We can do all that without the doctor.'

'I think we should see one,' cried Daisy. All this hardy self-sufficiency could be taken too far.

514

Sergei shook his head. 'The doctor will say what I've said. We will get him tomorrow, if Darley feels no better. But if he's worse, then I say we take him to the hospital at Komsomolsk. If we can get there, of course.'

'I insist you get the doctor!' cried Daisy, drawing herself up to her full height. 'If he might need to get to hospital, we must know now!'

Sergei stared at her as if wondering whether to allow his anger to flare into life at being ordered around by this girl. Then he sighed. 'The doctor is an hour's drive away. If I go now, I can be back for lunchtime, I guess.'

'Yes, yes,' she said, relieved. 'Go now, definitely. Please. I'll look after him until you get back.'

Ten minutes later, Sergei was pulling away in the Land Rover and heading off to get the doctor.

Daisy took Darley cold water to drink and painkillers to help reduce the fever. 'Don't worry,' she said, as he swallowed the pills. 'The doctor will be here soon.'

'Can I get home?' he said in the same rasping voice, his eyes glittering and cheeks hectic.

'Not today,' she said gently. 'Maybe tomorrow, if you're feeling better. But just relax. Everything's under control.'

Two hours later, Daisy was pacing the sitting room, staring out of the window every few minutes, but she could see nothing. Sergei was still not back and the weather, as he had predicted, was closing in. The sky, a heavy palette of white, grey and violet, had sunk down on to the village and she could see no further than a few feet from the front door. The air seemed thick with unshed snow and she could tell that a bitter wind was whirling around outside.

'Come on, come on,' she muttered, glancing again at her watch. Time was moving with terrible slowness. She picked up a large fur throw from the sofa and wrapped it around herself, not from cold but because she needed comfort.

Darley was sleeping. Daisy had taken him hot soup to drink but he had not been hungry and had soon sunk into a heavy slumber. It was his breathing that worried her. It hummed and rattled in his chest, emerging from his open mouth with an unhealthy whistle. Was it 'flu? Or something more serious?

'Oh, where *is* the doctor?' she said helplessly. She looked over at Sergei's computer, blank-screened in the corner, and wondered if she dared switch it on. She wanted to Google Darley's symptoms.

Just then, she heard the muffled roar of an engine.

'Thank God!' She rushed to the window and saw the dark shape of the jeep pulling up by the house. She ran through to Darley to tell him the good news, but he was still sleeping. She decided not to wake him.

She returned to the sitting room in time to see the door swing open and a big burly figure come inside, followed by another well wrapped in protective clothing.

'Sergei, thank goodness you're back,' she said. 'Is that the doctor?'

The first man threw back his fur-edged hood, revealing a face as craggy as Sergei's and similar blue eyes, but it was not him. The other had Chinese features beneath a thick wool hat.

'I'm afraid not,' said the first man in a thick Russian accent. He grinned at her and his eyes glittered hungrily. 'Sergei has unfortunately been delayed. But don't worry. We've come to take you somewhere safe. Please put on your coat.'

64

Will had worked mostly from home lately but at last he had to go to his office, so Coco decided to go shopping and buy something to wear for the party. There was no sign of Xander, and the door to his cottage was firmly shut. Will drove Coco downtown, taking her past his offices which were in a stunning black-glass skyscraper, and dropping her on Melrose Avenue. She had spent some of her days in LA seeing the famous sights – Grauman's Chinese Theatre, the Hollywood sign, and the studios – and trying out the huge number of restaurants and novelty joints like frozen custard bars. Now she was ready to shop, and while Will went back to the office, she spent a happy couple of hours browsing, buying a sexy Diane von Furstenberg wrap dress for the evening. Like most of the LA roads, Melrose seemed to go on forever. After trying to walk it for a while, she eventually hailed a taxi to take her up and down the street and wait outside when she saw a shop she wanted to browse through.

When she got back, exhausted and carrying several

bags, Xander was up but monosyllabic. He kept his shades firmly on, retreating behind a newspaper whenever she came near. Coco wasn't offended. She knew that he went through phases when he felt the after-effects of his punishing party lifestyle. He always bounced back, the charming, smiling Xander reappearing with his ready jokes and eagerness to amuse.

That evening she took care over her appearance. She always wanted to look her best for Will and put on her make-up as she'd recently been taught, fading subtle colour over her eyelids and darkening the sockets, highlighting her cheekbones and brows with the lightest shimmer. She stared back at her reflection, satisfied that she looked good: polished and healthy with bright eyes and softly shining lips. Her new dress brought out the greeny-blue of her eyes.

Then she went downstairs, ready to start welcoming the guests.

Night had fallen in that soft LA way, floating down over them all like a piece of navy gauze. The party had been going for a while now.

Xander, she could see, was hitting it hard for some reason. He was very drunk after only an hour and Coco guessed he was alternating his beers with whisky. His constitution must be like iron. It was Friday night, and the partygoers seemed keener than ever to let their hair down, jumping into the pool and turning the music up loud so that they could dance on the terrace. The fragrant odour in the air meant that a joint was being passed around somewhere. No doubt pills and coke were being taken as well.

Coco began to feel anxious about Will. He was still shut in his office. Was there some kind of work crisis? She decided she would disturb him, although she rarely went into his office. At the door, she stopped and listened. There was no sound from within. She knocked and pushed the door open. 'Will? Are you all right?'

She looked inside. He was sitting with his back to her, his feet resting on the table, watching something on his computer screen. He turned around at the sound of her voice. 'Huh?'

'Everyone's here. I was wondering when you're coming out.' She smiled at him. 'Tough day?'

'Oh. Yeah.' He clicked his mouse so that his screen went blank. 'I'm coming now.'

As he came close to her at the door, she reached up and kissed him. He kissed her back but she sensed the tension in his shoulders. 'You need to relax,' she whispered, taking his hand. 'Come on.'

As soon as they were outside, people came up to Will to say hello and chat about work issues. Coco didn't mind; this was what he needed, to join in the party and forget whatever was troubling him. She sat beside him, sipping her caipirinha cocktail and watching as he chatted to his guests. Some girls were dancing to the music floating out over the terrace from the hidden speakers: there was a bare patch near the pool that made the best dance floor. They were moving their hips and writhing their arms in time to the beat, some of them singing along.

Suddenly Xander turned to her and said, 'Hey, Coco, why don't you dance?'

She smiled at him. 'Yeah, let's dance, hon.' She put her glass down.

'Nah, not me. You dance. Show Will how good you are.'

Will grinned. He seemed less tense now. 'I know how good she is.'

'No, you don't, not really. She's brilliant, aren't you, Coco? Go on, dance for Will.'

She looked over at Xander, a little suspicious. He'd put on his sunglasses despite the darkness and she couldn't see his eyes. 'Well . . .'

Will said, 'Sounds like it's unmissable. Go on, babe.'

She stared at him. He'd never asked such a thing before but it seemed harmless enough. She got up and walked over to the dance floor. Feeling self-conscious, she started to move to the music, swaying her shoulders and swinging her hips.

'Very nice!' Xander called over. 'Keep going.'

She began to find her rhythm now. God, she loved to dance. She remembered the studio in London where she'd learned to dance properly, the steps Roberto had taught her, the way the other girls had impressed her with their dedication. She felt alive when she danced: the music seemed to come from inside her and she was at one with it. She was oblivious to the other dancers and they kept away from her, as if slightly in awe of the way she moved, so effortlessly and fluidly.

Others were watching her now, the ones sitting round the pool and terrace, with their drinks, cigarettes and bottles of beer.

'She looks sexy, doesn't she, Will?' called Xander. 'Keep going, sweetheart!' He gestured to someone to turn the music up, and the soulful voice of the singer burst over them.

Coco carried on dancing. If Will liked it, she would do it, though she was a little uncomfortable that everyone else was watching too. Wasn't this something that should be private, for just the two of them?

Then Xander said loudly, 'Hey, Coco. Take your dress off.'

She stopped. 'What?'

'Take your dress off. You've got your bikini on underneath, haven't you? What's the problem? Come on, you've got a great body. We want to see you dancing properly.'

She stared over at him, uncertain if he was joking. She gave a half laugh just in case he was.

'Take your dress off,' he insisted. His eyes were still inscrutable behind the shades, but he was smiling. 'It's just your swimming stuff underneath. What are you worried about?'

'Xander, if she doesn't want to, then leave her alone,' Will said. He looked puzzled.

'What's wrong, Coco, too good for us, are you?' Xander called. His voiced slurred ever so slightly. 'It's just a bit of fun.'

'It's OK, Will,' she said. 'I don't mind.' Perhaps Xander was right. Lots of the other girls were dancing in bikinis. She put her hand to the tie at the side of her dress and slowly pulled it. The wrap dress fell open to show her red bikini underneath. She let the dress slide off her shoulders, deftly caught it and tossed it to the side of the terrace.

'Dance, baby!' shouted Xander, so she started moving again, aware that everyone could now see her body: her long legs, the flat stomach, the full breasts with small red cotton triangles over each nipple. 'Yeah, that's good.'

It's just a swimming costume, she told herself. *I'm just dancing at a party.* But there was a sick feeling in her stomach. She knew what this reminded her of. The other girls had stopped dancing now. She was alone on the terrace, swaying and moving to the beat in full view of everyone while Xander whistled loudly from the side. *What's he doing?* She felt frightened and confused but also had a terrible sense that she had to play along with whatever he wanted. *He's drunk. He doesn't know what he's doing.*

'Now,' shouted Xander, 'Coco, take your top off for us! Come on, show us those gorgeous tits!'

'Xander!' Will leaped to his feet, his eyes flashing. 'What the hell are you doing?'

Coco stopped dancing. She stared over at the men, a nasty churning feeling in her belly.

'You heard me,' Xander said loudly. Everyone around had stopped what they were doing and were focusing on the situation. 'Take your top off.' He pulled out his wallet, removed a $50 bill and held it up. 'Here, hon – will this help?' Then he tossed it towards her. It floated to the ground near Coco's feet. She stared down at it, horrified. The music was switched off. Silence covered the terrace; everyone was still.

'Come on,' Xander said, in a voice she'd never heard him use before: hard and hateful. 'Doesn't that buy a peek at those tits of yours? It can't be more than that, surely?'

Rage and humiliation rushed through her.

'Xander, shut the fuck up! What the hell are you

doing?' cried Will, appalled. 'Coco, don't listen to him, he's drunk . . . he's off his face.'

Xander stood up, pulled another fifty out of his wallet and drawled, 'How much for the panties? What's the exchange rate? I guess you're used to pounds, aren't you . . . How much was it, Coco? Twenty? Thirty? What did guys usually pay you to have a look and a feel?'

'Fuck you!' she shouted. 'Fuck you, you bastard!'

She saw Will raise his fist to his friend, ready to punch him, and rushed forward to grab his arm. 'No, Will, no . . . don't.'

'You shithead, how the fuck *dare* you?' Will hissed, staring at Xander.

He swayed and grinned. 'Come on, mate, can't you see it? She's a fucking pole dancer. An East End tart! Common as muck, all done up to make you think she's a lady. She's nothing!'

'What are you talking about?' Will demanded, confused. He looked over at Coco, who stared back, her face stricken.

'You heard me. She's not what you think. She's just like those girls last night. She'll probably give me a blow job if I pay her enough.'

Coco's heart filled with ice. She turned and walked away, scooping up her dress as she went and covering her chest with it. She strode past Will, not looking at him, back into the house and up to their room, where she stood trembling with shock and too stunned to cry.

What the hell had Xander just done?

65

Daisy had worked out that if she balanced the rickety chair on the tea chest, being careful to keep at least three of the legs on the edge so that the chair didn't crash through the lid, she could stand on it, hold on to the high windowsill and then, on precarious tiptoe, look out.

For all the good it did her. There was nothing to see beyond the window but more whiteness. But it kept her occupied. Worse than anything so far was the terrible boredom of having nothing to do but dwell on her situation. Questions swirled round her mind in an eternal carousel, each one coming back as regularly as a favourite pony on the fairground ride. What was happening to Darley? Was he still ill? Had he been taken to hospital? And what about Sergei? Had he even returned? Had he guessed what was happening? Was he looking for her?

Sometimes she had the nightmarish vision of Sergei never coming back, Darley dying in bed with nobody to bring him water or painkillers, and herself vanishing into utter oblivion with no one any the wiser.

When would they start wondering where Darley and Daisy were? They were officially on a fact-finding mission, booked away from the office for a week. They'd been gone five days. It would be two more before anyone began wondering where they were, and goodness knew how long after that before anyone would do something.

What about Darley's family? Wouldn't they raise the alarm when he didn't come home?

There's no one at all to care for me, she thought wretchedly. *No one to wonder where I am when I don't come home.*

This, she saw now, was the terrible truth of the situation she had made for herself. The day she'd become Daphne Fraser and decided to pursue her dream of revenge upon her father, she'd cut off all other human ties and devoted herself to her mission. Even Christophe, who'd loved her . . . she'd chosen her goal over him. And this was where it had led her: to a cold, empty shed in Siberia where anything might happen to her. She could die and no one would know. Oh, God, where was Darley? Was he still ill?

And off it went again, the merry-go-round of questions, and no way of finding out the answers.

She'd barely had time to think when those men had walked into the house the day before yesterday. When she'd protested and said that she wanted to wait for Sergei, the first man had become aggressive, shouting at her that she'd better hurry up, or she'd be sorry. She'd obeyed, not knowing what else to do. She hadn't had time to scoop up her phone and slip it into her pocket, but then it was still resolutely without a signal. They'd brought her here, to this place like the building on the mine site, and pushed her into the back. It was a storage room kept warm by the stove on the other side of the wall, with a tiny lavatory cubicle and sink off it, and apart from that only boxes and old furniture. They'd opened the door to pass in food and hot drinks, so they didn't want to starve her, she supposed, but apart from that, there was nothing.

When either of the men came in, the one who looked like Sergei or the Chinese one, Daisy shouted questions, demanding to know why she was there and what they were doing, and to let her damn' well go, but they never answered. She had the feeling that the Chinese man didn't speak any English, and when she tried a few words of Mandarin he remained blank, so she was wasting her time.

Even though the room was quite warm, she didn't dare take her coat off. She wanted to be ready at all times in case she had to run. Besides, she felt cold no matter what.

She felt sure that the Russian man was Sergei's brother – the one who worked for Korsilkoff, who'd wanted to buy into the mine. He must be holding her in return for Sergei's compliance. But then . . . what would Sergei do? Why should he care enough about her to give up a piece of his beloved mine to save her?

The thing that sent chills up her spine and fear crawling all over her was that he might not. And then what would happen?

Daisy heard laughing and carousing on the other side of the thin partition wall. They were getting drunk, from the way their slurred voices were increasing in volume. No wonder – what else was there to do in this forsaken place? It sounded as though her captors had been joined by at least one other man, there was too much noise for only two of them. She curled up on her mattress in the darkness, trying to ignore the racket next door, wrapped her arms around herself tightly and closed her eyes.

She must have dozed off despite the noise but suddenly she was wide awake. The door had opened, casting a large triangle of golden light over the floor, and a dark shape stood there, swaying slightly. She stared at it, blinking and bewildered, then sat up and tried to focus. She realised she didn't know the face looking down at her, but saw the usual two behind him, gazing in as well, laughing drunkenly.

The man in the doorway smiled nastily and said something in Russian, then looked back over his shoulder, saying something else in a tone that made the others laugh but caused a feeling of dread to twist through Daisy. Adrenaline prickled all over her, and she was instantly on her guard.

The stranger swaggered in towards her, his eyes glittering dangerously as he gazed at her appraisingly. He was still talking loudly in Russian and the other two sniggered; something in their apprehensiveness made Daisy fear the worst.

They're drunk. She began to look furtively about for something to protect herself with. *They've told this man about me – God only knows what they've said.* Awful images flashed rapidly through her head: perhaps Sergei had washed his hands of her and this man was some kind of trafficker, prepared to take her into a life of slavery. And perhaps he intended to test out the goods first . . .

No, she thought, fury making her fierce and damping down her fear. *I won't let that happen.*

Quickly and smoothly she rose to her feet, keeping her knees bent, ready to run. The man was closer now; she could smell the sour smell of alcohol coming off him, and the musty scent of his fur-lined jacket. He was still talking as he approached, murmuring slurred Russian in a voice clearly intended to keep her calm. His slow drink-deadened reactions might be her only chance, she thought. She was sure now that he meant to harm her in some way: even the two men behind seemed nervous despite their obvious interest in the situation.

They might not help me. I've got to be prepared to do this alone . . .

The man was close to her now and the two of them stared at one another like animals preparing for combat. His face was sunburned, his small slanted eyes showing some kind of Asiatic descent, though he wasn't Chinese. He looked tough and his leering smile told her he liked what he saw and wanted more of it. Just as Daisy was about to slide away from him, he pounced, his hands gripping her arms like steel pincers and his bitter-smelling mouth pressed on hers.

She gasped and tried to resist but he had her in an iron grasp. She turned her head away but he followed it with his own, searching for her mouth with his, scratching her skin with his rough stubbled face.

So this is it, she thought, panicked. *This is what they intend to do to me. How the hell can I stop them?* She gathered all her strength and shouted, '*Niet! Niet!*'

The man who held her didn't stop his efforts to kiss her but she sensed the other two moving uncomfortably behind him. Perhaps they weren't as tough as they looked; perhaps they had begun to bond with her over the last couple of days and didn't relish seeing their captive assaulted in front of them. She pressed home her advantage, trying to catch their eyes as she struggled to avoid the stinking kisses, and shouted again, '*Niet!*'

They weren't going to do anything, she could tell. Perhaps their blood was up and they wanted to see what would happen. Daisy knew she would have to think of another way. Behind her on the rickety table she could see the remains of her supper: a dirty tin plate and an empty water bottle. A glass bottle. She managed to move back a few steps. Her assailant was losing patience, she could sense that. His hands were now scrabbling at her coat, trying to gain access, and that left her free to move her arm. With one swift movement, she reached back, picked up the bottle and swung with all her strength at the man's head, closing her eyes tightly as she did in case of flying glass.

She felt the crunch against his skull as it hit him. The bottle split into three separate pieces, leaving the neck still in Daisy's fist. Her attacker instantly crumpled, groaned, rolled his eyes and slumped to the floor unconscious. For a moment the other three stood without moving, staring at each other. Daisy faced them, panting, holding up the broken bottle neck like a knife, prepared to take them on if they went for her. But they didn't move; the awful noise of the bottle on bone seemed to have brought them to their senses. After a moment they moved forward, almost sheepishly, muttering to one another, and began to pull their friend out of the room. A few seconds later she was alone again in the dark, the door closed firmly on her. She sat listening, the bottle neck still tightly held in one hand, but there was no more carousing. She heard groans and muted conversation and then doors slamming and a truck driving away.

She was alone again.

66

Will found Coco upstairs, flinging her things into a
suitcase.

'Hey, what are you doing?' he cried, coming over
to her.

'What does it look like?' She picked up some silk
shirts and stuffed them into the case. 'I'm packing of
course.'

'But why?'

'Why?' She spun round to find him staring at her,
anguish deep in his eyes. 'Because of what Xander said!
You know the truth about me now. I'm just a cheap
dancing girl. Not like you and your friends at all.'

He reached out and touched her. 'Do you think I
care about that?'

She stopped packing and gazed back at him, hardly
daring to hope that she might be wrong about his
reaction. She'd assumed that he'd loathe the very idea
of how she used to earn her living and that the thought
of her would sicken him from now on. After all, he'd
had no experience of a life like hers. Of course he
would find it repugnant. Wouldn't he?

532

'Coco, it seems like you haven't been entirely straight with me, but do you think I can't understand that? If you really were a dancer in a strip club, like Xander said, do you think I'd judge you for it?'

Her shoulders slumped. Pain and confusion were making a tight knot in her chest, the kind that only tears could release. 'Yes.' She sank down on the bed. 'Yes, I thought you would hate me for it. I thought you'd think I was a piece of shit. Everyone else always has.'

'Well, I don't.' He kneeled down beside her and took her hands in his large ones. 'Coco, I know we haven't known each other long. Hardly more than a couple of weeks. But you've affected me like no one else I've ever known. This feels like something big . . . special . . . once-in-a-lifetime stuff. I don't want to let you go.'

She lifted her gaze to him, filled with wonder. 'Really?'

He smiled, his coppery-green eyes tender. 'Yes. Now don't leave me hanging here . . . are you going to tell me that you feel the same?'

'Of course,' she said, a smile breaking over her face. 'Of course I do.' She wanted to say 'I love you' but the idea seemed ridiculous when they'd known each other such a short time. The thing was, she didn't want to imagine a life without Will in it. That was love, wasn't it? Then she suddenly realised that soon he would ask her more questions, and she'd have to decide what to tell him. It would mean more lies, she realised that. *I don't want to lie to him. I don't want to betray him.* But what else could she do?

'Coco, are you all right?' Will asked, watching the expressions changing on her face. 'What's wrong?'

'I . . . I . . . nothing.' She smiled again. 'I'm just so relieved, that's all. And I'm sorry I didn't tell you the truth from the start.'

'Why should you? You had no idea we were going to become involved. Your past is your own affair.' He stroked his thumbs across the back of her hands. 'And tomorrow I'm going to ask Xander if he'll go. I don't think we want him here now.'

His tenderness and understanding was breaking her heart. It made her want to cry almost more than the fear of losing him.

He doesn't know the truth. I don't know if I dare to tell him.

Then he leaned in to kiss her and the softness of his lips and the deliciousness of his mouth made her push all other thoughts aside, and lose herself in the pleasure of the moment.

Coco didn't see Xander the next day but she knew that Will had gone to see him first thing and tell him that it was best he went. They talked into the night about Xander's problems.

'If anything, he's worse than he used to be,' Will told her, his face worried. 'He seriously doesn't seem to have an off switch. And he'll drink and take drugs every single blessed day if he gets the chance. I think he's frying his brain to the extent that he doesn't really know what he's doing any more.'

Coco, happy to be wrapped in Will's embrace, traced a finger down his forearm, weaving it between the red-gold hairs. 'It's a shame. He's got so much to offer, and when he's sober he's adorable. Funny, charming . . .'

'But he's hardly ever sober,' finished Will.

Coco knew that he had offered to pay for his friend to go into rehab but Xander had turned it down.

'He says he's fine,' Will said as he and Coco ate their supper in the kitchen that evening. 'He looked like hell and was very repentant. He couldn't stop apologising and he asked me to give you his love too.'

Coco nodded, relieved that it appeared Xander had said no more. She'd feared that he had somehow decided to throw her to the wolves entirely and that he was prepared to reveal everything to Will. It seemed not. 'I hope he sorts himself out.'

Will nodded. 'I'd stopped him having a good time the night before – I think he was resentful, and the drink the next night made it all come out.' He leaned over and kissed her tenderly. 'But I have you all to myself now.'

It was blissful, with just the two of them. Coco felt now that Xander had done her some kind of favour. Will was sweet and loving, and didn't ask any questions about her past as a dancer, but she found that she wanted to tell him. For the first time, she wanted to open up to someone else and share what had happened to her.

'My life hasn't always been easy,' she confessed to him one night, as they lay together in the darkness after making love. 'In fact, it's been bloody hard.'

'Really?' Will propped himself on one elbow and looked down at her in the gloom. 'From what you've said, it sounded OK. Your mum and dad, your brother . . .'

She took a deep breath. 'Actually, that wasn't true.

I made it up.' She felt him go still. 'I'm sorry I lied to you, I didn't want to frighten you off. You see, I've got no idea who my father is. My mum was a drug addict and she brought me up alone on a council estate in Peckham. There wasn't a brother, or a cosy house, or violin lessons, or any of that. Just dirt and booze and drugs and misery. I ended up hanging round with a gang, and when my boyfriend was knifed to death, I ran away and got a job in a lap-dancing joint.' She tried to smile but her mouth wobbled and twisted. 'It's not a great life story, is it? I'm sorry, Will, I'm not the nice girl you thought I was.'

There was a long pause. She sniffed, blinked back her tears and held her breath. Would he reject her, just like everyone else always had? Or was she right to confide in him at last?

Will took her hand very gently. 'You're not exactly who I thought you were, but you know what? You're much more interesting and I admire you a hundred times more than I did before. You got away from all that, Coco. You've made something of yourself. I think that's amazing.'

'But you don't know how I did it,' she said unhappily.

'I don't need to know, it's not my business,' he insisted, his voice tender. 'Not unless you want to tell me.' He pulled her towards him, so that she was nestled against his chest, and wrapped his arms around her. 'You've suffered in a way I never have. I can't begin to imagine what you've been through. How the hell can I judge you?' His lips were on hers, soft as velvet, then he murmured: 'You only have to tell me what you want, when you want. Nothing else. And we've got plenty of time . . .'

His lips nuzzled her mouth, her cheeks, and then trailed along her neck, setting each place he touched burning with desire. Her longing for him sparked back to life, despite their recent bout, but now with even more emotion. He knew the truth about her past and he still wanted her. One hand stroked her shoulders, her back and waist as his mouth moved down to her breasts. He pulled one of her nipples in between his lips, sucking on it gently at first and then with more strength, as he took the other breast in his hand, stroking and rubbing it until she couldn't help sighing, her head thrown back.

She reached out for him as his hand moved down her belly and lightly touched her mound, sending delicious sensations all over her. She took his hot shaft in her hand as his strong fingers played over her, softly rubbing and probing. A rush of desire swept through her, and she slid downwards, kissing his firm body as she went lower until she was next to his groin. She put one hand beneath him, cupping his balls and stroking them gently until he groaned, and kissed the crease between his thigh and the place where his cock stood proud. She brought her face close to it, breathing out softly so her breath touched him and then inhaling his delicious scent, teasing him with the proximity of her mouth to his rearing penis.

'Coco,' he murmured, 'you're driving me insane.' Then he gasped as she put her lips on his cock and, with one finger circling its root, ran her tongue up it and then engulfed it in her mouth, taking in as much as she could, sucking it while the tip of her tongue played over the velvet-soft head. Will groaned again, one hand in her hair, stroking her head as it rose and fell over his cock. She tickled the place behind his balls as she sucked him, feeling herself growing hot and wet with desire. She longed to feel him inside her and, when she had brought him almost to the peak with her mouth, she lay back and pulled him on top of her. He didn't need any urging but pressed his stiff prick into her entrance, filling her up in a way that made her sigh with delight, and then they moved together with increasing intensity and power, until she felt him stiffen and his cock swell and then he came, in a fierce climax. She was so close but had lost herself in the pleasure of his orgasm, not quite attaining her own peak, but now she was hungry for it. At once, he moved his hand back down to where her bud was stiff and waiting, almost unbearably sensitive, and, with his cock still hard inside her, he brought her to a shuddering crescendo of orgasm that made her cry out and clutch at him as she rocked with its force.

They lay spent in one another's arms, and slept.

Will didn't change at all towards her, even after her confession, and at last Coco began to allow herself to trust him and his feelings for her. *He must really value me*, she thought, amazed by the idea. *Perhaps even . . . love me . . .*

She felt ten times taller, stronger and more radiant with the thought.

She began to feel safe and settled, revelling in the wonderful new life she was having with a man she was starting to adore. Every day she told him a little more of the pain in her past, and the despair she'd known, and every day he seemed to take a little more of that hurt away from her. She tried not to think about the dark secret that lay between them. She shut out thoughts of Margaret and Daddy, back in London, waiting for the return on their investment, confident that their stool pigeon was doing her work as promised.

I'll find a way to get out of it, she told herself. *I'll think of something. Just not today.*

In the meantime, Will was telling her quite freely about the developments in the battle with his father. He had a team of investigators working on it, and they had been looking into the affairs of the Dangerfield Foundation.

'It's all very mysterious,' he told her. 'The Foundation is registered in Switzerland and appears to be some kind of medical research joint, though we're still discovering exactly what they do. Whatever it is, it seems to be making them rich. From what we can discover, it's very well endowed.'

'Must be a Dangerfield trait,' Coco said saucily.

Will laughed. 'Well, we'll find out more. I have my suspicions about what's going on. But I'm more inter-ested in Daisy at the moment. My people are telling me that there's no trace of her going back years. She seems to have vanished long before she died. I'm determined to get to the bottom of it.'

Coco listened as he told her everything, knowing that all this was exactly what she'd been sent to hear.

They were snuggled up together in the den one evening watching television when the front doorbell went. It was the pizza delivery boy, no doubt, and with Maria off, they'd have to answer it themselves. Will unwrapped himself from Coco, stretching out as he stood up.

'Hey, have you got some cash for a tip?' he asked, patting his pockets. 'I'm clean out today.'

'Sure,' Coco replied. 'I've got some dollars in my purse. Help yourself.'

She turned her attention back to the screen, half listening to Will as he paid the pizza boy. After a few minutes she turned to look at the door. Where was he? Why hadn't he come back? She frowned, but a second later Will walked slowly back through the door. He wasn't holding any pizzas. Instead, he held a small rectangle of white paper and was staring at it, an expression of horror on his face.

'What's this?' he said in a strangled voice as he walked towards her.

She sat up. 'What?'

He reached her, and held it out in his trembling hands. 'This!' he rasped in a terrible voice. She looked at it, and felt an awful swoop of horror.

'Not this, Coco,' Will said, his eyes agonised. 'Anything but this. Anyone but him.'

It was a cheque for a hundred pounds, to be drawn on a prestigious private bank, and signed by Daddy Dangerfield himself.

67

The door of the storage room opened and the Chinese man came in. He never spoke to Daisy but simply put down a tray of some kind of stew or lamb pasta with bread and water, and left it for her. She had been shut in this horrible place for three days now.

As he entered, she jumped up. She'd been waiting for this moment, planning what she was going to do. 'Please, please,' she begged, 'please let me go. Where is Sergei? *Sergei?*'

He stared at her for a second, then turned on his heel and headed back to the door.

'No, no!' she shouted frantically, running after him and grabbing the handle. 'Don't go, you can't leave me here! This is kidnapping!' She grabbed hold of his hood and coat, trying to pull him back into the room. He swore loudly in another language and tried to shake her off, but she held on as tight as she could. How else could she convey her desperation? The Chinese man attempted to make her release her grip and when he realised that she meant to hang on, he pulled back one fist as though he was about to punch her.

There was a shout in Russian from outside the room and the other man appeared suddenly, grabbing the Chinese man around the wrist to stop him hitting Daisy. It was the man she assumed was Sergei's brother. He spoke in fast, furious Russian. The Chinese man listened and then obediently lowered his fist. Daisy let go of him and he moved away from her, shaking out his coat where she'd yanked it.

'Please,' Daisy said to the Russian, certain he could speak English, 'you must let me go! What are you doing, keeping me here like this?'

A joyless smile curved the lips of the Russian man. 'Don't worry,' he said in thickly accented English. 'We won't hurt you. We just need you for a little longer, OK?'

With that, he shoved her firmly back inside the room, and pulled the door shut with a slam. She rushed to it and banged on it with her fists, shouting that they had to let her out, but there was no sound from beyond. Eventually, she gave up and sank to the floor, sobbing. He'd said they weren't going to hurt her – but how could she believe it?

The noise of shouting woke her in the middle of the night. She came to instantly, throwing off the duvet and getting up from her thin mattress. She pulled on her boots, picked up her coat and ran to the door, pressing her ear against it. There was a great commotion going on in the next room, with loud voices yelling in Russian and the noise of furniture being overturned.

Daisy started to tremble. What the hell was happening? Adrenaline surged through her. All she could do was be ready to react in whatever way necessary. She quickly zipped her coat and pulled up the hood, wishing she still had her fur hat. She pulled on her gloves. Whatever opportunity came her way, she intended to take. She would make a run for it. It was madness perhaps – out on her own in the dark Siberian night, into freezing temperatures and God only knew where – but she couldn't stay here any longer without losing her mind.

The quarrel outside seemed to be gaining pace, the voices louder. It seemed interminable as she stood there, her head pressed to the door, trying to listen through the wood and the thickness of her hood and interpret what was going on.

Then the voices quietened down to a more reasonable level. One of them became sulkier, the other – she was sure it was Sergei's – became more scornful and rebuking. Then, to her intense relief, it came closer, issued firm orders, and a moment later the handle was turning.

She looked out into the lighted area beyond. There were several people standing about a large room dominated by a stove and a pair of bunk beds. Her captors were there, surrounded by tough-looking men in outdoor gear, while standing at the door, a half smile on his face and relief in his eyes, was Sergei.

'Sergei! Thank God you're here,' said Daisy in a choked voice.

'Are you OK?' he asked urgently, looking her over.

'Yes . . . yes, I'm fine.' Tears sprang unbidden to her eyes with the strength of the relief that enveloped her. She was going to be all right. She wanted to hug Sergei.

'Good,' he said tersely. 'Then let's get out of here before my stupid brother decides to do anything even more crazy than he already has.'

He grabbed her arm and pulled her out of the room, shielding her with his massive bulk. He barked out something in Russian as he took her with him towards the door leading outside. Her captors watched her go with mutinous expressions on their faces, but they said nothing and did not move as Sergei's men kept a close watch on them.

The next moment, they had reached the door. Sergei opened it, pushed Daisy out in front of him and said, 'Get in.' The Land Rover was standing just outside in the snow. She ran towards it, opened the door and jumped inside. Sergei paused to issue orders, then came round and got in next to her. He made the engine roar into life and then they were pulling away from the horrible place where she'd spent the last nightmarish few days.

'Thank you,' she said, trying not to cry. She didn't want to be a weak, snivelling girl in front of Sergei, who was always so tough.

'I apologise on behalf of my brother,' he said grimly, staring out into the black-and-white night beyond the windscreen. 'He's always been an idiot, but this really takes . . . some beating.'

'How did you find me?'

'There are only so many places a fool like him will go. And some money in the right hands usually gets results. He has been in touch with me to make his stupid demands so I knew he had you.' Sergei glanced over at Daisy, checking her face to see if she really was all right. 'Did they treat you OK?'

She nodded, not able to say any more.

'Well, he's dumb but he's not a monster,' murmured Sergei, shaking his head.

'Why did it take so long to find me?' she asked in a small voice.

'I've been in Komsomolsk,' he said. 'When I got back to the house with the doctor and found you gone – well, there was nothing I could do. Your friend Ross was in a bad way. We had to get him to hospital. I guessed at once that my brother had taken you and he let me know soon enough. I was pretty sure you'd be safe until I got back.'

Daisy gaped at him, not knowing where to begin. How could he have been so sure that she wouldn't be hurt? It seemed a reckless gamble to her. But there were important things to find out first. 'Is Darley all right?'

Sergei nodded. 'He had pneumonia. Serious. But they say he's over the worst and is going to be fine. He'll be able to fly home in a week or so.'

'I'd better let his office know – his family. They'll be worried about him.'

'Don't worry, I spoke to his wife,' Sergei said. 'I called her from his mobile in Komsomolsk.'

Daisy nodded, relieved. 'Good. I'm glad she's not in a panic.' She looked out of the window for a moment. She couldn't wait to be back in the warm, familiar environment of Sergei's house. When would they reach the village? She said, 'So – why did your brother take me?'

'I think you can guess,' answered Sergei with a sardonic smile. 'He wanted to force me to let him buy into the mine.'

'So he thought, if he kidnapped me, he could black-mail you into letting him?'

'I told you he was an idiot.' Sergei shrugged. 'But I've told him that if he resigns from Korsilkoff and joins me as my partner, I might consider letting him buy a stake. That's why he agreed to let you go today. So maybe it was all for the best.'

All for the best? Daisy didn't know what to say: the idea she'd had to endure three days of imprisonment and fear for the sake of two warring brothers becoming reconciled seemed extraordinary to her. Was there to be no punishment for the illegal abduction she'd suffered? Daisy kept her comments to herself. She had a feeling that things operated a little differently around here and she wasn't about to make a fuss until she was on safe ground once again.

'Besides,' Sergei went on, his gaze sliding towards her once more, but this time with a look of cunning in it, 'I discovered that there are people looking for you. When I explained to my brother that this would become very serious . . . well, that made a difference.'

'People looking?' Daisy echoed, startled. 'Who?'

'Yes. I mean you are a high-up executive, right? Not just my little girlfriend, which is maybe what my brother thought. I told him you can't take someone from a powerful company like that and not expect nasty reprisals. I explained that we need the money from your business to finish our mine and get it working. And, of course, you are the daughter of the owner of Dangerfield.'

Daisy froze. 'What?' she whispered, her lips suddenly stiff and her mouth dry. '*What* did you say?'

'You are the daughter of the owner. Mr Dangerfield himself. So you are very hot property, aren't you? Dangerous for anyone to possess. I didn't tell my brother this, in case he decided you were valuable enough to make a proper kidnapping worthwhile.'

Daisy tried to laugh. 'That's ridiculous! You know who I am . . .'

'I do now,' Sergei said, a edge to his voice.

She licked her lips, questions whirling around in her head. 'But . . . why do you think that?' Black panic was creeping over her. How could he know? She'd never told anyone, in all these years! It was impossible. Absolutely impossible.

'Because of this.' He reached into his pocket, took out her BlackBerry and tossed it to her. It landed in her lap and she stared down at it.

'It has no signal—'

'It has in Komsomolsk,' he replied tersely.

'But how . . . ?'

At that moment, Sergei pulled the car to a halt. She realised that they'd been bumping along for some time with no sign of the lights of the village. Now they appeared to be in almost total darkness and she sensed the forest all about.

'Come on. We're here.'

'Where?'

'Just get out.' He jumped down from his side of the car into the snow, and crunched round to her side. He opened the door and half helped, half pulled Daisy out. 'Follow me.'

She realised now that they were outside a low wooden building. Its shutters were firmly closed but she could see small lines of light here and there. Sergei walked over to the building and pulled open the door. At once, red-gold light fell from the room within, lighting up the snow so that it glittered and shone.

'Inside,' he said brusquely. 'Go on.'

She felt dazed, utterly stunned by the revelation of Sergei's knowledge of who she was, and so she obeyed, moving over the snow and walking into the room.

There was a man inside. He was stooping over the open stove, throwing in some logs. She stopped and stared at him, her skin beginning to prickle. The man slammed the stove door shut, stood up and turned round.

She gasped. It was Christophe.

Part Four

Part Four

68

Coco climbed out of the taxi in front of the Belgravia house, ran lightly up the steps beneath the wide white portico, and rang the doorbell in its brass surround.

A maid answered and she walked into the hallway, catching a glimpse of her reflection in the huge Second Empire gilt mirror, topped with a laurel wreath and an eagle, that hung over the mahogany console. She looked tanned from the LA sun, her skin glowing with health and vitality, and she was slimmer than ever, her figure shown to its best advantage in a dark pencil skirt and a cream merino jumper, a large slouchy Prada bag over one shoulder. Dior sunglasses shaded her eyes.

'Will you follow me, please, madam?' asked the maid politely, and led her into the drawing room. Coco declined the offer of a drink and instead wandered about the room, taking in the hand-blocked wallpaper, the sumptuous French fabrics and the expensive antique furniture. An oil painting of a dog caught her attention: a vital-looking spaniel, standing ready to dash off at his master's call, eyes full of eager obedience.

She knew that look of trusting adoration. It had been in her own eyes once.

Not any more.

It was all over. She had given her heart to him, and now it was broken. She could hardly bear to remember that awful last interview with Will. He'd guessed the truth immediately, and how could she deny it when he held proof of her connection to his father in his hand? He'd ordered her out, shaking with emotion, his eyes cold and the hurt plain on his face. He hadn't let her speak, but shoved her out of the door, tossing her purse after her. She called to him, trying to explain, beating on the front door with her fists, but he was obdurate. She'd called a cab and gone to a hotel, and sent a car for her things the following day. Then she'd booked her flight home. She'd had no word from him since.

She wanted to hate him, she was forcing herself to. He was a bastard, treacherous, cruel, cold-hearted, vindictive . . . *Stop. Don't think about it. You know where that goes.*

It led to despair: bitter tears, wracking sobs and the sense that life was over and everything beautiful in it destroyed. But she also knew that his heart must be broken too, and if only she'd been honest, then perhaps they might still be together.

But it's too damn' late now.

'Coco.' Margaret was coming into the room, looking unusually cheerful. She was neat as usual in a plain navy suit. 'What a pleasure. How was your trip?' She sat down on a ball-and-claw foot Queen Anne armchair and indicated another to Coco.

'Fine. Very good.' Coco sat down, putting her bag on her lap.

'I was a little concerned when we went for so long without hearing from you,' Margaret said smoothly. 'I had to trust that you had simply lost yourself in your mission. It was a relief to receive that email from you.'

Coco didn't respond but pulled out a black folder and handed it over to Margaret, who took it.

'Your report? Excellent.' She lifted a pair of glasses that hung from a chain around her neck, put them on and opened the folder. She began to scan the pages inside.

'It's all there,' Coco said. 'Everything I found out. I've gone into detail about Will's attitudes, his plans, his suspicions . . . and his anger over the death of his sister.' She raised her eyebrows at Margaret. 'The sister you forgot to tell me about.'

The other woman kept looking at the report, murmuring only, 'I had my reasons. Let us leave it at that.' She ignored Coco for twenty minutes while she skimmed the pages, then looked up, satisfaction on her face. 'You've done well. I can see from just a short perusal that there is much here we can learn from.' She smiled. 'It seems our investment in you has paid off.'

'Actually, I wanted to speak to you about that,' Coco said slowly. She had planned how she would approach this. She'd thought very carefully about the best way to frame what she wanted.

'Yes?' Margaret raised her eyebrows, peering over the top of her glasses.

'I found the work you gave me to do very . . . stimulating. To be honest, I enjoyed it.'

'Mmm?' Margaret's expression remained neutral.

'I believe I could be of further use to you and your organisation.'

'Really? How? Your job here appears to be done. You've had a fair reward. You may keep all the clothes and other things you've been given. You may stay on a little longer in South Kensington, and you have the tools now to go out into the world and make something of yourself. All invaluable . . . if you think back to how things were when I found you.' Margaret's voice was soft, almost caressing.

'I appreciate all of that, of course. I just think that you may need my services in other ways. I believe I discovered quite a talent in myself for the kind of investigations you required. You might need me again for other . . . projects.'

Margaret blinked, her expression giving nothing away. 'Well, I shall need to think about that. I make no promises, but I will ponder what you say.' She stood up. 'Now, Mr Dangerfield requested that you be brought to him immediately on your return. He's very keen to see you.'

Coco stood up and followed Margaret out of the room and across the hallway to the study. As they went, the older woman looked back over her shoulder and said, 'Keep it brief if you can. Don't tire him out. He hasn't been well lately.'

'Another lawyer's letter by any chance? Will said he was sending one.'

'I'm afraid so.' Margaret stopped in front of the study door. 'He continues to make unreasonable

554

demands. It was accompanied by a poisonous personal note from Will to his father, accusing him of many awful things. Quite appalling.' She knocked and pushed the door open. 'Sir – Coco is back.'

The old man was sitting in a large green leather button-back armchair, and Coco suspected he might have been asleep. He jumped slightly as they entered, then hauled himself to his feet, smiling expansively. 'Coco, Coco, how charming!'

She smiled. 'Hello, Mr Dangerfield.'

'Come here, come here,' he said, beckoning her over. As she reached him, he leaned out and pulled her into his arms, the scratchy tweed of his jacket rough on her skin, as he kissed her cheek. 'It's lovely to see you again. How are you?'

She pulled away from him, startled by the bear hug and kiss. 'I'm fine, thank you, sir.'

'Coco's brought back an excellent report,' Margaret said. 'We shall be able to learn a great deal from her.'

'Good, good. You got under the skin of that son of mine, did you?' Daddy looked suddenly sad. 'A writ today. There's no end to this awful nonsense. But if he wants a fight, I shall certainly give him one, and with your help, my dear, we shall win.' Then he smiled broadly. 'This calls for a celebration!' he announced. 'Margaret, what do you say to Le Caprice this evening? I think Coco deserves a treat for being such a very good girl.'

There was a pause, then Margaret said, 'A wonderful idea, sir. I shall see about booking the table at once.'

It felt odd to be back in the South Kensington flat. It was as though she'd never been away, but the Coco who had returned was very different from the one who had left. She'd been through an emotional upheaval. Was it really possible that in such a short time she'd found something she'd been looking for all her life, and then lost it?

She walked to the windows of her flat, pulling the heavy linen curtains to shut out the night outside. She began to unzip her dark green Marchesa cocktail dress, thinking how strange the evening had been. Mr Dangerfield had seemed in very high spirits to see her, and was extremely affectionate throughout the meal, as if she were an old friend he had missed terribly. He was always leaning over to pat her hand or smile broadly. When he'd asked her about Will, she had spoken freely and frankly – except that she hadn't mentioned a thing about what had happened between them. She was sure that Will would not be swayed from his course whether or not his father knew anything about it.

At the end of the meal at Le Caprice, as the women sipped espresso and the old man drank a glass of port, Dangerfield had leaned over, taken Coco's hand and asked her fondly to call him Daddy. Coco had a feeling that no matter what Margaret's feelings on the subject were, she was about to become a fixture on the Dangerfield scene.

For some reason, he's taken a real shine to me. Even more than before.

As Coco pulled off her Kenneth Jay Lane chandelier earrings, she heard her phone go. She took it from her handbag and saw Xander's number flashing up on the screen. Her stomach flipped over. What could he want to say? She ought to ignore it and let him leave a message if he wanted, but she couldn't fight the desire to find out.

'Yes?' Her voice was cold and curt and she didn't care.

'Coco . . .'

'What is it?'

'I'm sorry I haven't been in touch before now.'

'I'm not surprised, you fucking yellow-belly, traitorous, betraying shithead!' She got pleasure from saying the words. She'd been wanting to for ages. 'How could you do that, Xander? How could you try to destroy me like that? I thought we were friends.'

'Coco, I'm so sorry.' Xander's voice was deep with misery.

'I don't know if sorry is going to cut it, you bastard,' she said, her voice dripping vitriol.

'I didn't know what I was doing . . . I was drunk, stoned . . .'

'You humiliated me,' she said in a low voice.

'What can I do to make it up to you?' he said plaintively.

'Nothing.'

'Did he throw you out?' Xander asked.

Coco said nothing. She didn't know how to tell Xander the truth of what had happened. She couldn't bear to talk about it. 'It's over,' she said shortly.

'Coco, you've got to believe me, it was a mistake. And you're not what I said – you're a brilliant girl. I'm so sorry.' Xander sounded wretched.

She padded back and forth along the rug. 'You need help, Xander. Seriously. You're out of control.'

'I'm calming down, I promise. I'm going up to

Scotland to see my family for a bit. I guess I won't be seeing Will again after what I did.'

'Well – good job, Xander. You really fucked us both over. Congratulations.' Full of fury and despair, Coco clicked off her mobile and stood frozen at the window, trying to tame the torrent of emotions inside her.

69

As Daisy realised that she was actually staring into Christophe's face, she found that astonishment seemed to have stolen her voice from her and glued her legs to the ground. She could only gape at him, wondering if he was something she'd conjured up out of her own mind. Was she ill? Perhaps she had pneumonia and was delirious, perhaps she'd dreamed everything that had happened for the last few days . . . But, oh, God, what a wonderful twist her delirium had just taken.

She felt winded, but managed to gather enough breath to speak. 'Christophe . . . is it really you?'

'Daphne.' One word spoken in that familiar voice rolled over and round her, and seemed to engulf her in warmth.

They stood and stared at each other, the rest of the world around them disappearing in a haze. She could see only his dark velvety eyes, and the sweet familiarity of his face.

A rough voice cut into her daze. It was Sergei. 'I'm going to leave you here,' he said. 'I've got business to see to, and no doubt you have things to discuss. I'll come back in the morning to take you to Komsomolsk.' The next moment, the door of the hut was closing and she was alone with Christophe.

'Am I dreaming?' Daisy said wonderingly.

He smiled tenderly and shook his head. 'It's really me.'

'Oh!' Overcome, she stumbled towards him and threw herself into his arms. An instant later, he was hugging her close, enveloping her in his strong embrace.

'You're OK now,' he murmured, mouth pressed against her hair. 'You're fine, don't worry.'

She wanted to cry and sob out all the tension and fear of the last few days, but she was also so suffused with happiness that she wanted to laugh and jump at the same time. She pulled back, gazing at him with shining eyes. 'But what on earth are you doing here?'

'I came to find you,' he replied simply. His large hands grasped hers. 'You were in trouble and you needed me.'

'But I don't understand!' She shook her head, bewildered. 'How . . . ?'

'I know. It's strange. But let's get your coat off and make you something hot to drink, and I'll explain everything.'

From lonely darkness to golden comforting light; the contrast was startling but Daisy accepted it more quickly than she would have thought possible. Soon it seemed to her like the most natural thing in the world to be sitting on a sofa in a hunting lodge in Siberia, with Christophe opposite her, as they both sipped hot black tea from the samovar.

'How did you find me?' she asked.

'I came looking for you,' was the simple answer. 'You needed me, I was sure of it.'

'But why?'

Christophe said nothing for a moment, then he reached into his pocket and pulled something out. When he opened his palm, she didn't recognise what he was holding for a second, then she realised that the object glittering in his hand was the Van Cleef & Arpels brooch she had been given by her father so many years before.

'My brooch!'

He nodded. 'You left it at Nant-y-Pren. You must have dropped it when you were packing and it rolled under the chest of drawers. It was only when I moved it that I found the brooch again.'

'I hadn't realised I'd lost it. I thought it was in my jewellery box.' Daisy stared at it as the light bounced off the diamonds, flashing and glinting. 'And how did this lead you to . . . to me?'

'I put it to one side to return it to you, but it seemed too precious to put in the post. I meant to contact you and arrange a way to drop it off, but it was hard. I still felt bitter about our breakup.' His eyes darkened for a moment. 'Then I read in the paper about Daisy Dangerfield's death and there was a picture of her, from years back. She was wearing your brooch. I recognised it instantly. And once I'd seen that – well, I realised that *she* was *you*. Or you were her. I found a few more pictures online, and knew you were the same person.' His mouth looked grim. 'It was a huge shock . . . awful. I thought for a little while you were dead.'

'But . . . my disguise . . .' she faltered.

He smiled. 'A very good disguise, but when you've known someone the way we knew each other . . . Did you think I wouldn't recognise the shape of your face, your eyes – no matter what colour they are – your nose and mouth? Your new hair style distracts attention from your face, it's true. That blunt cut you used to have was almost like a helmet, and the glasses were a nice touch. And . . .' he looked at her more closely '. . . didn't you used to have brown eyes?'

'Lenses,' she whispered. 'I'm not wearing them.'

'I like your real colour,' he said softly. 'That grey-blue suits you better.'

'Oh, Christophe,' she cried. 'I couldn't tell you! I couldn't . . . I wanted to, but . . .'

'Don't worry about that now,' he said, his voice gentle. His face softened. 'I nearly went mad when I thought you were dead. But I knew that you were calling yourself Daphne Fraser, and still working at Craven. I calmed down and called John, and he told me about your impressive promotion. It was obvious he thought you were perfectly fine. I called the Dangerfield Group and pretended I was still a Craven executive so that I could get your new BlackBerry number. They told me you were out of the country. I called you several times but you didn't answer, and in the end I left a message. I said I knew you were Daisy Dangerfield.' He looked shamefaced. 'I regretted it as soon as I'd said it but it was too late. Sure enough, I got a call back from someone who definitely wasn't you. It was that great hulk of a Russian.'

'Sergei,' Daisy supplied.

'Right. Well, he told me you were busy, but I said he'd better put you on or I'd call the police, Interpol,

562

whoever. I'd kick up one almighty storm. That's when he told me that you were in the hands of a rival business associate who was making demands in return for your safety.' Christophe frowned, eyes glittering at the memory. 'He seemed to think it was no big deal, that you'd just be away for a few days until he managed to make his rival see sense. I explained that it was a bigger situation than that, and said I was coming straight out to get you myself.'

'Oh.' Daisy clasped his hand and squeezed it. 'The whole time I was locked up, all I could think of was that no one knew where I was. No one cared. And all the time . . .'

Christophe smiled, his eyes crinkling at the corners. 'I couldn't leave you in that situation, at the mercy of some guy who seemed to think that you could hang on and wait to be rescued until he was good and ready. Besides, once he knew who you were, I was afraid that he might decide to use it to his advantage.'

'You didn't call the police?' breathed Daisy, looking up at him.

Christophe stared earnestly at her. 'I was prepared to, at any moment. But I was very frightened for you. The rule of law is a secondary consideration around here. I wanted to be where I could help. So I chartered a plane and flew to Komsomolsk. Thank God when I got here, Sergei had already discovered your whereabouts and arranged your release.'

'You flew?' Daisy's eyes filled with tears and she felt choked. That must have cost him a great deal, in more ways than one. She knew how Christophe felt about flying. 'For me?'

He grasped her hand and held it. 'It was hairy,' he

said with a smile. 'The weather conditions were atrocious. It was reckless and foolhardy. But I did it because I had no other choice.'

'You did have a choice,' whispered Daisy, her heart swelling. 'You could have left me. I left you, after all. I let us be separated.'

'Sometimes things happen that make past quarrels seem unimportant.' He put his arms around her and pulled her close so that she was gazing up at him. She marvelled at his beautiful face and those soft brown eyes, and wondered how she could have gone so long without him. What had she been thinking of, walking out of his life the way she had? Being with him felt so intensely, incredibly right that every minute she'd spent away from him now seemed a terrible waste.

'Daphne . . .'

'You can call me Daisy.' She smiled up at him. 'That's really my name.'

'Daisy. Yes. That suits you better too.'

She felt suddenly desperate. 'I wish you'd hurry up and kiss me,' she said, 'if you're going to?'

'Of course I am, if you want me to?'

'God, shut up!' She couldn't wait any longer and pulled his mouth to hers, losing herself at once in the bliss of Christophe's taste and touch.

Much later, as the stove was burning low and they were lying in each other's arms on the sofa, neither of them willing to move and disturb the tranquil pleasure of being so close, she said, 'I suppose you've got lots to ask me.'

'You mean, about why you're officially dead? And why Daisy Dangerfield is the girl I fell in love with?'

Christophe rubbed his cheek against hers, pulling her a little tighter against his chest. 'Yes, I suppose I do have a couple of questions.'

'I promise I'll tell you everything,' she said in a small voice. 'I couldn't before, please believe me.'

'I can guess that everything is a great deal more complicated than I could ever have imagined. But you don't have to tell me the whole thing right now. Maybe we should get some sleep first.'

She frowned, shaking off some of the drowsy enjoyment she felt to be in proximity to him again. 'Yes – where are we?'

'It's a hunting lodge of Sergei's. He thought it would be safer for us to keep off the beaten track until he's quietened everything down and sorted out the situation. We'll see him in the morning probably.' Christophe smiled down at her. 'So – shall we go to bed?'

'Oh, yes,' said Daisy, so fervently that she made him laugh. 'Yes, please.'

'I'm glad you want that as much as I do,' he said gently. 'I missed you so much. I tried to shut you out of my life, but I couldn't forget you. When I thought you were dead, the pain was unbearable. I'm so glad we've got another chance.'

He got off the sofa, separating her from the warmth of his body, but only for a moment. The next minute he was swinging her up into his arms and carrying her across the small sitting room, kicking open the door to the bedroom and hurrying inside to the inviting bed and the enveloping darkness beyond.

70

The South Kensington flat remained Coco's refuge
for the time being. Here, she could shut herself away
from the world and be alone to think about everything that had happened. Here, she smoked cigarettes
and paced the sitting room until the early hours,
replaying events in her mind, having long imaginary
conversations with Will that would turn into ridiculous, one-sided arguments in which she'd yell, cry,
explain, berate and ask forgiveness. The only thing
missing from the whole crazy scenario was Will
himself.

When she wasn't at the flat, she was at the Dangerfield
mansion in Belgravia with Daddy, who couldn't seem
to get enough of her company. Coco was happy to
provide it. After all, staying close to the Dangerfields
was part of her plan.

She sensed the loneliness in the old man. She'd
seen it before in the men who had paid for private
dances in the club, and then were more interested in
talking to her then goggling at her tits. Whatever
Daddy Dangerfield was – and she suspected he was

the nasty, selfish egotist that Will had portrayed him as – he was missing human companionship.

He can't get much from Margaret. She's more like an android helper than a human being. No wonder he was warming to Coco so quickly: she was young and vital, and when she flattered him – well, he lapped it up. When she told him how wonderful he was, he would light up like an electric bulb and grow visibly more expansive, and those dark brown eyes of his would fill with animation. It didn't take much encouragement for him to start regaling her with endless stories of his past life and business achievements.

She could tell he was growing more dependent on her. If she didn't appear at the Belgravia house even for a day, her mobile would ring and there would be a querulous voice on the other end: 'Coco, where have you vanished to? When are you coming round to see me?' Or it would be Margaret, in that level, emotionless voice of hers, saying the boss wanted to see Coco, and could she please come as soon as possible, or meet them at Langan's or Rules or some other restaurant.

The presents began to arrive: a silk scarf, followed by a luxurious pearl grey cashmere shawl. A Chanel handbag. Pairs of expensive shoes. A dress. Daddy liked to wander around with her after a rich lunch, take her into boutiques and let her see the way the staff instantly recognised him as a man with money and jumped to serve him. He liked to watch her try things on, fall in love with them, and then keep her hanging on until he'd declare she could have them. Then she'd laugh, hug him and thank him for being so amazing to her.

The South Kensington flat filled up with clothes,

shoes and jewellery. Coco became accustomed to sending the bills for her living expenses, and the beauty treatments she now couldn't live without, to Margaret's office to be settled.

Sometimes, in the night, she wondered if she was doing the right thing; if she could really see this through. Then she'd remember Will's face, his eyes glittering with cold derision, and pain like a punch to her stomach would remind her why she was determined on this path.

In the drawing room of the Belgravia house, Margaret looked unusually ill at ease, pacing about as though she really didn't know how to express what she had to say.

'You don't have to worry,' Coco said generously. Margaret had summoned her to this little interview earlier that morning. 'I'm all ears. Spit it out.'

Margaret stopped next to a beautiful rosewood William and Mary cabinet inlaid with exquisite marquetry. On the top stood a Sèvres vase full of pale pink roses. She frowned, opened her mouth and closed it again. Then she said, 'Very well. I'll come straight to the point. Mr Dangerfield wishes me to ask you if . . . if . . . you would care to live with him.'

Coco stared. She was amused by Margaret's obvious discomfiture but also surprised. She hadn't foreseen this, but perhaps she should have.

'So,' Margaret went on, compelled to fill the awkward silence, 'I ought to make plain the terms on which he wishes to ask you this. He has grown . . . fond of you over the last few weeks. He wishes to spend as much time with you as possible. I needn't tell you that he recently lost a daughter. He misses her companionship and he'd very much like you to offer some of the warmth and company he has been lacking.'

'So, what you're saying is – he looks on me like a daughter?' Coco said. 'He won't want me to sleep with him.'

Margaret flushed slightly and stammered a little before she managed to say, 'No no. The arrangement will be platonic. Although that needn't be discussed with other people.'

Coco laughed out loud. 'He's happy for people to *think* he's shagging me, right? But he doesn't actually want to.'

Margaret stiffened. 'No. As I made clear, Mr Dangerfield thinks of you as a daughter. And anyway, certain medical circumstances make it impossible for . . . a consummation.'

'You really know everything about him, don't you?' Coco said, stretching out her long legs in front of her, admiring the effect of her Louboutins on the Persian carpet. 'And it's funny, isn't it, how the heart can go on working after the other equipment has given up the ghost?' She sat up straight and looked Margaret right in the eye. 'All right. You and I are used to doing business together, so I'll expect a contract drawn up just like before. I'm happy to be the old man's pal, sparkle on his arm, make him happy – but I'll need proper recompense, and a guarantee of certain things.'

'I'm sure we can hammer out terms that are acceptable to both sides,' Margaret said, raising one eyebrow.

'Don't worry, I won't go nuts. I'm not a total gold-digger, you know. But I need to think about my future.'

'Oh, I understand.' Margaret's tone was cool but

not judgemental. 'Send me your terms and we'll sort everything out. In the meantime, can I tell the boss that you'll be moving into the house? A suite can be arranged for you immediately.'

Coco rose gracefully to her feet – the result of Lady Arthur's excellent coaching – and said, 'Don't worry, I'll tell him myself. Is he in the study?'

'In the gym,' Margaret replied, 'having his massage.'

The massage room was in the depths of the basement gymnasium. When Coco arrived there a few minutes later, she knocked on the door and opened it.

'Daddy?' she said playfully.

He was lying on the table, a great mountain of fleshy white back, a towel covering his hind quarters, two white hairy legs emerging from below – much thinner than his top half so that they looked as though they might belong to someone else. The masseur, a blond Swede in a pale blue tee-shirt, was rubbing the slippery flesh back and forth.

'Coco?' Daddy's voice came out muffled from where he lay face down.

'Daddy, some very exciting news.' Coco walked over and then sank to her knees so that she was on a level with his eyeline. 'I'm going to come and live with you!'

He yelped, his face flushing with excitement. 'That's wonderful, sweetheart. Oh, we're going to have such fun together, my princess. You wait and see.' He grinned at her, showing a bridge of perfect white porcelain teeth. 'You've made me a very happy man. Very happy.'

The feeling's mutual, thought Coco, though her heart remained as cold and untouched as it had been since the day she'd left LA.

71

This time yesterday, I was in total, abject despair. Now look at me!

Although Daisy hoped no one *was* looking at her. No one but Christophe, considering she was lying naked beneath him, moving in time to his delicious thrusts inside her. How could she have lived without this pleasure for so long? It was still mystifying her at the same time as she thrilled to the wonderful sensations induced by her lover.

'Christophe,' she sighed, wrapping her legs around him to pull him ever deeper. 'Oh, Christophe.'

His eyes went from tender to burning as passion overtook him. He bent his head to suck on her nipples, rolling one around his tongue, pulling on it and grazing it with his teeth, before turning his attention to the other. It was almost unbearable, sending electric sensations buzzing downwards to her groin and making her sigh with pleasure. He sank his mouth on hers, exploring her with his tongue as he pushed hard inside her. Daisy could tell they were both near their climax: the thought was almost exciting enough to push her over the edge. Fire seemed to be burning in her belly as he rubbed against her with every thrust, taking her inexorably towards the peak she longed for. But the journey was so good, she never wanted quite to tumble over . . . Then she felt him swell inside her, and speed his movements, and knew that he was about to stiffen and come, and that knowledge made her gasp, clutch him and rush into her own orgasm. They shook in each other's arms for long moments, and finally they were calm.

'What time is Sergei arriving?' she said, still breathless, as she kissed his face and shoulders.

'Let's hope it's not in the next five minutes,' Christophe said, grinning. He kissed her back, sweetly and luxuriously.

'I'll make us some coffee. Is there any?' She climbed out of bed, shivering in the cold air, reaching for her clothes. 'And I'll check the stove.'

'I don't know, have a look around, see what you can find.'

She went out, stoked up the dying embers of the stove and put in some more wood, then went to find the loo and explore the tiny kitchen. She came back a while later with two cups of instant black coffee and an anxious expression.

'You know, there's not much food here. No bread. No milk. Some tins of meat and vegetables, and that's about all.' She handed Christophe a cup of coffee.

'Don't worry,' he said, taking it. 'Thanks, darling. Sergei will be here later. We're only staying today. I'm sure we'll cope. Now climb back into bed. We've got a lot to catch up on.'

While they snuggled up together under the warm

patchwork blanket, Daisy began to tell him how she had become Daphne Fraser, and why. Christophe frowned as he heard how her father had brutally thrown her out and disowned her a short time after her mother's death.

'How could he do that?' he asked, horrified.

'I wasn't a Dangerfield any longer. It had mattered so much to him, you see. Being his daughter, having his own father's blood run in me. When it turned out I didn't have a drop, I was virtually worthless to him.'

'But,' Christophe exclaimed, 'he'd been your father in every way since you were a baby! How could he just turn his love off?'

Daisy shrugged. 'I wish I knew. That question has tormented me for years, along with the mystery of who I really am. My mother didn't say.' She gazed down at the patchwork, tracing the stitches with one finger. 'I still don't know why she didn't tell me.'

'So you invented your alter ego?'

'I needed a purpose in life, something I could focus on to shut out the pain. I decided I would prove myself to my father and show him how wrong he was.'

Christophe wrapped her tighter in his arms and listened as Daisy explained her plan: how she would get to the top of the Dangerfield company anyway, without Daddy's help, demonstrating that she could get wherever she wanted by herself. She didn't need to be parachuted in to a directorship: she could and would earn one herself.

'And you did!' Christophe said, surprised and proud at the same time. 'Boy, did you! I've never seen anyone so single-minded about their work.'

573

'It was all that kept me going. I didn't let myself despair. I concentrated on winning instead.'

He ran a finger along her cheek. 'You are so brave.'

'Brave or stupid. Who knows?'

'You weren't going to let him write you off!'

'No. I couldn't let him erase me from his life.'

There was a pause and then Christophe said, 'But then he killed Daisy Dangerfield.'

'Yes.' The familiar sadness crept over her. 'God knows how that was arranged. I hope it was just a matter of bribing an official and cremating an unclaimed corpse from the Thai mortuary. I don't think he's capable of worse. Or I hope not.'

Christophe held her hand, stroking the back of it with his thumb. 'In a way, it brought us back together. But how will you ever come back now that you're officially dead?'

She turned and looked him in the eyes. 'I can never come back. I know that now. Daisy Dangerfield *is* dead and I can never be that girl again. I didn't realise I could be happy being someone else, but now I think I can. I still want to shake him up, though, give him the shock of his life. And I know enough about his company to cause a hurricane!'

Christophe laughed. 'You've got guts.'

'I'm pig-headed. Perhaps I got it from my real father. I suppose I'll never know.' She smiled and held on to Christophe tightly, pressing her lips against his warm, comforting skin.

Sergei did not come that morning. Eventually they got up, fed the fire with more logs and made themselves a meal with tinned potatoes, carrots and mince,

574

followed by tinned fruit. There were two bottles of vodka in the fridge, but nothing else. They drank water and ice-cold vodka, then warmed themselves up with more black coffee.

As darkness fell again, Christophe looked out of the window at the sky. There was not much else to see but the thick blackness of the nearby wood and hillocks of snow everywhere. 'The weather doesn't look so good,' he said, sounding a little anxious. 'I think we're in for more snow.'

'Does your phone get a signal?' asked Daisy, looking out at the lowering grey sky, tinged with the violet of imminent snowfall. Christophe shook his head. 'Nor does mine. And I've no battery either, it hasn't been charged for days.'

'He'll come tomorrow,' Christophe said confidently.

But snow fell in the night and they woke to find the lodge almost entirely engulfed. There was no sign of Sergei and the chances that he might be able to get through this snowfall seemed increasingly remote.

'He won't have forgotten, will he?' Daisy said, counting up the tins of food in the cupboard.

'I'm sure he won't have, how could he? He'll come,' Christophe said, but he looked worried.

Sergei did not come, that day or the next.

72

Coco left the South Kensington flat with more regret than she'd expected. After all, she'd been happy there. She'd felt safe from the world outside, cushioned against all the things that had marked her childhood, and she'd been able to live alone, unobserved for the most part. But now she had to move on.

As she shut the door, she wondered if Will would ever forgive her for what she was about to do.

The suite Margaret had arranged for her was more sumptuous than any hotel room: it had a vast bed, made up with sheets and blankets instead of a duvet, and with huge soft pillows. There was a sitting room, a small study, a large bathroom and a dressing room. Coco's luggage was already there when Margaret showed her in.

'A maid will unpack it later,' she said. Margaret seemed unusually cool and her expression was almost sour. *What's her problem?* wondered Coco. 'If you have any particular requests about how you like things, let her know. It's her job to keep it just as you like it.'

I could get used to this, Coco thought, looking about.

'It's lovely,' she said. It was modern, unfussy and calm, in greens and greys and pearly whites.

'This used to be his daughter's room. But don't worry, we had it refreshed for you. It's quite different now from how it was.'

Nevertheless, Coco shivered and tried to put that fact out of her mind. There was something a little eerie about being in the dead girl's room.

After showing Coco her new home, Margaret led her back downstairs to the basement office to settle some of the admin necessary for the new arrangement.

When Coco had checked and signed the paperwork, Margaret slid a Coutts gold card across the table towards her. 'For you,' she said.

'Cool.' Coco picked it up and looked at it. 'What's the limit?'

'The limit?' Margaret looked amused. 'Well . . . let's put it this way, I don't think you'll manage to spend it in a month. Now, shall we go and find Mr Dangerfield?'

Daddy was plainly excited when they found him finishing up his lunch in the dining room. 'Coco!' he cried, wiping his mouth on a napkin which he flung down. 'You're here at last! I thought you were never coming.'

'Here I am, Daddy,' she said brightly. Here he was, then. Her new charge. Her partner. Somewhere deep inside she felt sickened by the prospect, but she tried to ignore it.

'Good, I can't wait to show you around! You need to see the place properly, now that it's your new home.'

He led her around the house, pointing out his collections and acquisitions: the exquisite furniture, the paintings, even the wine cellar. 'Do you know how much that cost?' he demanded, waving his arms at the row upon row of bottles. 'Two million, I think! Over two million on wine alone.'

'We'd better have a bottle or two at dinner then, hadn't we?' remarked Coco. 'It's going to take you a while to drink that lot on your own.'

He snorted with laughter and took her off to see his collection of Chinese jade, and his Graham Sutherland, newly bought at auction.

That night, Coco wondered if he was going to surprise her by making a claim to her body. After all, wasn't she just another artefact, bought to add to his sense of self-worth and prestige? Didn't he want to own her too?

After dinner they watched television together in the small sitting room, Daddy's head nodding and his eyes closing in front of the news. Keen to make her escape, Coco went over and kissed his cheek. 'Night, night, Daddy,' she said.

'Good night, my darling,' he said, smiling back contentedly at her. 'I'll see you in the morning.'

So it was true. There was no lead left in the pencil. He was no longer interested in climbing between the warm thighs of a gorgeous young thing like her. It seemed that age was taming Daddy Dangerfield.

If Will could see him now, what would he think? Coco knew that he still saw the father of his youth in his mind's eye: fierce, tempestuous, commanding. Not this mild old man drowsing on the sofa. But she couldn't think about Will. It was still far too raw.

She went upstairs to bed. This was her life now and

she had to get used to it. It was what she'd wanted, after all.

Coco was lounging about in the study, waiting for Daddy to get off the phone, when she noticed the difference in colour between a large square patch of wooden panelling and its surroundings.

When Daddy had finished his call, she pointed at it and said, 'Is something missing?'

'No . . . yes . . . that is . . .' He frowned. 'There was something. It's been sold. A painting.'

'It looks like it was a big one.'

'It was, yes. A Gainsborough. A very large one.'

The artist's name meant nothing to Coco, though she knew it ought to. Or, at least, that if someone said 'a *something*' like that, then the painter's work was worth a great deal of money. 'Did you sell it recently?' she asked.

'I don't see what difference it makes,' Daddy replied irritably. 'It's gone and there we are. There are plenty of other paintings in the house to look at. Take a look at the Picasso in the drawing room if you want to see something.'

'That's tiny,' Coco said with a shrug, which made Daddy laugh and restored some of his good humour.

There was a knock on the door and Margaret came in. She acknowledged Coco with the faintest nod of her head and went straight to Daddy's desk. 'Sir, I've had some contact from HQ about a couple of executives.'

'Yes?' Daddy said gruffly, his concentration obviously elsewhere. 'Who?'

'I don't think you know them − Darley Ross and Daphne Fraser.'

'Darley Ross . . .' He frowned. 'That name rings a bell. Yes, I know him. But not the other one. What about them?'

'They're stuck in Siberia, sir.'

Daddy looked crossly at Margaret. 'Well, what the hell does that have to do with me? And what on earth are they doing there?'

'A fact-finding mission. They didn't report for work at the end of it. There's been little contact except from Ross to say he's had pneumonia and will fly home as soon as he's able. No news from Fraser at all.'

'Well,' Daddy said in a bad-tempered voice, 'they'd better be finding some bloody good facts, that's all I can say. Or their next mission will be to find another job. Is that all?'

Margaret absorbed this and then said, 'Should we put any effort into locating Fraser, sir? In case she's in trouble?'

'I don't think so. If she's in trouble, we'll find out in due course. If not, she'll turn up. They usually do. And then we can sack her.'

'Very well.' Margaret shot a look over at Coco, but she pretended she wasn't listening and the assistant went on her way to fulfil Daddy's orders.

73

Sergei wasn't coming. It didn't matter whether he wanted to or not, there was no way he could get through the snow to them, Daisy was certain of it. Christophe was less sure.

'He's used to this weather,' he said reasonably. 'Russians know how to deal with it in a way we don't. What looks impassable to us might be something they can get through with the right equipment. Why would Sergei want to let us starve up here?'

'He didn't seem to mind all that much when I was kidnapped,' Daisy said, but she was calmed by Christophe's words. He wasn't panicking and that helped her, even though she was nervously watching the wood pile go down and the tins in the cupboard diminish as they used up their stores.

'If it comes to the worst,' Christophe said with a smile, 'I'll go out and cut more wood and hunt something down to eat.'

'Good luck with that,' retorted Daisy. 'I haven't seen a living thing for days! And do we have an axe?'

'Honey, if it comes to it, you can eat me. I'll gladly

surrender an arm or a leg.' He laughed but Daisy shivered. She didn't want to think about such an awful eventuality as their starving, but she was becoming increasingly anxious.

On the other hand, it was also blissful to have the kind of warmth and happiness she hadn't known since the days they'd spent together at Nant-y-Pren. The two of them were locked away from the world here, perfectly content with each other. When they weren't sitting in front of the fire, talking and making plans, they were in bed where they couldn't get enough of each other's body, making love with a ferocity that was sometimes overpowering, or with a tenderness that left Daisy weak and helpless and close to tears.

'I'm so sorry we've spent so long apart,' she said to him, touching his cheek gently.

'But we wouldn't have had this sweet reunion if we hadn't,' said Christophe with a smile, and she knew it was true.

On the fifth day, even Christophe looked concerned. It hadn't snowed for a while but there was no sign of a thaw. They went outside, clearing a path with shovels, but the snow was deep. If they attempted to walk on the surface, they sank down at once. They were warm with the effort when they went back inside at last.

Christophe looked around. There was a handful of logs left on the hearth and he could see now that just getting the few feet to the forest was going to be difficult, let alone cutting wood when he arrived there. 'Daisy, how many tins of food do we have left?'

She went through to the kitchen and returned with

three tins. 'Two of mince, one of potatoes,' she said helplessly. 'And we're even out of vodka.'

'Out of vodka?' Christophe tried to lighten the mood. 'Well, that *is* bad. No one can expect me to stay here without vodka.' He beckoned her over to the sofa. 'Come and sit down.'

They sat together. Christophe took Daisy's hands in his and looked at her seriously.

'Do you know what I really want?' she said suddenly. 'A change of clothes!' She'd been washing her underwear in the basin at night and drying it out on the stove while she slept but her other clothes hadn't been washed for days. 'I haven't worn anything else since I was kidnapped.'

'Yes,' Christophe said gravely. 'It's time for us to be serious. We can't sit here forever waiting for Sergei. We don't know why he hasn't come. It's probably the weather but the fact is, he might not get through. And I don't want either of us to die here. I want to live a long and happy life – with you, if at all possible.'

Daisy's cheeks flushed as she felt happiness surge through her, but she said nothing.

'So the time has come.' Christophe lifted his wrist and pulled back his sleeve to reveal his watch, a large silver timepiece with a black face, compass points etched around the face, and bulky knobs on the case. 'Do you know what this is?'

'A watch,' Daisy deadpanned back.

'Yes. But it's a very special kind of watch. You see this large button on the side?' She nodded. 'In a moment, I'm going to pull it out. When I do that, it will release antennae that will transmit a signal on the distress frequency and reach a distance of 160 kilometres. It should be picked up and trigger a rescue team to save us.'

Daisy stared at it, then laughed. 'Very good. I almost believed you then.'

'I'm not joking.' Christophe gave her a candid look. 'This is a Breitling Emergency watch.'

'Really?'

He nodded, a big smile spreading over his face. He tilted it so that she could read 'Emergency Chronometer' written on its face. 'It's a pretty pricey piece of kit, designed for pilots. There's a large fine for calling out the rescue service unnecessarily but I think this counts as an emergency.' He looked down at the watch. 'I've had it since my flying days.'

Daisy picked up a cushion and threw it at him. 'All this time you knew you had this rescue watch, and you didn't tell me?' she cried, indignant but also deeply relieved.

Christophe laughed and dodged the cushion. 'We were having such a good time, I thought it might take the edge off if you knew about the watch. Now – I'm going to trigger the signal and then we should have time to go back to bed for a bit before the rescue team get here.'

74

Naturally everybody assumed that Coco was Daddy Dangerfield's mistress. Almost immediately items appeared in the gossip columns using the kind of snide language that meant everybody assumed that the 'new friend' was a sleeping partner. When the more oily gossip magazines pictured her and Daddy at a gallery opening or a book launch or a charity dinner, they called her his 'close companion', which said the same thing in a more acceptable way.

They didn't realise that she was more like a daughter to him than a lover; Daddy simply enjoyed having her about. If he admired her sexiness or having someone so young and beautiful in the house, it was more in the way of the owner of this remarkable object than as a red-blooded male staking a sexual claim. Perhaps he knew what people were thinking; if he did, he never made any effort to correct it.

One day he took her into company headquarters with him, riding the executive lift to the top of the impressive City premises, and showed her the view across London and the luxurious appointment of his office. Coco was impressed, though she pretended it all meant very little to her.

'Tell me what you do, Daddy,' she said, and he went on to lecture her for the rest of the day about the remarkable history of his father's business and how he himself had continued to build it up to the peak of success. It nearly drove Coco to tears of boredom.

To cope with her new role, she took as much time away from him as she could. He understood that she needed to visit her hairdresser and beautician and re-stock her wardrobe. But the evenings he considered his, and she had to spend them with him. All the time she listened carefully and watched as well.

One morning, lingering outside the dining room where Daddy was having his breakfast, she heard Margaret's voice coming from within.

'Sir, the Foundation needs more funds. The professor has told me he's on the brink of some exciting discoveries. As usual he's at the forefront of developments.'

'What kind of discoveries?' Daddy asked, sounding eager.

'Some of the serums he's testing have had remarkably positive effects,' was the reply. 'New cell growth, incredible rejuvenation, and the possibility of renewing entire organs. Imagine!' Margaret sounded more enthusiastic than Coco had ever heard her before. 'Every part of your body could be reinvigorated. Eternal youth, sir! And you would be the very first to experience it.'

So that's her game, Coco thought grimly. *She's another snake-oil saleswoman, peddling her stuff to a rich man.* Just then a maid came along the corridor, bearing a tureen of oat bran porridge. Coco breezed through the dining room door in time to see Margaret pushing the needle of a syringe into Daddy's arm.

'Ah, Coco,' he said, his face lighting up at the sight of her. 'I'm just getting my special shot. You should try them, they're remarkable.'

'Maybe I will one day,' she said airily. Margaret was observing her closely but Coco took care to seem unconcerned. 'But I prefer eating an orange. I hate injections. Ugh!'

Margaret quietly packed away her equipment and left the room.

Coco ran through the Belgravia streets on her way back from Hyde Park. She was semi-oblivious to the world around her, plugged into her headphones and listening to the music from her MP3 player. She loved her running sessions. She felt at peace as she pounded through the park, more so than anywhere else, and it was a blessed relief to be away from Daddy for a while. She found life with him claustrophobic and stressful.

Not too much longer, maybe. We'll see.

She slowed down as she approached the house, panting and taking a drink from her water bottle. In a moment, she'd back inside the gilded prison. Still, she'd chosen it. She could hardly complain. If ever a girl had made her bed and now had to lie in it, it was her. Bed made her think of the wonderful hours she'd spent there with Will, pressed against his muscular body, tasting the delights of his skin and tongue, feeling him deep inside her, driving her on to a fierce torrent of pleasure . . .

Stop it, she told herself sternly. *Don't you dare think about that! It's over. He's out of your life forever.* The desolation that possessed her at that thought was almost unbearable, and her head drooped. As she was approaching the door to the house, a man stepped out from against the railings where she hadn't noticed him. 'Coco?'

She looked up at pair of dark eyes and a thin face covered with dark stubble. 'Roberto?' she said, astonished. Then she smiled. 'Oh my God! It's been a long time.'

'It sure has.' He smiled back. 'I won't kiss you, you look a bit . . . glowing.'

'Oh, yeah.' She wiped a film of sweat from her forehead with one sleeve. 'Sorry.'

'Listen, have you got a moment? Can we go somewhere? I need to talk to you.'

Coco looked at her watch. 'Sure – but I can't be long. Ten minutes max. Is that OK?'

'It won't take long.' Roberto looked up admiringly at the huge white mansion. 'Hey, you've done very well for yourself, haven't you? Well done, doll.'

'Thanks.' She turned and began to walk with him towards the private garden at the centre of the square. 'I can't believe you found me. How did you know where I was?'

'Funny what you can find out when you need to. I saw your picture in the paper the other day, along with the bloke whose party you danced at.' He raised his eyebrows. 'Looks like you got lucky there after all.'

'Yeah. If you can call it that.' She longed suddenly to be able to go with him to a café, and sit and drink coffee and chat like they used to. Instead they leaned against the garden railings. 'Tell me how things are going,' she said.

'Honey.' Roberto put his hand on her sleeve and Coco suddenly felt nervous. 'There's no easy way to say this so I'll come straight out with it. I had a visit at the club the other day, from someone looking for you to tell you about your mum. She's . . . she's dying.'

Coco felt a jolt of her heart and a rush of panic, and then said with a mirthless laugh, 'She's been dying for fucking years!'

'Yeah, but now she really is. And she wants to see you.'

75

It was strange going back to being Daphne Fraser, Daisy thought. *I've almost got used to being Daisy again.* She'd loved it when Christophe had begun calling her by her real name.

On her return, she'd had to report to Karen O'Malley with a full explanation of what had happened abroad. She told the version that she'd also sent to Darley in a private email, hoping that he would back it up when he was in a fit state to explain himself. She expected that he would, since she was protecting his back and buying him some more time. For now, he was on indefinite sick leave.

'OK,' Karen said, when Daisy had finished her explanation. 'So this was really a sight-seeing trip that went wrong when Darley got sick and you got snowed in?'

'That's about the size of it,' Daisy said lightly. 'Except that we were there initially to inspect a possible investment in Anatolski's hotel business. It looked like a good one, in my opinion.'

Karen sat back behind her desk, pushing her glasses higher on her nose. 'That's reassuring to hear. But we'll have to see what the thoughts from upstairs are on this one.'

'You mean . . . Mr Dangerfield?'

'That's right. I'll have to make my report to him. Word is that he wasn't impressed by two executives going missing. But I think you've explained everything adequately. He'll be satisfied, I'm sure.'

Daisy's stomach fizzed with a curious mixture of fear and excitement. 'I see. Well, I'm happy to explain myself further as necessary.'

She left Karen's office feeling strangely elated. The odd thing about her experience in Siberia and the reunion with Christophe was that she now felt liberated. She'd been released from the strain of her previous state of mind, where she'd felt herself to be locked in a furious, invisible battle with her father. Somehow, suddenly, she didn't care. All this time, she'd been keen to show him that she mattered, that she was worth something, that she could make him proud of her even though she wasn't his daughter.

Now, as she considered facing Daddy's wrath in her new incarnation, she wanted to laugh. *Perhaps I should take my revenge after all*, she thought. *I know I could. But is it what I really want?*

The rescue from the hunting lodge had come about just as Christophe had promised. The signal had been picked up and a search-and-rescue helicopter dispatched to find the source. It hadn't been able to land, but first Daisy and then Christophe had been airlifted aboard, and the aircraft had sped them away over the miles and miles of snow-covered country

591

beneath. It seemed that within mere minutes they were back in Komsomolsk. Sergei had met them there the next day, full of vehement apologies and assurances that he had done his best to reach them, but that the unexpected snowfall had been too much for any vehicle to tackle. He promised that only one more day would have gone by before he would have alerted the rescue services himself.

Darley Ross had been returned to the UK already, so all that was necessary was for Sergei to fetch Daisy's luggage, including her travel documents, and then they were free to go.

All the way home she and Christophe held hands, unable to let go of each other again. Now they were back together, Daisy felt complete and it had seemed utterly natural for him to move in with her at the rented flat in Shoreditch. Neither of them could contemplate being apart, but the future was not at all clear.

'I thought I knew what I wanted,' Daisy told him over dinner the day of her interview with Karen. 'I've been driven on by this need to show my father what I was capable of. And today, it felt like it had all just melted away.' She smiled at him. 'All that desire and passion . . . vanished. Now that I have you again, I don't need to face him any more.'

'You have no need to prove yourself to that man,' Christophe said, wrapping tagliatelle around his fork.

'I know.' Daisy toyed with hers, leaning her head on one hand. She looked up at him. 'I could also bring Dangerfield toppling down, you do realise that? I know about the hidden debts, the precarious nature of the whole company, and the fact that one rogue executive has got the business involved in a crazy mining scheme that's more like a money pit than a sensible investment.'

Christophe smiled at her. His brown eyes looked even more velvety in the candlelight. 'So bring it down. Why not?'

'Because I still love it, I suppose,' she replied simply. 'And I want to work there, just as I always did. I'm not sure how long I can go on being Daphne Fraser, though. And at some point he has to know about me. That's the final step.'

'Is it?' Christophe gazed at her tenderly. 'Maybe *you* need to know about you. Maybe you need some answers, and you don't even realise it.'

Daisy frowned. What he'd said suddenly sounded right. 'Yes,' she said slowly. 'Maybe that's exactly what I need.' She looked him straight in the eye. 'But even if I decide to leave Dangerfield, there's something I need to clear up first. I'm going to Scotland to solve a little problem. And I need you to come with me.'

76

I thought I would never come back round here, Coco told herself. Her mother had been taken into King's College Hospital in Camberwell, so Coco took the train out to Denmark Hill and walked to the hospital from the station. She felt like a creature visiting from another planet in her Dior jeans, outsize blazer, McQueen scarf loosely wrapped at her neck, a Mulberry satchel over one shoulder.

But as soon as she'd heard from Roberto that her mother was dying, she'd known she had to go back. He had offered to go with her, but she'd said no, she would go alone. The hospital was enormous. Outside the entrance she passed people in pyjamas, attached to drips or in wheelchairs, puffing away at cigarettes, enjoying one of the few pleasures they had left. Inside, she passed signs to the different departments, and marvelled at all the knowledge and skill contained under one roof, along with all the sickness and misery too.

She found the right floor and department, and a receptionist directed her to where she would find her mother. The ward was full of patients and yet the place seemed eerily deserted. She'd thought it would be full of medical staff, but the nurses seemed to be grouped at a desk outside, there was no doctor to be seen, and the sick lay in their beds unattended getting on with the tiring and tedious business of being ill. Some of them had visitors, some were curtained off from view. Coco found her mother at the far end, lying prone against thin hospital pillows and attached to a variety of machines, apparently asleep. Coco went up to the bed and gazed at her for a moment. Michelle was a shadow of her old self, thinner and more wizened than ever, her hair sparse and streaked with grey. Coco bent over her.

'Hello, Mum.'

Michelle opened her eyes and a look of joy appeared on her face. 'Chanelle! You're here.'

'Yeah.' Coco sank down into a chair beside the bed. 'So, how are you doin', Mum?' She couldn't help slipping back into her old accent.

'Not so good.' That was apparent from the thick rasp in Michelle's voice, the roar in her chest every time she took a breath. 'This emphysema's gonna get me, love.'

'Yeah.' Coco leaned over and took her hand. 'I guess so.'

There was a long pause while they held hands, then Michelle drew in another tortured breath and said slowly, 'Oh, well, babe . . . I've had a good life.'

Coco fought the impulse to jump to her feet and screech, 'No, you fucking haven't! You've had a bloody miserable life and you made mine miserable too!' *What's the point? What can she do about it now? She's dying.*

After a while, Michelle squeezed her hand and looked up at her pitifully. 'Chanelle, was I . . . was I a good mum to you?'

Coco stared down at her. She could see death all over the older woman's face. What was there to be gained from hurting her now? 'Yeah. You were. The best.' She squeezed her mother's hand in response and smiled at her.

'Thank you, love. I know I wasn't always there for you. It was hard for me. I was very depressed at times, I know that. But . . . I always loved ya, Chanelle. You gotta know that.' Her mother's eyes filled with tears that slid out and trickled down her sunken cheeks.

'I do. And I love you too.' As she said the words, Coco realised she meant them. All these years she'd convinced herself that she hated her mother, but she knew now that she really did love this poor, sick woman. Even though she resented the years wasted on drugs and booze, all the chaos and selfishness and desperation, and still felt desperately sorry for the child she'd been – little Chanelle Hughes, who'd had to grow up too soon and look after herself and her mother too – she also pitied Michelle and knew that, despite everything, her mother had loved her in her own way. Tears sprang to her eyes, burning her lids, and her nose prickled. 'Mum,' she whispered, feeling overcome, 'did you hear me? I love you. And I'm sorry too . . . that I walked out on you and left you alone.'

Michelle sighed as though Coco's words had somehow released something in her, and smiled. She closed her eyes and there was a long pause when it seemed she might have slipped back into sleep. Then she stirred and opened them again.

'Mum,' Coco said hesitantly. She felt closer to her mother now than she ever had. Perhaps this was the time for them to be honest with each other. 'There's one thing you can do for me. It's . . . I want to know . . . who my dad was?'

'Your dad?' It came out on a long whirring exhalation.

'Yeah – do you know who he was?' All this time, she'd had an inkling who he was. There was only one thing left her mother could do for her now, and that was to tell her the truth.

'Your dad,' Michelle repeated, looking confused. 'Oh, God.'

'Mum . . . was it . . . was it . . .' Coco hardly wanted to say it out loud but she couldn't stop herself. 'Was it Gus?'

Her mother's eyes widened and she looked startled. 'Gus?' she rasped.

'Yeah.' Coco couldn't help speaking more urgently, leaning close to her mother, every nerve of her body straining, desperate to hear the answer. 'It was him, wasn't it? That's why he was so kind to me. He gave me those dance lessons, remember? He always treated me differently. He wasn't like the other people you knew . . . and why were you friends at all if it wasn't for sex?'

'Gus.' It seemed to leave Michelle's tired voice on a sigh. 'Yeah. Yeah, that's right. He's your dad. Gus is.' She took another breath. 'I always liked him, even if he was posh. He was an artist. Came from some rich family, though he didn't have much money himself. Mad as a hatter though.' Michelle dragged in another rasping breath. Coco willed her to carry on and eventually she said, 'He was a . . . drop out. He took a shine to me and I liked it round his. There was tea. Food. He was kind to me. He gave me cash as well – not to have sex, but just because he liked me. So we did have sex.' Michelle looked up at her daughter. 'And you're his. You've got his eyes. There's no mistaking that.'

'So he knew about me?' Coco swallowed. There seemed to be a hard lump in her throat.

Michelle shook her head slowly. 'Nah. But he was good to you all the same, 'cos you was mine. Maybe he suspected. I dunno. I went round to tell him I was pregnant but he was all of flutter 'cos he'd been seeing some other girl – posh like him – and got her up the duff. And she was married. So I didn't tell him. But he was always nice to you, so maybe he guessed.'

'Thanks, Mum,' Coco said in a soft voice. She felt a sense of completeness that she'd never known before. It was what she had always suspected. *At last I know who I am.* 'Thanks for telling me.'

They didn't speak for a while. Coco sat there lost in thought, holding her mother's hand as the old woman slept, exhausted by her long speech. She stayed until the nurses finally came and told her that she had to leave.

Finally she kissed her mother's dry cheek and stroked back her hair. ''Bye, Mum,' she whispered. 'I'll come back and see you soon.' Then she turned and walked out of the ward.

That night, Daddy took Coco to the Dangerfield Florey for dinner. No one would have guessed that just a few hours earlier the beautiful girl in the gold Gucci dress

598

had been at the bedside of her dying, drug-destroyed mother in one of the poorest areas of London. *I'm good at hiding where I come from*, she thought ironically.

They dined on roast langoustines and poulet de Bresse *en cocotte*, the waiters scurrying about to make sure that the boss had perfect service, and then the maître d' made crêpes Suzette at the table for them, preparing them in a silver chafing dish over a tableside gas burner.

'A Florey speciality, my dear,' Daddy said softly as the maître d' expertly spooned the orange caramel sauce over the crêpes, then added and ignited the brandy.

'It looks wonderful,' she said sincerely, and thought it tasted just as marvellous. Life wouldn't be so bad, would it, if she had these small pleasures to help her through? Better than lying sick in a hospital ward, that was for sure.

Coco savoured the citrus toffee of the crêpe and then said, with studied casualness, 'Daddy, tell me about the Dangerfield Foundation. Margaret mentioned it and I wondered what it does.'

He instantly perked up. 'Ah, yes. A wonderful thing! It's going to guarantee fame for the Dangerfield name, probably for the rest of time. Margaret introduced me to the professor and his marvellous ideas. He is discovering the way to eternal youth.'

'I've seen her give you those injections.'

'Absolutely. She is keeping me in perfect health with a serum made from extremely rare ingredients. I'm lucky enough to have the natural version – a synthetic one is being created for general use.' Daddy looked puffed up with importance. 'I've made generous grants to the Foundation over the last few years, and the professor decided to name it after me in thanks. We have a little deal . . .'

Coco raised her eyebrows. 'A deal?'

Daddy looked uncomfortable and coughed. 'Yes . . . an arrangement. But it's nothing that need concern you, dear, it's just business.' His face darkened. 'Not that my wretched son understands such things.'

Coco froze for a second and then carried on eating, trying to keep her composure. 'Oh? Has Will been in touch?' She hoped her voice was giving away nothing about the way his name made her feel.

Daddy's face darkened. 'His lawyers have been pestering me about the Foundation, demanding accounts and audits and God only knows what. Poking their noses in! And I know that he and his sister intend to sue me. Thanks to your report, I can guess exactly what charges they intend to bring. I'm more than ready to defend myself. I'm expecting the writ daily. Well, well . . .' A cunning expression settled on his face as a waiter approached, carrying a silver salver with a large domed lid. 'What's this? Why, I do believe it's an extra course for you, Coco.'

The waiter put the salver down and bowed. 'For madam,' he said, and lifted the lid, revealing a turquoise ring box with 'Tiffany' stamped across it in black letters.

Coco gasped.

Daddy was smiling fondly at her. 'Open it, my dear.'

She picked it up and opened it. Inside, on a bed of white silk, was a huge square-cut yellow diamond ring. Around it were a score of smaller white diamonds set in a double border around the central gem, and the diamonds continued round the platinum band. Light flashed off it, revealing the extraordinary golden hue within. It was dazzling.

'Oh my God,' Coco said in a faint voice, hardly able to believe her eyes. She was stunned. This was completely unexpected.

'Now, don't worry,' Daddy murmured, leaning forward and taking her hand. 'I know it's sudden. This doesn't mean I want anything to change between us, in the private arena. It simply means I want to protect you. If I die – which, of course I won't, with the help of the professor's amazing work – I want to be sure that you are looked after. And I'm very fond of you, my dear. More than fond. I can't imagine life without you. Coco – will you marry me?'

77

The woman at the airline check-in desk was making eyes at him, but Will ignored her. It was a hazard of travelling first class and having all his own teeth: the girls always gave him a special smile.

'I hope you enjoy your trip to London, sir,' she said, returning his ticket and boarding pass to him. 'Please let us know if we can help in any way.'

'Of course,' he said. He hadn't made this trip for a long time and, as he headed for the first-class lounge to grab something to eat before boarding – he always liked to settle down and sleep for as long as possible during the flight – he wondered if he was doing the right thing.

Of course I am, he told himself. *Besides, I'll get to see Sarah and the kids. They won't even know what their uncle looks like at this rate.*

He settled down with a newspaper and ordered a sandwich to be served to him later on. In thirteen hours he'd be in London. He had once believed he would never go back and yet here he was. The thought of Coco passed through his mind, but he pushed it away. She was gone. Finished. That was over. It had been the weirdest interlude of his life: he'd really fallen for her, and those few weeks they'd spent together had been bliss of a kind he'd never known before. He'd connected with another human being and thought, for the first time, that he understood what songs and poems were talking about when they harped on about love. Even when Xander had exposed her past, he hadn't cared. And when she'd opened up to him, it had felt precious, a privilege, to hear the truth about her suffering. But all along she'd been a spy in his home, the viper in his bosom, working for the man he despised most in the world – and that was unforgivable.

Sometimes he wondered if he should have let her explain why she'd done it, but he dismissed that thought. There was no excuse she could possibly make for betraying him. He tried to close it all out of his mind: the memories of the golden days they'd spent together, and the pain he'd felt when she'd gone. It didn't work out. It happened all the time. Whatever. She might be in London, she might not. Who cared?

It was time for him to board. He picked up his jacket and bag and headed for the departure gate.

The flight was straightforward and Will slept nearly all the way, thanks to a sleeping mask and some ear plugs. The plane landed at a stupidly early hour but that didn't matter. He'd slept well and would soon adjust to the time zone. A black BMW was waiting to take him into town. He'd go to his hotel, have breakfast and read the papers before going on to his appointment. As the BMW slid easily on to the M4 and headed towards central London, Will opened his bag and took out the sheaf of papers his lawyers had given him to look through.

By the time he arrived at the offices of Graham & Philpot, Will had assimilated most of what the lawyers had sent him. The problem was that reading the papers kept making him hot with rage, and he'd slam them down and stare furiously into space, thinking over all his grievances and rehearsing vitriolic but factual speeches that he was sure would convince any judge that Will's father was a crook.

He was shown into the office of a senior partner, Neville Hanratty. Two younger solicitors were with him, both with folders open in front of them.

'Ah, Mr Dangerfield, welcome,' Hanratty said, getting up to shake his hand.

'Please, call me Will.'

'Very well – Will. Please sit down and let's get started.'

Hanratty recapped the situation quickly: Will and Sarah had reason to believe that their father had been plundering the family trust, using the proceeds to fund his lavish lifestyle.

'Yes,' Will said briefly. 'You only have to look at what he's got. How can he afford to buy the stuff in his wine cellar, on his walls, all the property, the cars, if he's not taking sizable chunks out of the trust? Dangerfield PLC hasn't paid large enough dividends. And he is the main trustee. I shouldn't think the others would know how to say no to him.'

Hanratty looked down at the sheet of paper in front of him. 'No, they don't look like financial experts to me.'

'They're business acquaintances with no financial

604

expertise to speak of,' Will said scornfully. 'And if you knew my father, you'd know that he'd make sure they were well under the thumb before he put them in place.'

'The other side have released some papers to us in response to our letters, and I thought you might be interested to see this.' Hanratty passed another piece of paper to Will, who took it and scanned it quickly.

His expression changed as he read. 'The Gainsborough? He's sold the Gainsborough? He's expressly forbidden from doing that by the articles of a trust. That's a family asset! He has no right to sell it.'

'We made that point to his lawyers. Your father claims the Gainsborough was sold by his own father years ago.'

'I'm sure that's a lie!' Will said vehemently.

'Well, if we can prove that, then we can certainly prove mismanagement, and that would be enough to have your father removed as trustee and a thorough audit made on the family trusts.'

Will threw down the piece of paper. 'It's not just selling assets. I'm sure he's giving vast chunks of money to some mysterious organisation called the Dangerfield Foundation, though I can't find out much about it. If it turns out he has been plundering money meant for Sarah and me, well – what then?'

'He'll be forced to sell his own assets to make up the missing amounts,' Hanratty said plainly.

'Good.' Will felt a surge of satisfaction. He'd like to see his father have to sell all those fripperies and indulgences of his in order to repay the family. 'I want you to issue the writ as soon as possible.'

'There is something else . . .' Hanratty said,

hesitantly. He looked over at one of the junior lawyers and nodded. The younger solicitor obediently started leafing through his file. 'Your father appears to have a new companion. We don't have any reason yet to believe they're married but she has been seen sporting a rather large engagement ring. They were pictured at a function last night that's reported in today's papers. You can see the ring very clearly in this shot. It looks as though it cost a pretty penny.'

The young lawyer pulled out a colour photocopy of a gossip column from his folder, and passed it over. Will took it and stared. He felt the colour drain from his face.

'Are you all right?' Hanratty asked, leaning forward, concerned. 'Do you need some water?'

'I'm fine.' The words came out in a choked voice. Will stared at the caption under the photograph: '. . . with his fiancée, Miss Coco Hughes'. A buzzing feeling in his head seemed to be getting stronger. He thought he was going to pass out.

'Mr Dangerfield . . . ?'

'I have to . . . I have to go. I'm sorry.' Will got to his feet and stumbled out. He couldn't breathe again until he reached the street below, where he leaned against the wall of the building and gulped in great breaths of the city air, trying to calm himself down.

Was it really true? Would she really do that to him? Did she really hate him so much she would do the worst thing she possibly could, just to hurt him more?

But he had to believe the evidence of his own eyes.

78

The trip to Scotland with Christophe had provided Daisy with what she was sure was the greatest coup of her career to date.

'This is going to secure everything,' she said gleefully to him on the way home from the airport in a black cab. 'It's the answer, I just know it!'

He smiled back at her. 'You've really done it this time. I have to say, I wasn't sure you could. He was a tough old nut to crack.'

'He just needed careful handling.'

'True. But this doesn't solve the question of what's going to happen with Sergei's mine,' Christophe reminded her.

Daisy leaned back against the smooth leather seat, watching the city slide past the window. 'No. That's going to have to be Darley's problem. I can't see any other way. He's going to have to face the consequences.'

'He invested with company money, though.'

'Fraudulently borrowed,' she replied. 'The Dangerfield Group has no legal responsibility towards

Sergei or the mine, and after what happened to us there, I don't think I can reasonably recommend that we remain involved. No, I'm going to tell Darley that he has to confess, and take what's coming to him. If he's lucky, they'll hush it up and let him retire. Meanwhile, I'm going to see Karen first thing on Monday and ask her to set up an executive board meeting as soon as possible.'

Christophe took her hand, smiling at her. 'I only wish I could be there.'

Daisy grinned back, though her stomach was already turning massive somersaults at the thought of what she was about to do.

'So let me get this right, Mr Campbell. You're prepared to sell your house and land to the Dangerfield Group, on several conditions.'

Daisy's voice floated out over the darkened boardroom. The eyes of all the executives were fixed on the film now playing on the drop-down screen, revealing the gloomy interior of a Scottish cottage. Daisy stood to one side, the control in her hand, watching her audience as they took in what they were seeing.

The camera fixed on Campbell's face. He had a weathered complexion, bright blue pin-prick eyes under bristling eyebrows, and snow-white hair. He tapped the arm of the chair he was sitting in and nodded. 'Aye.' He spoke in a thick Scottish brogue. 'I know that the business will be good for land and jobs round here, right enough. So long as you meet my terms, then we may be able to make a deal.'

Daisy's voice was heard again. 'You want your house

taken down and reconstructed, brick for brick, on a similar piece of land.'

'Aye. Every plank and board the same,' he growled.

'And you want a wildlife preservation charity set up and funded by our organisation, to make doubly sure, beyond even the government restrictions already in place, that everything is protected.'

'Cor-rrect.' Campbell's r's rolled portentously.

'And a job in this charity, patrolling and monitoring birds and animals on the Dangerfield land. For life.'

'Cor-rrect again.'

'Well, Mr Campbell, I think I can happily agree to all those conditions – although we do have one of our own. Work on moving and rebuilding your house must start immediately so that we can commence our own works.'

'As soon as ye like.' He nodded slowly. 'I cannae pretend all this has been easy. I'm glad it's over. Ye've listened to me, young lady, and that was all I asked. I didnae like being bullied by those other types. I've got what I wanted, and that's enough for me.'

'Thank you, Mr Campbell. I'm delighted to have done business with you.'

Daisy clicked off the film and the lights came up. The executives turned to her almost as one, their expressions elated, and the next moment a round of applause filled the room.

Karen O'Malley stepped forward, her face beaming. 'Fantastic, Daphne, thank you! Ladies and gentlemen, I give you Daphne Fraser . . . who has just managed to rescue the Scottish links project from disaster.'

Daisy nodded in acceptance of their praise, beaming but embarrassed. As the room subsided into a buzz of excited chatter, the executives getting up to mingle, Karen congratulated her again. She had known in advance the contents of the film but was still thrilled to see it. 'That was marvellous! And you and I both know how precarious the situation really was.' She gave Daisy a knowing look. 'Darley didn't let it get out, but a few more weeks and there was a real risk of this bringing the organisation down. With renewed confidence that the project will be completed, the banks will certainly extend our credit.'

'I was happy to help,' Daisy said, flushed with her triumph. It had been a fantastic moment when Campbell had agreed to her suggestions. Christophe had filmed it all on his phone so that there was irrefutable proof of what had been decided in that dark fisherman's cottage on the edge of the dunes. Daisy had known that this way she could ensure that the Dangerfield Group, which she loved, survived. How she would deal with Daddy was another matter.

Karen rested one hand lightly on Daisy's arm. 'Can I introduce to you to Mr Dangerfield? I don't think you've met, and you certainly should. I've briefed him about what you've done.'

'Yes, what a good idea,' she said. Though she was outwardly calm her stomach flipped over with nerves as she followed Karen out of the boardroom and down the hall towards Daddy's office.

It was all still so familiar. Almost nothing had changed. Her breath began to come in short bursts as they approached the penthouse office suite and her heart raced unpleasantly in her chest. *I have to be calm. I mustn't let him guess – not yet. The time isn't quite right. I want it to have maximum impact.*

Karen knocked at the door and entered. Daisy followed her, feeling that powerful presence before she'd even seen him. Then she caught a glimpse of him, a large, imposing figure behind the familiar desk, and almost gasped out loud. He'd aged. There was no disguising that he looked pale and tired under his tan, and his bushy eyebrows had straggly white hairs emerging from them. He was thinner and hunched-looking, as though worry was burdening him. He stared at her as she approached. She faltered for a second, fear and nausea rising in her stomach, and then regained control. She had to be strong.

A second later, Daisy was standing in front of him, as Karen smoothly introduced her – 'Daphne Fraser, our bright young hope for the future. She's sorted out our little local difficulty in Scotland. Just in time, too, sir.'

Daddy stared at her through eyes that were more faded and rheumy than she remembered. 'So you're the up-and-coming executive I've heard so much about,' he said in that familiar booming voice. That, at least, hadn't changed.

She felt sure she was trembling visibly, certain that in a second he'd recognise her. But he kept gazing at her with a friendly interest, obviously seeing only the dark hair, the glasses, the identikit black business suit. 'Yes,' she said in a high voice. 'It's an honour to meet you, sir.'

'Well done on your negotiating skills. I'm impressed. You're the kind of person I'd like to see more of in this organisation: forward-thinking and go-getting.' Daddy nodded. 'Yes. More like you, please!'

611

'I'll do my best for you, sir,' she said.

'I'm delighted to hear it. You'll find out we reward loyal members of the Dangerfield family very well. You, Miss Fraser, look as though you'll fit right in. Well done.' He smiled at her, his face creasing into wrinkles, eyes receding into fleshy pouches.

So that's that. The words I've wanted to hear for so long. She'd expected to feel overwhelmed, triumphant, victorious. Instead a quiet satisfaction crept through her, along with a sense of completion. 'Thank you, sir,' she said in a low voice.

'Thank you. Good day.' Daddy signalled the interview was at an end.

Karen led her back to the door. In the hall, she said, 'That went well. Believe me, he's hardly ever complimentary.' Her eye was suddenly caught by someone emerging from the executive lift at the other end of the hall. 'Hmm, maybe this is why,' she murmured.

Daisy followed her gaze and saw a slim young woman, sexily and very expensively casual in jeans, boots and a big shaggy white coat, stalking down the hall towards them. Her face was hardly visible under the giant Dior shades she was wearing, but her pink-glossed lips were set in a resolute straight line. 'Who's that?' Daisy whispered as the girl approached, tossing back her golden-caramel hair as she came.

'The new lady in his life,' muttered Karen. 'Shh!'

They both stood to one side to let the girl stride past. She ignored them completely and went straight to Daddy's office. As she flung the door open, she cried, 'Daddy darling, it's me!'

Daisy watched, open-mouthed.

'Did you see the rock?' Karen asked conspiratorially. 'It's the most enormous thing I've ever seen.'

'You mean, they're engaged?' Daisy was stunned.

Karen nodded. 'Looks like it. No fool like an old fool, eh?'

79

The hired Mercedes roared along the country lanes, leaving hedges shaking in its wake. Will realised he'd missed the beautiful English countryside and all its lush greenness. The sight of it was helping to lift his spirits just a little from the black gloom he'd found himself in lately.

I've been away too long, he thought. *I'll go and see Mum. I've missed her.* He had been a neglectful son, only calling every few weeks to tell her his news and relying on Sarah to provide her with company. He would put that right as soon as he had talked to his sister. There was plenty for them to sort out and it had to be done quickly.

He'd stopped at a country pub for a drink and to stretch his legs when his cell phone went. It was Hanratty with the news that the writ had been issued and the other side had suggested a meeting of all the parties, to see if the matter could be resolved without the expense and intrusion of a court case.

'The papers are already reporting on the affair,'

Hanratty explained down the line, 'and your father's lawyers are keen to get this sorted out in private.'

'I bet they are,' Will said grimly. 'The old man's reputation will count for shit once he's revealed as a swindler who would cheat his own children. OK, we're up for it. I'm sure my sister will agree to be there as well.'

He did not add that his father was also a man who would marry a woman young enough to be his daughter, but that thought was tormenting him too. He'd been plunged into depression ever since the revelation that Coco was seeing his father. He was tortured by hot dreams of her, where she'd be in his arms again, kissing him, yielding her beautiful body to him, letting him push himself in between those taut thighs to her secret, delicious centre. And then the ugly truth dawned: she was his father's. Her beauty and all the pleasures it brought with it belonged to him now, and it sickened Will to his stomach to think of the revolting old man pawing that body, tasting the delights that had meant so much to Will himself. He had woken gasping more than once, longing to his core for the woman he now told himself he hated with a greater passion than ever he had loved her.

But it made sense to do as his father suggested and meet to talk out the situation. Surely the old man would see his position was weak – but Will had a sneaking feeling that his father's obstinate pride would not allow him ever to give in. He half dreaded and half desired the meeting. It would be the first time he had been face to face with his father for many years.

He climbed back into his car and headed off. The

Sat-nav guided him perfectly to the cross-barred gate at the entrance to Ivy House Farm, and before long he was approaching the old farmhouse at the end of the drive, a large two-storey building in weathered Dorset stone, with a muddy Range Rover and children's bikes standing outside.

Will parked and went to knock on the front door, banging the iron ring with relish. There was an instant flurry of barking from inside, a voice shouting at the dogs to be quiet and the sound of footsteps on stone flags. A moment later the door opened and there was his sister, a delightfully ordinary figure in jeans, a light blue polo-necked jumper and a waistcoat, her dark red hair tied back into a loose ponytail. Two black Labradors panted and pushed around her, keen to see who the visitor was. Her coppery-green eyes, so like his own, lit up when she saw him.

'Will!'

The next moment he was engulfed in a fierce hug. He laughed and tried to kiss his sister's cheek, but her face was buried so deep in his chest it was hard to find it.

'I'm so glad to see you! Come in, come in.' Beaming, Sarah took his hand and led him down the hall to the farmhouse kitchen, a warm, cosily shambolic room, full of the detritus of childhood: scrawled drawings pinned to the walls and the fridge, plastic toys scattered about, a Spiderman mask abandoned on the floor alongside some well-read comics. The dogs padded in behind them, taking up residence in baskets by the warm Aga and watching the goings on with shiny black eyes.

'Where are the kids?' Will asked, looking fondly at the mess.

'At school. They'll be happy to see you. I'm so pleased you're here! You're staying, aren't you? I've got a room all ready for you, and the boys made you some welcome presents and a banner – it's in the bedroom, you'll love it. Do you want tea?'

'Yes, and yes,' Will said, laughing. He felt happy for the first time in ages, as though just walking into his sister's comfortable home had given him a much-needed dose of family life.

'We've got so much to catch up on,' Sarah said, filling a big red kettle and placing it on the Aga to heat up.

'I know. It's not the same on the phone, is it?'

Sarah shook her head, her hair glinting amber and gold where it caught the light.

'And it's not just the good stuff,' he went on, suddenly solemn. 'You know why I'm here . . . why I came back?'

Sarah nodded, an agonised expression crossing her face. 'So it's going ahead?'

'Yes,' he said simply. 'You and I never wished for this, but it's the only way. He can't be allowed to get away with it, you know that.'

Sarah took her time before answering, busying herself with fetching mugs and teabags. Then she said, 'From what you've told me, it's the right thing to do, and I'm with you all the way.'

Will smiled. 'Thanks, Sarah. It's the right choice, I just know it. I hope it will be as painless as possible. I just wish I could find out more about this Foundation I told you about, but my investigators are drawing a blank. Besides,' he said, his eyes darkening, 'we have to act now, before he gets married again. Otherwise we could see another sizable chunk of the money in trust disappearing into smoke.'

Sarah gasped. 'Gets married again? Who . . . when . . . ? This is the first I've heard of it.'

Will stared down, observing that his fists were suddenly clenched, the knuckles white. 'Some gold digger, a stripper or something, if you can believe it.'

Sarah sank down into a chair as if her legs had suddenly weakened beneath her. She paled. 'A *stripper*? After all that talk of the Dangerfield honour and the marvellous family legacy . . . he'd marry a *stripper*?'

'Looks like it,' Will said harshly. 'And I'm not going to let that tramp get her hands on any of what belongs to us. But let's talk about something else. How are the kids? Tell me all about the farm, the horses, and let's forget about this awful business for a while.'

It was only later, after the boys had come home, climbed excitedly over their uncle, had supper and gone to bed, that the talk returned to the serious matter of the Dangerfield family trusts. Sarah's husband, Ben, a solid, reliable farmer, joined them for dinner but excused himself afterwards so that brother and sister could talk about family business in peace. Will explained all the aspects of the case.

'If only Daisy were alive,' Sarah said, an expression of sadness passing over her face. 'She would be able to help us. She'd certainly be able to confirm that the Gainsborough wasn't sold until recently.'

'Do you really think so?' Will shook his head. 'She

was his creature. She would never have turned against him.'

Sarah fixed her brother with a heartfelt look. 'I feel so bad now – about the way we broke off all contact with her. She was just a child. She wasn't to blame for what happened. We should have been more generous to her.'

An image floated through Will's mind: the look in his little half-sister's eyes when she'd found him at her mother's funeral, the spark of pleasure and awe he'd seen there then. She'd obviously thought the world of him. He felt a stab of guilt, remembering. 'You're right. I feel terrible as well. I last saw her years ago, at Julia's funeral. She thought I was coming back to the family and I told her we could never be anything to each other as long as she was on Dad's side.' He shook his head sadly. 'The look on her face . . . I feel so awful about it now. I punished her for the anger I felt with Dad. But, you know, if she hadn't died, she would definitely be on his side.'

'I suppose we'll never know for sure,' Sarah said softly, and they were both silent as they remembered the little girl they had hardly known, who'd sunk to her death in the warm waters off Thailand.

80

Coco knew that she didn't have to be frightened, but she was. Margaret was not in the house, she was sure of that; she was definitely in Paris, on some unspecified tasks for her master, going about her work with all the diligence and discretion she'd always shown.

This is my chance. At last.

Coco padded along the carpeted corridor, lit by small lamps on side tables and in alcoves. The house was never completely dark. Daddy preferred it to be kept semi-lit at all times, as though it were a great hotel, always on standby to answer his needs, rather than a family home.

He would be snoring away by now in his huge, swagged four-poster bed, said to have been slept in by Charles II. The royal connection appealed to him. As she went past the landing that led towards his bedroom suite, Coco glanced down at the vast yellow diamond glinting on her finger.

Daddy's proposal had put her in a quandary. She hadn't been expecting it in the least. He'd seen her obvious shock at once, and had clearly panicked that she might run in the opposite direction and abandon him altogether.

'You don't have to say anything,' he'd said quickly. 'Please . . . I've been stupid. I've rushed you. Take your time and decide when you're ready. But please, Coco, wear the ring as a sign that you're thinking about it.'

She had let him persuade her to accept the ring. Despite what it signified, she'd been enraptured by its beauty. The huge yellow diamond shone like a small sun on her finger, a promise that she would never have to return to the darkness again. Now the world believed her engaged to the old man, and she was sure everyone was having a good laugh about it . . . but she knew she would never marry him. She had once thought she might be able to, as an act of spite towards Will. In her wildest dreams of revenge, she'd imagined marrying Daddy and becoming Will's step-mother, with access to all the riches he'd wanted to reclaim from his father, and then taking great pleasure in squandering as much of his inheritance as she could. She would give it away, spend it on nothing at all, dress herself in the finest clothes and jewels in the world . . . and let him see her do it, helpless to stop her. She would make him suffer, and feel a tiny bit of the pain he'd inflicted on her.

But when it came down to it, Coco couldn't do it. The moment Daddy had asked her to marry him, she'd known it was impossible. Her heart had rebelled against it. She'd tasted love now, even if it had been so cruelly destroyed, and something in her that had been dead had come alive. It wouldn't let her stamp it down again. It wanted all the things she had shared with Will – to live and to feel and to love again.

And as for the money . . . well, it wasn't hers and it wasn't even Daddy's. What she had learned about the goings on recently had made her sure that Will was right in his suspicions that his father had been misappropriating the family trusts. Margaret and Daddy still kept much of their business dealings secret from her, despite Daddy's telling her she was now in the circle of trust. Nevertheless, they sometimes let their guard down and Coco had gleaned that this painting, the Gainsborough, was a source of great anxiety to them. She'd heard them discussing at length how they were going to deal with the matter of the date of the sale.

'Without that,' Daddy had said, 'they can't prove anything!'

Coco had buried her nose even deeper in *Vogue* and pretended not to be listening just as hard as she could. Then there was the Foundation. She'd heard Margaret badgering Daddy for more funds to be sent to it, and it seemed obvious that the woman was involved in promoting its cause to her employer. Coco often found Margaret's cold eyes fixed on her, hard with suspicion. The fact that she was wearing Daddy's ring on her finger had clearly horrified Margaret, and Coco had a feeling it wouldn't be long before the other woman became her enemy.

She hasn't had to share Daddy's attention – or money – with anyone for a very long time. No wonder she doesn't like me on her territory, especially if it looks like I'm a permanent addition.

All of which had sent her on this strange night-time mission down the winding stairs to Margaret's office.

It was locked, of course. How could she expect

anything different? But that was precisely why she'd made it her business to locate the set of security keys that could open any door in the house. A bit of flirting and chatting with the security guard and she'd managed to persuade the poor lump to hand over the secondary key to Margaret's office. *The benefits of working on the inside,* she thought wryly. *The circle of trust. Hah!*

She slid the key into the lock and turned the handle. It opened smoothly and a moment later she was inside the office. Switching on the lights, Coco took in the extraordinary neatness of the minimalist surroundings. She took out her phone and quickly began to photograph the desk and the shelves so that she had a record of exactly how everything had been when she'd found it. She was sure that Margaret would be very sensitive to the position of things in her own office. Then she sat down and turned on the computer. The password box flashed up. Coco looked at the screen on her phone and replayed a piece of film she had made the last time she'd been in here: it was a shot of Margaret typing in her password. Coco played it over and over, following each tap of the keys and writing down each letter and number as they were hit: Ru5tyN4iL. So that was it.

Sure enough, once she'd entered the password, the screen cleared to show her Margaret's desktop. Someone as organised as that was bound to have a clearly labelled and wonderfully logical filing system, Coco thought. She was going to have a quick look around and see what she could find . . .

Coco sat in Margaret's office for three hours, though it seemed barely half an hour. It was fascinating, scrolling through the engine that kept the Dangerfield machine rolling along so effortlessly. And in the folder named 'Foundation' she found absorbing and revealing information that occasionally made her gasp aloud, and shake her head. Once she even laughed at the sheer audacity of it. In the printer tray lay several documents that she had sent to print: each one had sent shivers of pleasure along Coco's spine as she'd stumbled across it. These would prove very useful indeed, she was sure of it.

But as she was about to exit the system, she noticed another file entitled 'Renegade'. She opened it and there saw another folder called 'DaisyD'. Daisy . . . the other daughter. The half-sister of Will and Sarah who'd died in that accident in Thailand. Why was all that information filed away under 'Renegade'? Coco was curious. She clicked on the Daisy file and saw all manner of interestingly titled documents.

Will had told her that Daddy's second wife Julia had died of alcoholism, leaving the youngest daughter to be brought up by her father alone. According to Will, Daisy had been pampered and spoiled, whisked around the world as her father's companion, treated like a grown woman when she was still in her teens. Renegade? Hardly.

Then the true story began to emerge in bits and pieces. Coco found documents at random, each one more intriguing and bizarre than the last: a letter to a DNA-testing clinic making enquiries about their services; the cancellation of a place at Brown University; an instruction to a bank to make a payment of one hundred thousand pounds into a new account. And then she found it: a document marked 'Contract'. She clicked it open and began to read, her mouth falling open in astonishment as she realised exactly what the contents meant.

Holy shit, she thought. *Were they really capable of this?*

But as she kept looking and the pieces of the jigsaw all fell into place, it seemed clear to her that they were . . .

81

In the aftermath of her triumph, saving the day for the Dangerfield Group, Daisy felt a little deflated and unsure of what she should do next. She was anxious about Christophe, sure that he wouldn't want to continue living in London without a purpose of his own for much longer. He was willing to help her, she knew that, but even she didn't know exactly what she wanted to achieve any more.

They lay together in bed in the Shoreditch flat in the moonlight that shone through a gap in the curtains, their warm skin pressed together as they quietly discussed the future.

'I don't think we should work together again,' Christophe said gently. 'We seemed to find each other a little distracting. Besides, it's never a good thing for one of us to be in a position to boss the other around.'

'So what will you do?' Daisy asked anxiously.

'I'm not sure. I know I want to stay with you, if you want me to,' he said, and kissed her shoulder. 'But, I must say, London's not for me. At least, not permanently. But if this is where you need to be, then this is where we'll stay for now. As long as I can escape to Wales fairly often.'

'Thank you, darling. I know what that means for you.' Daisy hugged him tightly. 'But I've been thinking,' she said, eventually. 'I'm not sure that I want to stay here any longer myself. I've done what I could for the Dangerfield Group. I've heard the words from Daddy that I wanted to hear so much – that I'm worth something. And do you know what? The minute he said them, I didn't care any more. I realised that he's just a lonely old man who's destroyed everything he loved and rejected everyone who ever loved him. I always thought I wanted to do the big reveal, shock him, show him what I'd done – but now I'm not so sure. Who cares what he thinks? My real revenge is to be happy and get on with my life.' She smiled at Christophe. 'I could stay here under my assumed identity, trying to climb up the ladder even further – or I could chuck it all in.'

She suddenly felt full of enthusiasm, as though a door she'd thought closed had just swung open, showing her a new and exciting path ahead. She sat up with the excitement of it. 'I'm sick of all this pretence. I want to be Daisy again. I'm going to leave Dangerfield and we'll go back to Wales together and do something else. I used to design shoes – maybe I'll start that again. Or I'll find some little hotel to run. Or . . . or . . . I don't know. All I know is, there's life outside this bloody company.'

'If you don't want to be Daphne Fraser any more,' Christophe said, taking her hand and kissing it lightly, 'you could always be Daisy Cellan-Jones.'

She blinked at him, astonished. When she managed to speak, her voice came out in a croak. 'What?'

Christophe laughed. 'It's sudden, I know, but . . . you seem to be in need of a new name, and you could always have mine, if you want it. In fact, I'd like you to.'

Daisy looked down at herself and laughed. 'I always hoped I'd be dressed when I got engaged.'

Christophe sat up as well and put his arms around her waist. 'You could never look more beautiful than you do now.' He put his cheek against hers. She felt his eyelashes move against her temple. 'If you agree, I couldn't be any happier. I love you, Daisy, I can't live without you.'

She felt tears start into her eyes. 'I love you too,' she whispered. 'Yes, let's go away and start a new life, Just the two of us.' She hugged him tightly, inhaling his delicious, comforting scent.

'There is one condition,' he said, pulling away and looking at her seriously.

'Mmm?'

'No more getting kidnapped in Siberia.'

'OK, I promise.'

'Then,' he said, 'I think we should seal the deal, don't you?'

He bent down and kissed her, pulling her tightly into his embrace. She kissed him back, full of delight. *Thank God for Christophe. Wherever he is, is home.*

82

Coco stood outside the old Victorian terrace house on the edge of the estate where she used to live. Ever since she'd found out from her mother that Gus had indeed been her father, she'd felt a compulsion to return and see him. At first, she'd thought that knowing the truth would be enough, but the sense that she had to find him had grown stronger until she'd been unable to resist it. Besides, she had discovered so much lately on other people's behalf, maybe it was time she did something for herself.

Taking a deep breath, her hands shaking, she went to the door and knocked loudly several times. She waited, almost unable to breathe from tension, desperate for the door to open, but no one answered. He wasn't in. The sense of disappointment was overwhelming. She'd been gearing herself up for the meeting all the way here, remembering how he had been in her childhood and preparing questions and what she would say to him. Now there was only a horrible sense of let down.

She went back along the path and examined the

house from the pavement. The blinds were down in every window and there was a general air of neglect about the place. Was it possible that he'd gone away somewhere? How would she find out? A cool breeze lifted her hair and she pulled her shaggy coat more tightly around her.

Just then a window in the neighbouring house opened and a woman put her head out. 'You looking for Gus?' she called.

'Yes.' Coco perked up. 'Do you know where he is?'

The woman stared at her for a moment and then said, 'You'd better come in, love.'

A few moments later, she was sitting in the warm, comfortable kitchen of the house next door. The woman had introduced herself as Mandy and insisted on making her a cup of tea, bustling about as she talked, asking Coco how she knew Gus.

'I used to live round here. Gus was a friend of my mum's.'

'Then you've seen how much worse the place has got lately. Properties falling to pieces. Problems with unemployed kids, gangs and drugs.' Mandy shook her head. 'Worse than ever.' She sighed. 'What can we do? I dunno.'

'So, Gus . . .' Coco prodded impatiently. 'Do you know where he is? When he'll be back?'

Mandy put a cup of tea on the table in front of her and sat down. Her expression was serious. 'There's no easy way to say this, love, so I'll come out with it. I'm afraid Gus has passed away.'

Coco gasped. 'What?'

''Fraid so. Sorry to be the bearer of bad tidings, love. It was only a month or so ago. The ambulance came and took him away, and he never came back. Heart attack, I think it was.' She gave Coco a sympathetic look. 'Like I say, sorry to give you the bad news.'

Coco felt winded with shock. No! This was too unfair. A month ago? What awful, terrible timing. She buried her face in her hands. 'Oh my God.'

'There, there.' Mandy put a hand out and rubbed her arm gently. 'You've missed the funeral too. What a shame.' She gazed at Coco sympathetically for a minute or two and then stood up, went to the dresser and picked up a bundle of envelopes. She brought them over and put them down in front of Coco. 'Any idea what I can do with this lot? There's been post coming for him and sometimes they give it to me when it won't fit into the box.'

Coco looked down at the cache of letters. Then she drew breath with a sharp gasp.

'What is it, dear?' Mandy eyed her curiously.

Coco snatched up a letter and held it out in a trembling hand. 'Is this really his name?'

'What . . . Gus Dangerfield? Of course it is. Didn't you know that?' Mandy looked worried for a second.

'I only knew him as Gus,' Coco said, trying to keep control of herself. 'I'm sorry . . . I don't know what you should do with it.'

But everything in her head was in a terrible whirl of confusion as she fought to work out what this meant.

'I have to see her!' Coco said desperately to the nurse at the ward desk.

The woman gazed back at her sympathetically but shook her head. 'It's just not possible. She's asleep for one thing, and heavily drugged to help with the pain. She won't be awake for hours. Come back for visiting tomorrow.'

'I have to ask her something,' Coco burst out, straining to see down the long dim ward.

'I'm sorry,' the nurse said with a note of finality in her voice. 'Your mother's in no condition to talk. She's very ill, Miss Hughes. Very ill indeed.'

Coco returned to the Belgravia house looking white and strained.

Daddy was waiting for her in the drawing room, obviously anxious for her return. He was letting her out of his sight less and less these days. That was going to make life difficult. She needed some time alone to think everything through. She had to make some enquiries as soon as possible, and Margaret was back this lunchtime. The option of researching further inside her office would not be there any longer.

'Coco, Coco!' Daddy called as she came into the hall.

'Yes, Daddy.' She took a deep breath, put a deter-mined smile on her face and marched into the drawing room. 'How are you?'

'Where have you been?' he demanded. 'I've been lonely, that's what.'

'Oh, you know,' she said carelessly. 'Shopping.'

'Shopping? Where are your bags?' He looked suspi-ciously at her empty hands.

'Silly Daddy! They're delivering, of course,' she responded easily. 'I couldn't carry all those bags.'

His face cleared. 'I suppose not.' Then his mouth turned down again and his expression darkened. 'Well, while you've been enjoying yourself, I've had some horrible news.' He picked up a heavy lead-crystal glass and took a sip of the whisky inside it. 'My wretch of a son, in cahoots with my thankless daughter, has issued another damn writ. Their claims are nonsense, of course, but I'll have to fight them as though there are some grounds to this rubbish.'

'Of course,' Coco said, trying to sound unconcerned.

'He's here in England now, and I'm going to have to see him at a meeting of both sides and our lawyers.' The old man seemed to slump momentarily, his shoulders giving way at the prospect. When he spoke again, his voice sounded reedy and plaintive. 'I shall need you there, Coco! I can't go on my own to face Will and Sarah.'

She had felt something like a physical blow to her stomach at the sound of Will's name. The idea of facing him over a table in a lawyer's office by his father's side made her feel sick, especially after what she had found out.

'You'll come, won't you?' Daddy said beseechingly. 'I know you made friends with him in the States, but he'll have to know about us sooner or later.'

The nausea in Coco's stomach swelled and rose, making her fear she might have to bolt for the cloakroom. She managed to speak despite her dry mouth. 'Of course I will.'

At once Daddy looked relieved, a smile on his thin lips. 'There's my good girl. I can face it if I'm with you. Now – come and give me a kiss.'

Coco went whiter than ever. 'I . . . I . . . I'll be back in a moment,' she said as brightly as she could, and then ran for the door.

She was violently ill into the downstairs lavatory.

83

Will sat at the desk of his suite in the Mandarin Oriental, staring at his computer screen. The big meeting was in two days' time, and he was determined to be prepared to the last detail. With any luck, the strain of it might cause the old man to keel over of a heart attack there and then and save them all a lot of trouble.

As long as he hasn't already married that . . . that . . . Will wanted to think of her as a bitch, a gold-digging whore, but he couldn't bring himself to form the thought. Why not? Coco didn't matter to him any longer, he knew that. She was just a piece of ass he'd once had. His inability to forget her was driving him mad.

He'd already decided that once the meeting was over, he'd see some old girlfriends, go clubbing, try to find someone to wipe the memory of her clean from his mind.

The telephone on his desk rang. He picked it up. 'Yes?'

'Reception here, sir. You have a visitor.'

'A visitor?' Will glanced at the time. It was after ten o'clock at night. 'Who is it?'

'The lady says she's your sister, sir.'

Will's mind raced. Sarah? Not likely, she was staying with a friend in Ealing and probably in bed by now. And anyway, wouldn't she call first? He picked up his phone to check it but there were no missed calls or texts. 'Could you put her on please?'

'I'm afraid I've already sent her up, sir. I hope that was all right.' The voice was apologetic.

'OK.' He put the phone into the cradle just as there was a knock on the door. He got up, walked over and looked through the spy hole. The person had turned their back so that all he could see was a pair of slim shoulders and a dark headscarf. *Who the fuck was this?* He considered not answering but his curiosity was too great. Who would pretend to be his sister? He opened the door. 'Yes?'

The woman turned around. A flash of dark-blonde hair emerged from below the headscarf; a pair of outsized dark glasses covered most of the face, but he knew the shape of those lips and the determined chin and that slender neck. As he realised who it was, she lifted one hand to her face and removed her sunglasses.

'Hello, Will,' said Coco quietly, her expression a strange mixture of bravado and vulnerability.

He couldn't speak for a moment. It frightened him to realise that the sight of her was still intensely pleasurable, and that made him angry. That was good. He could build on anger. 'What the hell are you doing here?' he said roughly.

'I needed to see you.'

'Well, I don't need to see you.' He stepped back as

if to shut the door and she put out her hand to stop him.

'Please, Will – give me a moment. One moment, that's all I ask.'

'Why should I?'

Her eyes . . . He'd forgotten their luscious greeny-blue quality, like a lake he'd once seen in Brazil. 'Just one moment. Don't you think you owe me that?'

'What do I owe you?' he snapped. 'What have I had from you but lies and betrayal?'

Coco looked down the corridor. 'We shouldn't talk like this here. Can I come in?'

He knew he ought to curse her and slam the door in her face, but he couldn't. Every nerve was alive to her nearness. He could feel traitorous lust stirring in his belly and groin, and hated himself for it. But he couldn't bring himself to shut her out. 'All right,' he said at last. 'One minute.'

The next moment she was with him in the suite, taking off the head scarf and shaking out her hair. Christ, she was beautiful. In that instant, the memory of all the pleasure they had given each other came flooding back and he had to fight the urge to take her in his arms and kiss her. *No. Remember who she's with now*, he told himself, and that helped a little.

'So?' he demanded.

'I know what you think of me,' said Coco, gazing at him intently. 'You think I'm a tramp, selling myself for money. But you don't know the misery of living with nothing and having nothing and thinking you are nothing. I know that in your world having sex for money is wrong, but in mine it's about survival. When you don't have a roof over your head, you'll do what

636

it takes to get shelter.' Coco took a deep breath, shuddering a little as she did, as though all this was costing her a great effort. 'I slept with men for money. I'm not proud of it, but I'm not ashamed either. I had to do it . . . or thought I did. But I didn't have to sleep with you. I did it because I fell in love with you, and I think you fell in love with me. For a while, we really loved each other, didn't we?' Her eyes glistened suddenly with unshed tears.

'I told you that didn't matter. I didn't care what your past was. When Xander let it slip, did I let it affect the way I felt about you?' Will asked roughly.

'No,' she whispered.

'When you told me that you'd made up those stories about your family, that you were really brought up on a council estate, did I change towards you?'

She shook her head.

'But all along you were deceiving me,' he said, in a voice that was full of pain. 'You were spying for my father. All that time. It killed me when I found that out.'

'I know. But you never gave me the chance to explain.' Coco turned away suddenly, hiding her face from him.

A desire to hurt her flashed through him, and anger ignited. 'And now you're fucking my father! How can it be any worse than that?' Will's voice was raw with fury. 'How could you do that to me, Coco? Is this your ultimate, filthy revenge on me? To let him touch you like I used to?' He couldn't stop his voice from cracking on the last few words and fought to keep control.

She turned back to face him. Her eyes burned with

intensity, their green colour flashing. 'Let me tell you something.' She walked straight up to him, so close they were almost touching, and stared up into his face, her own tilted to his so he could look directly at her almost heartbreaking beauty. 'He's never touched me. He's never kissed my lips or laid a hand on me.'

'Don't lie to me!' he spat. 'You're engaged!' He gestured to the yellow diamond on her finger.

'This? Yes, he wants to marry me. I won't marry him. But even if I did, he would never, ever touch me that way. And he hasn't. Not once. Ever.' Her mouth trembled suddenly. He had to resist the impulse to bend down and kiss it. It would be so easy, and the nearness of her was unbearably tantalising. Will believed her when she said his father had never touched her, and he wanted to touch her now himself, so badly that it was like a physical force propelling him. He had to exert all his strength to stop himself.

'Why are you here?' he whispered, staring at her. 'Just to tell me this?'

'I came to tell you that I never stopped loving you,' said Coco in a low voice. 'Yes, your father sent me to find out what I could about you – I had no idea that I was going to fall in love with you. As soon as I felt something for you, I told them nothing. I never wanted you to know because I was ashamed of it and had no idea how to explain. Then, after we finished, I came back here. And I gave them all the information they could possibly want, except –' her eyes flashed again ' – I made it all up. Nothing I told them was true. They think they know everything, and they know nothing.'

He gazed at her, hardly able to think. 'Do you really

think I'll believe that? Or that it makes everything all right?'

'It doesn't matter whether you believe it or not. It's true.' Coco smiled sadly and shrugged. 'And it makes no odds now anyway, we could never be together in any case. But I wanted to make amends and show you that my love for you was real.' She pulled a sheaf of papers from her pocket. 'These are for you.' She pushed them at him.

'What are they?' Will eyed the bundle suspiciously.

'Take it. You'll find out when I've left.'

He reached out and grasped the papers.

'Goodbye, Will. We'll see each other at the meeting but we'll never meet like this again.'

He found he couldn't speak, could only watch as she picked up her scarf and glasses and went to the door. Without a backward glance, Coco was gone.

Then he looked down and began to read what she had given him.

Downstairs, Coco ran out of the hotel lobby and on to the side street where a car and driver were waiting for her. She jumped into the back.

'Take me home,' she said to the driver, then sat back as he pulled out into the London traffic. She had only hours left to bring everything together.

84

Daisy sat at her desk, replying to emails and tying up loose ends. In a few minutes she had an appointment with Karen O'Malley, and intended to hand in her resignation. She was sure that Karen would do her best to persuade her to stay, but there was no way Daisy's mind was going to be changed. Now she had decided on her escape route, she couldn't wait to be free.

I feel as though I've been in the grip of a kind of madness, she thought in wonderment, as she sent off some instructions to the manager of a Craven hotel. *All this time I've been obsessed with my struggle with Daddy. And now it's just vanished in a puff of smoke. I don't care any more.*

More than anything, she longed to be back at Nant-Y-Pren with Christophe, inhaling the fresh clean air and walking for miles. She needed a holiday.

Maxine, her secretary, knocked at the door and put her head round, looking anxious. 'Er, Miss Fraser . . .'

Daisy looked up from her computer screen. 'Yes?'

'There's someone here to see you.'

'Who?'

'Er . . .' Maxine looked confused.

'Me.' The voice rang out clear and strong, and the next moment a woman had appeared in her office doorway. She was wearing a bottle-green silk cashmere dress, belted with a skinny tan leather belt, and high heels. Around her neck was a leopard-print scarf. Her glossy hair was pulled back into a neat ponytail the same colour as her caramel leather handbag, and a giant yellow diamond flashed on her finger. It was the girl Daddy was going to marry.

Daisy got to her feet, surprised. 'What can I do for you?' she asked, flushing.

'I need to talk to you privately.' The girl threw a look at Maxine, who quickly retreated, pulling the door shut behind her.

Daisy gestured to the chair in front of her desk, and sat down as calmly as she could. 'This is very surprising, Miss . . . er . . .'

'You can call me Coco.' The other woman appraised her with cool greeny-blue eyes. 'And what shall I call you?'

'I suppose you can call me Daphne.'

'Really? Or should I call you . . . Daisy?'

Daisy's eyes widened and she gasped. After a second, she laughed lightly. 'I'm sorry, I don't understand.'

Coco leaned forward, her expression serious. 'I think you do. I know this is a shock, but there isn't much time and we have to work quickly.' She frowned. 'Do you know who I am?'

'I believe you're my boss's fiancée,' Daisy replied coolly. She picked up a pen and fiddled with it. 'I can't think what business you have with me.'

641

Coco nodded. 'All right. There's a lot to tell you, but I know you won't listen to me until I explain that I know who you are, and why you're here.'

Daisy raised her eyebrows, her mind racing. 'Oh, really? Do tell me. I can't think what you're talking about.'

'Sure, sure.' Coco made a dismissive gesture, as though to wave away Daisy's lack of comprehension. 'The first thing I have to say is that you can trust me. I'm not on your father's side, I'm on yours. I know that's hard to believe, but please – try. Just for a while, until you've heard what I've got to say.'

Daisy stared at her, puzzled but intensely curious to hear what this woman had to say next.

'Right.' Coco took a breath. 'I know that you're Daisy Dangerfield. Don't worry –' she held up a hand '– your father has no idea you're here, or that Daphne is really Daisy. I must say, you've got yourself a good little disguise there. I could hardly believe it when I realised that you were the same girl as the one in the old pictures.'

Daisy could feel herself paling. 'But . . . but . . .'

'I know that they chucked you out and made you sign a phoney contract. I also know they faked your death, using the body of some poor unknown kid they bribed a Thai mortuary attendant to let them have. But what they don't know is that you're actually here, working for them.' Coco burst out laughing, throwing back her head. 'It really is priceless. You've done so fantastically well. I totally salute you.' She jokingly raised her hand to her temple.

Daisy laughed uneasily, still mystified by the way all this was coming to light.

'I don't blame you for being a bit bamboozled,' Coco said generously.

'Let's say you're right,' Daisy said at last. 'How did you find all this out?'

'I'll explain in due course. Let's just say I discovered that at some point you enrolled in a college to study for a diploma, and that when you started out you were Daisy Dangerfield but when you'd finished you'd become Daphne Fraser. When I went looking for this Daphne person, I had no idea where the trail would lead me. But, I can tell you, I was completely gobsmacked when it turned out you were right here, in the dragon's lair. And quite the golden girl too!' Coco laughed again. 'All credit to you.'

Daisy regarded her as calmly as she could despite the whirlwind in her mind as she tried to process all of this and think through the ramifications. 'That's all very well,' she said, 'but what exactly do you want from me? If you intend to expose me to Mr Dangerfield, you may as well not bother. I'm about to leave this organisation and I don't care if I never see it, or him, again.'

'You hate him, don't you?' Coco said quietly. 'Well, you're not the only one. Your brother and sister are about to sue your dad. He's been stealing from the family trusts to fund all sorts of little activities on the side. And I'm working on their behalf, you see.' She waved again, seeing Daisy's puzzled expression. 'Oh, it's all pretty tangled, no denying that. I'll tell you everything, but first you have to promise that you'll come in on our side?'

Daisy thought for a moment, then stood up and walked over to her office window. After a while she turned back to face Coco, who was watching her from

643

her seat by the desk. 'Of course I have issues with that man after what he's done to me. But, you see, I'm not a Dangerfield. Their problems aren't mine any more. I wish Will and Sarah well, but they're not my siblings and haven't been for years. And Daddy isn't my father.'

Coco stared at her, amusement curling her lips ever so slightly. 'Oh,' she said, 'I wouldn't be too sure about that, if I were you.'

85

Hanratty had prepared the best boardroom for the meeting of his most important clients. The Dangerfield children were likely to bring hundreds of thousands, if not millions, of pounds in fees to his firm.

Unless they manage to sort everything out today, of course, and we all go home happy bunnies.

But that wasn't likely. And while that might be the best outcome for the family, he couldn't pretend that a big court case wasn't far preferable to him, bringing with it all those juicy fat fees.

They would be sitting at a round table, Mr Dangerfield and his lawyers together with the Dangerfield children and the in-house solicitors. It promised to be a fiery meeting.

The Dangerfield siblings arrived first, strikingly similar with their auburn hair and coppery eyes. Will looked determined and in a surprisingly good temper. Hanratty had great respect for him and all that he had achieved; and, of course, the young man couldn't see how much he resembled the father he seemed to loathe so much. They shared many of the same traits: stubbornness and pride being two of the most obvious.

'Hey, Nev,' Will had said with a smile when he arrived. 'I've got a humdinger of a surprise for you. But, you know what? I think I'm going to keep it to myself for now.'

Despite Hanratty's protest that it was rarely a good idea for a client to keep things to himself, Will wouldn't budge. 'You'll be pleased,' was all that he would say.

The Dangerfields were seated at the table talking quietly together when a call came to say that the other party had arrived. This was it. Action stations.

A few minutes later the door opened and in came the lawyers for the other side: Mankiewicz and Forbes, followed by old man Dangerfield – there was no mistaking that well-known face with its heavy jowls and pouches of skin under the eyes, even if he was looking surprisingly thin. He wore a loud sports jacket and one of his trademark red waistcoats, and the dyed hair couldn't hide the fact that age had him well in its grip. Behind him came a slim young woman with glossy hair and very expensive clothes. Hanratty laughed to himself. These rich old men usually had a dolly like this somewhere in the background – the fools never asked themselves what young lovelies like this saw in wrecks like them. Behind the totty came another woman, this one middle-aged with severely neat hair and clothes, her blank face giving away none of the importance of her role. She was the old fellow's eyes and ears, there was no doubt of that. There was usually someone like this, the back-up, the one who really kept the show on the road.

Hanratty stepped forward to greet everyone but the Dangerfield children did not move. They barely looked at their father. Will's eyes went at once to the beauty – no surprise there, he was probably a red-blooded male and who could help checking out the long legs and the surprisingly large rack? Sarah kept her eyes downcast as though she was afraid to look at her father even after all this time.

Mr Dangerfield paused at the table and said, 'Hello, Will. Hello, Sarah,' in an almost unnaturally loud way. The daughter looked up and muttered something, while Will said, 'Dad' in a closed-off, formal way.

This is going to be fun, Hanratty thought as he asked the other party to sit down and pulled up his own chair to the table. When tea and coffee had been distributed, he cleared his throat.

'Well, I suggest we get started. We'll begin by summarising our position as it stands.' He looked down at his notes and began. The story was familiar to them all: the trusts that Josef Dangerfield had put in place for his children and grandchildren had been mismanaged by their main trustee, Mr Dangerfield himself; he had plundered the money to spend on his own extravagances and sold off assets specifically assigned to remain in trust. The children demanded their father answer these claims and planned to require his resignation from the board of trustees and the appointment of new ones who would audit the trusts. Any missing funds should be repaid by the sale of Mr Dangerfield's assets.

'All very simple and straightforward,' Hanratty finished. 'And our purpose today is to see if these matters can be resolved without going to court.'

Dangerfield was red in the face, his leathery tanned cheeks a strange scarlet and orange hue. 'I shall never resign!' he spluttered. 'My own father made me the main trustee! These claims are outrageous and unfounded.'

Manckiewicz, his solicitor, put up a hand to calm his client and then said in a measured voice, 'My client disputes these claims. He can prove that any sales of assets were made with the prior agreement of his late father. No money has been removed from the family trusts without the prior agreement of all trustees—'

'Puppets,' put in Will scornfully.

'—and Mr Dangerfield intends to remain in his position, one of trust, which he has carried out faithfully despite the lack of any goodwill or affection shown by his children. There is absolutely no need for my client to dispose of any of his own assets.'

Hanratty said, 'It appears there is no meeting halfway, if your client refutes all claims outright and refuses to alter his position. We had hoped he might agree to resign from the trusts, even if temporarily, in order for a proper audit to be carried out.'

'No!' said Mr Dangerfield at once.

'Perhaps . . .' Will's voice broke into the room, low and authoritative. 'Perhaps your client might change his mind about a few of these matters when he learns the evidence we already have. You see, I have here some very interesting pieces of paper. This one, for example, is a memo from my father's personal assistant –' he looked over at Margaret '– regarding the fate of the Gainsborough. In it she states that it will be possible to alter the records to make it look as though the sale of that painting took place at the behest of my grandfather, thus covering up the fact that ownership has

648

in fact been transferred to the Dangerfield Foundation . . . a completely unauthorised action.' Will pulled the relevant document from his folder and pushed into the middle of the table. 'I have copies, of course.'

Margaret had gone pale. 'How did you get that?' she hissed, her eyes flashing. Then she recovered herself. 'A forgery!' she declared. 'Anyone could write this. Where's my signature?'

'It had no signature, of course,' Will said pleasantly, 'but I believe any cursory investigation of your computer system and back-up files will reveal it, along with a great many other incriminating documents.'

His father had gone an even darker crimson, but Will continued talking.

'I have some other very interesting documents here that prove my father's financial involvement with this mysterious Foundation, based in Switzerland. It seems that he's been funding it to the tune of several hundred thousand pounds . . . a month. And a great deal of that money has been siphoned out of the family trusts, of which, incidentally, Miss Anderson here has recently suggested she become a trustee.' He raised his eyebrows. 'I'm not sure exactly how that would sit with the fact that she is also a co-owner of the Dangerfield Foundation along with a Professor Offenal, who also seems to have profited very nicely from the organisation.'

Margaret's mouth dropped open and she stared at Will in abject horror. Daddy's solicitors turned to murmur rapidly to each other, worried expressions on their faces, while Daddy himself looked astonished. He turned towards Margaret. 'Co-owner?' he said in disbelief.

She looked over at him pleadingly. 'Lies, sir, lies!

Who do you trust – these shameful excuses for children who've treated you so badly over the years, or me – your faithful helper for all this long time? Everything I've done, I've done to help you.'

Daddy stared back at her, clearly confused.

'Don't be too sure about that,' Will interjected. 'You might want to have those wonder serums analysed by a competent chemist. I wouldn't be surprised to find they were basic compounds, nothing special at all. And as for the Foundation's claims to be discovering the secrets of eternal youth – eternally full bank accounts might be more like it.'

'Shut up, damn you!' snarled Margaret, her eyes blazing. 'And where did you get all these lies, huh? All this make-believe?'

Suddenly the beautiful girl at Mr Dangerfield's side, who'd been watching the goings-on with a neutral expression on her face, stood up. 'I think I may be able to answer that,' she said in a calm voice. 'He learned it all from me.' She turned to Margaret. 'I gained access to your files, and I gave the information they contained to Will. That's how he knows. There's no use pretending, it's all there.'

Daddy groaned in a broken-sounding voice, 'Coco, no! Not this! What have you done?' while Margaret stared at her furiously, ashen-faced.

The lawyers swapped glances, clearly bemused by this turn of events.

Coco took a deep breath. She clenched her fists hard, so that her knuckles turned white. 'I also learned some other things,' she said, in a voice that shook with emotion. 'I learned that Daddy's other daughter, Daisy, did not die in a scuba accident but was instead

650

thrown out of her own home when he learned from a stolen letter that he was not her biological father. She was forced to change her identity and promise never to contact any member of the Dangerfield family again. She did that. And, to cover his own tracks, Daddy then arranged for her death to be faked.'

He groaned again. Margaret's eyes now showed plain fear as her mouth gaped open.

Will and Sarah exchanged astonished glances. 'What the hell are you talking about?' rapped out Will.

Coco walked towards the door of the office. 'I didn't say earlier because I wasn't sure I would be able to find her. But I did. And here she is now.'

She swung the door open with a flourish.

Daisy had been waiting outside, still disguised with her glasses and dark hair, ready to play her part. As Coco opened the door she stepped in, her breath shallow in her chest and butterflies fluttering in her stomach, to face the round table of astonished-looking people.

Daddy, who had been looking quite sick, suddenly cried triumphantly, 'That's not Daisy! That's a woman from my office – Daphne Fraser. What the hell are you doing here, Fraser? What stupid game is this?'

Daisy looked at him full on. From the corner of her eye she could see Margaret, white-faced and frightened, already suspecting. Will and Sarah stared, wide-eyed and amazed, still not understanding.

This is it, then, she thought. *I'm actually going to do this.* She lifted her hand and took off the heavy-framed glasses. There were no lenses in her eyes today. Then she put her hand to the crown of her head and lifted off the blunt-cut dark wig that looked like her usual hair. Underneath, she'd had her own hair dyed back to its natural colour. As the wig came away, she looked her father straight in the eye and said, 'Hello, Daddy.'

He was staring at her as though seeing a ghost. Sweat had broken out all over his face, and he looked first appalled, then frightened, then angry. 'Wh-wh-what?' he spluttered. 'What the hell is this?'

'I'm back,' she said simply, with a small smile. 'In fact, I never went away. You thought you'd got rid of me for ever, but I'm afraid you were wrong. With a new name, I started work in one of Dangerfield's least important, least noticed hotels. I learned everything I needed to know – what I hadn't already learned at your knee – and I worked very hard. I got all the way to the top. You even welcomed me into your office and told me I was just the kind of person you wanted in your organisation.' She smiled again. 'I can't tell you how sweet that moment was. So, yes, I'm Daphne Fraser. And I'm also Daisy, the daughter you spurned, and then – almost literally – killed.'

All eyes turned back to Dangerfield, his lawyers looking almost as horrified as he did. The old man appeared to be on the brink of passing out, then suddenly he gathered his strength and leaned across the table towards his once-adored daughter, eyes full of hatred and his mouth twisted into a terrible snarl. 'How dare you?' he growled in a voice of fury. 'I paid you! I paid you to go away and never come back. How dare you walk back in here like this?'

'You threw me out and offered me money to leave your life for ever,' Daisy replied calmly, but there was a hint of underlying emotion in her voice. 'I was eighteen. I had no mother. Of course I took what you gave me. But you know what? You can have it back. All of it. I spent barely any of it, and I can easily make up the shortfall.'

He ignored that and sneered, 'You think you're working in my company tomorrow? You can forget that! You're sacked. And you!' He turned to Margaret. 'How the hell could you let this happen, you clumsy bitch? How did you let her walk back in like this? You were supposed to have her extinguished so thoroughly she could never turn up again!'

There was a shocked silence. Daddy's lawyers, who'd been trying to quieten their client, now froze with horror at what he'd just said. Will and Sarah stared at Daisy, stunned and disbelieving, even though they now recognised her. It was almost too much to take in.

'I think you might want to stop there,' Coco said, gaining the room's attention at once. 'You see, you trusted the DNA laboratory, didn't you? And they were right. The sample they received showed absolutely that the person tested was unrelated to you. But it wasn't Daisy's DNA they received.' Coco turned towards Margaret. 'It was yours, wasn't it? That's why the result came back such a resounding negative.' She shook her head. 'You really shouldn't keep such excellent notes.'

Daddy turned to Margaret, his mouth dropping open. She appeared to try to speak for a moment, stuttered and then gave up. She threw Coco a filthy look and muttered, 'It didn't make any difference. That bitch her mother confessed the child wasn't his in her letter.' She turned back to Daddy, her expression pleading. 'It was only to set your mind at rest, sir, to make you sure of what was certainly the case!'

'Or was it to get your own hands on as much of the Dangerfield fortune as you could? You've been fooling an old man into thinking those bog-standard vitamin injections you're giving him are going to keep him young for ever, while siphoning off lots of lovely cash for your foundation.' Coco smiled, looking deceptively pleasant. 'I read Daisy's mother's letter – it's in your files. She only said that Daddy might not be Daisy's father, not that he definitely wasn't. Whether you should have intercepted and opened it at all is a matter for the police to determine.'

Daisy smiled at her father. 'So you see, Daddy, I might be your daughter after all.'

He stared at her, unable to take this in. Instead, his eyes went to Coco. 'Why are you doing this to me?' he whispered, white about the lips. 'I wanted to marry you.'

She turned to look at him. 'We both know that would not have happened. There has never been anything of that nature between us. And it's over now. You might as well know that I'm prepared to pass on everything I know about you and your methods.'

'Traitor!' he hissed, slumping back in his chair. 'Margaret, help me!'

'Sir, for once, I'm afraid there's nothing I can do,' she replied coldly. 'After all, despite my years of service and devotion, I'm nothing more to you than a clumsy bitch.'

'You've had your reward already!' howled Daddy. 'And now, if what they say is true, you'll be sued to Kingdom Come!' His eyes filled with tears. 'You're all

654

betraying me,' he whimpered. 'You're a bunch of thankless traitors, and you can all go to hell!' He slapped the table like a petulant child.

Will stood up. 'Don't worry, Dad. When you've resigned as trustee and from the Dangerfield Group, and repaid the money you owe, there'll be enough left for a small house and no doubt you'll get yourself a new companion. But right now, I think you need to admit that your little game is well and truly over. I shouldn't think even your lawyers want much to do with you.'

Coco moved to the door, standing straight and digni-fied. She turned to address the Dangerfield children. 'I think my part in all this is finished. I'm leaving now.' She looked straight into Will's coppery eyes and smiled. 'I hope it all works out for you. Goodbye.'

As she walked away down the corridor, in a daze from all that had just happened, she heard footsteps behind her.

'Coco!' It was Will.

She turned and looked at him.

He stood there gazing at her, tall and handsome, looking unusually formal in his dark suit but still devas-tatingly attractive. 'Thanks. Thanks for everything.'

'I wanted you to know that I was on your side. I always was and I always will be.' He made as if to take a step closer but she stopped him with an upraised hand. 'But things have changed, Will. We can't be together. Ever. That's just how it is.'

Then she turned and walked away, without looking back.

86

Christophe was hardly able to take it all in when Daisy rushed to meet him. He'd been waiting in the hotel opposite the lawyers' office, nervously drinking coffee and pacing about the lounge.

'Wait,' he said, laughing at her excitement and holding her hands, 'I don't understand! So you really are a Dangerfield after all?'

'I don't know,' she cried, elated. 'I might be. We'll need to do new tests! Imagine, I might have been Daddy's daughter all along!'

Christophe was suddenly solemn. 'I don't know how he'd live with that. No one could.'

Daisy's eyes danced with joy. 'Will and Sarah are joining us in a moment. We've got so much to talk about.' She threw herself into his arms. 'It's over, Christophe! At last, it's all out in the open, and I've got some of my family back. I'm so happy! I can't believe it's real.'

Things had moved quickly after Coco had made her dramatic exit. Daddy and Margaret had left, Daddy deflated like a balloon, suddenly looking old and confused, while Margaret seemed intent only on getting away as quickly as possible. Will had watched her go intently. 'She's planning her escape,' he muttered. 'We'll need to keep an eye on her.'

But the next moment Sarah had rushed over and taken Daisy in her arms, tears streaming down her face. 'Oh my God, you're alive! I can't believe it!'

Daisy nodded, laughing. 'Who was it who said "reports of my death have been greatly exaggerated"? I'm alive, as you can see.' She hugged Sarah back, her eyes welling up. She saw Will gazing at her, contradictory emotions flitting across his face: amazement, bewilderment, shock – and then a kind of happiness that curled the edges of his mouth upwards.

'Daisy, I'm happier than I can say to see you again. But . . . did he really do those awful things to you?' He shook his head and she could see the questions crowding in on him.

'I'll tell you everything,' she said, 'but first . . . can I hug you too?'

'Oh my God – yes!' he cried, and threw his arms around her so that all three siblings were embracing at once.

Back at the hotel, Daisy, Christophe, Will and Sarah sat around a table, a bottle of champagne open in front of them. There was a lot to tell, myriad questions to answer. The two Dangerfields listened intently, eyes round with horror and sympathy as Daisy's story unfolded, interjecting questions when something occurred to them. When the facts were finally laid out and they understood everything, they were both stunned.

'I can't believe he was capable of it,' Sarah said,

shaking her head, tears in her eyes. 'How could anyone do such a thing?'

'You know how he felt – about the Dangerfield bloodline, the inheritance we supposedly had from Grandpa through him.' Daisy gazed into the faces of her brother and sister. *Maybe not my brother and sister at all. But I can't help thinking of them that way. And who knows what the new DNA tests will reveal?* 'When he found out I wasn't his daughter, he must have been heartbroken and humiliated – and he took all that out on me.'

'But to cut you off like that! To throw you out with nothing!' Will's face flushed with anger. 'I knew he was a monster. This proves it. And to let the world believe you'd *died* – to let *us* believe it! He's not human, he's really not.'

'He's very flawed,' Daisy agreed. 'But he's his own worst enemy. Look where his pride has led him – he's lonely, miserable and with no family at all. And his entire defence has gone up in smoke.'

'Who was that girl Coco and why did she help you?' Sarah asked. 'She was Dad's fiancée, wasn't she?'

Will nodded, looking strangely sad. 'I don't think she was exactly what she seemed. You see . . . a while ago, she and I were involved, but we fell out badly because I thought she was on Dad's side. And I think she's done all this to help me.'

There was a pause while the two girls took this in.

'She's got balls,' Daisy said frankly. 'You should have seen her come into my office and tell me everything she knew. It was amazing.' She smiled at her brother. 'I can see why you liked her.'

'I liked her very much . . . until I found out she'd been recruited as a spy by Dad and Margaret.'

Sarah smiled. 'She's obviously made up for that. How do you feel about her now?'

He bit his lip and said, 'I don't know, but it doesn't make any difference. She's out of our lives. Dad's too. It's all over for him.'

'He'll have to climb down now, anyone can see that,' Daisy said. 'And even though I might not be your sister, I want to help if I can.'

'Don't be silly,' Sarah said warmly, reaching out a hand to her. 'You're family. It's ridiculous to pretend you're not.'

'Sarah's right,' Will said emphatically, turning to face her. 'You're our little sister. And what Dad did to you only makes that stronger.'

'I'm on your side completely,' Daisy said. 'Whenever you need me, I'll be there.' She smiled at the other two.

'You've been amazingly brave,' said Sarah. 'I know I speak for Will when I say that we're both sorry for treating you badly when we were all growing up. We felt terrible when we thought you were dead, and I'm so happy we have the chance to make up and be a family again.'

'That goes for me too.' Will leaned over and put an arm around Daisy. 'I'm sorry.'

She felt an almost painful welling of emotion in her chest. She wasn't alone any more. All the years of struggle and loneliness were over. She had Christophe and she had a family. 'Thank you,' she said in a choked voice. Christophe put a comforting hand on hers.

Sarah spoke up suddenly. 'You know, I've just thought of something. I know where we can go for some answers.'

87

Mum always had terrible timing, Coco thought to herself, although in some ways a funeral suited her mood exactly. Her mum's friend Rachel had sent a message that Michelle's struggles were finally over, and the cremation was the following day.

The service was short and perfunctory. The congregation was tiny – just five of them gathered in the crematorium chapel, with the vicar in his white cassock and dog collar. They sang a hymn, their six voices reedy in the large space, listened to the vicar speak a few words about Michelle and say a few prayers. He'd asked Coco if she'd like to speak but she'd said no. She had no idea what she might say and there was certainly nothing about her relationship with her mother that she wanted to share with anyone else. When the brief service was over, the coffin moved on its conveyor belt through the curtains and that was that. As they left the chapel, an official stepped forward to tell Coco when she could collect the ashes. The other mourners – neighbours of Michelle, an old friend and an ex-lover – came up to shake Coco's hand and offer commiserations. They were going down the pub. Would she like to join them?

Why not? she thought. *I suppose we can raise a glass to Mum. It'll be the last time anyone ever does, I should think.*

They went to a pub close to the estate and sat with pints around a smeared table, talking about Michelle. Coco didn't recognise much about the fun-loving, generous friend they all described, but that was the way of death, she supposed. It erased the bad and turned the good into golden virtue. It was the last tribute of the living, to remember only the good times.

She tried to join in, remembering what was good about her mother and that, despite everything, Michelle had loved her. *I'm glad we had those last words together. I'm glad I was able to tell her I loved her too. I hope she died happier and more peaceful because of that.*

A smiling Coco listened to the others talking. Her mum's friend Rachel, looking almost as ravaged as Michelle had, kept popping out to smoke Benson & Hedges. Coco went to join her, though she hardly smoked now. But if there was ever a day when she needed a fag, then the day of her mother's funeral was it.

As the two women stood in the late afternoon sun, puffing away on their cigarettes, Coco said suddenly, 'Rachel, did my mum ever talk to you about my dad?'

The woman looked a little shifty. 'What do ya mean, love?'

Coco pressed on, suddenly eager to see if she knew anything. 'Mum told me that my dad was Gus, that artist type, the one who lived near the estate.'

Rachel looked surprised. 'What, Gus Dangerfield?'

Coco nodded. The Dangerfield connection had been driving her mad. She hadn't been able to find out anything about who Gus Dangerfield was, and in the drama of the last few days, hadn't had much time to search. All she knew was that she could be Will's close relative, and that meant nothing could ever happen between them.

Rachel took a long drag of her cigarette. 'She told you Gus Dangerfield was your dad?' She shot Coco a sympathetic look. 'I don't know what story she was spinning you, dear, but you weren't his kid.'

'What?' She stared at Rachel in shock.

Rachel shook her head. 'Nah. You were on the way before she even met Gus. It wasn't long after, she told me. She was pregnant when Gus took her in one day off the streets and gave her a hot meal. He was her friend after that, and stuck by her all those years, helping out when he could. But she never knew who your dad was. A poor junkie like she was, no doubt. Or else she turned a few tricks and got up the duff.' Rachel smiled at her. 'Sounds awful, but she got you out of it, and she loved you even when she couldn't show it.'

Coco felt as though she'd been winded. Not Gus? She was bewildered. So her mum had just told her that to keep her happy, to give her a father . . . any father.

'I can't believe it,' she said in a small voice. But then an image that had been troubling her floated into her mind: it was Gus's face with those twinkling dark brown eyes. 'You've got his eyes' Michelle had said. 'There's no mistaking that.' But her own were greeny blue. Nothing like Gus's at all. She knew in that instant that Rachel was right.

Rachel put out a comforting hand. 'I hope I haven't upset you, but I always say the truth as I see it. You shouldn't go around believing old Gus was your dad, when he wasn't.'

Coco took a deep breath. 'Thanks, Rachel,' she said at last. 'You're right. I'd rather know the truth.'

'That's the spirit. Now let's go back inside and finish our drinks.'

88

The drawing room was cosy rather than elegant, scattered with a large collection of china ornaments on the many side tables. The sofas were perfectly matched and the cushions were of the same fabric as the curtains at the windows.

Daisy sat on the edge of her seat, facing a woman who was plain but neatly turned out, her grey hair showing the last streaks of what had once been a rich coppery red. She had come all this way to a pleasant house in the heart of a pretty Cumbrian village, hoping to find the missing pieces to the puzzle. Will and Sarah had diplomatically left them to it.

'So you are Daisy,' the woman said in a kind voice. 'I always wondered what you were like, and now I can certainly see your mother in you.'

'Thank you for seeing me, Mrs Dangerfield,' Daisy said humbly.

'Please, call me Elizabeth.' The hazel-green eyes so like Will's and Sarah's were warm. 'The children told me you were coming, of course. And I know why you're here. You're looking for answers.'

Daisy nodded. It was a strange experience to be here with her father's first wife, the one he had cast aside for Daisy's mother. 'I'm so grateful you agreed to see me. So many women might not have, after what happened.'

'Oh!' Elizabeth Dangerfield took a sip from her china teacup. 'Don't worry about that. I can safely say that life was much more pleasant once my marriage finished. My ex-husband was not an easy man, as I'm sure you know. I wanted to warn your poor mother, but there was no way I could.' She smiled her serene smile. 'She never would have believed me. I wanted to tell her that there was an overpowering reason why my husband found her so appealing – and that was because his brother was in love with her.'

Daisy gasped. 'His brother?'

'Yes. Gustavus. He was lovable and crazy, not at all like my ex-husband. He had no interest in business, wanting only to pursue his bohemian life, and his art and poetry. He liked to live in rundown areas and mix with the local people, although of course he always had a few friends of his own class too. Dear Gus. We all loved him. Except my ex-husband, of course.' Elizabeth Dangerfield smiled again, as though to calm the emotion she could see on Daisy's face. 'You see, Gus was illegitimate and it drove your father wild. He was the legitimate son and Gus was only his half-brother, and yet his father, old Josef, seemed intent on giving Gus as much as a son born in wedlock might get.' Elizabeth shook her head. 'It was the beginning of the trouble, all the me-me-me selfishness that my ex-husband has let destroy his life, and once he had the power, he cut Gustavus out, buying the poor foolish chap's agreement with a big sum in return for his surrendering his

665

interest in the family trusts. Then he simply expunged him from history as much as he could.'

'So how did Gus meet my mother?' Daisy asked breathlessly.

'Oh, young Julia worked as a publishing secretary and Gus published a small book of his poems. That was how they met. He was in love with her long before my ex-husband decided to have her for himself. I'm sure it was partly because Gus loved her that he decided to take her – as well as Julia's excellent pedigree, of course.' Elizabeth shook her head. 'Poor Julia. I don't think she realised what she was giving up until it was too late. From the warmth and laughter of Gus, to a life of being controlled and bullied. No wonder she went back to Gus when she could.'

'You knew?' Daisy asked, astonished.

The older woman nodded. 'I was friends with Gus for some years, though we lost touch a long time ago. He told me about Julia. I said nothing. Why cause trouble? It could only end badly for Julia and for Gus – it was the same for anyone who crossed your father. I knew he thought he had made Julia pregnant.' She shrugged lightly. 'It was none of my business, and if Julia was carrying Gus's child – well, it would be better if no one ever spoke of it unless she herself decided to.'

'And that was me?' Daisy asked faintly.

Elizabeth smiled again. 'I think so. You have a look of them both. And certainly very little of my ex-husband.'

'So . . . I *am* a Dangerfield,' Daisy said wonderingly. 'My grandfather is still my grandfather.'

Elizabeth laughed. 'Yes. Whatever happens, you are still a Dangerfield. I'd stake my life on it.'

89

Homeless again, Coco thought. *Alone again too.*

Still, she had her bolthole for the moment. She'd taken the precaution of having the key to the South Kensington flat copied, and she'd also had her luggage sent there the night before the great showdown with the lawyers. She'd known when she took the information from Margaret's computer that she would soon be leaving the Belgravia house and never going back.

To keep everything above board, she'd written a formal letter to Will informing him that she was in the Dangerfield property and of her intention to use it while she sorted out her affairs. That was almost two weeks ago. She needed to find a new place to live. She had some money now – Daddy had been very generous to her and she hoped no one was going to demand it back – and every now and then her yellow diamond, or the insurance as she called it, winked on her finger and reminded her that it was still there.

I have to work out what I'm going to do, she thought as she stared out into the Kensington night, thinking over all that had happened. She could never go back

to her old life now. She'd lost the sense of completeness she'd had for a brief moment when she'd thought
that Gus was her father, but had discovered a new
strength within herself. *I'll find something. Maybe it's
time for me and Roberto to start that dance studio together,
like we always wanted to, now I've got some money to invest.*

But all she could think about was Will, despite her
efforts to shut him out of her mind. Seeing him at
his hotel and then at the lawyers' that day had been
intensely bitter-sweet. Being close to him again was
amazing. She'd had to fight the urge to reach out and
touch him, or to get near enough to breathe in his
sweet, enticing smell. He'd looked so incredibly handsome, better than she remembered. Just picturing him
made her stomach cartwheel. She'd forgotten how
deeply attracted she was to him and the bond that
still tied her to him.

But soon I'll leave the flat. And then the last tie will be cut.

She sighed, and wondered whether to pour herself
a glass of wine from the bottle chilling in the fridge.

The buzz of the doorbell made her jump. Her heart
started to pound and she felt a lump in her throat as
she tried to swallow. She went over to the intercom
and pressed it. 'Yes?'

'Coco?'

She was seized by pleasure and fear. 'Will?'

'Can I come up?'

'Of course.' She pressed the key release, realising
that her hands were shaking. She had a feeling that
the next few minutes were going to decide the course
of her life. There was just time to race to the mirror,
inspect her reflection and shake out her hair before
a knock sounded on the door.

She opened it and there he was, standing on the doorstep, gazing at her. He looked less formal than the last time they'd met, in jeans, brown Loake boots, a dark Ralph Lauren jacket over his sweater. Her skin tingled with the desire to reach out to him but she held back. Who knew what he'd come to say? Perhaps he was about to throw her out of the flat.

'Hi, Coco,' he said, his expression still impossible to read. 'May I come in?'

'Yes, of course,' she said, stepping back. His presence was affecting her badly and she knew her hands were shaking. She hoped he hadn't noticed. He followed her to the sitting room. 'Would you like a drink?'

'Yeah, thanks. Anything. Anything strong.'

'Sure.' Was he nervous too, then? Was that a good sign? She found the bottle of wine in the fridge and poured them both a glass, then took it over to him. They sat down opposite one another, both tongue-tied.

At last Will broke the silence. 'I got your letter.'

So that was it. He was here about the flat. She tried to look businesslike. 'Oh. Yes. No need to worry, I'll be out of here soon. Maybe just a few more weeks . . .'

'Stay as long as you like. Seriously.' He stared over at her. 'It's the least I can do. You've done a lot for us.' He looked down into his wine and added quietly, 'For me.'

She shrugged and took a nervous slug of her drink. 'Yeah. Well, it was the least I could do. You know why.' She couldn't look at him. 'You must hate me,' she said huskily.

'You know I don't,' he said in a low voice. 'I wanted

to. But I can't. And you did something amazing for me. You brought my sister back.'

Coco still couldn't meet his gaze but laughed hollowly. 'Yeah, you wanted to get rid of your father and instead you end up having to share the inheritance with her after all.'

'Don't be silly. We have more than enough. We'd rather have family than money any day. That's what this was all about, you know – not the money but the issue of love and respect. Dad didn't love or respect us enough to protect our inheritance or to tell us the truth. The money doesn't really matter. But you . . .' Will seemed to be choosing his words carefully. 'You threw away financial security to help me.'

Now she looked up, staring straight into his eyes, trying to convey the sincerity of her words. 'I never wanted to be with him. I only stayed so I could help you. And you know that nothing happened with him. Nothing.'

Will gazed back, his eyes suddenly soft. 'But something happened between us,' he said quietly.

'Yes . . .' She was lost in the intensity of his gaze.

'I owe you an apology. I was vile to you in LA.'

'But I deserved it. I'd been sent there to spy on you, by Margaret and your father.' Coco's voice cracked. 'I had no idea I was going to fall in love with you.' She looked away again, miserable at the memory of their happiness and how it had been destroyed.

'Coco . . .' Will's voice was tender. 'Look at me.'

She glanced up, almost unable to bear the way he made her feel. Her whole body yearned for him and she felt that familiar pull of magnetic attraction. It was almost too hard to be so close to that mouth and not be able to kiss it.

Suddenly he got up and in two strides was across the room and sitting next to her, taking her hand in his. 'Coco . . .'

Her stomach swooped with desire. She'd been longing for, dreaming of, his skin on hers for so long, and the simple touch of his hand was driving her wild.

He was gazing at her but Coco still couldn't look up. 'That's not all I came to say,' he murmured.

She could hardly speak from the dizziness of longing that was consuming her.

'Coco, look at me, please.' Will put a gentle hand under her chin and tilted her face upwards. She stared into his beautiful eyes. The closeness of his mouth was almost unbearable. 'I've missed you so much. I didn't want to, but I couldn't help it. I can't get you out of my mind . . . I need you. I think this is too important to throw away. But I need to know if you feel the same?'

She wanted to sob or laugh with the extraordinary relief that possessed her then. She realised that she hadn't known how to live without him. 'Of course I do,' she gasped. Impulsively, she leaned forward and pressed her lips to his, burying one hand in his hair and pulling his head to hers. Instantly they were engulfed in a kiss of such depth and mutual longing that it took their breath away.

'Coco . . . Coco,' said Will when they pulled apart for an instant, yearning in his voice. He gazed at her with delight.

'I thought we were never going to be together again,' she said, her eyes shining. 'If you knew how desperate I've been . . .'

671

'I know, I felt the same. It was unbearable.' He pulled her to him. 'But we had to be apart to know how we felt.'

She nodded. 'We met through lies and pretence – we needed to come together again in complete honesty.'

'I didn't know we'd fallen in love until I felt the pain of losing you,' he said simply. 'But I do now.'

They kissed again, and didn't speak for a long time, lost in the ecstasy of one another's touch and the bliss of two bodies desperate for each other, finally meeting and becoming one.

'Let's not be apart again,' said Will afterwards, when she lay in his arms.

'Never,' Coco said simply. 'I'll go wherever you go.' And kissed him again.

'So it looks like your father has been well and truly beaten.' Christophe raised his glass in a toast. 'You did it!'

Daisy lifted her glass in return as they sat across the table from each other in the luxurious dining room of the Florey. 'Yes. We did it.' She smiled. Things had progressed at great speed since the meeting a fortnight ago. Daddy had backed down entirely and resigned both from the family trusts and from the company. Will had gone into the office at once to convene an emergency meeting of the board and had put himself forward as chairman. He was voted in unanimously, and had told Daisy that her job was still open for her if she wanted it. She hadn't yet decided about that. Meanwhile, the lawyers were pressing ahead, with full cooperation from Daddy's side, now that he had been so comprehensively blown out of the water. It was obvious he had no spirit left for the fight any longer. 'But more important than anything, I know who I am now,' she said.

Christophe put down his glass and reached for her

hand. 'I know what that means to you. And you really had no idea about your father's brother?'

She shook her head. 'Perhaps it was mentioned in passing when I was tiny, but no . . . I really had no idea. Daddy controlled me absolutely – and he tried to control my mother too.' Her voice softened as she thought of Julia. 'It's hard to imagine what she suffered. No wonder she turned to drink to numb the pain. But I wish she'd told me about Gus. That's my one real regret.'

'I'm sure she wished things had turned out differently too.'

She looked up into Christophe's brown eyes. 'I'm just so pleased I had the chance to correct the mistake I made with you. Going through this without you would have been unbearable.'

He tightened his hand around hers. 'We need to decide what happens next,' he reminded her.

'I know. But whatever happens, we'll be together. And before I can decide anything, there's something I have to do first . . .'

The cemetery was on a hillside, sloping gently away from the massive stone pillars and wrought-iron gates at the entrance to an abandoned roofless chapel at the top. Around the chapel more graves stretched away, some now lost in thick brambles and ivy, others laid out on clear ground. These newer ones still boasted shiny granite headstones, bright lettering and fresh floral tributes.

Daisy walked up the hill, looking at the dark grey sky overhead. It was cold and would be getting dark soon. It had taken longer to get to South London than she'd expected.

She went past the abandoned chapel and approached the stretches of clear green ground where the headstones stood in neat rows. She knew she was looking for a fresh grave and found what she was looking for over at the very edge of the graveyard, close to an overgrown thicket and next to a bench. The headstone was of pale grey granite, the lettering carved in black. It read *Gustavus Dangerfield.* Underneath were some lines of poetry she did not recognise, perhaps Gus's own.

She stood in front of it for a long time, simply staring. Then she said quietly, 'Hello, Dad. I'm sorry we didn't get to meet while you were still alive. That was some really shitty timing, I must say. Here. I brought you some flowers.' She lifted up the bouquet of dark red roses she was carrying as if to show it to the headstone. Then she placed it on the grave, where the blooms lay soft, blood red and velvety against the freshly laid turf.

She went to sit on the bench next to the grave. It felt like a moment of great peace after a tumultuous few days, and Daisy needed that. As she stared at her father's grave, lost in thoughts of what might have been, she noticed someone walking up the hill towards her. As the figure drew closer, she saw it was a slender girl in jeans, biker boots and a camel-coloured leather aviator jacket that matched the lights in her long hair. Daisy stood up.

'What are you doing here?' she asked in astonishment when the other girl was in earshot.

'Paying my respects,' Coco said, surprise written all over her face. 'And you?'

'The same.' Daisy frowned. 'But what on earth . . .?'

675

'Wait – Dangerfield,' cut in Coco, her face clearing. 'That's the connection, right? Don't tell me – Gus was *your* dad, wasn't he?'

Daisy nodded. 'He was Daddy's illegitimate brother. But how did you know?'

'So that's why Margaret had to use another DNA sample! In case the results came out too close and it looked like you might be Daddy's daughter after all. I expect she knew all about Gus, just like she knew about everything.'

'Yes . . .' Daisy frowned. 'But I still don't understand why *you're* here.'

Coco laughed. 'I know. It's confusing. This whole thing is difficult to take in. I knew Gus, you see. He lived near us and he was a friend of my mother's. He told her he'd got some posh bird pregnant. That was your mum, I suppose.' She fixed Daisy with her greeny-blue stare. 'And for a while, I thought he might be my dad too. I wanted him to be, I guess. He was kind to me. I just heard he'd died and wanted to visit his grave.'

'You knew him?' whispered Daisy, staring at the other girl.

Coco nodded. 'Yeah. Not well.' She gave Daisy a sympathetic look. 'But I knew him enough to be able to tell you that he was a good man. A free spirit. Creative. A fantastic dad to have.'

'It's very cruel not to have been able to know him,' Daisy said sadly. 'I'm too late.'

Coco shrugged. 'Life's cruel. You've got to count your blessings, I know that better than most. I still don't know who my own dad was, and I probably never will. My mother had other kids, babies taken into care.

Somewhere I've got three half-siblings growing up that I know nothing about.'

Daisy bit her lip. 'I'm sorry.'

'I think we had pretty different experiences growing up. My life wasn't exactly a picnic.' Coco smiled to show there were no hard feelings.

'I didn't mean to be insensitive,' Daisy said, looking wretched.

'Hey.' Coco fixed her with a steady green-blue gaze. 'I know your life wasn't a breeze either. Maybe you had money, but you still lost your mum. And then your dad.'

'Everything really. Even my name.'

'But you're a Dangerfield again now.'

The two girls sat quietly for a moment, taking in the huge changes they were both confronting.

'I need to thank you for what you did,' Daisy said sincerely, breaking the silence. 'You found me at just the right time. You brought me back to my family. You've transformed my life.'

'It's OK.' Coco seemed to wave away Daisy's thanks. 'I didn't do it for you.'

'Was it . . . for Will?' Daisy ventured.

Coco's face softened. 'Yeah. I owed him.' Her eyes glowed with happiness.

'I take it you two have sorted things out,' Daisy said, smiling.

Coco nodded, unable to prevent a huge smile from breaking over her face. 'Yes, we have. And it's amazing.'

'I'm really pleased. I could see you meant a lot to him.' Daisy's mind was immediately flooded with questions but she held them back. There would be plenty of time to find everything out in due course. 'Then we're going to get to know each other a little better, I hope. Perhaps we can even be friends, now that all the misunderstandings have been cleared up.'

'Friends?' Coco thought for a moment. 'I haven't really had many in my life so far. I don't know if I'd be any good at it.'

'You may as well try. I think we've both been lonely. That's why we're here.'

The two girls stood together for a while, looking down at the grave. At last Coco spoke.

'Girls like us aren't usually friends. But we've got some shared history now, and you know what? I think I'd like it.'

'Good. Me too.' Daisy smiled at her. She stood up, straightening her jacket. 'Then let's go and get a coffee. I need to warm up.'

'That sounds great.' Coco stood up as well, and the two of them walked slowly out of the cemetery, talking as they went, leaving Gus's grave behind them.

Author's Note

You can read more about Jemima Calthorpe and the Trevellyan sisters' battle to save their family perfumery in *Heiresses*.

The story of Xander and Allegra McCorquodale forms part of the story of *Midnight Girls*.

Beautiful Creatures features the fortunes of the grand old department store, Noble's.

If you've enjoyed reading about the people and places in this book, I hope you might enjoy those other novels too – or if you've already read them, that you liked revisiting these old friends as much as I did.

Lulu Taylor

Acknowledgements

Huge thanks to everyone at Random House for all their amazing work, but especially to Gillian Holmes for her terrific editing and tireless support. Thanks as well go to Lynn Curtis for copyediting and Sally Sargeant for proofreading this rather long book!

Thanks as always to Lizzy Kremer, a magnificent agent. I appreciate so much all her hard work and willingness to be on the end of the phone. Special thanks to Laura West too for her invaluable editorial eye just when I needed a fresh take on the book.

Very special mention to Gill Paul for her wise words and constant support, and to Paul Laikin for taking the time to apply his eagle eye, and big thanks to the fabulous James Tuttle, my eyes and ears in LA. He knows *everything* and is utterly gorgeous (look him up on Facebook and you'll see what I mean).

Thank you to the Mather family in Temple Guiting: Spring Cottage was a fantastic hideaway when I needed to lose myself in the world of the book.

I appreciate so much the help and support of

family and friends, who always do what they can when I need a hand, but I'll always be more grateful than I can say to James, without whose support this would not be possible – thank you for everything.